ON WINGS OF DEATH—

Heat seared the back of Larson's neck, and he ran, even as he thought, *Dragon. Goddamned fire-breathing dragon like every legend and fairy tale I've ever read.*

A wall of trees rose before him. With a joyous sob, Larson ran between them. Yet even here there was scant safety as flame gouted through the trees with a heat that made him scream. Clutching his sword, Larson ran on with a speed born of desperation. Branches rustled overhead, too loud for wind. Fire lanced before Larson, the stabbing fires coming closer and closer, threatening to set the entire forest ablaze. Spotting the light of a campfire in the distance, Larson fled toward this one possible chance of aid. Flame shot down, and a wall of heat knocked Larson to one knee at the edge of the camp. "Dragon!" he screamed his warning through lungs that felt raw. "Fire . . . breathing . . . dragon!"

**Be sure to read these magnificent
DAW Fantasy Novels by
MICKEY ZUCKER REICHERT**

THE LEGEND OF NIGHTFALL

The Renshai Trilogy
THE LAST OF THE RENSHAI (Book 1)
THE WESTERN WIZARD (Book 2)
CHILD OF THUNDER (Book 3)

The Bifrost Guardians
GODSLAYER (Book 1)
SHADOW CLIMBER (Book 2)
DRAGONRANK MASTER (Book 3)
SHADOW'S REALM (Book 4)
BY CHAOS CURSED (Book 5)

MICKEY ZUCKER REICHERT

THE BIFROST GUARDIANS #1

GODSLAYER

DAW BOOKS, INC.

DONALD A. WOLLHEIM, FOUNDER

375 Hudson Street, New York, NY 10014

ELIZABETH R. WOLLHEIM
SHEILA E. GILBERT
PUBLISHERS

DAW Book Collectors No. 716.

Acknowledgments
The Spaewife's Song; as quoted in *Gods of the North* by Brian
Branston, published by Thames and Hudson; copyright © 1955 and
1980 by Brian Branston.

Conrad, Joseph, lines from *Under Western Eyes*; copyright © 1911;
reprinted by permission of the trustees for the Joseph Conrad estate,
and by permission of Doubleday & Company, Inc.

First Printing, August, 1987

6 7 8 9

DAW TRADEMARK REGISTERED
U.S. PAT. OFF. AND FOREIGN COUNTRIES
—MARCA REGISTRADA
HECHO EN U.S.A.

PRINTED IN THE U.S.A.

*For the veterans of Vietnam, especially
the PTSD patients of Coatesville VA Hospital.
May they find an uncondemning world and
a god who believes in them.*

And for

*Marcellus, Brahmin, and Ahngmar for the
inspiration.*

ACKNOWLEDGMENTS

I would like to thank Janny Wurts for being a role model, a teacher, and a friend; Joel Rosenberg for slapping me around when I most needed it; Raymond Feist for glowing praise and encouragement; Steve Zucker for storybook heroics; Jane Butler for her godawful patience and "not to worry"; Sheila Gilbert for things that can't be said in public; John Mulvey for objectivity, encouragement, and enthusiasm; my mother for patience; my father for pretending to discourage me; but mostly Mark Fabi for not writing a satire.

CONTENTS

PROLOGUE

---

*"I! I who fashioned myself a sorcerer or
an angel, Who dispensed with all moral-
ity, I have come back to the earth."*
— *Arthur Rimbaud,* Adieu

The three mailed guards who ushered Bramin into
the king's court regarded him with cautious curiosity. No one dared touch him. Nor did they question the cloth parcel which swung from his belt.
Offending any wizard could spell instant death,
and the jade stone clamped in the black-nailed
claw which tipped Bramin's staff identified him as
a sorcerer of high rank.

As they passed through the double set of oak
doors, Bramin fought to keep his head high. The
battle he had just survived and the enchantments
of transport weakened him both mentally and
physically. His aura had dulled to a flicker of gold
and, though he had nothing to fear in Ashemir's
throne room, he hoped the king's magician would
not recognize his fatigue. It was simply a matter of
pride.

The carpeted path to the king's throne seemed

to stretch for miles. The court watched the procession in a vast silence which jagged Bramin's already taut nerves. A comma of black hair slipped into his eye, and he flicked it back with an anger that sapped much of his remaining strength. Weakness of any sort enraged Bramin, and it reminded him of his reckless squandering of power. Overconfidence had cost many of his colleagues their lives.

"Step forward and name yourself." King Ashemir's command broke the silence, and tense whispers followed it. Ire rose momentarily at this ritual formality. The king knew Bramin well. The magician had been born and raised in the royal city, the product of a rape. His father was one of the dark elves, the last faery creature seen in this part of the world. As a child, Bramin paid for his willowy figure and dark complexion with jeerings and ridicule.

Bramin came forward, unhurried. He nodded briefly at the advisor beside the king, glared at the court sorcerer, who regarded him with both envy and amusement, and bowed pleasantly to the king. "I am Bramin, Dragonrank of the Jade Claw." He thumped the base of his staff on the floor for emphasis. "I have performed your quest. The giant, Redselr, lies dead at my hands." He thumbed the sack at his belt. Enervation and anxiety caused him to misjudge position and strength, and the tie snapped. The bag fell to the floor, and the giant's head rolled free to the king's feet.

King Ashemir recoiled with a gasp. The court sorcerer turned an unbecoming shade of green. Behind Bramin, strained whispers broke to cries of fear and amazement. Guards scrambled to maintain order, others ran for the abomination which seemed to stare at their king with glazed eyes.

With a word and a gesture, Bramin caused the head to slide back into its bag. The effort slammed against him like a wall, stealing his breath. His life aura flickered dangerously. A high-pitched ringing filled his head, making the voices around him seem distant. Yet Bramin retained control over his languishing muscles. Gradually his mind cleared, and he cursed himself brutally. He could have let the guards clear his mistake away or physically done so himself. Pride alone goaded him to recklessness, and he had nearly paid its price.

The king cleared his throat. His look of fear dissolved, masked by a pleasant smile. "You've earned your reward, Bramin Halfman. Five chests of gold, a parcel of land, or the hand of my daughter, Halfrija. The choice is yours."

The pronouncement of Halfrija's name made Bramin smile despite his exhaustion and indignation. "I need neither money nor power, for I have both already. But for Halfrija's hand, I would stop the sun from setting and the moon from rising. I would still the tides or steal the hammer of Thor."

The court passed opinion in a gentle hum of conversation. The king bit his lip against an ecstatic grin, but his blue eyes gleamed with excitement as they met Bramin's glowing red glare. The court sorcerer looked stricken. All three men knew Bramin would need to abandon the School of Dragonrank, since one of its primary requirements was eleven months per year of training on the school's grounds. For the king, it meant a new court magician with power beyond any of his predecessors. Only those blessed with the claw symbol could join the Dragonranks. Its devotees were the most capable users of the art, and the most able among them became omnipotent lords or directly served gods. "Summon Halfrija," Ashemir commanded his guards. They rushed to obey.

Bramin knew marriage would force him to sacrifice a future of ultimate power for domesticity and the banality of court proceedings. He lowered his head, staring at the claw-shaped scar which puckered the black skin on the back of his right hand. The symbol had appeared at the age of ten along with the first traces of the life aura which glimmered about him, visible only to those versed in magic. His mother and human half siblings sent Bramin away that year. So he traded the gibes of the citizens of Forste-Mar for their respect and the grueling discipline of the Dragonrank.

A person marked with the claw was a rare enough occurrence in any town, and Forste-Mar received its second surprise three years later. Bramin's eldest half sister, Silme, was similarly stamped by destiny. She joined the Dragonrank, which pleased Bramin. It gave him a familiar companion on his infrequent breaks from studying enchantments or practicing swordsmanship. And he had always liked Silme best. Many times she had dried his tears or soothed his deadly rages when children grew cruel with their taunts or citizens wounded his pride with derision.

The doors swung open, interrupting his memories, and the court again fell silent as the guards ushered Halfrija before them. A dress of blue silk with interlacing patterns of silver tastefully outlined her delicate frame. Her face was fair with artistically high cheek bones. Her wide-set eyes were the pale blue of cornflowers. At the sight of the lady he loved, all other thought fled Bramin.

His heart pounded, pumping warmth and desire through his body. He stared without speaking, love-blinded to her taut-lipped pall of fear.

The king rose from his throne. "Bramin Jade-claw, you see my daughter, the Lady Halfrija. On Midsummer's Day, I sanction the marriage between you. May you live long together and prosper!"

Halfrija opened her mouth to speak, but her words were lost beneath the cheers of the crowd. As Bramin turned his back to the king and trod the walkway toward Halfrija, she shrank back. Her hands clenched to bloodless fists, and her soprano pierced the dying shouts of the court. "Wait!"

Bramin stopped before her trembling form.

"I would test your love," she announced shrilly. "It is my right."

Breath broke from Bramin in an angry hiss. He had risked his life for her once and would gladly do so again. But her entreaty was an affront. While it was indeed her privilege, no princess had invoked the law since its enactment three centuries past.

Halfrija continued. "You must fight a champion of my choosing to the death in the arena at midmorn. Should you survive, my hand is yours." She shivered, and her voice acquired a strange, droning quality. "You may select your weapon, but use of sorceries or enchanted swords will free me from my promise."

Struck to the heart by the maliciousness of her challenge, Bramin dropped all pretense of dignity. He knelt before Halfrija with the true respect he had denied the king. "As you wish, my lady. May the court hear my vow to kill or be killed by your champion without use of magic."

Halfrija's mouth twitched to a cruel smile which swiftly disappeared.

Stiffly, Bramin turned. Fatigue and hopelessness wove a black curtain across his vision. As he retreated along the carpeted walkway he stumbled, and the glares of courtiers sapped him of all remaining grace. It seemed an eternity before he reached the far end of the hall. A guard swung open the carved oak doors, and Bramin passed through them. The portals clanged closed behind him, silencing the whispered condemnations of Ashemir's court as completely as death.

Outside, wind flung strands of matted hair into Bramin's face as if to mock him. Despair rose to self-pity, then flared to righteous anger. His journey through the familiar streets of his childhood seemed as one through a tunnel. The dirt roads blurred to the dark obscurity of disinterest. Peasants stared or scuttled from his path, unnoticed. A horse cart driver hurled epithets at the dark sorcerer who paced the cobbles at the center of the alley. But at a flick of Bramin's hand, the driver stemmed his tide of oaths and swerved to a roadside ditch. *They fear me.* For the first time since he had left to kill the giant, Bramin smiled with cruel satisfaction. *My life aura has dwindled to nearly nothing, yet those who once scorned me now shy from a gesture.* Still, for Halfrija's love, he would weather the gibes of peasants gladly.

The setting sun lanced red light through the guttering remnant of Bramin's aura. Utterly alone in his fury despite the dispersing throng of Forste-Mar's citizenry, he plodded to his mother's home. He opened the simple plank door, stepped across its threshold, and slammed it closed behind him. Despite his effort, the portal slid shut with an impotent click which betrayed his weakness. Rage flared anew.

Despite the death of Bramin's stepfather several months earlier, the cottage had changed little since his childhood. The sod-chinked walls enclosed a simply-furnished room separated from his mother's bedchamber by a patched, blue curtain. Silme sat before a blazing hearth fire, a tomcat nestled in the folds of her robe, while a brother and sister begged stories of distant lands and Dragonrank training. As Bramin entered, his mother rose from a chipped wooden bench, her youngest child cradled to her breast. "Bramin?"

Bramin gave no explanation. He spared neither glance nor words for the mother and half siblings who followed his march to the loft ladder with questioning stares. Anger lent the sorcerer strength. He caught the lowest rungs in callused palms and climbed to his sleeping quarters with a deliberateness designed to override fatigue-inspired clumsiness. Once in the loft, he pitched onto a pallet, oblivious to the bells and balls left by the child who occupied this bed since Bramin's departure to pursue the skills of Dragonrank. Tears burned his eyes. Repeatedly, his fist pounded the pillow, scattering straw among the toys.

Behind Bramin, the ladder groaned. Silme's sweet voice wound through the loft. "Brother, are you well?"

Bramin whirled like a cornered beast. Inappropriately, his malice channeled against the half sister who had comforted him in youth, the one woman he knew would not condemn him. "Nothing's changed, Silme! The citizens of Forste-Mar still hate me. Halfrija spurns my love." He struck the pallet again.

"Stop!" Silme's voice grew uncharacteristically harsh. "Before you embed your soul in self-pity and accuse me of lying, tell me what happened in Ashemir's court."

Bramin sucked air through pursed lips, then exhaled in a long sigh. He recounted the scenario in the king's presence, his overwhelming exhaustion, Ashemir's eager determination, and Halfrija's cruelty. As he concluded the tale, he surrendered to the cold grip of hopelessness. His words emerged in a thin whine. "While vestiges of dignity remain, I must leave Forste-Mar and never return. I cannot bear the sight of Halfrija's beauty, knowing her love will never belong to me."

Silme lowered herself to the pallet beside her half brother. She squeezed his knee reassuringly. "Don't talk that way, Bramin. Your loves are intense. Your hatreds fester. In youth, you would damn all children for a single taunt and despise every man of Forste-Mar for a glare. Now, Bramin, would you condemn yourself to exile to avoid a challenge?"

"A challenge!" Bramin shook free from Silme's grip. "Halfrija degraded me by calling upon a privilege rejected for centuries. Even Queen Agnete, who wrote the law, never invoked it for herself or her daughters."

Silme's reply came soft as a cat's purr. "But Halfrija knew you could fulfill it."

"What?"

Silme framed a smile of triumph. "Halfrija doesn't hate you. For the last decade you have trained in a distant land eleven months of the year. Yet Halfrija never married in your absence."

Bramin scowled, unconvinced.

Silme rose from the pallet and knelt before

Bramin. She caught his hands. "Here a woman is judged by the worth of her man. She must make certain her husband can protect her from bandits and raiders."

Silme's blue-tinged aura dwarfed Bramin's, so dimmed was it with exhaustion. The jade rank sorcerer grunted. "You know I can."

Silme concurred. "I know. But magic seems more alien to Halfrija than the sharp, dark features and red-hued eyes she has learned to accept. She understands swordplay."

Bramin wavered.

Silme pressed. "Who is the best warrior in this town?"

"Me?"

Silme stood. "We both know none of Ashemir's knights can defeat you. Halfrija knows it, too."

As anger dispersed, fatigue crowded Bramin. Though Silme's explanation seemed implausible, his desire for the princess allowed him to believe. "Then why. . . ?"

Silme interrupted. "Because she's insecure. She needs to justify your appearance by displaying your talents in public. Do you find Halfrija's hand more valuable than the life of a soldier?"

Realization drove Bramin's voice to a whisper. "Far more." He sprawled across the pallet, drained of all emotion except the early, fine stirrings of hope. As Silme crept back to the ladder, sleep overtook him. Yet, despite his half sister's reassurances, the memory of Halfrija's fleeting sneer haunted Bramin's dreams.

Rest restored the vitality drained by Bramin's battle with the giant. As he dressed in a simple tunic and breeks, many thoughts plagued him. As

skilled with a sword as with magic, Bramin knew
from his one month a year at home that no warrior of Forste-Mar could best him. Unless some
strange and highly capable swordsman had joined
them in the past year, he could not be defeated.

Bramin fastened his sword belt and drew the
blade from its leather hip scabbard. He smiled as
the radiance of his restored life aura bounced
blue highlights from the steel. He felt strong, mentally and physically. Striding from his mother's
cottage, he let the door swing shut behind him
and trotted through the streets to the cleared patch
of castle grounds. Guards passed cautiously about
him, attentive to their duties. With magically enhanced hearing, Bramin invaded their conversations, but the sentries seemed as curious about the
princess' champion as he himself.

Bramin executed an elegant series of sword
feints. The hilt felt comfortable in his grip, metal
wrapped with rough leather which would not slip
from his sweat-slicked palm. He stopped, not wishing to tire himself before the match. His love for
Princess Halfrija had begun as a childhood crush.
He sent flowers and trinkets. Though she acknowl-
edged none of them and regarded him with the
same scorn as the other citizens of Forste-Mar, her
reluctance only strengthened his passion. During
his vacations from the School of Dragonrank, he
wooed her. Soon, his love became an all-encompassing desire.

The sun shouldered over the horizon. Citizens
drifted toward the southern side of the castle
grounds where the arena towered over the quarters of guards and servants. Finely-dressed courtiers strode in regal pairs. Peasants in worn homespun crowded toward the building, hoping to catch

a glimpse of the combatants. Armored guards tried to maintain some order in the milling chaos with little success.

From habit, Bramin checked his own excitement. As he walked toward the arena, he took his staff in hand. It would help him through the throng, for men rightly shied from its touch. He used it like a walking stick, though none would question his youth or vigor; even those too foolish to fear the power of his magic could not fail to notice the unearthly aura of evil inherited from his father.

The citizens of Forste-Mar shrank from the slim, dark wizard who strode purposefully to the door of the stadium. Despite the demoralizing inevitability of combat, Bramin gleaned some amusement from their awe. Years ago, these same men and women would have spit on him.

The guards gestured Bramin inside, and the crowd closed in behind him, hoping for a glimpse of the combat. Noblemen lined the balconies and applauded politely at his entrance. Bramin leaned his staff against the lowest stands, walked to center ring, and examined his audience. He raised a hand in greeting to the king and queen. Ashemir waved, then shrugged in apology. Halfrija's seat was unoccupied, and Bramin supposed she was coaching her champion. The thought formed a painful ball in his throat. He felt utterly alone. Now, before Forste-Mar's masses, Silme's reassurances rang as hollow as in youth when she swore her playmates did not hate him even as they hurled rocks and challenges. Anxiety allowed Bramin to forget the times she had stroked his hair until he ceased to tremble. He knew nothing of how she had confronted his tormentors with their inhumanity and made them blush with humility.

Thus reminded of the townspeople's hostility, Bramin's will faltered. The noise of the peasants changed pitch. The door swung open, and Halfrija entered. She wore a suit of leather far too large for her tiny frame. She grasped a long sword in both fists, and it leaned awkwardly.

The audience erupted in riot. The queen fainted. All color drained from the king, and he sat, rigid, like an ivory statue. Bramin met Halfrija halfway into the ring. "What are you doing?" he demanded.

Her eyes blazed with madness. "I *am* my champion. Kill or be killed," she chanted like a priest before a sacrifice. She thrust the sword clumsily.

Bramin's mouth went painfully dry. He side-stepped and caught both of Halfrija's wrists, drawing her too close for combat. If anyone in the audience spoke or moved, Bramin did not notice. His blood-colored eyes probed the princess for answers, but true to his word he avoided magic. "Halfrija . . ."

She spat in his face. "Beast! I would rather die than marry you."

Halfrija's words pained like blows. Bramin's grip tightened on her flesh till she winced. His voice was rambling and plaintive as a lost child. "Why? Oh, why, Halfrija? I've the power to grant your every desire. A thousand kings have offered great treasures for me to come serve them. Yet I refused them all for you. I love you, Halfrija."

Halfrija's hands whitened as her face flushed with ugly rage. "I'll not be disdained by my own people because a dark creature loves me." She added cruelly, "If, indeed, your kind can know love."

Bramin caught his breath with a sob. "Now I know love and pain." Desperately, he spouted Silme's trite comforts as if they were truths. "The people of Forste-Mar don't hate me. They mistreated me as a child from ignorance. But many years have passed since . . ."

"You stupid animal!" Halfrija's voice rose in pitch and volume. "We hate you now more than ever. We would kick and spit, even slay you if we didn't fear your power. You're no man, you're a beast. Worse than a beast, for a rat is content with its lot and you have the audacity to pretend you're human!"

Slapped by Halfrija's cruelty, Bramin made a pained noise. His grip went lax. "Halfrija . . ."

Her sword struck. Though too near her target for an effective strike, her blade nicked Bramin's side. The razor edge opened his tunic. Blood beaded his skin. Bramin watched in fascination as a single drop slid down his breeks and splashed a tiny, scarlet circle in the sand.

He looked up as Halfrija raised her sword like a club and lashed at his face. Tears stung his eyes. He stood, hopeless and uncaring, as the blade cut above his head. Just before the blow fell, self-righteous fury warmed his blood. The will to live and claim vengeance on all who had ever wronged him replaced the anguish roused by Halfrija's scorn. He sprang aside. Her sword whisked through air where he had stood and hammered the packed sand with a crash.

Off-balance, Halfrija staggered. Bramin caught her by the throat. He drew her so close their faces nearly touched. Her cheeks and eyes paled with fear, which gave Bramin a morbid satisfaction. The legacy of his dark ancestors rose hot in his veins. "Too good for me, lady?" His voice transformed to an ancient croak of evil. "You're not too good for death." His hands knotted convulsively, cartilage crumbled beneath his fingers, and Halfrija fell limp against him.

Blood trickled from the corner of her thin lips, staining Bramin's hand. He looked up quickly to a condemning horde. A great shout rose from the stands, and men descended upon him. "Stop!" screamed Bramin. His cry was lost in the rising din. Clutching Halfrija's body with one arm, he raised the other. Spell words rushed from his throat. His life aura flared to blinding white. Smoke broiled from his fingers and rolled like fog across the arena floor. It struck the first wave of courtiers and roared to flame.

Screams filled Bramin's ears like song. The courtiers' charge was transformed to chaotic flight. Enchantments rolled from the half-elf's tongue. Bramin's staff leapt to his hand. Its jade stone winked once, staining the roiling magics an eerie green-blue. And when the works of sorcery cleared, all that remained of Bramin and Halfrija were five drops of blood on the sands of the arena.

Stiffly, Halfrija let the last of her garments fall to the floor of Bramin's quarters at the School of Dragonrank. She stood before him, naked. He had imagined her unclothed so many times in his dreams and desires, yet now the sight only sickened him. Her slimness transformed to a cadaverous frailty. Her breasts sagged, violet with pooled blood. Her eyes were hollow and dead. All his magic could not restore life, only simulate it. This was not Halfrija, just a crude animation which would perform as Bramin wished, without will or knowledge of its lot.

Black rage engulfed Bramin. His life aura rose to off white as he channeled his energies. Magic lanced Halfrija's body as it fell, and the pale form crumbled to dust. Bitterness grew like a cancer. Bramin rose and paced. With each jagged pass, his fist crashed against the smoothed-stone walls. "Hate me, do they?" he screamed at the ceiling. "Hate spawns hate."

He stared at the charred pile which had once been the person of the princess of Forste-Mar. One kick scattered the ashes around his quarters. "Hatespawn I am, and so will I remain. But all mankind shall pay for their abhorrence." His thoughts shifted slightly. For a moment he pictured his half sister Silme, as beautiful as Halfrija and in many ways as cruel.

Bramin paced again. "It was she who told me they meant no harm. She blinded me to their treacheries and laughed behind my back. She taught me the torture of love as though it were a pleasure and held me from my vengeance. She goaded me to destroy my love and shame myself before Forste-Mar's peasants. It's too late to sunder Halfrija's soul, but not Silme's. She will die in torment and the manworld of Midgard with her!"

Light flashed through his quarters, dimming his life aura to dirty yellow as another's power pulsed against him. Bramin turned with a hiss. Before him stood a man more beautiful than the woman he had loved. Fine gold locks fell to his shoulders. His dark blue eyes twinkled with cruel mischief. He wore a strangely-tailored costume interwoven with magics which shimmered as he moved. Arms folded across his chest, the stranger stared at Bramin with a grin of arrogant scorn.

"Die, human!" screamed the half-man. Power streamed from his fingers, slowed, and fizzled to sparks a foot before the handsome stranger.

The man laughed, sweet as rain. "Very pretty, Hatespawn. But you've much to learn."

Bramin glared. "Who are you?"

The stranger yawned, and his shirt sparkled so it nearly blinded Bramin. "I am called by many names." He chuckled. "Some even I am too polite to speak. I am Loki, first father of lies, thief of Brisingamen, evil companion of Odin, slanderer and cheat of the gods, and father of the Fenris Wolf."

Bramin's scowl wilted. His throat went dry, and he swallowed several times before attempting speech. "A god? But why . . . ?"

"Did you mean your threats, Hatespawn?" Loki frowned accusingly. "Or were they the idle ramblings of self-pity? Decide quickly. I don't waste time with fools."

Anger blazed anew. Bramin's fists clenched so tightly his fingernails bit red welts in the palms. Though sorely embittered, he chose his words with care. "I never speak idly. I will cause the downfall of man."

The corners of Loki's mouth twitched upward, and his voice lilted. "And the gods as well if you serve my cause."

Bramin started. "Gods have enlisted the aid of high claw Dragonrank. But I am only jade. Why me?"

"Because, Hatespawn." Loki's inflection almost made the title sound pleasant. "You will rise quickly through the ranks. Already the master prepares your staff for garnet. And . . ." The god leaned casually against the stone wall. "You take your swordplay as seriously as your magic. I've use of that."

Bramin focused on the shimmering patterns of Loki's shirt. "It will still take time," he said sullenly.

"I've plenty of it." Loki grinned wickedly. "And so have you. It would be wise for us both to learn patience."

Bramin scowled, saying nothing.

Loki continued. "Save your vengeance. I've something for you to remember our bargain in the meantime." The god bowed his head and his golden hair fell about his cheeks like waterfalls, obscuring his face. His hands crossed before him, fingers spread. Slowly, he drew his hands apart as he uttered sharp, harsh syllables of summoning.

Loki's fingers curled. Suddenly, his wrists flicked outward. A globe of blackness winked into place before him, marred only by the silver lines of sorcery from Loki's shirt and Bramin's aura. The ball stretched to a rod-like shape and dropped in to Loki's hands. It was a sword.

Loki raised his head. "Take it."

Bramin bit his lower lip. Hesitantly, he took a step forward and met Loki's eyes. They were chill blue, with the same contempt as the men of Forste-Mar. Anger made the half-breed more confident. He strode forward and seized the sword.

Its sheath was carved ebony. Its hilt was split leather-wrapped steel studded with fire opals, and it fit Bramin's hand comfortably. With a quick pull, he freed the blade, slim and silver, polished so fine its glow mocked enchantments. Near its hilt, runes flickered, effused with red light. For a moment, their meaning was clear to him. Then they muddled to obscurity and his memory of them as well. Bramin muttered a spell in frustration, but the writings remained just beyond comprehension. "What does it say?" he demanded, hating his inability.

Loki smiled. "It's the sword's name, Helblindi. And its purpose. Your vengeance begins when the writings become clear to you. Know only that men will flee from your blade, and the braver the man, the more he must fear it."

"Helblindi." Bramin raised his brows in question. "Isn't that the name of another god?"

"Very perceptive, Hellspawn. Very perceptive." As suddenly as he had arrived, Loki was gone. All that remained was a rumbling of laughter which echoed between the walls.

CHAPTER 1

Dragonslayer

*"For those whom God to ruin has
designed,
He fits for fate, and first destroys their
mind."*
—*Dryden,* The Hind and the Panther

Death hung like an omnipresent shadow over the fire base at Aku Nanh, Vietnam. A wave of heat rustled a circle of thirty grass huts and drummed against the quonset of messhall and infirmary. It carried the reek of burning excrement but no relief from the broiling sun.

Inside a shelter of wood frame and bamboo, a corporal slammed his cards on the table, and Al Larson looked up from his book.

"Four jacks." A grin split the corporal's owlish face as he raked in a tidy sum of cash.

"Shit," said Jamie Fisher, a streetwise black from south Philadelphia. "Big Man knows rank, eh, blood?" He glanced teasingly at Tom Dragelin who had been kneeling on the floor for the last quarter hour. Larson awaited Dragelin's inevitable retort, but the boy only continued his prayer.

"Throw in a word for me." Gavin Smith gathered the cards with a gesture of annoyance. "I'm losing."

Dragelin loosed a purse-lipped grunt of disapproval. Larson swung his leg over the side of his bunk. "Won't help. You really want to win, learn to deal off the bottom of the deck like Steve." He gestured at the corporal.

The room fell silent. The corporal's dark eyes went cold as he glared at Larson.

"What you readin', Al? *How to Win Friends?*" Fisher picked his teeth with the corner of a card.

Gavin rose. He looked at the book in Larson's hand and laughed. "It's a text book. We're stuck in hell, and he's readin' a goddamn text book."

"Hey, this is major theology." Larson set the book aside. "Christianity's mixed up. It's fine for people at home, but what good does it do us? What good did it do Danny?"

"Stop!" The corporal's single word was a threat.

Larson's eyes burned as he fought tears. Though only twenty, he was the oldest of the group except for the corporal.

Dragelin turned toward the wall.

Gavin dealt the cards. "We're dodgin' bullets while Danny's in heaven havin' tea with God. Come on, let's finish the game."

"Wait. Hear me out." Larson ran a hand through the tangled growth of his blond hair. "What's the fundamental teaching of Christianity?"

Fisher lit a cigarette. "Do unto others."

"Peace, brotherhood, and the word of God," called Dragelin from the corner.

"Exactly." Larson smiled as Dragelin stepped into his well-prepared trap. "How much of that do you see here?"

Gavin picked up his cards, swore, and slapped them to the table. "I got a piece just yesterday."

"We got ourself a brotherhood right here," added Fisher.

Gavin finished. "And Tom'll pass God's word, won't you, buddy?" He laughed.

Larson spoke over the snickers. "We're worshiping a peace god during war. Doesn't work. The Vikings had some real war gods. Get a load of this." He raised the book and read aloud. " 'Stir war!' cried Odin. 'Set men at each other's throats. Whether they wish it or not, have men rip one another to pieces. And when they lay steeped in their blood, have them rise to fight again.' "

Dragelin crossed himself.

The corporal scowled, hand over his cards.

"Fuckin'-A, man," said Fisher. "You're crazy."

"What's your point?" asked Gavin, obviously unimpressed.

For effect, Larson stood to deliver his philosophy. "Odin signified wisdom in Norse mythology. He wasn't even their war god. The real war gods helped their side in battle. That's what we need. Not some pansy who lets people smack both cheeks."

The corporal gathered the cards with a frown. "Ten o'clock, time for patrol. Draw. Lowest two on point."

The five men grew grave as each slipped a card from the deck. Larson frowned at his three. The others displayed their draws. Gavin flipped his six. "Your war gods didn't help us much. You and me play target."

Larson forced humor around the lump growing in his throat. "On the contrary. What could please a war god more than placing his follower in the most dangerous position." He donned his helmet and gripped his M-16. "Sorry about what I said, Steve."

The corporal waved a hand. Everything was forgiven before a patrol.

Al Larson and Gavin Smith left the hut first and stepped into the withering heat of afternoon. A football hit the ground before them with a thud, and Larson started. Immediately, he cursed himself. Wariness was an asset on a sniper hunt, but hyperarousal could prove worse than none at all. Larson took several deep breaths, hefted the ball, and tossed it to a grinning, sandy-haired corpsman.

Gavin sidled several paces ahead while Larson watched the corpsman's retreating figure. It seemed ludicrous. Here was this troop of trained soldiers playing games like they were in some kind of sandlot, while he and his buddies prepared for fire action in the jungle. As instinct rose like ire, he could almost forget the card game in the hut. Everybody took a turn on patrol. It just felt better when it was the other guy's turn.

Larson hurried to catch Gavin, and they strode side by side to the perimeter gate. One of the sentries yawned as he tripped the latch, and the other raised his gun in mock salute. The men made no sound as they crossed three hundred yards of tank-cleared ground and entered the steamy murk of the jungle. The ghostly cry of a macaw drowned the noise of their boots in the soft, red mud. Gavin stiffened. Larson knew his companion believed macaw calls foreshadowed death. With so many of the birds in the Vietnamese jungles, it seemed unlikely. Yet death was nearly as common. Alert, Larson moved away.

Humidity converged on them with a stench of

sewage and blood. Larson crept through brush like a shadow, tensed for a sniper's volley. For half an hour he moved, muscles knotted. Biting insects and heat weakened him, but he found nothing except jungle fauna. Larson wondered whether he should feel relieved that no snipers waited or terrified of one concealed in the trees.

Suddenly, an explosion rocked the forest behind Larson. He plunged into the mud, heart racing. An ugly scream numbed his mind till it allowed no thought. But his body reacted. He wriggled forward cautiously.

"Al." Gavin's frantic whisper came from his right. Though tinged with panic, the familiar voice soothed.

"What happened?"

"Trap," said Gavin.

Larson shuddered. The dying scream of his companion would haunt him to the end of his life. He did not want to see what remained of the others, but he could not continue until he knew their fates with certainty. Reluctantly, Larson followed Gavin.

Bellies to the ground, they crawled between the trees. Gavin stopped abruptly and loosed an oath. His body spasmed regularly as he retched. Steeling himself, Larson looked beyond at the torn bodies. His mind exploded in terror. The corporal still lived. Nothing protruded below his waist, but he breathed in a regular, shallow pattern. Larson pushed past Gavin who caught his arm.

"No, Al." Gavin's face turned the color of fatigues.

"He's alive."

"Not long," Gavin said weakly. "He won't make it to camp. If we carry him, neither will we."

"Let go." Larson tried to twist free of Gavin's grip, not certain why he had to rescue the corporal. He could imagine his own body hemorrhaging on the jungle floor, living food for rats.

A macaw shrieked four consecutive notes. Gavin shivered, and Larson pulled away.

"Wait, listen." Gavin seized the back of Larson's shirt.

Above the continuous hum of insects, they heard the faint rustle of approaching men. "Stay." Larson licked dried lips and flitted between the trunks. Ahead he saw a dozen black-clothed figures moving stealthily toward them. Larson stood, paralyzed.

Gradually, he gathered his wits and headed back to where he'd left Gavin. "Charlie. Too many for us. Hide."

Gavin nodded. "This way."

Gavin slithered to the right. The thick foliage let too little sunlight through for underbrush to grow. Trapped in the open with only trees for cover, Larson saw no means of escape. But Gavin grabbed his arm and led him to a dry river bed. Larson grew giddy with hope. They might hide between the banks while the Vietnamese passed. Gavin gestured Larson to stillness and crept farther along the stream bed. Kneeling in mud, Larson watched his companion merge into the green infinity of jungle. The rustlings grew louder, and Larson heard a gruff vocal exchange.

Gavin's pained cry broke the hush. A volley of gunfire followed. Larson's heart beat at least as loud. He could only imagine what happened, perhaps a snake bite caused Gavin's indiscretion. It no longer mattered. Larson flattened against the bank, clutching his M-16 like a teddy bear.

Limbs frozen with fear, Larson forced himself

to think rationally. The enemy knew as well as he that soldiers did not travel alone by choice. They would come looking for him. Even as he watched, a man in black circled and entered the river bed north of his position. Larson lined his sights but did not fire, unwilling to reveal his own position. The moment he did, he died.

Larson knew without seeing that another man stalked him from the south. Cornered, he needed a miracle. *God help me,* he thought. Despite his situation, the irony of his prayer struck him. Not quite ready to accept death, he hugged the bank and waited.

Death prowled closer. He let understanding settle over him. He would die, but not alone. Deliberately, Larson switched the gun setting from semi to full auto. *Freyr. You're a war god. You ought to love this.* "For my buddies, Freyr!"

Larson burst from the river bed, shooting. He embraced death.

Al Larson stared at bleak stone walls. *Alive,* he thought. *Impossible. Those guns should have cut me in half.* He ran anxious hands along his body and felt nothing abnormal but the slick sweat which coated his palms. He sat up and realized he lay on a hard stone floor, alone. He ran his fingers through the fine, soft hair on his head and his hand stopped on the edge of a pointed ear.

Startled, Larson leaped to his feet. He did not recognize his clothing: tight doeskin pants, a blue linen shirt, and a matching cape. "Wha?" he said stupidly. His hands clamped over both ears. Each came to a delicate point. "I'm a goddamn Vulcan!"

"Elf," said a voice. Larson whirled but saw no

one. Except for a belt and sword in the far corner, the room appeared empty.

Larson stared at his hands which looked smaller than he remembered. "Who are you?" he shouted. "Where are you?" If this was a Vietnamese torture, he found it extremely successful. He knew he had gone completely insane.

"Silence." The powerful voice echoed. "I am Freyr. You called me before you died."

"I did?" *Yes, I guess I did.* Larson caught a handful of the pale hair which fell to his shoulders. "Who am I?"

"I haven't time for foolishness," said the voice impatiently. "Neither have you. You've a purpose to fulfill."

Larson felt small and confused. "What purpose? Where am I? Help me please." He felt ridiculous pleading with a disembodied voice.

"Take up Valvitnir, your sword, and guard it well. Pass northward. You will find an old man and a young woman who are more than they seem. Trust them. They'll aid your task."

Larson's head whirled. "What task?"

No reply.

"Oh, hell." Larson walked to the corner. He hefted the swordbelt, a gaudily-tooled work of leather. He fastened it about his waist, and it dragged like dead weight at his side. Larson gazed at the ceiling. "Freyr? Freyr!"

Silence.

Larson patted the jewel-encrusted sword hilt. "I don't know how to use a sword!"

Nothing.

Larson shrugged. He pulled the worked steel from its sheath. The sleek blade glowed faintly blue. His unfamiliar hand fit the grip exactly. "Why me?"

He had not anticipated a reply. "I found it necessary to bridge time. We've few worshipers after the coming of the White Christ. Now, please go. Your companions will explain further."

Larson resheathed the sword and walked to the door. He took hold of its ring and pulled. It opened with a complaining creak to reveal a green meadow surrounded by hills. After months of artillery and jungle, the scene shocked Larson. Jaw gaping, he walked as if in a trance, and the door swung shut behind him.

The sun beamed down on Larson like a golden eye, striping the high grasses with light. In the distance, a tall patch of weeds rose like a tiny forest. Beyond, a real forest of evergreens waved like a chorus in the breeze. Anxiety balled in Larson's gut, and sweat beaded his neck. Fearful of the open terrain, he back-stepped and caught for the door handle. His fingers clawed through air. Startled anew, he whirled, staggered, and fell to the grass. Where the building had stood he saw nothing but fields, not even a shadow or a square of crushed foliage to indicate it had ever existed.

Larson rose to a crouch. *This cannot be real.* But the screams of his buddies echoed eerily through his memory, vividly clear. *If this is not a dream, then I am dead. And dead men cannot dream.* Without explanation for the bizarre series of events, Larson could do nothing but believe. He stood and stumbled forward, broad-based like a child learning to walk. Brownish grasses crunched beneath his boots. The sun formed an orange ball in the pale sky, but Larson could not guess whether morning aged or evening began.

His stride grew more confident as he headed for the stand of trees in the distance. He quelled an instinct to run. For now, the field seemed safe enough. He saw no need to incite enemies by crashing blindly through the meadow. The last few minutes seemed ridiculous to the point of impossibility. Yet, never having died before, Larson supposed he had no right to judge. *And if I am dead,* he surmised, *is this heaven or hell?* It seemed pretty enough. Lonely perhaps, but he had just begun exploring.

More curious than afraid, he trotted toward the higher grasses which he now recognized as cattails. The reeds bowed around a small pond which reflected the sky like an uncut sapphire. Without rations and slightly thirsty, he veered toward the water. Though he knew he could never have survived the guns in the jungle, he peered about him with caution. Until something came about to convince him more completely of his status as a corpse, or to prove there was no death after death, he saw no need to risk . . . whatever it was he had.

Larson frowned and abandoned his jumbled maze of thought. Despite his bold oratory in the jungle cabin, he'd never cared much for philosophy. And Vietnam taught even the most obsessive men to live moment by moment. He dropped to his stomach, gritted his teeth in anticipation, and wriggled among the cattails.

The surface of the pond spread before him, broken only by the ripples of wind and the wakes of water striders. For several seconds, Larson watched the insects glide like skaters, legs stretching like wires from their bulbous bodies. He touched the water, and it felt oddly chill after the enveloping heat of the jungles. Widening rings spread from his finger, lengthening his reflection. His gaze riveted on a face which seemed to stare from the bottom of the pond.

Larson recoiled with a cry. The face mimicked him with a perfection only nature could achieve. It was his reflection, yet the features were not at all as Larson remembered. His forehead was shorter, covered with bangs of fine, white hair. Larson had always felt self-conscious about the roundness of his "baby face." Now, it looked oval and angular, with high, sharp cheekbones and a narrow chin. His eyes seemed broadly-set, though he could not distinguish their color through the pond's distortion. He caught a lock of hair between his fingers. It was not actually white, but such a pale gold as to seem almost white. It reminded him of the color some women dyed their hair back in the States. He had never liked the unnatural, washed-out look, and had always been partial to brunettes.

Recalling his earlier discovery, Larson held the hair away from his head. He cocked his face sideways, and strained his eyes. The oddly-shaped ear remained just beyond his vision. He tried snapping his head about quickly, but found this even less successful. With a sigh, he resigned himself to a tactile impression of the ears. He rose to his full height and examined the clothing which had surprised him earlier. The cape flapped in the wind behind Larson, reminding him of a gripping scene from a Superman cartoon. The most striking feature of his garb was the sword at his left hip. Even sheathed in leather, it seemed to glow ever so slightly, like a television screen only recently shut off.

Larson turned his attention to his own stature.

He seemed as tall as ever, about six feet, but he had no way of knowing for certain. He looked thinner, too, and that bothered him. For a moment, he forgot he was lucky to have any body at all and cursed. Many painful hours had toned and shaped his muscles, now all gone to waste. He flexed an arm, and leaned closer to examine it. The sky darkened till only the sword remained clearly visible on the surface of the pond.

With a frown, Larson dropped to his haunches and waited for the cloud to pass. It did not. Slowly, the shadow encompassed the surface of the water and hovered there. Wary tension returned in a rush. Larson jerked his head upward. Swaying in the air above him was some enormous creature. Screaming, Larson leaped aside. A column of fire struck the water with a hiss.

Larson rolled to his feet as the creature banked for a second pass. He clawed at the cattails. Two bat-like wings carried a long, sleek body covered with scales the color of bark. Plates jutted from back and tail like a stegosaurus. It came around, and the sight of its triangular head mobilized Larson. He sprinted for the woods.

The beast caught him effortlessly, spraying the ground behind with flame. Panicked, Larson did not stop to wonder why the creature had such poor aim. The forest loomed closer, but still too far. His legs ached. Cold air rasped his lungs painfully and brought the taste of blood. Rationality returned only one thought to his numbed mind. *Among the trees, I can maneuver. It cannot.*

Heat seared the back of Larson's neck. Frantically, he ripped the cape from his shoulders and let the flaming linen drop to the ground. The beast rose over his head with a noise between a bark and a human laugh. Larson ran on. He could not control his thoughts, so he let them ramble as they would. *Dragon. Goddamned fire-breathing dragon like every legend and fairy tale I've ever read.* Yet there was a major difference. This one was real.

A wall of trees rose before him. With a joyous sob, Larson ran between them. Another man appeared suddenly before him, and Larson braked with a sharp intake of breath. He stood, panting, before the stranger while sweat dried on his back. The other regarded him with scornful curiosity. His features looked enough like the ones Larson had seen in the pond to be those of a brother. Yet, his hair and skin were as black as Larson's were white. His eyes glowed a feral red.

"Dr-dr-dragon!" stuttered Larson, glad of the stranger's company. "Run!"

The dark elf remained in Larson's path, unmoving, like a carving in black onyx. He spoke in a sibilant voice with an accent Larson recognized but could not place. "Give me the sword."

Hope flared. *The sword.* "Certainly, if you can use it." Larson's fingers trembled as he unsheathed the sword and thrust it toward the stranger.

The dark elf withdrew with a high-pitched expletive. "On the ground, fool! Put it on the ground."

The words puzzled Larson. He balanced the glowing blade on his hands and offered the hilt. The sword vibrated slightly, and the light grew brighter.

"On the ground, idiot!" The stranger retreated farther. His voice lost some of its power.

The reaction raised Larson's suspicions. His mind cleared, and he noticed the other elf as if for the first time. At the Dark One's hip swung a black wooden sheath from which jutted a hilt wrapped

with black split leather and garnished by red gemstones as wild as the stranger's eyes. *So why does he
want my sword?*

The dark elf's lips twisted to a scowl. He took
one bold step forward and gestured angrily toward
the ground. Larson hesitated. They stood face to
face, dark to light, like chess queens before the
final battle. Larson caught the hilt of Valvitnir
in his callused palm. The stranger stiffened, and
sweat oozed above his drawn lips.

Larson knew he had the advantage with his
sword already freed. He would keep that upper
edge, at least until the dark elf realized he did not
know how to wield the blade. "Call me idiot, will
you?" said Larson, not at all certain it was not an
accurate assessment. Suddenly, six grueling weeks
of combat training seemed woefully inadequate.
He executed an awkward fencing lunge. The sword
whined like a hungry dog. The dark elf cursed
and vanished as completely as the building in the
fields.

Larson basked in his triumph for scant seconds.
Flame gouted through the trees with a heat that
made him scream. Despite the forest, the dragon's
aim seemed to have improved miraculously. Still
clutching the sword, Larson ran, dodging trees
with a speed born of desperation. Behind he heard
a beastly roar of frustration, followed by the whisk
of giant wings as the creature rose above the forest.

Branches rustled overhead, too loud for wind.
Fire lanced before him in a column, but the tree-
tops obscured the dragon's vision. Sparks bounced
outward from the impact and died among the
greenery. Larson ran in random circles, doubling
back like a fox. But the creature followed his
ruses, apparently by sound. Soon, the maneuvers

wore on the elf, and his run slowed dangerously. The stabbing fires came closer, threatening to set the entire forest ablaze.

In the distance, Larson saw a more benign fire, the flickering orange of a camp. Desperate, he ran toward it. As he neared, he observed a single figure hunched before it with back turned. From the short gray hair, Larson supposed it was an elderly man and instantly regretted steering the dragon toward the stranger. Too tired to swerve, he ran on.

The man rose and turned suddenly, confirming Larson's impression. Though clean-shaven, the man's lined face revealed his age and gave him an air of power. He wore a loose-fitting yellow garment, trimmed with black and belted at the waist. Two swords girded his waist, a matched set slightly curved like an old Japanese katana and shoto. Gold brocade enhanced both hilts. But the feature which drew Larson's attention was a wooden staff at the old man's feet. Its tip was carved like a claw, and the four black-nailed toes cradled a sapphire.

Flame shot through the spruce, and a wall of heat knocked Larson to one knee at the edge of camp. "Dragon!" He screamed his warning though his lungs felt raw. "Fire . . . breathing . . . dragon!"

The older man seemed unperturbed. "As far as I know they all spit fire." He smiled encouragingly.

From the ground, Larson stared at the stranger's baggy yellow pants. He raised his head to a sagging face. The old man's eyes were brown, slightly slanted, and with prominent epicanthic folds. New danger lent Larson a second wind. He lurched to his feet and reached instinctively for the gun which no longer lay slung across his shoulder.

The stranger watched his antics with obvious amusement. "Beast won't come to ground and fight fair? We'll see what we can do about it." He winked.

Larson fought for breath, quelling panic. He was no longer in Nam. An Oriental face was nothing to fear in and of itself, though he wondered why he should find such a face in Old Scandinavia, or dragons for that matter.

The stranger seemed to notice none of Larson's consternation. He strode past the campfire where the trees thinned and undergrowth grew lush in the sunlight. Larson felt more comfortable despite the open terrain and the dragon shadow which darkened the weeds. The forest seemed much more like those of the New Hampshire camp he had known in his youth than the Vietnamese tangles of stench and death. He followed.

"Wyrm!" screamed the old man.

Larson cringed back as the dragon descended. Its breath reeked of ozone, and scales rattled together like shingles. The beast's jaws gaped. Its black fangs were like giant stalactites, and Larson dodged the globs of spittle which struck the ground with a smoky hiss. With a whoop of wild joy, the old man pulled a piece of metal from his belt and hurled it toward the bus-sized target. His hand was a blur as he pitched three more missiles at the dragon. The first glanced from the hoary chest plates. The second struck, and an explosion rocked the trees. Flame gouted and spread across the dragon, engulfing it. The huge body plummeted with an unearthly wail.

Instinct flattened Larson to the ground; his heart pounded like gunshot. Smoke burned his eyes, and fumes choked him. As he watched through a veil of mist, the smoldering corpse faded to memory. Two of the metallic missiles thumped to earth, and the old man gathered them with a curse. Larson wanted to speak. His lips parted, but no words came forth. He rose, gathered scattered wits, and tried to understand how Freyr expected him to survive with only a sword in a world with both dragons and grenades. All courage fled his overtaxed mind. No amount of field drills could have prepared him for such a madman's reality. He stood utterly still, hoping to escape his fever dreams, yet equally afraid he might again awaken in the jungles.

The old man approached and bowed courteously. "I've not had such fun in days. I, Kensei Gaelinar, thank you, hero." He bowed again.

"Kensei Gaelinar?" Larson's Bronx accent mangled the name. He extended his hand in greeting, but quickly withdrew it when the old man showed no recognition of the gesture. Muddled, he continued. "Um . . . I'm Al." His name seemed pitiably inadequate, so he added inanely ". . . er . . . um . . ."

"Allerum." Gaelinar's brows knitted together in thought. "Odd name. Elven, I suppose. I haven't seen many of your kind in Midgard." He gestured toward the fire. "You look hungry, Allerum. Would you join us?"

More intrigued by the old man's use of the plural pronoun than the misinterpretation of his name, Larson quickly scanned the brush. He saw no one. The odor of roasting meat rose from the campfire and made his stomach rumble. Glad for human company, Larson followed his host to the fire where four steaks hung from a spit. Forgotten in the excitement, their lower sides were vastly overcooked.

"Loki's children!" swore the Kensei. He dismantled the spit and slid the blackened carcasses onto a piece of leather on the dirt. He speared a hunk of meat with a sharpened stick and passed it to Larson apologetically. "I'm not the best cook."

As adrenalin ebbed, Larson found himself ravenously hungry. Saliva poured into his mouth like the rich juices which sizzled on the lesser cooked areas of the steak. He did not know what sort of meat he had accepted from his Oriental-looking companion, but the aching void of his gut would have been pleasured even by manflesh were it the staple of this strange world.

Gaelinar answered his unspoken question. "It's the last of the fresh venison. We smoked the rest for the journey ahead."

Gaelinar used "we" again, Larson noted. *Does the old man simply refer to himself in this odd manner?* Larson had not seen any living creature to dispute his conclusion, except the dark elf he had encountered at the edge of the woods. The thought made him shiver, and so he discarded it. The meat did taste a lot like the deer he used to shoot in the upstate forests, though, perhaps because of his hunger, he found the flavor richer despite the ash.

"Where do you come from, elf?" Kensei Gaelinar asked around a mouthful.

Reluctantly, Larson lowered the food to answer. "I come from far, far away." He winced. His words were not only trite, but grossly understated.

Gaelinar raised his eyebrows encouragingly, but Larson lapsed into silence. His teeth ripped muscle and gristle indiscriminately from the preboned feast. But when the growls of his stomach settled to a satisfied purr, Larson grew more curious about his new companion. "Those . . . um . . . missiles of yours saved my life. How do they work?"

Gaelinar's elbow fell to his knee; his sharpened stick still supported a ring of meat. His slanted eyes slitted, and his features twisted to a scowl of withering disdain. "Your sword didn't help much either."

Larson settled back gingerly, and his chest flinched taut beneath his tunic. He tried to remember what he'd said which might have angered the Kensei. "P-please, I . . . I meant no disrespect," he stuttered.

Gaelinar met Larson's eyes, and his expression went from affronted to puzzled. As suddenly, he smiled. "Oh! You think . . ." He laughed. "No, no, hero. Magic, not my shuriken, flamed that dragon."

Magic. The explanation seemed embarrassingly obvious and oddly comforting. For reasons Larson could not understand, sorceries seemed far more benign than grenades. Unexpectedly, visions from Vietnam flared, horrific as nightmares. He remembered sitting in darkness complete save for the narrow slit of moon over the rows of grass huts. A dank wind rustled the barracks, blended chorus with the shriek of insects and the gentle whisper of sentries at the fire base gate. *Peaceful.* For a moment he could almost forget the ubiquitous threat of the V.C. who owned the jungle nights.

Back pressed to the door jamb of his hut, Larson lifted a joint to his lips; its tip was a singular bobbing light in the pitch darkness. He inhaled. Smoke rolled across his tongue leaving a sweet taste, then funneled into his lungs. He squeezed his mouth shut and held it, swallowing gently. *Nothing could spoil the sanctity of this night.*

A flash of red-orange light colored the sky and outlined the bamboo of huts on either side. Even as Larson's mind responded to the sight, an explosion rocked his foundation, filling his head with sound. Something unseen thudded against his cheek, spinning his face with the force of a slap.

With a warning cry, Larson crashed through the door of his hut. Static blattered and a muffled voice screamed. "Incoming fire! Incoming . . ." A second mortar blast rendered the words incomprehensible. Larson collided with a man in the entranceway with a force which wrenched his ankle. Pain lanced through his abdomen, and Fisher's baritone cursed him with steamy epithets only a street kid could design. As Larson dived for his bunk and the M-16 on the quilt, two more men pushed past and out the door.

The explosion had torn a hole in the hut, and the harried exits of Larson's companions through the door seemed as ludicrous as the gunshot at the fire base perimeter. Not content to lie low while mortars shattered the camp to chaos, soldiers wasted round after round shooting blindly into the jungle. With a sigh, Larson seized his gun to help, but a roaring mortar lit a scene which froze him in place. Danny lay face down on the floor, unresponsive to Tom Dragelin's frantic proddings.

Larson leaped forward, pulled Dragelin's arm with a force that sent the other man reeling against his bunk. Dragelin protested furiously, but Larson flipped Danny over. The body rolled like a rag doll. Blood slicked Larson's fingers, and he recoiled with a choked sob. A chunk of wood from the cottage foundation was embedded in Danny's chest like a stake. His glazed eyes glared accusingly in the scarlet glow of the mortars. The continuous stream of gunshot, screamed orders, man-shouts, and the louder, broken reports of mortars blended to a numbing, unrecognizable ring.

Dragelin's quavering voice was the only thing Larson heard. "Is he. . . ?" They had seen death before, too many times in this sordid movie without beginning or end. But this was Danny, and this was different.

Larson dared not feel for a pulse. "Help me carry him."

He caught Danny behind the shoulders, waited until Dragelin seized the legs, and they lifted together. Danny sagged between them, dead weight, yet they struggled through milling soldiers toward the infirmary.

A roar rose wildly above the rest. The high-pitched scream of jets slammed against Larson's ear drums. He grimaced against the agony of sound, unable to clamp burdened hands to his ears. Then the noise dulled to a long thunder roll. He caught a glimpse of two red disks in the sky, like feral eyes. Abruptly, the jungle flamed in a wide circle. Mercifully, the mortar fire ceased. The answering call of guns died to the last panicked bursts, and the sour odor of napalm pinched his nose. Long after, the screams of the dying echoed through his dreams.

Larson's mind returned to the present with a start. His fists were clenched against sweat which ran like blood. His every nerve felt taut. Adrenalin coursed, warm, through his veins. The face

which stared curiously into his own was Oriental,
yet rounder than a Vietnamese visage. The eyes
were the yellow-brown of ancient pages, and they
held an odd power which reminded Larson of a
picture in a book his mother had read to him as a
child. The book was a juvenile rendition of the
stories of King Arthur; the drawing was of Merlin
the Magician.

"Are you all right, hero?" asked Gaelinar with
concern.

"Yes," responded Larson without conviction. Realization struck a cruel blow. Back home, technology made men equals. Here power stemmed from
skill with sword or sorcery, and he possessed
neither. One thing he knew, he wanted to remain
in the graces of a man who could flame dragons
to ash. "Forgive my ignorance. I'm grateful for
your magic which saved my life. As a . . ." He
rummaged for a word. Warlock seemed deroga-
tory, wizard too plain. Sorcerer conjured images
of Mickey Mouse juggling buckets of water and an
animated broom. Magician reminded him of staged
card tricks. ". . . great and wonderful user of magics . . ." The term seemed vague enough for safety.
". . .you might understand my problem. I'm from
another world."

To Larson, his explanation seemed anything but
humorous, yet the Kensei's features cracked a smile.
Between them, light flashed, bright as a search
flare. Larson staggered back with a cry. His eyes
snapped shut against the glare, and red spots
winked on the backs of his eyelids. He opened
them hurriedly, not certain what to expect and,
so, prepared for nothing. What he saw shocked
him dumb. A woman stood between him and
Gaelinar, more starkly real than anything he had

experienced since death. She was beautiful in a way Larson could not have understood before he glimpsed her.

Plagued by a passion that native whores could never satisfy, any white woman would have seemed more than human to Larson. Yet it was not simply heightened sexual tension which made this woman inhumanly desirable. She was slim beneath a baggy gray robe which in no way marred the perfect arcs of hips and breasts. Her skin looked snowy white. Her eyes echoed Gaelinar's power, bitter gray as gale-tossed surf. Her hair fell to midback in a gold-white cascade, a color Larson had always hated for its artificiality. Now it became his favorite hue. Dyed or real did not matter, it belonged to the woman whose smile, Larson felt, would satisfy him for weeks.

She did smile. Though tinged with sarcasm, her words plied Larson like song. "Oh, please, great mage Gaelinar. Enlighten us with more of your sorceries." The sapphire gleamed in the staff at the Kensei's feet.

The old man rose with a stiffly formal bow. "Lord Allerum, I think it best you meet the Lady Silme, Dragonrank of Sapphire Claw. I shall take neither credit nor blame for her magics."

"Uh . . . hi," said Larson, instantly cursing the bumbling stupidity which had characterized his every action since this day began. From the towel-cracking days of junior high to the raw jibes of boot camp, he had tried to appear competent. Death, it seemed, had shaken his confidence. He tried again. "Lady Silme." He mimicked Gaelinar's bow. "It is my very best pleasure to meet you." *Not bad for my first attempt at courtly talk,* Larson rewarded himself with nonverbal praise.

"You owe me a shuriken, witch," said Gaelinar with none of Larson's respect. "Your fireworks destroyed it. I could have taken the beast without you."

Amusement left Silme's features, replaced by a concern which lined her face beyond its years. "Silence, swordlord." For a brief moment she grinned again at the awkward sound of his title. "You speak as if dragons are commonplace. Someone of Dragonrank summoned the creature."

Gaelinar spoke with bitterness. "Bramin?"

"I recognized his power."

The Kensei paced around the campfire. Silme took the seat he had abandoned and speared a venison steak with a stick. Larson watched both, contemplating a means to correct their misunderstanding of his name without making himself, or Gaelinar, look foolish.

Gaelinar mumbled. "He's close then?"

Silme nodded as she gnawed the meat.

"And the elf?" Gaelinar indicated Larson with a subtle toss of his head.

Silme shrugged. She regarded Larson with a mixture of curiosity and suspicion.

Larson remained silent, not certain what she expected from him. A memory surfaced in his mind with the intensity of a new idea. *You will find an old man and a young woman who are more than they seem. . . . Your companions will explain further.* "You two!" he called triumphantly. "Freyr said you'd tell me about my task."

Gaelinar stopped. Silme blinked in the waning light. "Freyr?"

Larson picked up the pacing where Gaelinar left off. "Yes, Freyr, or at least his voice. I . . ." He broke off, realizing he must sound as touched as the lieutenant who swore he had met Jesus Christ among other raving blasphemies and was duly shipped home. The strained glances between his new companions came not wholly unexpectedly. Further clarification would only place his sanity more completely in doubt. "So you don't know my task?"

Silme returned her attention to the meal while Kensei Gaelinar shook his head slowly. "I'm afraid not."

"Shit." Larson sat, head cradled in his palms. "How many remarkable old men and young women can there be?" Yet he had no way of answering the question. If his experiences to date gave any indication, this world was crowded with extraordinary people.

Silme and Gaelinar offered no comfort. As the sky dimmed to gray, they turned to matters more relevant to themselves. Larson brooded in silence, thinking they had forgotten him. The setting sun colored the horizon with flame-colored arches, a doorway for the daring. Idly, he wondered if he could pass through it like a gate and find himself home or in Oz or back in the stinking hell of Vietnam.

After a time, Silme turned from her companion, retrieved her sapphire-tipped staff, and approached Larson. She moved with a dancer's confident grace, but her eyes shifted in the manner of a deer. Larson stared, surprised at how, despite death and the oddities of his new surroundings, her beauty excited him.

Silme stopped several yards from Larson. Her features remained soft, but she jabbed the tip of her staff toward him. Her words emerged as a calculated threat. "Are you who you claim?"

Her tone made Larson uneasy. He shifted to a crouch. "Y-yes, of course," he stammered defensively, immediately realizing his hasty reply robbed him of any opportunity to correct her misunderstanding of his name. Thrust into a new life and a strange world, he supposed he needed a new identity. Allerum was not the name he would have chosen, but it would do as well as any other. "At least as close as could be expected. You see, I . . ."

Silme interrupted. "And your purpose in the world of Midgard?"

Larson fidgeted. His gaze swept the tree line. *She knows I'm from another world. How?* But the answer came to him as swiftly as the question. He sifted his thoughts for the duller cosmology of his mythology text. The Vikings believed in nine worlds, each inhabited by its own race of creatures: giants, gods, elves, dwarves. *Midgard,* Larson recalled, *was the land of men. To her, I'm an elf.* The thought seemed foreign. *In that respect, I am from another world.*

"Your purpose?" Silme prompted.

Larson had forgotten her question. "I'm on a mission. My, um, commander informed me I would find an older man and a young woman who could explain things further. I'm afraid I've mixed you up with someone else."

Silme scowled, unsatisfied. "What connection do you have with Bramin?"

The word meant nothing to Larson. "What's a Bramin?"

Anger darkened Silme's eyes. "I won't stand for lies! Do you think me stupid enough to believe coincidence placed an elf in a wash of Bramin's magic, playing with a conjured dragon?"

"Playing!"

Soundlessly, Gaelinar cleared the distance to Silme and caught her arm. "It wouldn't be the first time an innocent stumbled into Bramin's designs against your life."

Silme never took her gaze from Larson. "An elf?"

Gaelinar shrugged. "We've come upon stranger occurrences."

Silme raised her brows and eyed her Oriental companion. "An elf?"

Gaelinar sighed. "In Lord Allerum's defense, the dragon seemed less than friendly toward him. You swore to protect mankind from Bramin's wrath. Would you deny wardings to a traveler without bedding or rations because he happens to be an elf? Shame on you, lady." He smiled at Larson. "Join us for the night?" He motioned to a pile of furs near the campfire.

Silme opened her mouth to protest, but Gaelinar waved her silent. "If the elf can slay us in our sleep, he deserves to wear our heads at his belt." Respectfully, he bowed toward Silme then turned and knelt in the furs. He tapped a space at his side invitingly.

Larson hesitated, sorting his fears. Gaelinar's camaraderie beckoned, despite his features. Silme's comeliness seemed added incentive; he found her aloofness a challenge. He felt certain from their display of power against the dragon, that either of his new acquaintances could already have killed him if they had wished. He turned a glance toward Silme.

Silme's eyes met Larson's stare. She smiled weakly. "Gaelinar's right, of course. You may join us for the night." She emphasized the last phrase as if to assure herself of the transience of his presence.

Larson rose and paced to the furs by the fire. He sprawled beside Gaelinar, more comfortable for soft bedding and warmth. Silme stood, watching the two men, arms spread. Her gaze seemed to pass through and beyond them. Her eyes blazed like gemstones.

"What's she doing?" Larson asked, concerned.

"Quiet," whispered Gaelinar. "You'll mar the spell."

Larson fell silent. He watched in fascination as the grim lines in Silme's face deepened. Light streamed from each hand, the dazzling white of phosphorus. Snakelike, the beams coiled around the camp and met halfway. Blue light welled to life on her fingers, wound about the white with an intensity that colored stars and moon. Silme stepped forward and examined her efforts briefly. At an approving nod, the enchantments faded, but Larson still felt the presence of their brooding power. Protected by the sorceress' wards, Larson pondered the coming day until fatigue overtook him and granted a dreamless sleep.

CHAPTER 2

Manslayer

"The belief in a supernatural source of evil is not necessary; men alone are quite capable of every wickedness."
—Joseph Conrad,
Under Western Eyes

A yellow edge of sun tipped over the horizon, chasing darkness in bands of blue and pink. As if it were a signal, the sleepers within the sorceress' wards stirred. Silme was first to open her eyes and greet the dawn, but her movements wakened Gaelinar and Larson. Her enchantments had dwindled through the night, yet when Larson tried to leave the protected circle to relieve himself, he discovered they still held the potency of an electric fence.

Silme snickered and dispelled her magics with a word. Gaelinar bowed politely. "Lord Allerum, we've enjoyed your company, but we must move along and you as well."

"Wait." Silme rummaged through a weathered pack, pulled out a bag of woven cloth, and handed it to the elf. "Rations," she explained. "I noticed

you carried none and couldn't leave you starving."
She clipped her words short as if to register her
disapproval. "You must have left someplace in an
awful hurry." Her tone demanded explanation.

Larson declined to answer. The few times he
had tried to enlighten his new friends had put his
sanity in question. He preferred an aura of mys-
tery to one of lunacy. "I thank you both." He
extended a hand, hoping Silme might accept it
like a royal maiden in the movies. He would gladly
submit to the ridicule of an entire platoon if it
meant a chance to kiss her fingers. But Silme
showed no more understanding of the gesture
than Gaelinar had of his attempted handshake.

After a breakfast of dried meat and fruit, Larson took his leave. He skirted the tangled clearing,
reminded of Vietnam's towering elephant grasses
which forced the point man to waddle as he cleared
a path for his followers. He traveled northward,
beneath interlocking branches which muted the
sun. Pines flowed endlessly past, lower branches
withered in the shadow of their younger brothers.
Songbirds flitted above Larson's head, their sweet
trills a welcome relief from the too-well remembered screams of macaws.

Near midday, his mood reversed. He began to
question Silme's and Gaelinar's sidelong glances in
the clearing and the sorceress' mistrustful queries.
The birds became less apparent, their song more
shrill. A squirrel, startled from its food hunt,
scolded, while Larson was still some distance away.
A shiver traversed him from buttocks to neck,
warning of imminent peril. Repeatedly, Larson
reminded himself this forest hid no snipers. But
his fear remained and intensified nearly to panic

until he would have bet all the water in his pouch
that unseen eyes watched from the branches.

Larson stopped, hoping the sudden cessation of
his own passage would amplify any noises around
him. The harsh call of a crow ruined the silence.
Suddenly, light sparked before him, flaring to blinding brilliance. He dropped to a crouch, now capable enough to recognize a sorcerer's craft. Desire
dared him to hope the power originated from the
slim-waisted beauty he had left that morning.

But the figure which sprang to clarity was cloaked
in a blackness which was echoed in his features.
Red eyes met Larson's for the second time, filled
with cruelty and misplaced hatred. This time, the
dark elf clutched a staff like Silme's, but the gem
gripped between carven claws was a flawless diamond. And he raised it threateningly.

Shaken, Larson stumbled two steps backward.
His mind reverberated with memory of his last
encounter with the demon elf. His trembling fingers found the hilt of his sword and drew it with a
rasp of steel.

"Fool!" Bramin's voice mocked him. "Do you
think your toy will save you from my wrath?" He
suffixed his threat with a single coarse syllable.

Pain lanced through Larson's fist, flaming to an
agony which swept his entire arm. The sword fell
from his weakened grip and crashed against stone
with a shower of ice blue sparks. Bramin's assault
continued ruthlessly. Waves of torture racked mind
and body, twitched Larson's limbs like those of a
stringless marionette. Scream after scream ripped
from his raw lungs in ghastly duet with Bramin's
laughter.

Pain stabbed through Larson's body like daggers, worse than any agony described as hell. Could

he have uttered a coherent sentence, he would have pleaded for death. But Bramin knew no mercy. His spell stole strength of body and reserves of mind, seared like flame, and convulsed its hapless victim with anguish.

Suddenly, the pain stopped. Larson flopped to the ground like a beached fish. His mind jumped erratically. His breaths came thankfully easier from his aching lungs. Through vision clouded by his ordeal, he saw movement, and watched the blue blur of the sword slide toward Bramin's gesturing hand. He understood what was happening, but it meant nothing to him. *Let the dark elf have the sword. I have no use for it.*

The shadows flickered, suffused with blue as the sword flared with an anger all its own. The hilt knocked against a stone in its path toward Bramin, splattering enchantments like the rays of a star. A soft breaking of brush from behind startled Larson where he lay helpless and still, recalling stories of injured soldiers left for dead. Silver flashed over his head, casting a slight breeze which cooled his tortured limbs.

Bramin recoiled with a pained hiss. As he clamped his hands to his chest, his red eyes blazed purple with rage. His link with the sword broke, and it halted with a lurch. Blood trickled between his fingers, and his slim hand raised in an ominous gesture. Larson recognized a shaped piece of steel jutting from Bramin's wound. The dark elf's gaze locked on the gold-robed Kensei behind Larson who had hurled the shuriken.

Sorceries crackled, bounced between Bramin's outstretched hands as though they were opposing mirrors, and intensified to blinding white. Bramin moved. His magic leaped like a beast and screamed toward the man behind Larson. Larson heard a curse. Then, a second jagged ray sprang from the brush. Magics met with a sound like thunder, and both spells broke to glittering traces. *Silme!* Larson shielded his eyes against the backlash.

Bramin's malevolent voice broke the ensuing silence. "Hel take all your souls!" The diamond in his staff winked black, and the dark elf vanished.

Gaelinar's callused hand gripped Larson's upper arm and hoisted the elf to his feet. Movement dizzied Larson. He staggered, but regained his balance with the Kensei's aid. His stomach heaved. Unable to avoid the inevitable, Larson ripped free, dropped to his knees, and vomited with an intensity unknown since more experienced soldiers had forced him to wallow through rotting bodies to prepare him for death. Embarrassment brought tears to his eyes. He knew the most beautiful woman in existence watched, surely with disgust.

But Silme waited until Larson's sickness passed and squeezed his hand with a reassurance which almost made the ordeal worthwhile. "My humblest apologies, Lord Allerum," she said. "Had I known we shared such an enemy, I would never have let you travel alone."

Larson bowed though his legs felt weak and rubbery. He chose his words with delicate care. "Lady, I could never hold any offense against you." He beamed at his own efforts.

Gaelinar continued. "We dared not trust you. Light elves act as capricious as Bramin's kind do evil." He gestured, toward the place where the dark elf had stood. "But faery creatures of any sort are rare in the manworld of Midgard. We assumed you were outcast, that Alfheim's lord,

Freyr, had exiled you. Bramin's attack and your sword tell us otherwise."

Larson tried to recall his readings on the subject of elves. He had concentrated his interest on gods and war, and all he could dredge from memory was the respective good and evil tendencies of light and dark elves. He had read somewhere that tales of the latter were so rare many authorities believed dark elves and dwarves to be interchangeable. He regarded Silme and Gaelinar. *I have to trust someone. With enemies as unassailable as Bramin and his dragons, I have no chance of survival without capable, knowledgeable companions. And these two people have already rescued me twice.* "This may sound strange or impossible . . ." He spoke slowly, studying Silme's face for any clue he might have overstepped the boundaries of credibility. "Freyr called me from a place beyond the scope of your nine worlds. Aside from a few legends, I'm ignorant of even the simplest matters of Midgard."

Silme's face twisted in doubt, but her eyes widened and her lips pursed in consideration. Her gaze dropped to the faintly-glowing sword on the ground, and her expression changed suddenly to one of surprise. Ignoring Larson's revelation, she knelt before Valvitnir.

Larson cleared his throat. "Why are elves so uncommon here?"

Gaelinar seemed to accept Larson's explanation easily. "Travel between the nine worlds requires great effort and power. Even the gods cannot wholly disregard the energy such travel demands. Elves of any sort were never common. In time, men grew to despise the dark elves for their cruelty and vile sense of humor. Where men still remember dark elves, they slay them on sight.

"Light elves view men as narrow-minded beings so concerned with death they refuse to enjoy their short lives. Man's somber nature made light elves extremely uncomfortable, so they gradually curtailed all commerce with the world of men. Now, the tales and memories of elves have been confused or, at best, forgotten. At times, dark elves are welcomed because of the legends of light elves, and light elves are slain for the ancient crimes of their dark cousins. Mostly, the sidelong glances and whispered comments which follow any stranger viewed as different will accompany you throughout the world of Midgard."

Silme's voice seemed distant as she returned the blade to its sheath at Larson's side. "That sword is the work of a pure and powerful god. I don't know its abilities or purpose, but assuredly they will shape the destiny of our world." Her features assumed the intensity of her words. "Magic saps the life force of the one who calls it forth. Understand this, Allerum, a god paid dearly for your quest."

Guilt preyed on Larson's conscience. *Does Silme know how easily I gave up the struggle to Bramin, that I would have tossed him the sword to avoid his wrath?* But the situation had changed. Quest or no, Bramin's cruelty charged Larson to seek revenge.

The three continued north and east through forest which seemed endless. Pine passed to more pine, like the recurrent background of a cartoon until Larson began to believe they had gained no ground since the confrontation. But the walk gave him the chance to ask many questions. Their answers gave the world a logical order, magic aside. There were villages and governments, monarchies, and temples to the Northern gods. Wizards were a rarity, despite Larson's run-in with two of Midgard's most powerful on his first day.

"Most men," Silme told him, "become farmers or artisans. Those with interest in sword, or bow join armies or sell their services as bodyguards, soldiers, and assassins. To become a sorcerer requires an innate ability and a lifetime dedicated to magic. Even then, only those few stamped with 'the mark' can attain the power of Dragonrank." She displayed her right hand, and Larson stared at the claw-shaped scar which marred her skin.

As they walked, Silme and Gaelinar schooled Larson concerning travel foods and horse trading. They introduced him to the most common monetary system of the Northern kingdoms. But it was Bramin's name which opened a veritable flood of explanation, and Silme talked of the half-elf throughout the evening and on through a dinner of smoked venison.

"A warped creature," Silme described her half brother. ". . . twisted by a legacy base as demon shadow and intent on inappropriate retribution since I scarce passed from glass level to semiprecious." She indicated the sapphire which glimmered at the tip of her staff. "Bramin leagued with Loki the Evil One." Her voice grated with dissent, as if mere mention of the name caused her pain. "So, I joined with Vidarr the Silent, a god whose strength is exceeded only by that of the thunderlord, Thor. Even then, I knew someone must stop Bramin before his vengeance harmed innocents."

She took a bite of meat, eyes distant. Larson longed to put his arms around her and offer comfort, but Gaelinar sat between them. Her voice grew stronger. "Bramin held three years of advantage over me. He swept through the Dragon-ranks like wildfire in a shipyard. I knew I could never equal his training, but I fought to follow. Nearly every spell I chose to learn could be used as a defense against one of his. I forsook many of my own offenses for wards against him, a vast repertoire of counterspells as protection for Bramin's victims."

Silme's eyes remained fierce points of blue, but her body sagged as if with fatigue. "He left the school at the rank of Master. Though three grades behind, I followed, hoping to withhold his evils from the world. Kensei Gaelinar nearly equals the odds between us."

Larson could think of nothing to say in the awesome wake of her story. He let his mind absorb the oddities of Midgard as the meal continued in silence and night plunged the forest into darkness.

At the base of the deepest root of the World Tree lay the Spring of Hvergelmir which fed the rivers of the world and was in turn filled by them. Its waters frothed like the boiling brew in a witch's cauldron. On its bank stood two figures, one light with a rotted core, the other wholly dark.

Bramin's life aura spread about him like flame. His voice was gritty with accusation. "You never warned me the sword was warded. I shudder to imagine the damage had I taken it in hand. Retrieve your own blade."

Hvergelmir belched putrid gas. Loki regarded his prodigy with wry amusement. "Relax, Hates-pawn. I didn't know. It wasn't warded when it was still in my hands." He smiled at some private joke. "But your efforts will not go for naught. This task is so important, I offer reward without equal. Should you retrieve Valvitnir, you shall have the hand of my daughter, Hel, and rulership of her realm."

Bramin paused, momentarily speechless. His aura flickered and dulled to pink as anger faded. As Helmaster, he would be lord of the dead; the souls of men would become his to rack and rend through eternity.

Loki read his thoughts, and spoke over Hvergelmir's gurglings. "Beyond eternity, Hatespawn. If we destroy that sword, the nine worlds shall become ours. All men and gods will topple, lost to a chaos only you and I control. Not even the Fates can stay our vengeance."

Loki's enthusiasm spread to the sorcerer. "I've a plan," called Bramin as he watched lines of bubbles rise from the boiling spring. "In the woods, I did a mind search. Freyr's champion is a human in elf guise, a man from the future and a poor choice. The true structure of Midgard makes such knowledge as he has obsolete, and he has none of the mental protections of our kind. In short, he understands nothing of the sword's power and will fall easy prey to illusion. Although," he added bitterly. "Silme's presence makes my task infinitely more difficult."

Loki paced, distressed. It seemed almost too easy.

Bramin's next revelation redirected his thoughts. "I can read the runes," he said softly. His sword scraped from its ebony sheath, and its writings gleamed to vivid relief:

Helblindi
The Sword of Darkness
All who die on its edge
Add their souls to Hel's shadow hordes.
Their screams shall echo to Valhalla's barred gate.

Loki smiled. "And now you know why brave men must fear it. By assuring them eternity in the hall of men who succumb to illness or cowardice, we strip all glory from death in battle." *And add strength to my own army at the final battle*, he gloated in silence.

Bramin's fist clenched with purpose. "The writings are clear," the dark elf reminded Loki of his promise. "My vengeance?"

The burbling waters seemed to join Loki's laughter. "When you bring the sword, you shall have them many times over. But if petty slayings amuse you in the meantime, enjoy them. Just don't let them interfere with your task."

Bramin's malignant smile was his only answer.

Larson dreamed. He saw his sword, Valvitnir, gleaming blue as muted porch light. It spun in his hands, flinging glimmers in wild arcs. Gradually, the scene faded to a vivid view of the pine forest. He wandered wonderingly through a world of green highlights as tree trunks shuddered around him and their branches fused to a common core.

The whole seemed not unlike an insect, a giant, hairy spider, amusingly awkward. The trees rose like legs, moved from the confines of the forest, and Larson followed curiously. Eleven trunks gave the creature mobility, each with a name that ran through his mind like the players on a team: Svol, Gunnthra, Fjorm, Fimbulthul, Slidr, Hrid, Sylgr, Ylgr, Vid, Leiptr, and Gjoll. Even as he repeated the strange-sounding names, they muted.

The forest became a valley whose darkness the moon could not graze. The spider's legs split the blackness as they transformed into streams which sparkled like diamonds. They no longer towered

up from the ground. Their waters plunged downward to meet a swirling torrent, a glorious cascade
of foam unmatched by any work of man. Mesmerized, the dream-Larson worked the sword from its
sheath and watched the tumescent waters wink
shadows through the glow of the sword's magic.
He drew back his arm and hurled the blade. The
sword tumbled end over end. It hit the burbling
spring with a splash and sank instantly out of
sight.

Even as relief rushed to replace the urgency of
his quest, the illusion acquired the frightening
quality of his unbidden memory of Danny's death.
An unfamiliar obscenity crossed his thoughts briefly.
The scene wavered. The spring flushed to the
color of blood, and bloated, white bodies gorged
the streams. An alien presence knocked his consciousness askew.

He awoke screaming. Gentle hands first caught
his wrists and then drew his face to a chest which
muffled his cries. Consciousness changed his
screams to sobs, and his tears made the thin gray
cloth cling to Silme's breasts. She rocked him,
humming as if to a child, oblivious to the turmoil
in Larson's soul. He ached, loosing tears held far
too long, tears he had locked away as war forced
him from the mischievous antics of adolescence to
the atrocities of men. These were the tears he'd
never shed for Danny.

"Are you all right? What happened?" Silme asked
in a voice which could soothe a stampede.

"Just a dream," Larson heard himself say, though
he made no effort to speak. "Just a bad nightmare." His own voice brought a new rush of sorrow. "Oh, Jesus, what's wrong with me?"

Silme pulled her fingers from Larson's hair with

a crackle of static. She seized both of his hands, squatted before him, and met his gaze. "What was the dream?"

Overwhelmed by the intensity of the sorceress' gaze, Larson closed his eyes. Tears pooled on his lashes, and he spoke around his sobs with gritted teeth. "I'm sorry. Let me pull myself together first." For a brief moment, he hated this woman who was callous enough to stare at a broken man. But when he raised his lids, the sincerity of her pained expression moved him to pity. He let the tears fall where they might and began to relate his dream.

Larson told Silme and Gaelinar of the forest and its strange conformation. He described the eleven streams and their source and was surprised to find he remembered their names. His narrative slowed as he recalled tossing the sword into the burbling spring and the relief inspired by its sacrifice. Even as Larson detailed the final sequence, memory battered against his sanity. He held his gaze on Silme, aware a single glimpse of Gaelinar's slanted eyes would snap his control over the flashbacks.

"There's more." Silme would allow no denial. "Something frightened you."

The tears slackened to a trickle. Larson shook his head with an intensity that whipped his face with hair. "The dream ends there. The rest is . . ." he sneaked a look at Gaelinar, then closed his eyes tight against dizziness, ". . . just recollections of horrors I've seen."

Silme pounced on his words without mercy. "For some reason, your mind relates them to this dream. Tell me . . ."

"No!" The word came out more like a whine

than a command. Larson sagged forward on his bedding. His tears discolored the furs in a pool. *How can I tell Silme about a world where technology makes equals of the foolish and the skilled? How can I describe a place where there are no heroes or villains, where the lines between good and evil blur to interpretation, where men rape and torture innocents in the name of justice.* Larson slumped to one elbow, unable to face his new companions. *How can I expect her to understand the feelings of virility and power behind a loaded gun or the camaraderie which makes dismembering the dead seem noble?*

Enshrouded in a self-erected tomb of guilt and shame, Larson lay utterly still. He curled into a fetal position as a stream of tears wound uncontrollable lines around his cheeks. The voices he heard sounded dulled by distance.

". . .close enough to Forste-Mar. We'll take him to the dream-reader."

"We'll talk later. Can you do something for him?"

Leaves crunched beside him as Silme approached and laid her palms gently on his shoulders. Larson raised his head. His tear-blurred vision distorted her beauty to shapelessness. She whispered seemingly meaningless syllables, and the scattered shards of Larson's rationality fused together as her spell blanketed him with peace. As he opened his mouth to speak, he fell into dreamless bliss.

Larson awoke to a dull mental ache, like an old scar in cold weather. Sunlight was already slanting through the branches. He had overslept. He leaped to his feet and bit off an expletive as Silme rose to meet him.

"Here." She pushed a fist-sized strip of jerked

venison into his hands. "We'd best be off if we're to reach town by midday."

"Town?" Rubbing his swollen eyes, Larson glanced toward Gaelinar, who was examining the sharpened edge of his katana with approval.

The Kensei pocketed the whetstone and sheathed his sword. "Forste-Mar. It's Silme's hometown." He pointed vaguely northward.

Larson followed the gesture mechanically as he mulled over all the incredible things that had happened to him recently. More accustomed to his new surroundings, now he began to consider details which earlier had been blurred by the necessity for self-preservation. He became aware of the language he spoke as fluently as his companions, a melodious singsong which he supposed was Old Norse. He could not guess why the cold slap of wind did not chill him after the suffocating jungle heat, nor why he remained clean-shaven after two days without a razor.

Larson idly chewed mouthfuls of meat as their journey through the evergreen forest resumed. The clustered trees restricted undergrowth yet remained sparse enough for clear vision and passage. Yearning for a new identity, he paid little attention to their trail. *Al Larson died in Vietnam. Let him keep his memories of atrocity and evil. I am Allerum, an elf without a past on a quest sanctioned by gods.*

Despite the veracity of the sentiment, Larson's conscience resisted. Ugly recollections fought for control, bloody scenes witnessed by the man he had just denounced; but in the sanctity of the forest, Larson held such thoughts in check. His eyes followed Silme, and he surrendered to a thrill of desire. She moved soundlessly, like a woodland being. For all the effort it cost her, the forest might have adapted to suit her rather than she to it.

Gaelinar pushed past Larson and caught the hand in which Silme held her sapphire-tipped staff. The gesture drew Larson from his struggle with self-identity. Until that moment, he'd never considered there might be more to his companions' relationship than mere friendship. The idea drove him to a sadness which flared to fury. He glared as Silme answered Gaelinar's whispered words with a laugh, and the Kensei took the lead of the party.

He must be twice her age, Larson reminded himself in a rage. Yet jealousy did not blind him to an important fact. He had no way to judge Silme's years. Surely a powerful sorceress could warp time's ravishings with illusion. His stomach lurched at the notion. Beauty by magic seemed deceitful. *Yet,* Larson thought as reason dispersed anger, *why should Silme not take advantage of her craft?* Recognition of his own shallowness made Larson flush. There was more to Silme than comeliness. She demonstrated poise, empathy, generosity, pride, and a confidence he sorely missed in himself.

Ruffled by his ponderings, Larson turned his attention back to their surroundings. The terrain grew more hilly, swarming with foxgrape and low, twisted bushes. Passage grew easier as brush gave way to discernible trails beaten to mud by feet, hooves, and wagon wheels. The woods broke suddenly to fields of wind-bowed grain, and the weed-grown path became an obvious road with branches and byways.

Larson hesitated, accustomed to the waist-high, leech-infested swamps of the rice paddies. Gaelinar and Silme continued down the roadway between wheat fields without any apparent worry. But as they turned simultaneously to urge Larson forward, he recognized a solemnity which had escaped him during the journey. He trotted to Silme's side, stared into her eyes, and demanded stridently, "What's the matter?"

She lowered her head until billows of golden hair obscured her face. Her knuckles whitened about her dragonstaff, and she spoke in a dry, quavering whisper. "After your dream I sought Vidarr's guidance. He didn't respond." She raised water-glazed eyes to Larson's curious stare.

A reply seemed necessary, but Larson could think of none. He tried to keep a patronizing tone from his question.

"Does he usually answer you?"

"With images at least." Silme threw back her locks to reveal a face drawn with concern. "I'm his favored attendant. Something terrible has happened."

Unfamiliar with the dealings between gods and men, Larson could offer no real reassurance. He reached for Silme, but Kensei Gaelinar caught his forearm with a tortured cry. "Look there!"

Larson followed the old man's stare. White smoke funneled toward the sky from beyond the next rise. Gaelinar broke into a run, and his companions followed. Larson stubbed a toe in his haste, and his soft, doeskin moccasins did little to dull the impact. Cursing and limping, he caught up with Gaelinar at the hilltop, and the scene below made him forget his pain. Flames danced around an overturned wagon. Beside it, two men pinned a struggling figure to the ground while a third swayed, locked to the wild lurches of the prisoner.

High-pitched, panicked screams drowned Larson's own attempts at breath and cut him to the heart.

Every man draws his limit at an atrocity no amount of coercion could force him to commit. Larson's was rape. More than once, he had turned away while peers in uniform shamed and killed daughters before their helpless fathers. Too moral to join in, at the same time he was unable to risk provoking men on whom his life depended. So he had remained silent, seared by the guilt of a tacit condemnation which might have been approval for all it served the victim or his own conscience. All these thoughts condensed to a boil of emotion.

"Wait!" screamed Silme.

But Gaelinar sprinted down the roadway, howling, "Allerum, charge!" And, hearing his cry, the bandits scrambled for weapons.

After nearly a year of staking his life on strangers' orders, Larson obeyed Gaelinar without thought. He ran within thirty yards of the conflict before he remembered he could not wield his sword. He stopped abruptly as Gaelinar leaped at one of the rapists. Steel chimed as the bandit's sword crashed against the Kensei's shoto. Gaelinar's katana cut a silver arc and cleaved the bandit's neck.

Before Larson could react with even a gasp, one of the bandits closed the gap between them, brandishing a knife in his left hand and a short scimitar in his right. Forced to defend himself, Larson grasped Valvitnir's hilt and pulled. The sword came free with surprising ease and blazed blue as Larson made an awkward lunge. His opponent retreated before the longer weapon.

Larson thrust repeatedly. The bandit redirected the wild strokes with deft flicks of his scimitar. Sweat trickled down Larson's face in a cold stream.

Patience and skill would win this match, and he fell short on both. He hoped Gaelinar would finish his own battle before Larson lost the advantage of distance. Then, he caught sight of the mud-caked figure on the road. *The victim of the bandits' cruel assault was a young boy.*

Anger broke Larson's timing. His opponent dodged under his guard. Steel lanced toward his throat. Sacrificing balance, Larson caught the bandit's left wrist in his hand. The scimitar jarred around his crossguard, and the close range rendered Valvitnir useless. With his right hand locked to his enemy's wrist, Larson scarcely had time to react to the scimitar which flashed for his chest. He dropped his sword. Steel tumbled, and the hilt struck his stubbed toe. Pain shot to his knee. His freed fingers fended off the bandit's other wrist. The scimitar quivered inches from his cheek.

A gasp broke from the bandit with the odor of rotting teeth. He yanked free with a strength which wrenched every tendon in Larson's forearm. The elf responded sluggishly. The scimitar would cut him down before he could regain his grip. Resigned to a second death, he dodged as best he could. Suddenly, steel flashed from the shadows. A hunting blade in the grip of the ravaged child severed the bandit's hamstring, and he reeled backward. Larson's foot lashed into his opponent's groin. The bandit dropped, limp as a rag.

Sweat stung Larson's eyes and splintered the scene to bluish points of light. He dropped to his knees beside the writhing bandit. His hand closed on the hilt of the abandoned scimitar, and he thrust for his enemy's heaving chest. The bandit cringed flat with a strangled whimper, eyes wild with fear. Realization battered Larson like a blow.

He pulled the strike a finger's breadth from the bandit's heart, and the scimitar flopped from his hand like a wounded quail. *The man is helpless. Have I become so callous I kill without thought?*

The bandit's lips set, puzzled. A shadow fell across his drawn face, and light flashed overhead. Larson sprang aside as Gaelinar's katana whisked past him and carved a line of blood across the bandit's throat. The body spasmed in death, its face locked in surprise permanent as a mask.

Larson heard himself scream. His mind tore free from his body, plunging him into an older, more familiar world. Comprehension darkened, than broke in a flash to memory of boot-scuffed dust flickering in the midday heat. It was noon, time for him and Brent Hamill to replace Gavin and Fisher as perimeter guard. Hamill was a newcomer to Aku Nanh, a one week "fucking new guy" who had not yet seen his first fire fight. Though Hamill's inexperience endangered them, Larson liked him and felt obligated to help him through his initiation into Vietnam.

The past few weeks had been unusually quiet which pleased Larson but made many of his companions bored and impatient. Hamill's eyes jumped excitedly as he eyed the wall of sand bags which enclosed the fire base. Larson spared an encouraging smile. As they neared their station, a single shot rang above the general din of conversations. Fisher's good-natured curse was nearly lost beneath Gavin's laughter.

Larson dodged around a grass hut, Hamill close behind. At the perimeter, Gavin hunched over his gun while Fisher baited him like a catcher on a baseball field. Hamill's eyes widened with innocent interest as Larson called to his companions. "What are you doing?"

Gavin glanced over his shoulder and gestured Larson forward. When Hamill and Larson reached the sand bags, Gavin pointed across the tank-cleared plain. A stooped figure waddled along a winding road, barely discernible as an elderly woman. "So?" asked Larson.

"Five bucks to the guy what hits her," explained Fisher with a fiendish smile. "Try your hand?"

Hamill made a pained noise. Larson looked quickly from newcomer to friend, then transformed the shocked movement into a negative toss of his head.

Gavin shrugged and returned to his task. The M-16 spoke once, the woman continued undaunted, and Gavin crawled aside. Fisher moved into position. He spat on his hands, wiped them on his overlarge pants, and hunched over the gun.

Larson avoided Hamill's frantic glances. He knew Gavin and Fisher were merely working off hostility. The woman walked well beyond reasonable target range, and, apparently, she had taken no notice of their potshots.

Hamill grew more distressed. He caught Larson's forearm, and his grip tightened painfully as Gavin and Fisher passed the M-16 twice more between them. When Larson finally turned his attention to Hamill, the newcomer mouthed the words, "Make them stop."

Larson shook him off, not comfortable with the situation, yet unwilling to side with an FNG against friends. Hamill balled his hands together and paced wildly. Crazed beyond understanding, he stopped without warning, swung his M-16 from his shoulder, lined and fired. Soundlessly, the old woman fell to the ground.

Hamill's mouth wrenched open and his face puckered. Larson cringed from the inevitable scream, but Hamill stood silent, like a movie without sound. The gun slid from his hands and thumped to the ground. His dull brown eyes stared through Larson, and he staggered toward the huts as if drunk.

Larson turned to follow, but Fisher caught the back of his shirt. "Shit, Larson. Leave the poor FNG alone. You like some dude hoverin' over you after your first kill?"

Larson paused as Hamill disappeared around a grass hut. "You don't have to be the guy's mother," Gavin added. "Everyone goes through it. You went through it; I went through it. He'll feel like shit with you watching him puke or cry or both. And you ain't going to feel too great either. When . . ."

A pistol shot sounded in the compound, from the general direction of Larson's hut. *Ohmygod!* Larson sprinted toward his quarters with a single coherent thought. *Let it be a rat. Oh, shit, let it be a goddamn rat!* Although trained to his peak physical condition, Larson was out of breath by the time he rounded the corner and burst through the door to his hut. His heart hammered, loud and consistent as machine gun fire. His gaze played over the familiar disarray and settled on the body in his own bunk. Hamill lay still as if in sleep. The .45 automatic lay across his left thigh. His eyes remained open, as if staring at some horrifying sight. Blood spurted from his mangled chin.

"No!" Larson screamed to ears which could not hear. His first aid training surfaced with mechanical efficiency. *For bleeding, apply direct pressure.* Larson covered the ground between himself and Hamill in a single heroic bound. Need usurped thought. Larson locked his hands on the tatters of Hamill's face. Shards of bone and teeth gashed his palms, and his blood mingled freely with the scarlet spring ebbing from his patient.

"Al, stop! There's nothing you can do. He's dead. . . ."

"There's nothing you can do. He's dead." The words were the same, but the voice was from another world. Larson focused on the blood which colored his fingers dull red. The chin cupped between his hands sported two days' growth of beard; the eyes were mercifully closed in death. Larson raised his gaze to the burning wagon. Before it, Gaelinar held the struggling boy. "Child, it's too late. Your uncle is dead."

Dazed, Larson recoiled from the corpse. He whirled to stare at the glowing blue sword, and its brilliance returned him to a reality found only in legend. Slowly, he reached for it. Another object caught his eye, a glass bottle with a hand-lettered label. He retrieved both, jammed the sword into its sheath, and examined the phial. A thick, honey-colored liquid sloshed behind the words: *Crullian's Marvelous Cure*.

Near the dying flames, the boy ceased his furious kicks and punches. He fell against Gaelinar's loose-fitting garb, sobbing. The swordmaster, who had just mercilessly killed three men, held the child in the folds of his robe, face drawn with genuine concern.

Silme strode from behind the wreckage, and her reprimand was singularly tactless. "You may be a sword saint, Kensei. But by Vidarr's shoe, someone's got to teach you to think."

Gaelinar returned her accusation with unbroken confidence. "I'm sorry we got in your way. We couldn't take a chance your spells might hit the boy. Besides," he smiled sheepishly. "I was mad."

The boy pulled away to face Silme. He was small; Larson guessed him to be about ten years old. Raven-hued hair covered his head in a tangle, and his skin was light olive. His quick, blue eyes seemed out of place, and they betrayed some Northern blood mixed with a darker, Eastern race. It was obvious he was some sort of half-breed. Larson followed the boy's gaze from a pair of severely burned legs protruding beneath the charred wagon to Silme. The child clamped hands to his face and announced shrilly, "You're Dragonrank!"

Silme nodded in reply.

The boy's words tumbled over one another, the murdered uncle momentarily forgotten in his excitement. "My great, great grandfather was Dragonrank. And my uncle Crullian knew some magic, too. He's a healer. . . ." He broke off suddenly, and his speech decreased in tempo and volume. "*Was* a healer."

Larson walked over to his companions and stood at Gaelinar's side as Silme quickly changed the subject. "What's your name, child?"

"Brendor," the child introduced himself. "And I'm a wizard, too. Watch!"

Silme made only a half-hearted attempt to stop him. Curious, Larson watched as the child pointed a finger at Gaelinar's face and screamed, "Shave!"

As if in direct defiance of Brendor's command, whiskers sprouted from the Kensei's chin. Gaelinar loosed a startled cry, and Silme hid an amused smile behind her hand. Brendor's face flushed scarlet, and he tried again. "Shave!"

Soft, black hair coated Gaelinar's right cheek. Despite the fact—Larson's tension had been heightened by the brutal slayings and flashbacks, he broke into uncontrollable laughter. Gaelinar's eyes narrowed in annoyance. Brendor seemed drained. Yet he drew a deep breath, stomped his sandaled foot in the dirt, and screamed his command in frustration. "SHAVE!"

Larson's face tingled strangely as hair grew in random patches. His chuckles died to an incoherent grumble, and he rubbed at the oddly-placed stubble. Winded and purple-faced, Brendor relinquished his spell and dropped his arms. He glanced at his uncle's smoldering corpse beneath the wagon, and the sight wrenched a new volley of tears from his pale eyes.

Gaelinar made a subtle gesture. Silme nodded slightly, put an arm about the child's shoulders, and led him down the road toward the town of Forste-Mar. While Larson watched, woman and boy disappeared around a bend in the road among the wheat stalks. Once they passed beyond his view, Larson turned toward the wagon to find Gaelinar stoking the waning fire with twigs and branches. Without question, he joined in the effort, dragging debris from the forest to feed the flames that were devouring Crullian's body.

The fire flared to brilliance. Gaelinar knelt before it with bowed head and spoke the words of farewell. "Good-bye from Midgard to the healer Crullian. May he have died with dignity and the gods find him worthy of Valhalla or whatever haven in which he believed."

After Gaelinar's ruthless swordplay, Larson found the Kensei's compassionate prayer a surprise. *Good and evil may be more well defined in this world,* he mused. *But they remain relative.* Absorbed by this new abstraction, Larson failed to notice as Gaelinar hauled the three dead bandits within half a yard of the pyre. The smell of death, grain fields, and the roaring red flames against a background of forest formed a familiar knot in Larson's gut. Caught in the past, he stared until his eyes watered from pain.

Gaelinar's hand on his wrist rescued Larson from flashback. He started, acutely aware of every line on the Kensei's face, from the grim creases in his forehead to the sweep of his newly-grown beard. "If you're not going to help, at least hold this for the boy." Gaelinar tossed a tied linen pouch torn from a bandit's belt. The cloth muffled the clink of coins as Larson caught the offering.

"I'll also help." Larson smiled, pocketed the pouch, and added teasingly, "Since you're too weak to do it yourself." He hefted one of the bandits by the armpits. Gaelinar returned the grin and lifted the corpse by the ankles. In this manner, they tossed all the rapists' bodies on the pyre without benefit of epitaph.

The duty of disposing of the corpses dispatched, the two men started off along the road through the wheat. At a safe distance from the smoke, Gaelinar stopped so abruptly his odd, black-trimmed robes swayed about his hips. Larson whirled. Gaelinar bowed with a politeness his words did not match. "You look ridiculous with clumps of fuzz on your face, hero. Do you have something to take it off with before we rejoin Silme?"

Larson shook his head, grievously aware Freyr had ill-equipped him for whatever monumental task recalled him from the future.

"Here then." Gaelinar produced a knife from

the folds of his cloak and tossed it in a gentle arc. He frowned as Larson let the blade fall to the ground at his feet.

Larson hefted the knife uncertainly. Unused to using a dagger as a shaving tool, he waited until Gaelinar drew a second blade and, as hair rasped from the Kensei's chin, tried to imitate his companion's practiced motion. The unsharpened side of the blade settled awkwardly into Larson's hand, pinned to his palm by the tips of his fingers. He set the edge against his cheek and scraped. The knife carved hair and skin from his face with stinging pain. Blood trickled across his fingers, and Larson loosed a violent curse. He granted Gaelinar a glare which dared the man to laugh, but the Kensei kept his thoughts well hidden.

Larson pressed his hand to his cheek until the bleeding slowed. His second, more timid pass with the knife blade went smoother. Gaelinar finished quickly, flicked stubble from his dagger, and waited in silence while Larson struggled with an ineptness which covered his face with nicks. Still, Gaelinar said nothing until Larson finished his task, wiped congealing blood from the steel, and wrapped the dagger in its proffered sheath.

Gaelinar spoke in a voice free of emotion. "Don't be embarrassed. I understand why you can't shave; elves don't have facial hair . . ."

Of course. The revelation made Larson feel foolish. He had forgotten to consider the differences between men and elves. Perhaps his transformation also accounted for his strange tolerance to colder weather. Another thought caused him to break into a sweat which burned the lacerations on his face. *Perhaps elves and humans cannot interbreed—which makes my love for Silme both futile and ludicrous.* The idea so unnerved Larson, he nearly forgot that Gaelinar had not finished his speech.

". . . but I don't know how you've survived this long without sword training," continued the weaponmaster.

Not trusting himself to speak, Larson made a noncommittal gesture.

Gaelinar took the knife from Larson. "I don't mean to insult you, but if you travel with Silme and myself you'll have need of skill. An incompetent swordsman is as dangerous to his companions as to himself. . . ."

Larson nodded dreamily as his thoughts drifted toward Hamill. *An unpredictable hand on a swordhilt, a shaking hand on a gun trigger . . .*

The whipcrack force of Gaelinar's voice returned Larson to awareness. "I'll teach you if you wish. But I warn you, I settle for nothing short of perfection. My lessons will be the most grueling you'll ever endure."

Larson recalled basic training and bit back a skeptical smile. He nodded tacit assent.

Darkness descended upon Larson and his companions while they were still several hours from Forste-Mar. They set up camp in the sparser woodlands near the roadway. Brendor fell asleep immediately, apparently exhausted from the bandits' attack, mental anguish, and his feeble attempts at magic. Gaelinar crouched with his back against a tree, his gaze locked on Silme as she murmured the incantations which formed her wards. Larson stretched out beside the Kensei, his fingers locked beneath his head as a pillow while he stared at the stars through the interlaced branches.

Larson yawned. *It took me six weeks of boot camp to*

learn the rules of war and six months of combat to realize war has no rules. Now, in three days, I've come to accept elves and swords as commonplace. He rolled to his side and watched Silme pause as the enchantments of her wards faded into the gloom of night. *And then, there is magic.* The memory of Bramin's cruelties in the woodlands made Larson break into a cold sweat. *If laws govern or moderate its use, they are lenient. For all my knowledge of future technology, I cannot stand against Bramin.*

Larson fidgeted, bothered by these new ideas. *I thought the Norse gods aided their warriors in battle, not abandoned them without knowledge of purpose in a world of undefeatable enemies. I've risked my life too long for causes I don't understand. Bramin wants my sword, not me. And Silme and Gaelinar seem far more qualified to protect it.* His hand fell to the buckle of his sword belt.

A foreign sense of urgency swept through Larson. Freyr's authoritative voice seemed to echo in his mind. "Stop, please. It is true gods meddle in the lives of men, but you have entered the affairs of gods. I am helpless to protect you."

Stunned by Freyr's unexpected appearance, Larson said nothing.

Freyr continued. "The gods have vowed not to work against one another or the Fates. To you it may seem ridiculous, but without such laws nothing could ever get done. For every deity who wishes to stir up war, another would cultivate peace. Every action, every creation would have an antagonist. Soon, we would generate the chaos we guard against; the gods would war against one another in a combat which would not end until it encompassed the nine worlds.

Larson's mind responded sluggishly. "But why me?" he whispered.

Freyr hesitated. "I've seen your world. I brought you from a place where women, children, dirt, and trees were as dangerous as any sword. You learned to fear the few things in life a man should be able to trust. Love lost its allure before the constant threat of death which claimed friends, lovers, and enemies indiscriminately. Nothing remained permanent. In moments, rivers dried and forests exploded to barren plains. Amid colored lights and noise, the ground quaked with enough force to uproot the World Tree, and countless lives were spilled with every shrill of the war god's laughter. Like Valhalla's Einherjar, soldiers fought brave battles by day, but the dead never rose and the living lost sleep guarding against the dragons which stalked the jungles. Who is better qualified to prevent Ragnarok than a man who suffered its equal?"

Larson bit his lip, focusing on Freyr's words rather than the concepts they represented and the memories they inspired. He whispered a question. "Ragnarok? The war fated to destroy all but a handful of gods and men. Is it my mission to prevent such a thing?"

Freyr's presence in Larson's mind went pensive. "I'm . . . not certain. I can tell you nothing more. Already I have revealed more than my vows allow. I must never contact you again. If Loki's chaos can be halted, another god shall make your quest clear. If not, my efforts have only thrown you into a war as twisted as the one which killed you. But this one can claim your soul as well as your life. Forgive me." As suddenly as it had come, Freyr's manifestation disappeared.

Sweat beaded Larson's brow. "Freyr. Freyr!"

Larson received no answer, but Silme and Gaelinar stared. "J-just a prayer." Larson defended himself lamely. He curled into a fetal position on the grass. Despite his muddled thought, Freyr's disquieting revelations, and his companions' suspicions, he fell into a wary slumber.

The subtle breaking of brush startled Larson awake. His heart pounded. He forced himself to inhale and exhale slowly, counting each breath until the rhythm lulled him to an inner calmness. His senses focused on the irregular, soft sounds of movement through the brush. Gradually, he worked his hand to his side where his gun should sit. His fingers brushed empty ground. Suppressing a curse, he explored the clearing around him. The side of his hand met the hilt of his sword; and, for a time, he lay confused.

A hand pressed his shoulder reassuringly, and Gaelinar's familiar voice hissed into his ear. "Be still. Just watch."

Curiosity replaced Larson's bewilderment. His palm curled around Valvitnir's hilt. His gaze swept the brush at the edge of camp where a hunched, dark figure slithered into view and paused momentarily. Larson's grip tightened. Gaelinar's hand remained on his arm, restraining. Through the slight haze, Larson assessed the man who stalked them. He wore a dark gray tunic. Moonlight emphasized the pallor of his hair and beard. He crawled with calculated caution.

The stranger's hand rose, the gesture arrested as suddenly as if he'd struck a wall. White-hot flames burst around his fingers. He screamed, reeling back as Silme's wards sprang to view in an

intertwining pattern around the camp. Gaeliner and
Larson leaped to their feet simultaneously as the
stranger sprinted into the woods, howling in pain.

A distant voice yelled, "Gilbyr!" Nearby, a curse
sounded above the panicked screams. "Damn the
dark elf! He never mentioned magic. Gilbyr!" Arrows arched through the air.

"Incoming!" Instinctively, Larson dove to the
ground. The arrows struck the magical barrier
and, unable to pass through it, plummeted to earth
in flames. Brush rattled loudly for a short time,
and the woods returned to silence.

Brendor spoke in a frightened whine, and his
question mirrored Larson's thoughts. "What happened?"

Silme hadn't even stirred during the attack. Her
reply seemed inappropriately calm. "A few of
Bramin's lackeys tried to pass my wards. Fools."

Gaelinar resumed his crouch against the tree.
Larson remained still, his gaze locked on the forest. "What is 'Gilbyr'?"

Gaelinar closed his eyes. "A name, Allerum. Apparently this Gilbyr has chosen to become our
enemy. Therefore, I suggest you remember him."

Larson stared at the glowing waves of Silme's
wards, quite certain he could never forget.

CHAPTER 3

Kinslayer

"Every man's sword shall be against his brother."

—*Ezekiel 38:21*

Brendor whined fretfully as he followed Silme, Gaelinar, and Larson along the road to Forste-Mar. "You promised I could stay till you taught me to do my shave spell right."

"You can't come with us." Silme rubbed at her eyes with an annoyance which made it obvious she had answered his challenge more than once, and she was weakening. "Gaelinar's right. Our task is too dangerous for a child." In a sudden flash of inspiration she added, "You can stay with my mother. She raised two children to Dragonrank."

Larson moved to the roadside as a rickety wagon rolled past, drawn by a gaunt workhorse. Steam issued from the beast's wide nostrils, and the creak of wheels drowned out Brendor's reply. The driver raised his whip in salute. "Heyo, Silme! What brings you home?"

Silme returned the greeting, but the cart lurched past before she could answer the farmer's query.

As the wagon jounced toward the forest, its wheels left no mark on the frozen soil. At the border of Forste-Mar's town square, Larson and his companions left the wheat fields behind for sagging paddocks of lean-fleshed goats.

"You promised." Brendor's face reflected a pleading, childish innocence which Larson could never resist. It reminded him of the doe-eyed entreaties of Ti Sun, a Vietnamese boy who had always managed to relieve him of his rare chocolate bar until ... Larson's body snapped taut as he tried to force the thought from memory. Imagined gunfire deafened him momentarily, but Silme's soft reply to the child checked Larson's wandering consciousness.

"I only said I'd try. Not everyone can learn magic. You're fortunate to possess even the ability to cast a shave spell wrong. Only a handful of people in the entire realm control as much spell energy as you can now." Silme paused, obviously trying to twist her explanation to her favor. "If you are destined for power the dragonmark will appear. Until then, you'll be happier in town. The wandering life is insecure and often unpleasant. A child—"

Irritated by his mind's erratic lapses into memory, Larson interrupted with a tongue thick and furred as that of a man awakening from a drinking binge. "He knows more about traveling than we do for chrissakes! His uncle was a goddamn snake oil salesman." Suddenly Brendor found an ally.

Until that moment, neither Gaelinar, Silme, nor Brendor had paid Larson much heed. Now they whirled to face him simultaneously. The Kensei cleared his throat. "His uncle was a what?"

"A healer." Larson adopted the native term. "A *traveling* healer." He put a protective arm about Brendor's shoulders, and the boy's mouth twitched into a contented smile. "I'll bet he's never had a home."

"Just Crullian's wagon," Brendor answered on cue.

Silme tossed her head and continued walking into the town proper. "Come on."

Though the argument remained unsettled, Larson knew it had turned in Brendor's favor. He and the boy exchanged furtive smiles as they followed the sorceress in silence. Brendor's round face and partially concealed grin reminded Larson of his younger brother, Timmy, when they had once conspired to dye their sister's underwear green. This familiarity in a world of dragons and berserk wizards soothed, and Larson clung to the normalcy Brendor added to their party.

As they walked, Gaelinar gave Larson a few "we will talk later" looks, then drew up beside the elf. "Silme has business in town, and I think it best I accompany her. You can handle buying mounts and rations." No doubt entered Gaelinar's steady voice despite Larson's numerous previous displays of incompetence.

Grateful for the Kensei's confidence, Larson determined at least to purchase supplies without error. He accepted the pouch of coins Silme offered and listened attentively as she described the lay of the town. "Kortr the horse trader lives on the south side of the main track. You can get a decent horse for five silver, four if you bargain well."

Larson examined the sod-chinked log dwellings ahead which were criss-crossed by hard-packed thoroughfares. Five golden-haired girls passed in a giggling huddle. When they noticed Larson, their laughter ceased abruptly. Quickening their pace, they marked Larson's progress with nervous glances. Puzzled, he watched the retreating figures and considered their strange reactions.

Silme stopped on a large throughway, and her companions surrounded her as she continued. "Hlathum the food seller lives in the cottage beside Kortr. Tell him you want two weeks' traveling rations for three—" She corrected herself. "—four and mention my name. He won't cheat you. As for the innkeeper, Ura always acts like someone pissed in his ale. Don't let him charge you more than a silver for our suite. And . . ."

"Silme!" Gaelinar interrupted in a tone sharp as his katana. "The elf and the boy are perfectly capable of walking, talking, and breathing without your expert advice. Let's go."

As Silme and Gaelinar started down a side street, the sorceress added over her shoulder, "Get some dinner at the inn. We'll meet you there tonight."

Recalling the fear he'd inspired in the passing girls, Larson failed to acknowledge Silme's farewell. Without his more experienced companions for the first time in days, doubts rushed down upon him. The girls' reaction reminded him that he inhabited an elf's body, and Gaelinar's explanation when they were still in the distant woods seemed acutely important now: *Mostly, the sidelong glances and whispered comments which follow any stranger viewed as different will accompany you throughout the world of Midgard.* Larson wondered how he would fare in the town where Bramin was raised.

Unaccustomed to the horse-and-cart traffic of Forste-Mar, Larson found road crossings almost unbearable. Invariably, he waited long minutes while slower vehicles dawdled down the byways or earned vicious epithets when he tried to dodge before more swiftly moving carts. Twice, Brendor pulled him away from the steel-shod hooves of galloping mares. After that, Larson let the boy set their pace and wondered idly whether he could readjust to cars and trucks if he ever returned to the States.

Despite the overlong and often hostile gazes the populace accorded Larson, his marketing went smoothly. After he mentioned Silme's name, his session with Hlathum became brief and painless. The foodstuffs lay wrapped in portions in a large sack which Larson slung across his back. As if to conclude business as swiftly as possible, the horse merchant requested only seventeen silver for the four mounts Larson later stabled at the inn. Self-content and hungry, the elf ushered Brendor into the dimly-lit interior of Ura's Inn and selected a table in the farthest corner.

The round-topped table was pine, beer-stained and pushed tight against the chamber wall. Larson caught an outer edge and inched it forward. He maneuvered a chair into the vacant corner and sat. Back pressed to the wall, he surveyed the barroom and its patrons sitting at tables arranged in three neat rows of three. Each table bore a single candle which chased darkness in a broad semicircle, enhancing shadows on the ceiling. Rawboned, blond-haired humans conversed in couples or groups of four or five. A man proportioned like a middle linebacker stood alone at the bar. A pewter mug rested near his elbow, but the huge stranger seemed more interested in Larson than in his drink. While Larson met the man's stare with forced nonchalance, Brendor took a seat at his left.

A boy scarcely older than the healer's nephew strode around the tables and positioned himself between Larson and Brendor. He shifted from foot to foot uncomfortably. "Can I get you something?"

Larson replied without thought. *"Bami-bam, boy-san."*

Brendor started. The sudden movement drew Larson's attention from the man at the bar. "Excuse me, sir?" asked the serving boy nervously.

"Um . . ." stammered Larson. Lulled by the familiar surroundings of a tavern, he suddenly realized he had ordered in Vietnamese. "W-what do you suggest?"

The boy knotted his hands on the tabletop, obviously unsettled by his customer. "Special today is lamb breast, fresh bread, and cheese with ale."

"Fine." Larson slanted a friendly glance at Brendor. "Sound good?"

Coins clicked as Brendor closed a hand over the pouch of silver Gaelinar had rescued from the bandits. "I'll have the same."

The boy nodded and trotted behind the bar to relay the order. Larson returned his attention to the tavern's interior. Struck by the smokeless clarity of the candle light, he would have paid all the money remaining in Silme's pouch for a pack of cigarettes or a single joint. A gesture in Larson's direction swung his gaze to the exit where a man in ragged homespun downed his drink in a single gulp, abandoned his two companions, and ducked out the door. The man's two friends avoided Larson's stare.

Though troubled by the surreptitious exchange, Larson persuaded himself his mistrust stemmed from war-inspired paranoia. *Why should peasants in a town at peace wish to harm a stranger, even if he is an outsider?* The self-questioning revived recent memory. When Larson had first arrived in this unusual world, Bramin had attacked furiously without provocation. Torn between common sense and experience, Larson considered running from the inn. The serving boy approached with a plateful of food. Ultimately, its mouthwatering aroma convinced Larson to stay.

The boy set the wooden dishes before his patrons and scuttled back to the bar. Larson's first few mouthfuls took the edge from his hunger and with it his appreciation for the meal. He reached for a nonexistent salt shaker, caught himself, and leaned back with a sigh. "Everything in this world tastes the same. Isn't there any salt?"

Brendor dropped a lamb rib from fingers slick with grease. "Salt? I can do that!" Before Larson thought to protest, the boy performed a graceless gesture and spoke in a high-pitched whisper. "Salt!"

Nothing obvious happened, although Brendor panted with exertion. Relieved, Larson stroked the crusted scabs on his cheeks, a memento of Brendor's last magical endeavor. Painfully aware of his own inadequacies, Larson flashed the boy an understanding smile. Dwelling on the matter might embarrass Brendor, and so the elf passed it off with casual indulgence. "Tough luck, kid." He took a bite of cheese. A flavor bitter as poison spread through his mouth and pinched his face until he gagged. Between coughs which expelled half-chewed morsels, Larson managed to speak. "I asked for . . . salt . . . not soap!" He washed the taste from his mouth with a gulp of ale, left with watering eyes, a sore throat, and a memory that made his nose wrinkle with disgust.

Appetite ruined, Larson avoided Brendor's shamefully lowered face. He pushed his chair from the table and walked to the bar where a fat innkeeper flicked at the warped pine counter with a damp rag. Ura seemed to take no notice of the approaching elf, but the huge man at the bar squared his shoulders and edged closer. The movement put Larson on the defensive, but he forced aside discomfort as he prepared to bargain with the barkeep. "I'd like to rent a suite," he said in a businesslike voice which revealed none of his trepidations. Familiar with streetside markets, Larson prepared to snap back half the quoted price.

Ura raised his head. "Fourteen silver."

"S-what?" Composure lost, Larson stared. Ura's rate was too far beyond expectation to be other than a mistake.

"Fourteen silver," repeated Ura. He regarded Larson with scornful disinterest.

"That's outrageous!"

Ura shrugged. "Fourteen silver," he said with indisputable finality. "Take it or get out of my inn."

Larson opened his mouth to protest, but another man spoke from the tavern doorway. "You heard him. This place smells bad enough without your kind, elf!"

Larson caught at one pointed ear, suddenly feeling like an American in a North Vietnamese prison camp. He turned to his antagonist with feigned unconcern and adopted a false smile. The man at the door stood several inches taller than him, and Larson did not care to discover how much of the bulk beneath his chain shirt was padding. Likely the stranger was a member of Forste-Mar's guard force, summoned by the man who had left the bar earlier and now stood near the guardsman.

Brendor came to Larson's side. Afraid for the child's life, Larson stepped before him protectively. To his relief, a stranger at one of the tables came to their defense. "He's not going to hurt anyone, Anrad. He's a *light* elf."

Larson bit his lip with understanding. Again Gaelinar's description returned to him, and nervous energy revived the most distressing sentence of his explanation: *At times, dark elves are welcomed because of the legends of light elves, and light elves are slain for the ancient crimes of their dark cousins.* Bramin had turned the town of Forste-Mar against faery folk, but a Dragonrank mage was too powerful for peasants' vengeance. Over years, unvented hatred had intensified, seeking a victim. Unless Larson acted with heroic discretion, he might pay with his and Brendor's lives for Bramin's evil. He faced the barkeep again. "I just want . . ."

"Fourteen silver and not one copper less," said Ura with pointed hostility.

Goaded by Ura's patrons, Anrad stepped boldly into the barroom's center. "Let him sleep in the stables for two silver."

Steeling himself, Larson turned. His fingers plucked nervously at his tunic, but his words were carefully selected and innocuously spoken. "It only cost a copper for the horses."

Anrad folded his arms across his broad chest. "But you'll want to bed every beast in the stable." His gaze dropped to Brendor, and his lips twisted in a sneer. "Oh, but I see you've brought your own entertainment."

Brendor pushed in front of Larson. Red-faced with the perfect rage only a child can experience, he struggled to speak without screaming. "Your mother's safe, there are no asses in the stable!"

Anrad's face flushed. He raised a hand threateningly. "You little bastard."

Anger flared in Larson. Suddenly beyond thought of the consequences, he cocked his fist and leaped for the guardsman. A callused palm caught Larson's wrist. He was wrenched forcefully about to face the huge man at the bar whose bear-sized hand locked on his arm. "You two want to kill each other, do it outside!"

"Fine!" Anrad marched out the door, chuckling, and the crowd of patrons funneled into the street.

No stranger to bar fights, Larson tore free of the bouncer's grip and strode toward the door. Memory of his reflection in the pond bred doubts. This elf-form robbed him of the bulk won from years of wrestling and weight training. He could only hope he had retained some of his strength, and he would have to remember to throw full effort into every punch. Intent on strategy, Larson strode blindly from the inn and nearly impaled himself on Anrad's naked sword.

Larson recoiled with a yell. His fist closed on Valvitnir's hilt, and the blade sprang from its sheath so quickly he was unsure whether he or the sword initiated the movement. Anrad swept for Larson's chest. Larson ducked behind Valvitnir. Sword crashed against sword, and Anrad's blade shattered to faintly glowing shards.

Anrad retreated, eyes wild. More familiar with fist fighting, Larson handed his sword to Brendor. "I can take him without a weapon." Hands for-

ward, he closed, prepared to pummel the guardsman before he could recover from surprise. Anrad
dropped his useless hilt and dodged under Larson's swing. His return punch crashed against the
elf's jaw, hurling him backward. Larson tried to
block, but the guard's other fist thudded into his
gut, stealing breath.

Larson staggered. The cries of the crowd blended
to undecipherable noise. Anrad's pale fist rushed
toward his face. Larson blocked with his left arm,
then cut downward and caught the guardsman's
wrist. He seized Anrad's elbow in his right hand
and whipped his opponent around in a wrestling
drag. Larson's arm closed about Anrad's neck.
The guard struggled momentarily then dropped
to the ground, breathless.

Pain-maddened, Larson kicked Anrad's mailed
side. Impact with the heavy chain links shot agony
along Larson's foot. Anrad winced with a gasp.
Larson smashed his heel into Anrad's face. Bones
cracked, and blood poured from the guardsman's
nose. Anrad lay with closed eyes, emitting small
panting sobs.

Only then did Larson consider the battle won.
In the same situation, James Bond or Errol Flynn
would have delivered some witty line and strode
off into the sunset. But Larson felt too disgusted
for endearing dramatization. His jaw ached with
every heartbeat, and he could taste blood. Without a word, he wheeled away.

Dust billowed around the scene of the fight.
Larson waited until it settled and searched for
Brendor. The boy was gone. Larson's wits scattered as panic replaced ire. He cast about frantically. "Brendor. Where's my sword? Brendor?"

Larson received no reply from anywhere in the

crowd. He spun awkwardly, like a drunken dancer, without sighting the boy. Brendor and Valvitnir had disappeared completely. Larson seized an old man by the collar and jacked him against the tavern wall. "Which way did he go?"

The man pointed a shaking finger toward a narrow throughway between buildings. Dropping his informant, Larson charged through the gaping onlookers. He hurtled down the alleyway, well aware there could be only one enemy. Bramin's use of a child seemed a ruse so obvious he wondered how he had come to overlook it. Booby-trapping children was a favorite trick of the Viet Cong; he should have expected no less from Bramin. Brendor was certainly Bramin's accomplice, placed in a piteous position where Larson and his companions would happen upon him. Once Brendor gained Larson's trust, he waited for an opening to steal the sword. And Larson had fallen for the plan like an idiot, his only comfort the fact that Silme and Gaelinar had been duped as easily as himself.

The roadway forked suddenly. Larson chose his direction at random. Wind blew a discarded rag under his feet, and Larson skirted it instinctively. The pathway narrowed between cottages and ended at a staunch wooden gate. Beyond lay a plowed field. Across acres of sprouting grain stood a cottage. As Larson watched, a small figure darted toward it.

Larson sprang for the gate. A poorly-timed memory slammed his consciousness with a force akin to Anrad's blows. He flinched back as the scene in his head exploded in red light. "They've wired the gate!" screamed Gavin. Even as Larson surrendered to flashback, he pitched himself over the barrier.

The illusion mushroomed to a cloud of fire, and impact with the ground jarred Larson back to the wheat field. Sweat stung his eyes. Field dirt clung to his limbs. He ripped his tunic as he struggled to his feet and sprinted toward the cottage. The child grew more visible as he approached, dark-haired, dressed in tan and blue, and pressed to the mud-chinked stone wall. It was unmistakably Brendor. The boy turned as Larson closed, and his face went pale.

"You conniving little bastard," Larson panted as he seized Brendor's forearm. "I ought to break your goddamned neck."

Brendor's face screwed into a harried mass of wrinkles. "Stop, shhh . . ." He pulled against Larson's grip.

Larson tightened his fist as Brendor fought against him. "Don't 'shhh' me, you little brat. I'll . . ."

Brendor took a sharp intake of breath. His gaze suddenly focused beyond Larson. Menaced from behind, the elf loosed the child. Brendor fell against the wall with a pained whimper. Larson whirled to face two men with drawn swords. A third stood between them, unarmed but no less formidable. A heavy cloth bandage enclosed his right hand. "If you were trying to be subtle," said one, "you failed miserably."

The second man stepped forward. "If you've come for your sword, I may decide to give it to you." Spit sprayed from his mouth as he pronounced each word with gloating force. "Jammed through your ugly, elven heart."

"What do we do with them?" asked the unarmed man.

"Take them inside," replied the first. "I think Bramin would be grateful if we accidentally killed them." He gestured. "Gilbyr, you lead. Then the boy, followed by the elf." His eyes met Larson's. "Do anything we don't like and you earn two swords between your ribs."

The name Gilbyr blazed in Larson's awareness from the previous night when Bramin's bandits tried to break through Silme's wards. He stared at Gilbyr's bandaged hand, recalling the power of the sorceress' white-hot magics. *I can't face Bramin without Silme.* Rising fear blurred memory into purpose. Still uncertain of Brendor's role in the swordnapping, Larson glanced at the boy.

The fear and betrayal stamped across Brendor's features hurt Larson worse than the bandits' gibes and death threats. "They grabbed the sword from me and ran. I tried . . ."

"Silence!" Gilbyr raised his injured hand to strike Brendor and immediately realized his mistake. The thief bit back a scream. Fresh blood colored his bandage. "Another thing you'll pay for. Come along."

Hesitantly, Brendor went to Gilbyr, rubbing elbows skinned from Larson's unceremonious push against the cottage. Bereft of alternatives, Larson followed. He wished he had a means to judge the sword skill of the man behind him.

In a line, captors and victims passed around the cottage. Gilbyr paused before the front door and tripped the latch. Larson fretted, the thought of dying indoors no more palatable than that of dying outside. *Now or never.* The oaken door swung open. As Gilbyr started through the portal, Larson pretended to stumble. The swordsmen lurched with him. Larson shoved Brendor into Gilbyr with all the strength he could muster. Man and boy tumbled into the cottage, a twisting wheel of arms and legs. A blade licked Larson's back as he sprang through the opening and pulled the door shut behind him.

Swords thumped against the wood, mingled with muffled curses. While Gilbyr and Brendor untangled themselves, Larson shot the bolt home, aware the swordsmen could not quickly break through solid oak. Fists clenched, Larson turned to engage Gilbyr. As Brendor freed himself, he stomped on Gilbyr's wounded hand. Howling curses, Gilbyr backed toward an open doorway several feet away. Brendor ran to Larson's side.

Larson advanced. Behind him, the door rattled beneath the swordsmen's blows. A plan took form, and he repressed an amused smile which might ruin its effect. He let his fists go lax and trained his eyes on Gilbyr. "Stop, fool!" Larson borrowed the voice of a summoned god from a cheap horror flick.

Gilbyr hesitated.

Larson loosed a rumbling laugh and wished he sounded less nervous and more evil. "You chose the wrong victims for your childish prank." He snapped a hand in Brendor's direction. "This is no boy, but a master Dragonrank in child form."

Brendor looked as startled as the thief. The door shuddered and groaned warningly.

Larson sacrificed a dramatic pause for brevity. "You've already sampled his power. Look at your hand. He could slay you with a single word, but your transgressions have gone beyond merciful death. Now he shall twist your very soul." He raised his arms for effect and took a threatening forward step. "Your person will transform to a wolf-being which feasts upon blood and howls at the full moon. *Men will hunt you down!*"

Wood splintered as a sword tip cracked the door and retreated. Larson kicked Brendor's shin. "Shave, kid," he whispered.

"Shave!" hollered Brendor.

Hair sprang from Gilbyr's face. The thief loosed a blood-curdling shriek and bolted through the crumbling door. The oak panel broke open. Gilbyr spitted himself on his companions' swords, and his screams transformed from panicked to agonized.

Brendor grabbed Larson's arm. "Come on!"

Larson needed no urging. Elf and boy sprang through the rearward portal and found themselves in a small storage room. Behind, Gilbyr's sharp screams rose over the exchanges of the thieves. Brendor clawed at a square of fur which covered the window, but a faintly-glowing sack in the storeroom corner arrested Larson's escape. "The sword!" He crossed the room in two leaping strides and ripped the cloth bag, spilling woolen garments to the bare stone floor.

Dropping to a crouch, Larson buried his hands in the cloth and was rewarded by a touch of metal. His wild gesture flung tunics through the storeroom and uncovered Valvitnir's jeweled hilt. With a relieved sigh, Larson caught the grip as Gilbyr's shrieks subsided to anguished moans in the other room.

Valvitnir quivered in greeting. Its presence inspired a strange joy, lulling Larson's mind to an inner peace instantly shattered by a string of curses from the adjoining room. No sign remained of Brendor but a rumpled pile of furs beneath the window. Larson flung the sword. It flew, straight as an archer's arrow, through the window into the gathering grayness of evening. He scuttled after it.

The rough-hewn stone of the window scraped Larson's skin despite his clothing. He caught the outer ledge, swung his legs between his hands, and hit the ground prepared to run. A short distance ahead, Brendor's slight form darted toward the town square. Closer, Valvitnir flared blue as a beacon.

Instinctively, Larson dropped to the ground, held himself flat and silent in the gloom. Then, remembering that the thieves in this world carried no guns or grenades, he caught the sword hilt and sprinted after the retreating child. Though encumbered by the weapon's weight, Larson overtook Brendor halfway across the plowed field, and matched the child's pace. Like hunted deer, elf and boy bounded across the tract. By the time they reached the gate, Larson's legs ached from the effort, and he had twisted his ankles countless times.

Only when they reached the alley did they dare to look behind. The cottage stood shrouded in haze, but it seemed no thieves dared pursue the elven swordsman and his "master Dragonrank." Larson tried not to imagine who would have suffered Gilbyr's wrath had the thief realized the magic-using adept could be better called inept.

As he regained his breath, Larson looked at Brendor, and the boy returned his stare. "You spoiled my ambush," Brendor accused.

"It's only fair," Larson snapped back. "You ruined my dinner."

Brendor smothered a giggle. "Ruined Gilbyr's face, too."

Struck by the absurdity of the comment after their harrowing series of experiences, Larson laughed so hard he needed to catch the gate to keep his balance. Brendor lapsed into convulsive titterings. Their chortles melded to a gleeful duet as tension broke in a rush of camaraderie. Elf and boy regained composure simultaneously. Then Brendor hiccuped, and they burst into wild laughter again.

Less than a yard deeper in the alley, someone spoke. "Where have you two been?"

Startled, Larson inhaled a mouthful of saliva. No longer laughing, he wheeled to face a thin man in black-trimmed gold robes. The adrenalin rush inspired by Gaelinar's swift, silent appearance strained Larson's cry of welcome.

Gaelinar took no notice. "I thought you'd meet us in the tavern."

"We went exploring." Larson lied, not wishing to explain to the swordmaster how he had disarmed himself in battle and was forced to retrieve his sword from bandits.

Gaelinar fondled the brocade at his sword hilt. "Looking for trouble would better describe it if I'm to believe Ura. He told me you challenged the guard captain."

"Well . . ." started Larson, with no idea how he would finish the sentence.

Gaelinar did not need explanations. He scrutinized Larson in the waning light. "Did you at least win?"

"Of course," Larson said with a false confidence. Impossible as it seemed, his reply was true.

"Good." The Kensei turned in a swirl of gold robes and started down the alley. "Then you should do well with your first sword lesson tonight."

Brendor and Larson trotted behind Gaelinar. "Tonight?" repeated Larson incredulously, feeling very tired.

"Tonight," Gaelinar confirmed with a toss of his gray locks. "But just until dark. I would have started sooner had I known you made a habit of antagonizing guards."

Larson wanted to protest but could think of nothing convincing to say. The alleyway broadened and met the road before Ura's Inn, conspicuously devoid of the afternoon crowd. Forste-Mar had literally closed for the evening.

Gaelinar continued. "Silme settled your tab at the tavern. I've never traveled on Alfheim, Allerum, but here we pay for our meals before we leave the table." He nodded toward the hulking shape of the inn. "Brendor, get some sleep. Silme rented a suite for an infinitely reasonable price, and Ura gave her the sack of rations you left in the barroom. She can get very convincing." The slight smile which played across Gaelinar's lips as he thumbed his sword guard caused Larson to wonder about the Kensei's role in Ura's persuasion.

Brendor headed for the inn, and Gaelinar called after him. "And don't bother Silme until morning!" Swiftly, the Kensei turned and strode along the hard-packed road. "How much do you know about swordplay?"

Larson jogged to keep up with his companion. "Nothing. Believe it or not, men in my world haven't used swords for centuries."

Gaelinar made a disgruntled noise. "I commend the peacefulness of your people. But just because you've put an end to warfare doesn't mean you should forget weapons skills."

"Wha-huh?" Larson's incoherent reply was startled from him. Throughout the last few days, nightmare visions of Vietnam had haunted his waking moments as well as his dreams. Though he would have preferred to erase the war from memory, its actuality was too vivid to deny, even to a friend from a happier world. "I'm afraid my people abandoned swords for more lethal weapons. So long as a world contains men and issues, war will result."

"True enough." Gaelinar ducked beneath an age-blackened rope which enclosed a square of freshly-raked sand. "But disagreement needn't end in death. Many worthy opponents have become allies. And there is a glory to dying in a battle you and an able enemy chose to fight. Men here believe death in valorous combat earns a place in Odin's Valhalla for oneself or a noble foe. There souls battle through the day; those slain rise again each evening in preparation for the final war against Loki and his minions. The infirm and cowardly join Loki's Hel hordes, forced to side against mankind for the cause of utter Chaos."

Larson supposed the roped off area was a practice ground for guards. He followed Gaelinar, convinced the most important phrase in the Kensei's rhetoric was "chose to fight." Vietnam seemed nothing better than a lame excuse to satisfy the cruel fantasies of men and goad eighteen-year-old children to murder and misguided vengeance.

"Philosophy will not save you from my lesson." Gaelinar's katana sprang silently from its sheath. Its tip pointed toward Valvitnir's scabbard. "You will now begin the way."

Larson waited for an explanation which never came. He watched in silence as Gaelinar walked to the center of the field. Faster than Larson could follow, the Kensei drew his shoto and executed a strike with its handle. The katana followed with an upward cut. Gaelinar recovered, both swords close to his body.

Awed, Larson rested his hand on Valvitnir's pommel as he watched Gaelinar's swords flow around the Kensei, scattering reflections of the rising moon. Then a subtle change in timing gave his strokes the cruel snap of flames leaping through kindling. Abruptly, the Kensei stopped. He wiped sweat from his eyes with the back of his sleeve and beckoned Larson forward. Expectantly, Larson approached his teacher.

"You must learn much in a short time," said Gaelinar. "I will teach you a lot, but you will teach yourself more. Draw your sword."

Larson found Valvitnir's hilt and unsheathed the sword. The leather molded to his hand, but the grip shifted like a living thing against his palm until his thumb, forefinger, and middle finger rested only lightly on it while his remaining two fingers held the sword firmly. With a surprised gasp, Larson let the weapon drop from his hand. The blade struck the sand with a thump and lay still.

At Gaelinar's curious look, Larson reclaimed the sword sheepishly, certain fatigue accounted for his strange perception. The hilt settled in his grip. With the patience of wind whittling a mountain range, Valvitnir again adjusted to the proper position in Larson's hand.

"Good." The Kensei nodded his approval. "I see you've had some training. You do hold the sword properly. Now you'll learn your first form. Watch." Gaelinar sheathed his companion sword and gripped his katana in his right hand. Larson watched intently as his teacher positioned himself, left foot ahead and sword low. Gaelinar stepped forward and arched his sword over his head, then drove downward and slightly past his leg.

Larson chuckled inwardly as Gaelinar repeated the maneuver half a dozen times to either side of his body. *This will be easy*, he told himself. Strange laughter accompanied his assessment. Larson spun and saw no one. He and the Kensei were alone, and his teacher was not amused. Confused, Larson dismissed the incident as hallucination, attributing his odd perceptions to fatigue.

Gaelinar returned, grim-faced, and sheathed his katana. "If you know this form within three weeks, I will be pleased."

Shocked, Larson stared. "Three weeks? I can walk and chew gum at the same time."

"Gum?" repeated Gaelinar. He shrugged the strange word off as unimportant.

Evening breezes cut through Larson's ragged tunic, and he shivered. Gaelinar freed his katana and rested its tip on the sand. "Hero, you are a fledgling. At first, an eagle flaps its wings awkwardly and achieves nothing. Eventually, it understands. You are an eaglet without the luxury of time. You must soar and hunt before learning to fly. You will know this kata as nothing you have known before. Guide your sword with your spirit as well as your arm. When you find the way, it will become a part of you. Begin."

Larson shifted from foot to foot, seeking a comfortable stance. He lowered the sword, mimicking Gaelinar, and made a cut toward and past his right leg. Valvitnir jerked back, as if of its own volition. Larson froze. Slowly, he turned an accusatory glance toward Gaelinar who stood patiently waiting for Larson to finish. Puzzled, the elf repeated the attempt, and again the sword pulled to the same position. He gripped the hilt tighter and tried again. Though he struggled against it, the sword still adjusted.

"Allerum!" the Kensei instructed. "You needn't crush your sword. It is not your enemy. Relax. You must control your strokes. Don't swing past and return your blade. Stop the cut nearer your leg. Now, continue."

Valvitnir gleamed red-blue in the last dying rays of the sun. Larson recommenced. Apparently, whatever the sword did was correct. *There are too many odd things in this world to question. Is a sentient sword less likely than dragons or magic?* Its abilities and motives could be determined later. Now, he must practice.

Whatever had controlled the sword released it. Larson executed the same strokes repeatedly, and all Gaelinar ever said was, "Again." The heat inspired by movement felt pleasant against the chill breeze, but it was night and time to join Silme and Brendor at the inn.

The practice went on until Larson's exertion no longer kept him warm from frigid winds. *Silme and Brendor have probably already gone to sleep,* Larson told himself. *And I'm stuck freezing my ass off with some maniac who thinks I'm still in boot camp."* Larson's patience wore thin as his tunic as the lesson dragged interminably onward.

"Enough!" shouted Larson. "You said we would go till night, not morning! It's time for a hot meal and a warm bed. This practice is finished!" He jammed Valvitnir into its sheath and stormed toward the inn.

"Wait," said the Kensei quietly. "There are two

minor mistakes I can correct if you perform the kata one more time. Then we will find you a warm bed."

Hesitantly, slightly embarrassed at his own outburst, Larson returned and unsheathed Valvitnir. Gaelinar stood an arm's length in front of Larson. "Go through the kata. I will retreat before you." When Larson's weight shifted to his leading foot, a sharp kick from Gaelinar sprawled him on the cold sand.

Larson clutched his knee, rolling from side to side. "What the hell! You god damned sonofabitch! I won't be able to walk for a week. Why . . ."

"If you listen, I will tell you why." The Kensei's face was a mask, but his eyes smiled broadly. And that annoyed Larson more than anything. "You have just learned two important lessons. First, do not put so much weight on your front foot. It's harder to defend, and if knocked away, you fall." He paused thoughtfully. "Also, never gainsay your teacher."

Gaelinar smiled and offered Larson his hand. With his assistance, Larson stood. "For the remainder of the evening, you are a friend, not a student. Let's see about your bed, hero."

Darkness had settled about swordmaster and pupil as they worked. The moon hung, little larger than her court of stars. Gaelinar crossed the sand and shouldered beneath the rope. "We'll talk on the way to the inn."

Larson limped after, only partially listening. For neither the first nor last time, he realized there was something unusual about his sword, Valvitnir. *Like some sort of primitive life form, it seems able to comprehend its environment and communicate with me in a rudimentary way. I just hope it knows how to fight.*

Gaelinar continued as Larson joined him on the roadway and they walked toward Ura's tavern. "I want to warn you about Silme."

Suddenly Gaelinar had Larson's full attention. Ideas swirled through Larson's brain, few plausible but all possible in this eldritch world which was not quite Old Scandinavia. Jaw set, he awaited the Kensei's words.

Gaelinar continued as the shapes along the roadside grew more familiar. "Silme and I . . ."

Larson squeezed his lids shut.

". . .visited her family today. I'm afraid Bramin reached them first."

Larson's eyes jerked open. They stood before Ura's Inn; the bar sign creaked as it swung in the breeze like a body from a hangman's noose. "What do you mean?" he asked, not daring to contemplate further.

"Killed, Allerum." Wind spread the tassels on Gaelinar's swords to a pair of golden flowers. "Faces twisted in pain. The bodies were dismembered and accorded none of the honor the dead deserved. Bramin left enough traces of sorcery for Silme to know without question." He added more softly. "As if we might mistake his evil for another's."

Larson shivered, chilled both by wind and the Kensei's words. He fought images of almond-skinned children screaming for fathers, fathers crying for daughters, women's last blood gushing rhythmically onto dirt floors. In Vietnam, the villains were not black-hearted half-breeds cursed with a demon inheritance, but true-blooded American boys who, hours later, would shed tears for an orphaned puppy or a fallen comrade. "Silme," Larson forced the question around his thoughts. "How is she?"

"Silme?" Gaelinar seemed puzzled by the query. "You mustn't forget, hero. She's not like most women. The Dragonrank training hardened her like the stone in her staff. And she's dedicated her life to neutralizing Bramin's atrocities. Come on." He caught Larson's hand and half dragged him toward the inn.

Trapped between two equally unsatisfying thoughts, Larson walled off his mind to a small square of consciousness. Like a man entranced, he let Gaelinar lead him to the inn, through a door behind the bar counter, up a narrow set of stairs to the door of their suite. The Kensei produced a brass key from the folds of his robe and inserted it in the lock. The door swung open to reveal a clean-walled room lit by a guttering lantern on a table surrounded by four matching chairs. Beside the lantern lay a bowl and pitcher. Cloth rags were spread neatly across the back of one of the chairs.

When the two men stepped into the room, details became more apparent between the spinning shadows cast by the lantern. The farthest wall was broken by four portals. Two were covered by drawn curtains. The others opened to smaller rooms furnished with beds of straw and cloth. Each held a night table with an unlit candle and a crude iron striker.

Gaelinar closed the door, crossed the room, and flicked his fingers through the water in the bowl. "Tomorrow, when we leave Forste-Mar, your real lessons begin."

Larson unlatched his sword belt and slung it across a chair. "Where are we going?" Frustrated by the elusiveness of the quest thrust upon him, Larson spoke his words as a challenge.

Gaelinar submerged both hands in the bowl and splashed water on his forearms. "Silme and I thought we should purchase a few more supplies in the morning." He examined Larson's torn and soiled garments with a disapproving frown. "Then," he continued in an apologetic tone which instantly turned Larson against the suggestion, "we thought we'd take you to the dream-reader."

"The what?" asked Larson suspiciously. His fingers massaged the pommel of Valvitnir where it rested on the chair before him.

Gaelinar scrubbed his face. "The dream-reader of Forste-Mar. She's an old witch with a few minor magics and a talent for mind search and thought interpretation. Silme thinks the lady might find some answers in that dream you had in the woods, something to explain your quest and send us in the right direction." He reached for a rag.

Though excited by the prospect of knowledge, uncertainty weakened Larson's grip on his sword. "What's the catch?"

Gaelinar tossed his towel aside and raised his eyebrows uncomprehendingly.

"What's this dream-reading process do to me? How does it work?"

"Do to you?" Gaelinar caught the sides of the bowl. "It doesn't do anything to you. And you might just as well bid me cast the protective circle. If you want to learn combat come to me." He patted his sword hilts. "For explanations of magic ask Silme."

Finding the answer unsatisfying, Larson scowled. Gaelinar lifted the bowl of water and carried it to a dented tin bucket on one of the chairs. As water splashed from basin to bucket, disturbing a thin film of oil which had settled on the surface, the Kensei softened. "Silme wouldn't suggest anything to hurt you. I think you know that."

Larson said nothing. So many times in Vietnam he placed his life in the hands of men whose morals he questioned. Now, he balked before the trust of the woman of his dreams and the man who gave his new being direction. "Yes," he admitted. "I know that."

"Good." Smiling, Gaelinar refilled the basin from the pitcher and left it on the tabletop. "Wash up and get some sleep. See you in the morning." He turned and strode through one of the portals, pulling the curtain closed behind him.

Gingerly, Larson removed his tunic, worn thin as a favored tee shirt though he'd owned it only three days. He moistened a rag and scrubbed his unfamiliar body, paying particular attention to his armpits, which were hairless, and his genitals which he had already determined looked normal by human standards.

Minor comparisons and benign memories of showers and flush toilets busied Larson's mind while he prepared for bed. But after he finished his scrub bath, gathered his tunic and sword belt, and settled into bed, thoughts descended upon him. He pictured a kindly old woman and a man stooped and tanned from years in the field. Between them, he imagined a snub-nosed boy, like his baby brother Timmy, and a girl beautiful as Silme, but with a wide-eyed innocence only youth can grant.

Larson fought the idea like madness, but he imagined the four again, crushed like roses after a broken romance. Blood colored the cold, stone floor. Limbs bent like fragile stems. Memory awakened, triggered others in a spreading circuit. Bodies sprawled in limp piles, pinned to walls in death, shattered to red chaos. Faces lay locked in permanent accusation, lacking ears, prizes claimed for the gruesome pride of death collectors. *And we were all death collectors.*

Larson kept his eyes open, letting the scenes wash across the rain-warped ceiling, waiting for them to play out and leave him the tranquillity of sleep. But peace remained elusive. Remembrance of Bramin's sorceries surfaced in a searing rush, and past horrors washed to a waste of grayness. Agonies Larson dared not wish upon Satan condensed to a dully throbbing reminder that Silme's family had experienced it all and worse. Surely death was the kindest of Bramin's atrocities.

Larson forced his mind to cheerier topics. He remembered his father and their yearly New Hampshire trips to hunt deer and grouse. But even then, his thoughts betrayed him. Larson recalled the phone call which pulled him from college midterms. His father had been killed, the victim of a drunk driver. He left nothing. To relieve their mother's financial burden, his older sister married, and Al Larson quit school to join the army. *I wonder if Mother knows I am dead.*

A noise startled Larson from his nightmare of memory. Relieved, he lay alternately sweating and chilled while his trained senses identified sound and location. He heard it again, coming from his left over toward Silme and Brendor. It was the gentle creak of floorboards beneath weight shifting with deliberate stealth.

Larson hit the floor in a crouch. His groping hands found his sword belt in the darkness, and he worked Valvitnir from its sheath without a sound. The blade trembled questioningly as he pressed it to his naked chest, hoping to shield the steel from residual light which might reveal him. Taking care that the inseams of his doeskin pants did not rub together, he pressed to the wall and worked his way toward the portal of his bedroom.

Again, Larson heard movement. Carefully, he flicked back an edge of his curtain and examined the main room. The lantern had burned out, and the suite lay in blackness. A light in the corner bedroom discolored its drawn curtain in a central circle, marred by wrinkles in the fabric. Beyond, Larson heard a sandal scrape wood and a pained human sob.

Larson stalked the sound, acutely aware of each of his own motions. Well aware any person skilled enough to harm Silme could easily kill him, Larson still continued, relying on surprise to even the odds. Positioned to spring, he snaked the sword forward and tipped an edge of the curtain up. The linen folded aside to reveal a slight figure pacing before a candle on a bed table. It was Silme.

Larson dropped his sword and stepped into the bedroom. Silme whirled abruptly. Her hair hung in a cascade of golden tangles, and her eyes looked red and swollen. A tear slid halfway down her cheek before she caught it with a finger and flipped it away. Though stripped of pretenses and pride, she seemed every bit as beautiful to Larson.

He caught her to his chest, and she, at first, resisted. Then grief broke in a flurry of tears. She wept for her family, for all the innocent victims of Bramin's hatred, and for the men of Midgard fated to die in Loki's Chaos. Her tears glided down Larson's chest. He pressed his arms around her, muttering senseless comforts. Her warmth raised him to a dizzying height of passion, and it took no small amount of will to suppress the urge to force his desires upon her.

Shamed by the lust incited by Silme's grief, Larson said nothing. Between sobs which shook the sorceress' body, he vowed vengeance on the red-eyed half-man responsible for her pain. For his own peace, he swore he would earn Silme's love and respect and one day bed the sorceress who was sapphire Dragonrank from Forste-Mar.

CHAPTER 4

Wolfslayer

"Brother fights with brother,
they butcher each other;
  daughters and sons
  incestuously mix;
man is a plaything
of mighty whoredoms;
  an axe-time, sword-time
  shields shall be split;
a wind-age, a wolf-age,
before the World ends."
  —*The Spaewife's Song*

The dream-reader crossed the barren tract before her cottage and studied the main street of Forste-Mar through cataract-hazed vision. Four figures approached, too distant to discern through her aged eyes. Yet she identified her visitors without mortal sight. The woman at the lead glowed with a life aura bright as a barn fire, surely Dragonrank and therefore unmistakably Silme. Beside her walked a boy suffused by light so pale the dream-reader attributed the illusion to reflections of Silme's glory and her own near blindness.

Behind Silme strode her bodyguard of several years, the ronin, Gaelinar. To believe the rumors, he'd fought a thousand duels in the Far East without a loss and had been lured to the North by stories of fearless pirates commanding longboats carved in dragon form. No one knew how Silme had persuaded the Kensei to her cause, but his loyalty was beyond question.

The dream-reader knew the sorceress' last companion from gossip exchanged in the village market. The citizens named him a light elf. But even through diseased eyes which blurred Larson to an outline, the dream-reader found little comparison between him and the slight, giggling elves who whisked through her cottage on infrequent visits. His tread was heavy as a man's, his manner cautious and careworn.

As the four people crossed the ground before her cottage, the dream-reader lowered her head so her hood might keep her wrinkled face in shadow. She spread her arms. Wind caught the edges of her sleeves, drawing them from wrists thin as broom handles. Affectations were unnecessary before the sorceress, Silme, but the dream-reader assumed her position from decades of habit.

"Good day," called Silme a bit too loudly, as if the dream-reader's failing vision might affect her ears as well.

"Good morning, Lady Silme." The dream-reader bobbed her head once at the sorceress and again for Gaelinar. "Kensei." She waited patiently for Silme's introduction of the strangers.

"Lord Allerum and Brendor the . . ."

"Apprentice," Brendor interrupted in an excited squeak. "Silme's going to teach me my shave spell!"

Unable to discern expressions from her patrons' blurred faces, the dream-reader watched Silme's life aura for clues to her disposition. Now, the edges tinged pink with annoyance. Beside high rank Dragonschool, the reader's own aura seemed faded as the old cloak across her shoulders. "Have you come to visit an aging woman or for business?" asked the dream-reader, hoping for the latter. It was common knowledge Silme consorted with gods. Only desperation would drive Dragonrank to the lowly magics of a dream-reader. And desperation had its price.

"Business." Silme stroked the shaft of her staff thoughtfully. "Lord Allerum has a dream for your interpretation."

The dream-reader took one step forward and peered at Larson through slitted eyes. Closer, she recognized the small frame and angularity of an elf. But his long fingers balled nervously against the side of his breeches in a gesture uncharacteristic for a creature of faery. "I should gladly serve you, mistress." The dream-reader stepped around Larson. "In exchange, surely you have the power to cure an old woman's affliction." She pressed forward, giving Silme the full effect of her clouded stare.

Multi-hued light flickered briefly through Silme's aura. "Forgive me, lady. The spell you seek is within my power but not part of my repertoire. I can't help you."

Fearing to lose a chance at sight, the dream-reader persisted. "A mage of your rank has disciples. Surely one of them. . . ." She trailed to silence, awaiting the sorceress' reply.

Silme's life aura shimmered and swelled as she weighed alternatives. "The cost of spells for conjuration and exchange would exceed that necessary to heal you. They would weaken me."

The dream-reader said nothing, aware Silme's need for her services could bargain better than words.

"Even then," continued Silme, "I couldn't be certain the contacted wizard would agree to help you."

"I ask only that you try." The dream-reader tried to sound humble. "Nothing more."

"All right then," Silme responded in a hoarse whisper. She walked away from her companions and crouched on the frozen soil. Her life aura blazed like wind-stoked fire, then folded around her in a glimmering shield. Gaelinar strode forward and positioned himself before her, eyes watchful, hands tensed at his sides.

A slight smile shivered across the dream-reader's lips as she turned her attention to Larson. She shifted her shriveled hands to his shoulders. Sweat soaked through the fresh cloth of his tunic. He trembled slightly as a rising breeze flicked soft, pale hair and the folds of his newly-purchased silk cape against the reader's wrists. "Concentrate on your dream, so I can locate it," she informed him gently. "And try to lower your defenses."

The dream-reader knew her final suggestion was ineffectual routine. Only men accustomed to mental searches could withdraw defenses with any success. Thought invasion induced reflexive closure of the mind and its secrets. Anticipating a long session of relaxation techniques, the dream-reader thrust her consciousness toward the elf.

To her surprise, she met no resistance. Her mental probe passed effortlessly into Larson's mind, and his thought processes spread before her like the workings of a clock. It was not an elven mind; it lacked the wire-thin pathways and array of colors. It was a human mind and badly flawed. Passages looped in blind circles or linked with unrelated thoughtways in random binds and breaks. The effect seemed not unlike the looping chaos of stuffing from a torn doll. Though curious, the dream-reader avoided the strange conglomeration and focused on the faintly-glowing configuration which indicated Larson's present abstraction. Exploring other avenues of thought would betray the trust of her client.

The dream assumed the clarity of a play. The dream-reader saw the trees as Larson's link with the forest of his then current reality. The trunks muted to rivers, and Larson's memory of their names highlighted their importance to his vision. The titles which seemed foreign to Larson rolled through her mind like old friends: Svol the cool and Gunnthra the defiant, Fjorm and loud-bubbling Fimbulthul, Slidr the fearsome river of daggers and swords, Hrid, Sylg, Ylg, and Vid the broad, Leipt which streaks like lightning, and frozen Gjoll. These were the eleven rivers which cascaded through Midgard straight to Hel and the roaring cauldron of the spring, Hvergelmir.

The dream-reader of Forste-Mar saw the glowing form of the sword, Valvitnir, as the dream-Larson tossed it into the tumult of the Helspring. Hungrily, Hvergelmir swallowed the offering, and the dream-reader felt the relief inspired by the powerful being who had invaded Larson's thoughts and fashioned his vision. She found the misstep which caused the dream weaver to trigger unbidden memories of Vietnam and the misplaced circuits which amplified them to pain and awakened

Larson screaming. Gently, the dream-reader withdrew. She stepped away from her subject to face Silme and Gaelinar.

Silme waited expectantly, her life aura dulled by effort. "Within the week, expect a visit from an aged wizard of amber rank. He has agreed to lift your curse of nature."

Excitement plied the dream-reader like a faery dance, but she resisted response for the sake of dignity. "Bless you, mistress," she managed at length. "And the elf's dream is clear. Some divine being bid him on a quest to fling his sword into the spring of Hel at the tip of the deepest root of the World Tree."

In the silence which followed her explanation, the dream-reader continued. "You must realize, I can only interpret the dream. I can't guess who inspired it, nor the motive behind the quest. Loki's realm is unfit for any but the dead, and a journey even to its borders unsafe for man or elf or god. Legend says any object which falls into Hvergelmir is utterly destroyed. Unless the sword contains the essence of a most unholy creature, I can't fathom why the gods would send the elf on such a task."

Larson seemed about to speak, then went still. "How do we find this Helspring?" asked Silme softly.

The dream-reader tugged her hood against the wind. "North of town find the river Svip. Followed seven days it widens to Sylg which will bring you, in several more days, to the valleys of darkness which lead to the underworld. Eleven rivers coalesce before the golden bridge the dead must cross to enter Hel. They join at Hvergelmir." Pity rose for the four companions saddled with a quest envied by no man. "Something strikes me odd about pure gods sending minions to Loki's realm. If you'll forgive the advice of an elderly woman who has experienced more than most, the oracle of Hargatyr lies less than a day trip off your course. She can tell you whether destroying the sword will serve Midgard well or ill."

Silme's life aura guttered like an aging candle flame. "We thank you lady, for both direction and advice."

The men muttered gracious words. Then the four companions turned and made their way northward along the main track of Forste-Mar. The dream-reader watched until they passed beyond sight of her diseased eyes, and still she waited several minutes longer. Tipping back her hood, she let the breeze swirl her curled gray locks like sea foam. She loosed a single scream of joy and skipped toward her cottage for the first time since childhood. . . .

At the base of the spring, Hvergelmir, Loki paced before Bramin, his golden hair streaming like the mane of a lion. "We must stop them, Hatespawn."

"Stop them." Bramin's feral eyes followed his master's frantic course. "We have them routed straight for Hel, certain their mission is to destroy the sword."

Abruptly, Loki ceased pacing. "We have them headed straight for the oracle of Hargatyr."

"So?"

"So!" Loki screamed above the rush of falling waters. "So, the oracle taps the knowledge of the Fates for her wisdom. So she tells Silme and her wretched companions disposing of Valvitnir serves the cause of evil. Perhaps she even informs them of their true quest."

"Which is?"

Loki's face puckered into a frown of grim aversion. "Against our purposes, Hatespawn."

Bramin fingered his sword hilt, the fringe of his life aura dulled by irritation. "More specifically?"

Loki brushed off the half-man with a wave and resumed his rambling gait. "I'm a god! I've earned the right to be vague."

Bramin scowled, watching eleven rivers fuse in a cascade white as ice. "But not the right to grow impatient. That is your flaw. You told me so the first time we talked."

Loki froze midstride. His perfect features seemed chiseled and powerful as the background of clashing waters whipped to foam. He spoke in a placid monotone. "Very true, Hatespawn. You've more than enough time to divert them from the oracle, no matter the cost. Do you understand?"

Helblindi rasped from its sheath, sudden as a striking serpent. It drew shadow like a magnet, dulling the frigid waters and Bramin's life aura to gray. "Completely," said the Hatespawn.

. . . The dream-reader of Forste-Mar hummed a tune from her youth as she cleaned the floor of her one-room hovel with pendulous sweeps of a broom. Her gaze flitted from the black pit of the hearth, to the rectangle of her sleeping pallet, to the spindly-legged figure of her dining table. She imagined each piece of furniture as it had appeared before cataracts blurred her world to contours. Each hollow straw, every woodgrain seemed to reappear in the bold relief of her memory.

While the dream-reader basked in the anticipa-

tion of a visit from an amber-rank mage, light
flared behind her accompanied by a thunderblast
which shook the foundations of her cottage. She
whirled. A tall, dark male poised before her. He
clutched a diamond-tipped dragonstaff, and an
ebony scabbard hung at his belt. A strikingly powerful life force bathed him in brilliance, its edge
flaming red with anger. The dream-reader read
murder in the undulating shadows which wound
through his aura. She gasped. "Bramin?"

Bramin stepped forward. As he neared, the
dream-reader recognized red eyes filled with accusation and the cruel sneer which twisted his
features. Rage deepened his voice. "You trifling
adept! Whatever galled you to meddle in my affairs. If you had contented yourself performing
your paltry dream-reading abilities and not tried
to second-guess my motives, I wouldn't have to
take your life." His right hand caressed the hilt of
his sword.

The dream-reader shrank from Bramin's threatening form; fear destroyed all pretense of dignity.
"Bramin, please stop. I don't understand. . . ."

Bramin's sword slid from its sheath. Its blade
scattered highlights of his life aura from the faded
fabrics of the dream-reader's cloak. "I fashioned
the elf's dream. The visions were yours to interpret, not to advise. You sent Silme to the oracle of
Hargatyr!"

The permanent darkness of death loomed over
the gray reality of the dream-reader's near blindness. She realized impudence would lose her any
chance to claim Silme's payment, and tears blurred
her vision further. Slowly, courage returned to
her, lending her strength to speak against the
dark elf. "And I would do so again. Silme has

done only good for mankind. There was a time, Bramin, when you and your sister shared tea in my cottage. You both begged stories of magic. And, while the citizenry attacked your elven heritage, I protected you and warned them of your potential abilities. Does my loyalty gain me no mercy?"

Bramin's aura blazed red hatred. He advanced. The point of Helblindi hovered at the dream-reader's throat, driving her backward. "You just wanted my power," he accused. "You thought any kindness you showed me then would be repaid once I became Dragonrank. It was your investment, a gamble. You lost."

The dream-reader's back struck the wall with enough force to jar her fragile frame. The sword point scratched her neck. Desperately she thrust a mental probe to Bramin's mind, trying to understand the mad affliction which corrupted his thoughts and incited him to demonic fury. But her consciousness met defenses solid as stone.

Bramin's foot flicked against the dream-reader's knee, dropping her to the floor. "Grovel, witch!"

All strength fled the dream-reader. Gradually, panic drained to complacency, and she fixed an answering stare on Bramin. "Not for you or anyone else, Dark One. I'm too old to fear death."

Bramin gave no verbal reply. His face puckered to a scowl. Helblindi sheared through the dream-reader's throat. Pain wrenched a scream from her, but the half-man's laughter was the last sound she heard before the half-dead goddess, Hel, claimed her soul.

Deep in the forests north of Forste-Mar, near the banks of the river Svip, Larson repeatedly performed his only sword form for a Kensei who challenged him with offensive strokes of a wooden practice weapon. After four days of morning and evening lessons, the figures had grown as familiar to Larson as the never-ending sequence of pine and the widening river. Yet Gaelinar persisted, adding only simple directional changes to the basic cut of Larson's first session.

The time spent traveling between lessons might have offset the merciless repetition of Gaelinar's training had Silme chosen to grace Larson with conversation or even an encouraging smile. But she withdrew to inner contemplations, responding stiltedly to his attempts at humor, when she replied at all. During Larson's sword lessons, Silme and Brendor shared breakfast or dinner. After he finished, sweat freezing on his tired limbs, Larson was prepared for some social interaction along with his meal. But Silme would take Brendor into the woods for a discourse on magic, and Larson would have only Gaelinar for company. For reasons Larson could not discover, Silme appeared to be avoiding him.

I'll confront her today, Larson decided with unwavering resolution. *If I've done something to offend her, I've a right to know.* As his thoughts meandered in this new direction, Valvitnir jerked suddenly. Gaelinar's wooden sword rattled from the blade, skimming the edge of Larson's pants.

"Nice recovery." Gaelinar seemed pleased. "Perhaps you'll learn a new form tomorrow."

Larson flushed, too modest to credit himself with a maneuver wholly attributable to a sword it had become his mission to destroy. If the dreamreader was correct and Valvitnir housed the soul of an unholy being, it had thus far proved friendly.

Larson wondered whether the sword might lull him to confidence and betray him in real combat. Earlier, he had mentioned nothing of Valvitnir's strange powers to Gaelinar since the sword rescued him from many embarrassing situations in the course of the Kensei's teachings. Now, the decision to confront Silme made him bolder. "Gaelinar. I . . ."

He was interrupted by Brendor who crashed through the thin tangle of brush, face glowing with excitement. "Watch this!" called the boy.

Larson turned toward the child with a mixture of relief and apprehension. Brendor's eyes screwed tight in concentration. His face lined like an adult's. His hand curled in a smooth gesture and shook slightly, fingers stretched toward Gaelinar. "Shave," he said quietly.

Gaelinar flinched back. His chin, which had sported a day's growth of stubble, was now clean as Larson's. "Brendor, you did it!" screamed the elf.

"I . . . did . . . it!" Panting with exertion, Brendor cast his head about as if to determine which direction to run. "Shave, shave, *shave*, SHAVE!"

As the last command burst gleefully from Brendor's throat, hair sprouted from the Kensei's chin in a stiff, unnatural beard. Gaelinar's face went livid. Brendor loosed a strangled cry and staggered into the forest. Struck by the appearance of his customarily neat and serious swordmaster, Larson broke into laughter.

"We'll continue in the morning." Gaelinar waved a hand stoically. "Get something to eat."

Glad for the freedom, Larson wasted no time on words. He sheathed Valvitnir hurriedly and chased after Brendor, hoping the boy might lead

him to Silme. Eventually, he heard the sorceress'
voice, loud and angry, and followed it to a clearing near camp where Silme berated her apprentice without mercy. ". . . not a game, stupid child!
The summoning of a chaos force costs nothing; it
comes naturally to those born to magic. But you
know that channeling its energy to a specific enchantment drains power from its caster's life aura.
Your sloppy technique of partially focusing your
spell is all that saved you. Had you cast that second spell correctly as I taught you . . ." She paused.
Brendor quivered before her wrath like a towns-
man in the sights of a loaded gun. ". . . it would
have destroyed you."

Silme looked up as Larson entered the clearing,
and her glare made it obvious his presence was
unwelcome. Without so much as a gesture of greeting, she continued her tirade. "I was an idiot to
think I could trust a child with power . . ."

Larson wandered away, sick with frustration.
Now, when he had finally gathered the courage to
approach Silme with his feelings, she was busy
with matters she considered more important. Larson supposed hours would pass before she composed herself enough to talk, and by that time she
would want to sleep. Crushed by ill luck, Larson
took a seat by the fire across from Gaelinar who
was scraping the last of Brendor's foiled attempt
at magic from his wrinkled cheeks.

Larson said nothing. He stared into flames orange as a sunset against the darkening background
of nightfall. After a short silence, Gaelinar sheathed
his dagger, pulled rations from a pack beside the
horses, and crouched at Larson's side. Apparently
ısing Larson's mood, the Kensei spoke with en-

couragement. "You've done well. You learn as fast as any I've taught."

Despite the value of Gaelinar's rare compliment, Larson merely watched the fire and made a non-committal grunt. He saw little purpose in learning to wield a sword he was commissioned to destroy and even less in journeying with a beautiful woman who would never share his love. *Does the old man expect me to battle Bramin after a week of sword training?*

"Hungry?" Gaelinar spread a square of cloth before the fire and emptied a small sack of dried fruit and smoked meat.

Larson shared the food without tasting it. Gaelinar's words flowed about him, no more comprehensible than the bubblings of the river. At length, the Kensei stayed his wasted conversation and joined his companion in silence. The campfire settled as it consumed its supply of twigs. The moon rose like a chariot, a lingering token of the sun's glory. And still Larson brooded.

Gaelinar rose. He performed a dexterous series of katas, all lost on Larson whose thoughts centered on his own misfortunes. When the Kensei finished, he gathered bedding and spread it about the fire. He caught Larson's arm and gently tugged the elf to his feet. "Rest will do you good."

Larson made no protest but allowed himself to be led. He crawled between his own snug pile of furs; and, though he made no attempt to sleep, he fell prey to the blissful oblivion which veils men's burdens. Larson's peace was short-lived. He awakened to the low drone of Silme's voice beside him. Fearing he might lose another chance to talk, he groped toward the sound.

Larson caught Silme's leg in the darkness. She recoiled with a shriek. Magics fizzled to sparks around the sorceress, and Gaelinar's swords whisked from their sheaths in a defensive curl before her. "You stupid elf!" shrilled Silme. "You ruined my protection spell and weakened me for nothing. By Vidarr's shoe, am I surrounded by incompetents?"

Gaelinar flipped his katana and shoto to their sheaths and retook a position at Silme's side. "Excepting you, of course, Kensei," the sorceress muttered sullenly. She dropped her head, and again crafted the intricate enchantments of the circular ward which had defended them each night since Larson first met Silme and Gaelinar in the forest. Humbled, Larson retreated beneath his furs, sleep now an unattainable goal.

It's useless. Tears burned Larson's eyes while Silme's voice rose in incantation, followed by the crackle of intertwining magics. *I can't live with her derision, not after I've held her in my arms. Flawlessly beautiful, skilled, compassionate and strong, Silme personifies every quality a man could want in a woman. I would never have found one like her in the States. And,* he reminded himself, *I will never have her here.*

The coarse furs tickled Larson's cheek, and he brushed them aside with self-pitying fury. *I left my mother nothing but another life to mourn. As a soldier, I failed, only to be rescued from death for a task I still don't understand. I've duped Gaelinar with a living sword which learns his lessons better than I ever can. And Silme . . .* Larson gritted his teeth so tightly, his thoughts folded in a haze of redness. *As long as I remain part of it, this quest is doomed to failure.* He caught Valvitnir. With strength spawned of a boil of desperate emotion, Larson hurled the sword. It flew straight as a spear, struck the unseen enchantments of Silme's ward, and plummeted with a crash that woke every member of the party.

Cursing like a longshoreman, Larson sprang from his bedding and snatched up the sword. "I dropped it," he explained lamely for the benefit of his companions, though he doubted even Brendor would believe he was practicing at night with a sheathed weapon. But no one questioned Larson as he returned to his pile of furs and realized in a rush of self-deprecation he could not even desert the task with dignity.

A voice broke his dispirited train of thought. *Allerum.*

"What?" Larson responded with a growl, not wishing to talk. It occurred to him suddenly that the voice was unfamiliar, and his sinews snapped taut. "Who are you?"

"Did you say something, hero?" asked Gaelinar, apparently oblivious to the stranger's presence. Gaelinar's lack of vigilance struck Larson as odd. The Kensei was usually the wariest member of their group. *Sssh*, hissed the first voice. *Don't talk aloud.*

What the hell, thought Larson. *Surely Gaelinar can hear as well as me.* But the swordmaster neither moved nor spoke again. Trusting Gaelinar's instincts more than his own failing sanity, Larson flipped to his other side and tried to sleep.

Allerum. I'm your sword.

Larson's eyes flared open.

Don't speak. I'm communicating through your mind. You need only think what you wish to say. Do you understand?

Larson's wits exploded into confusion. He lay with heart hammering. At length, he formed a tentative reply and concentrated on it with the intensity of a card in a magician's trick. *NO! AND WHO ARE YOU?*

You needn't shout! The response lanced through Larson's brain. *Just think normally.*

Whatthehell?

I am Vidarr, the silent god. Already I've sent more words to you than all my followers in the last century. From now, I answer only in images. Ask what you will.

Larson gnawed a fingernail, believing his insanity well beyond question. *My sword is a god?*

A scene unfolded in Larson's mind. Before him stood the figure of a man, blond as the citizens of Forste-Mar. His face was fair and creased by a smile. His clothing shimmered with an unearthly silver radiance. On his left foot, he wore a crafted sandal. On the other was an oddly-cobbled boot constructed of scraps melded without seam, though the artisan made no attempt to match color.

Oh my god! Fearing his exclamation might be some sort of blasphemy, he amended, *Sorry.* Growing braver he added, *The dream-reader called you an unholy being. And if you're a god, what are you doing in my sword?*

An overwhelming sense of exasperation filled Larson's head and transformed to grudging acceptance. His surface thoughts dimmed like lights before a play. Memory receded behind a presence which possessed his mind like a dream. From the perspective of the god whose image had recently occupied his thoughts, Larson marched across a meadow marred by the footprints of giant men. Beside him strode a figure more beautiful than Silme, though decidedly male. His face was clean-shaven and shaped without flaw. His hair hung in a golden mane of ringlets. Through Vidarr's perception, Larson knew the comely figure as Loki, and he watched the Trickster with contempt.

"Isn't it a glorious day, son of Odin?" Though

clear as chimes, Loki's voice held an edge of threat. His slim hand stroked the hilt of an ebony-scabbarded sword at his hip.

Vidarr gave no answer, nor did Loki expect one. The Trickster adopted a look of suave assurance, stopped suddenly, and slid the sword from its sheath. The blade gleamed silver, then dulled to black as light fled and shadow gathered along its steel.

Unafraid, Vidarr frowned with impatience. He knew his life was protected by Loki's vow to Odin; the day had not yet come when one god could directly cause the death of another. Reluctantly, Vidarr examined the sword and found the craftsmanship exceptional. He demonstrated his admiration empathically and, when Loki sheathed the blade, returned his aura to one of abhorrence for his evil companion.

Loki laughed. "You like my brother and hate me. Fickle, aren't you, Silent One?"

Confusion wracked Odin's son. He waited for Loki's clarification.

Loki scuffed his feet in the dust, eyes dancing with evil mischief. "By my magic, the soul of my brother, Helblindi, resides in this sword."

Vidarr replied with tangible skepticism which flared to accusation. Surely Loki's claim was ridiculous, a sacrilege from any but a deity of Asgard.

Loki stepped around Vidarr with the grace of a cat, his cloak shimmering with enchantments. "Do you doubt me, Lord of Silence? I can prove my abilities well enough."

Vidarr followed Loki's movements with forced indifference. Yet curiosity glimmered faintly through his facade, and the Trickster seized upon it.

"I'd thought Odin's son too wise to judge with-

out evidence." His voice assumed the recrimina-
tory whine of a victim of injustice. "One demonstration will quell all doubt and clear my name.
Would you deny me that right?"

*It will take more than a display of magics to clear your
evil name.* Larson understood that Vidarr had kept
this thought to himself. The message the silent
god actually sent Loki was a mixture of impatience and reluctant concession.

Loki pressed his pale lips together and smiled
like a child with a secret. "If you'll help gather
materials, this task will be more quickly done. While
I find the many necessary components here on
the world of giants, I'd appreciate it if you'd pro-
cure some items from the dwarves. I'll need an
anvil and a piece of white metal more precious
than gold."

Before Vidarr could muster protestations, Loki
disappeared. To appease the Sly Trickster and
satisfy his own inquisitiveness, Vidarr traveled to
Nidavellir, the dark home of dwarves. Time passed
like a blur in Larson's mind, as if Vidarr tired of
the tale and condensed his adventures to outline.
He watched the silent god root through the par-
ings of dwarven blacksmiths for a fist-sized chunk
of platinum; then Vidarr hefted a half-ton anvil
and tossed it carelessly across his shoulders.

Returning at dusk to the world of giants, Vidarr
found his evil companion sitting cross-legged in the
dirt, head lowered and eyes glazed in trance. Vidarr
dropped the anvil; its impact tremored the meadow.
Loki took no notice. Words burbled from his throat
like boiling pitch. Orange light sprang to life, high-
lighting the Sly One in wicked splendor, a dancing
radiance of Helborn power.

Larson longed to shield his eyes from the glare,

but he was forced to witness the scene through Vidarr's eyes. Loki rose, and his aura flared green. "The metal?" Vidarr opened his hand, displaying his find. The platinum winked with reflected light from Loki's sorceries. "The spell works only . . ." Loki spoke gently, so as not to disturb the intricate mesh of his enchantments, "if the metal is carried by one burdened with a load of nine hundred-weight who then becomes . . ."

Loki's aura broke to a red explosion of fire. Sparks scattered in a wild arc and sizzled to oblivion against spring greenery. ". . . its victim!"

Too late, Vidarr realized his danger. Metal spun from his hand as he whirled to run. Magic pounded his back like a giant's fist and sprawled him over the stolen anvil. He struck the ground, body and soul sundered with a violent lurch. Larson felt his thoughts fold in blackness, spinning in the cyclone of Loki's fury. Oblivion strangled Vidarr's scream. There remained only a nothingness beyond darkness, the visual void of the blind accompanied by the ultimate silence of the deaf.

There followed a greater nothingness, a time of pure ignorance without benefit of discovery. From his prison of soundless, sightless eternity, Vidarr reached for the perceptions of those who molded his new blade form and plied the Fates for his destiny. But each attempt slammed him solidly against the impenetrable mental defenses of the gods and men who held him. Doomed to an existence without any contact with sentient beings, Vidarr settled uncomfortably into his confinement.

Claustrophobic panic nearly overwhelmed Larson's senses. Then Vidarr's awareness broke free to wander, unrestrained, through the mind of a future-born wielder selected by Freyr for his inability to defend against mental probes. Aside from a tangled web of guilt- and fear-inspired flaws mingled with strange words and concepts, Vidarr found functioning eyes and ears and a hand he could influence while it gripped his hilt. Larson realized Vidarr's window to the world was his own consciousness.

Larson felt violated. Remembering that the god could read his emotions directly, he struggled to control rising resentment and concentrated on a single question. *Why must I destroy you?*

For several seconds, Larson received no answer. The sword shifted uncomfortably in his grip as Vidarr abandoned pictures for words. *What makes you so certain Hvergelmir will destroy me?*

The dream-reader said . . .

The one who called me an unholy being? interrupted Vidarr.

Good point. Larson rolled to his back. Still clutching the hilt, he rested the sword across his chest and abdomen. *What does happen when I toss you in the Helspring?*

Uncertainty inundated Larson. Vidarr seemed irritated. *How should I know? Hopefully, it frees me. Only the Fates know the means to break Loki's spell, aside from the Trickster himself.*

The next question followed naturally. *So who influenced my dream?*

The hilt in Larson's fist went cold. *That, of course, is the problem. Apparently your people lost all means of mental exchange and warfare. You can't defend against manipulation. All your thoughts are suspect.*

Much of Vidarr's explanation meant nothing to Larson, but he had to agree with the final statement. *Why,* started Larson, trying to phrase the query delicately though he guessed Vidarr could read his intentions as well as his thoughts. *Why must we set you free?*

Reality crumbled before illusion as Vidarr again took control of Larson's mind, showing him the alternate fates of the world. Vision blurred to a vast white plain, and hail stung like cinders. Larson came to realize he was seeing a monstrous winter without end, a bitter frost which slew crops and beasts without mercy. Evil seized tree roots in a grip of ice, dropping century-old forests like stands of saplings.

As Larson watched in wonder, hordes of men appeared, arrayed in armor of skins, links, or chains. Shields gleamed on their arms. Axe, sword, and spear bobbed eagerly in the hands of warriors trembling like hounds before a hunt. Driven to madness by eternal cold, the armed men fell upon one another in a wild sea of battle without strategy, issue, or goal. Warriors dealt death to kin without remorse; men with matching crests fell, pinioned by each other's swords. Blood geysered, staining shields and snow like wine.

No! Larson bucked against Vidarr's control, ripped partially free only to fall prey to his own memories. The glint of light from metal became the flash of gunfire. War howls transformed to the roar of mortars. The scene broke to a tide of fire, and Larson screamed inwardly.

Intent on his demonstration, Vidarr seized a strand of Larson's sanity and hauled his charge back to his own imagings. The sun filled Larson's mind, a golden ball of glory shining down upon the chaos. From the sidelines, a wolf leaped upon the daystar, and caught it in fangs sharp as needles. Light crunched like bone, and bloody foam flecked the wolf's maw. The world plunged into darkness.

A distant cock's crow rose above the din of battle, followed by a second and a third. In blackness, the ground quaked. The World Serpent rose from its bed in the sea, and the gentle lap of surf became an all-consuming hell, battering rock to sand. Elsewhere, at the seat of the world, an enormous tree of ash moaned and shivered as a man and woman found refuge in the hollow of its trunk. Tension built like the crescendo of a song. While the men of Midgard slaughtered one another, greater armies gathered, preparing for a war which would color the heavens sunset red with the blood of giants, monsters, and gods.

The battle plain of Vigrid stood ready. Giants poured to its northern shore from a ship created of human fingernails. From a second vessel, Loki leaped to shore, leading the tortured souls of Hel who followed his commands like automatons. From the south came hordes of living flame led by the black giant, Surtr, whose sword blazed with the glory of the murdered sun. Before them all waited Loki's children: the flame-eyed wolf, Fenrir, breath soured by meals made of Midgard's warriors, and the World Serpent whose venom spewed as thickly as tar.

A handful of gods strode forth to challenge those who sought to destroy the world. They were flanked by the ranks of Valhalla, men who had died in the glory of war and whose souls had been rescued from battlefields by Odin for this conflict. Odin commanded his troop, terrible with his magic spear and helm of gold. The sight might have driven Larson to total mindlessness if not for Vidarr's influence. Guided by the god's vision, he saw the Silent One himself poised among the defenders.

With a howl of hellish fury, the Wolf sprang upon Odin. The warriors of Valhalla swept forward to meet the riot of giants and the Hel hordes under Loki. Sadly outnumbered but honed to a skill which evened the odds, their swords blurred to a whirling fury which scattered limbs and spilled lives like water.

Unable to turn from the violence, Larson pleaded for mercy. Despite his efforts to tear free, Vidarr's nightmare visions unreeled relentlessly. The battle raged on. Odin locked in mortal combat with the Wolf, whose fangs tore like daggers. Beside them, Freyr faced Surtr's firesword with only his fists for weapons. Freyr capered like a dancer, but a final lunge by Surtr tore open his gut. Larson watched helplessly as his patron became the first god to die.

Nearby, the World Serpent vomited poison on the taut-muscled god, Thor, who bruised the snake's mottled flesh with hammer blows mighty enough to fell an army of men. Thor crushed the Serpent's skull. The god stumbled nine steps in triumph, then collapsed, lifeless, as the venom overwhelmed him.

While parrying the strokes of giants, Vidarr searched for his enemy. He saw Loki's agile form dodge then return the blows of another god. Both sprang forward in offense. Sword scraped sword and each pierced flesh. God and Helmaster died together.

Vidarr broke from the throng. His cloak was stained with sweat and blood, his sword notched and dripping. As he raced to add his strength to that of his father, the Wolf swallowed Odin and turned on him. The scene progressed in slow motion. Eager for vengeance, the Silent God stomped his booted foot on the Wolf's lower jaw. His hands caught Fenrir's muzzle and held. Vidarr strained with an effort that taxed every sinew. Sweat sprang from his forehead, rolled down his cheeks like tears, and pooled on his lips. The Wolf loosed a human scream. Its body gave like cloth, sprouting a river of blood which washed souls from the battle plain.

The image froze as Vidarr's illusions ceased, the end slapping into Larson's mind with the impact of a broken film. Through the knowledge of a god, the elf knew that Loki had been defeated. Though Surtr's fires would destroy the world, elves, dwarves, giants, and most of the gods as well, there was a strong suggestion, like that in a fairy tale whose last sentence reads, "And they lived happily ever after," that all would ultimately be well. Somehow Larson knew the earth would rise again, complete with heaven and hell. From the two humans hidden in an ash tree would spring a new generation of men in the image of a god who was the son of a god; they would be the forebears of Larson's own world.

Just when Larson believed the nightmare had ended, Vidarr gathered his thoughts and forced him to understand what would happen if the same battle occurred with the silent god still imprisoned in his sword. Again the gods fought evil on the plain of Vigrid, but this time, the elf Larson had come to know as himself stood nearby, removed from the skirmish. As before, divinities died. Loki and the god fated to kill him locked in conflict. The glowing blue sword in Larson's grip quivered with sorrow as he watched Bramin wield Helblindi to protect Loki from his would-be slayer.

With Bramin's assistance, Loki endured until Fenrir swallowed Odin. But this time, Vidarr, Valvitnir *the wolfslayer,* shivered, imprisoned and impotent in the metal in Larson's hand. Alive because of the entrapment of Vidarr's soul, Fenrir howled with wolfish laughter and leaped onto Loki's enemy. With a snap of his jaws, the Wolf broke his opponent's spine then set upon the firelord, Surtr.

Loki rose in triumph. At his command, Chaos swirled like colored fire in a cyclone. It descended upon Vigrid, breathing new life into Loki's demon hordes. The souls of Valhalla fell prey to agonies beyond that which any being of flesh could understand. On Midgard, Chaos whipped men to killing frenzy. Fathers slew sons who pleasured mothers and raped sisters. Winds smashed rotted trees and swirled oceans to ship-swallowing maelstroms. Then Bramin's shadow sword splintered the World Tree, and the half-breed dragged the chosen survivors to the tortures of Hel.

"Stop!" Larson screamed through a haze of pain. "I've seen enough."

But the Lord of Silence showed him one thing more. Waves hurled foam against a cliff where Silme crouched, protected from the Hel hordes by a dwindling ring of magics. Larson watched helplessly as Bramin burst through her wards, his laughter cruel as thunder. "Now sister, your soul is mine!" He jerked the Helsword from its sheath and struck for Silme's breast. She flinched back; horror etched her features like sculpted glass.

"No!" Larson jerked away with enough force to break Vidarr's control. He fell back into his own private hell. A bullet-riddled, Vietnamese girl

dropped to the ground screaming, her baby left to
die in the field. A companion sprawled legless in
the mud, babbling about returning home before
medics shoveled him into a bag marked KIA.
Shells screamed about Larson with the intensity of
Loki's Chaos. Grenades roared like Fenris. Men
fell like twisted puppets. *And this time it was his own
hand on the trigger.*

Larson's fist struck the ground again and again.
"Why me? Why me? Why me?'

This time, Vidarr did not answer.

CHAPTER 5

Childslayer

"Men fear death as children fear to go in the dark; and as that natural fear in children is increased with tales, so is the other."

—*Francis Bacon,* Of Death

Silme's voice cut through the dark haze of Larson's confusion. "Allerum! Allerum, what's the matter?"

Drawn from the wild surges of memory inspired by Vidarr's imagings, Larson raised his head. Gaelinar crouched among the pines, patient as a shadow in the predawn mist. Closer, Brendor and Silme stood over Larson. The child cocked his head sideways in question. Silme's brow was lined, and concern darkened her blue eyes. For the first time since they had left Forste-Mar, she regarded Larson with something other than hostility.

"Just another dream," Larson muttered. He rolled to a sitting position and refastened the sword to his belt. Sweat dripped from his hair.

Gaelinar grunted disinterestedly and returned to his bedding. Brendor comforted Larson in a childish soprano. "I have nightmares, too. I used to lie real close to Uncle Crullian and tell him about them. He said if I told someone, I wouldn't ever have the same bad dream again."

Now more accustomed to flashbacks, Larson recovered his composure quickly. He stared at Silme, both pleased and discomforted by her anxious expression. "Describe the dream," said the sorceress softly. "Your last vision detailed our quest."

"I don't think . . ." Larson trailed off. *Only a fool could surrender such an opportunity.* "Fine. But I want to talk to you alone."

Silme pinched her lip between her fingers. For some time, Larson received no reply except the low-pitched hum of mosquitoes. Eventually, the sorceress nodded assent and gestured toward the brush beyond camp. She passed through the sparse undergrowth with no more noise than a summer breeze. Apprehensively, Larson jumped to his feet and followed her into the twilight haze of the forest.

Once beyond sight and sound of their companions, Silme confronted Larson with silent forbearance. Though half-hidden in shadow, her face reflected the same distress Larson had recognized at his bedside. "The dream?" she reminded him politely.

"Dream," repeated Larson vacantly. Sunrise lit glimmers of gold in Silme's hair. Wind pressed the fabric of her dress tight against her finely-sculpted breasts. She held a pose of self-assurance and command, but her eyes imparted interest as well as concern. Suddenly Larson felt awkward as a teenager on his first date. "It seems I . . . my sword . . ." A rush of passion spoiled his composure. "Silme, I love you," he blurted without preamble.

Silme's lips parted slightly, but she said nothing. An answering warmth flashed through her eyes and quickly disappeared.

Caught in a swirl of joyous emotion at the realization that Silme might actually share his affection, Larson caught her to his chest. Her body went taut as wood against him. Her hand snaked free and lashed across his face. Larson staggered, as much from shock as pain and stared with wide-eyed innocence.

"How dare you!" Silme's indignation cut Larson like a blade. "I'll not suffer the touch of a rogue who would worry friends to maneuver a woman alone!" She whirled with an anger that whipped her hair in a golden wave and stormed toward the camp.

Crushed by Silme's rejection and sick with embarrassment at his brazen approach, Larson rubbed his aching cheek. As the sorceress stomped into the shadows, he called after her in a voice weak with humiliation. "Silme. Please wait."

She continued as if he had not spoken. The details of her retreating form became lost among the trees.

"Wait." Larson shifted from foot to foot and pressed his one remaining advantage. "I want to talk about Vidarr."

Silme hesitated.

Larson continued with a valiant attempt at resolve which could not hide his tension. "I know how to contact Vidarr."

Silme turned, too concerned about the fate of her god to ignore any source no matter how unlikely. Her manner was stiff and threatening as a crouched tigress. Yet her features held a stunningly feminine vulnerablity which awakened Larson's desires despite his attempts to hold his emotions in rein. "If this is another ruse, I swear I'll kill you," she said coldly.

From another woman the challenge might have seemed ludicrous, but Silme had proven herself quite capable of lethal magics. Larson shivered and pressed his lips in a noncommittal line. "It's truth. I've spoken with Vidarr."

Silme scowled warningly.

Quickly, Larson detailed his story, the sequence of mixed reality and illusion which had threaded through his mind since nightfall. As he spoke, Silme's pinched face relaxed to nearly accepting warmth. But her arms remained crossed, and her fists tightened against the fabric of her cloak. From the corner of his eye, Larson caught Silme staring at him with strangely tender sympathy. But whenever he met her glance, she turned her face away like a star-struck school girl found examining the object of a crush.

"So you see, Vidarr's been with us all along." Larson swallowed, both confused and intimidated by Silme's odd behavior. "I guess I can't expect you to believe me. I'm never quite certain when to believe myself. I . . ." Larson stopped speaking as he realized proof swung from his hip. He pulled Valvitnir from its sheath so abruptly Silme recoiled. "Here. Speak with him yourself." He offered the hilt to the sorceress.

Larson's mind tingled from a blast like static. An idea glided gently though his thoughts. *Allerum. You're the only one who can communicate with me.*

"What!" Larson screamed aloud. Silme startled

again. "What do you mean?" he challenged the sword.

"I . . . I said nothing," Silme stammered.

Silme's mental defenses are too strong for my intrusions, Vidarr explained. *I told you before. You lack mind barriers. That's why Freyr chose you.*

Damn. Larson returned the blade to its scabbard, hand heavy against its jeweled hilt. *Now what do I tell Silme?*

"Allerum. Are you well?" Silme reached for Larson. He cringed reflexively, though her touch was gentle on his shoulder. "What's happened?"

"Vidarr can only speak with me." Grieved by his discovery, Larson did not notice the change in Silme's demeanor. "Now you'll never trust me." He spoke more to himself than to the sorceress. Then, in a rush of emotion, he continued quickly, "I suppose I really can't blame you. But I've loved you almost since the day we met. When I told you how I felt, hope made me think you returned my affection. I'm sorry I grabbed you, Silme. It was all a stupid misunderstanding." Larson gathered a great breath and released a sigh so loud it nearly obliterated Silme's whispered answer.

"There was no misundertanding."

Larson caught his breath. "What did you say?"

Silme met Larson's gaze for the first time since he'd confronted her in the brush. "I do love you. I . . ." She turned away with a lowered head, her face buried in her palms.

Larson hovered, uncertain. He wanted desperately to hold and comfort Silme, yet memory of her warning stayed him. Touching the sorceress against her will could well prove fatal.

Silme looked up. Her eyes were miserably red,

yet tearless. "Someday," she began with an obvious attempt to be tactful. "I want to have children."

Confusion strained Larson's smile. "That would suit me, too."

"But it can't be with you," Silme continued. "And we mustn't start something we can't finish."

Larson opened his mouth, but found himself unable to speak. He stared at Silme's face which seemed to shine like a second sun as dawn dispelled all darkness but the shadows of trees and ferns.

"You don't understand." Silme seemed troubled by his ignorance.

Larson stroked his sword hilt while he searched his mind for a reply.

"You're an elf," Silme prodded softly.

It always seemed such a simple thing to remember, yet Larson continued to forget he was no longer a man. Doubts rushed upon him like a plague. Once before he had wondered whether elves and humans could interbreed, a question pushed aside by the many adventures and wonders of Silme's world. Now, if he was to believe the sorceress, their union was impossible. But even through a haze of frustration and sorrow, Larson discovered a flaw in his conclusion; he wondered why Silme attempted to dupe him with biological falsehoods. "I may be from another world, but I'm not a fool. I know elves and humans can have children together. Your half brother . . ."

Silme wrung her hands with a fresh aura of distress. "That's the problem, don't you see?"

"No."

Silme paced. "Our children would be half-breeds like . . . Bramin."

"No!" Larson's denial held the authority of a

command. "Bramin's father was a *dark* elf. *His* demon blood ruined your brother."

Silme stopped, shaking her head vigorously. "Bramin was a good child until the gibes of neighbors poisoned him. Our offspring would fare no better. This world is unprepared for crossbreeds of any type. I'm sorry, Allerum." Resigned, Silme turned and walked solemnly toward camp.

"Wait!" Larson's screamed order stopped Silme in her tracks. "Denying love won't make it go away. You can't turn it off and on like a light switch!" Afraid to speak too boldly and anger Silme, Larson pursed his lips and kept the remainder of his thoughts hidden. *How can you condemn the citizenry of Forste-Mar for their treatment of Bramin when your own prejudice transcends love?* Desperately, he continued, "By his appearance, Brendor's a half-breed of Scandinavian and some darker race. And Gaelinar's a goo . . . a full-bred foreigner."

"Light's witch?" Silme seemed confused by Larson's tirade. She folded her arms across her chest and did not bother to face him. "They're both human. And Gaelinar can silence teasing."

"So can we." Larson's voice cracked as he sought to make his point before he lost Silme forever. "We can protect our children."

Silme pursed her lips and said nothing. Nor did she move when Larson came up behind her and made his final plea. "I'm good enough for your god, Silme. Why else would Freyr have chosen me to save him?"

The sorceress turned slowly. "And once we free Vidarr, every human in Midgard would respect us and our offspring."

Larson stared, not daring to believe the uncertainty which softened Silme's tone. He met her gaze. Warmth replaced the menacing coldness which had marred the beauty of her eyes. He caught her to his chest. Her presence drove aside all memory of the biting winds. She returned his embrace wholeheartedly, without trace of her former reluctance. Her slim hands sent shivers of desire through him, inducing his mind to conjure a third world between the archaic fantasy of Midgard and his nightmares of Vietnam. It encompassed only Silme and himself, a slim shadow of reality which would hazard no intruders.

Wind ruffled the foliage which defined the clearing, but Larson remained blind and deaf to everything except Silme. He wound his fingers in the soft waves of her hair, savoring her beauty now promised to him by love. Silme's hesitation changed his existence as suddenly as had death. Since his enlistment, the bliss of sleep melting to reality each morning filled his mind with dread. But from now, the rising sun must reawaken euphoric memories of Silme. And even after the initial intensity of their relationship faded, Silme's fierce loyalty to causes would bind them for as long as an elf and a sorceress might live.

Thrilled to the elation of love long denied, Larson pressed his lips to Silme's and explored her mouth with his tongue. He desired to know her like a treasured story which, read a thousand times, would never lose its magic. He studied her with his eyes, hands, and mind, dreading at any moment that she might stiffen and grow cold to him. But it never came. Silme's answering warmth intensified their kiss until Larson withdrew for fear of losing control of his passion so close to camp and driving Silme away with boldness. *She loves me!* Joy exploded within him.

Gradually, Larson's narrow ribbon of world expanded, and realization crowded him. He recalled Silme's earlier reluctance and her words which seemed so simple yet nearly formed an impenetrable wall between them. *Someday, I want to have children.* The accusation in her voice triggered memories, plunging Larson deeper into his flawed mental tapestry. Poised at the edge of sanity, he brushed aside the plaintive visages of slant-eyed orphans. The effort flung him further into his past to an age when he welcomed rather than feared the night. Though discomforting, his vision held none of the terror usually inherent in flashback. Soft and vague as a whisper, he revived the porcelain doll features of his young brother, Timmy, as they sat before the headstone of their father's grave. The haze of gathering night hid the tears in the child's eyes, but his voice emerged as a quavering whine. "Why? Why did he have to die? Why would he go to heaven and leave us?" His plea faded in the stillness.

In his memory, Al Larson scuffed his shoe in the dust, fighting his own sorrow for an answer. "He loved us, Timmy. God took him . . ." *God and his drunk driver.* Larson's present thoughts twisted the past. ". . . Dad didn't want to leave us. No one chooses to die." *No one but an enlistee.* Again, the Larson in Midgard amended his imaginings. This observation opened other channels of memory. He recalled the day he left for boot camp, plagued by doubts yet morbidly excited by the glamour of espionage and the challege of matching wits with other men. While in a zone of peace, distant dangers enticed him. But this thrill shattered before the hollow glare of betrayal he found in Timmy's eyes. Larson realized suddenly his brother had never said "good-bye."

A tear formed in Larson's eye, blurring his image of Timmy. Joy fled before an onrush of resolve. *Lost in the promise of passion, I dared to believe I could raise a child. I cannot subject some kid to my insanity or the consequences of flashback. Every person I care for becomes a weapon for my enemies. A child will not join my life until I learn to control my thoughts. And I can't allow myself to love Silme until we vanquish Bramin.*

Larson dropped his hands to his sides, and his index finger traced a gem in Valvitnir's hilt. Vidarr's voice crashed into his mind. *You hypocrite! Now who thinks of controlling love? Are you selfish or merely stupid?* Anger speared through the pathways of Larson's mind, and he winced beneath the onslaught of emotion. *Denying love won't protect you from grief. And fatherhood is more than ancestry. You already have a child; Brendor cares deeply for you. Does the camaraderie you shared in Forste-Mar mean nothing to you? If you reject Brendor like you did Timmy, you'll destroy his trust completely.*

"Allerum?" Silme caught Larson's arm.

Larson shoved the sword hilt aside; and Vidarr's presence fled his mind, leaving ghostly echoes in its wake. *I never abandoned Timmy! I did what I had to do. Do you think I wanted to go to war?* He battered aside the nagging memory of his brother's face, replaced it with others: his sister Pam, Ti Sun, Brendor. Each had experienced the greatest trauma chance could perpetrate upon a child, the loss of a parent. Like Timmy, all three returned to life with a resilience Larson could scarcely comprehend, innocents caught in a world without mercy. *They came to me with trust and hope. And I betrayed them all!* "Damn it, I do love Brendor. He needs me. He shall become our first child."

Silme seized Larson's hands and chided gently. "Of course we will raise Brendor. Did you think I'd abandon a partially trained apprentice who knows just enough of magic to endanger himself?"

Not realizing he had spoken aloud, Larson shied. Relaxing, he smiled. Again he pulled Silme to him, content with the pressure of her body against his. His thoughts remained in a lazy stupor of complacence. Stolen in death from a world at war, Freyr seemed to have given him everything: life in a new world, a woman more beautiful than a fairy-tale princess, and a child who, if a bit inept, reminded him of himself in youth and might one day inherit great power.

Silme continued speaking softly in his ear. "Naturally, I still think it best to leave Brendor safely in a town until our conflict with Bramin is completed. A battlefield is no place for a boy."

Larson agreed. Before he could reply, Gaelinar's gruff baritone interrupted their embrace. "Allerum. Time for your lesson."

Muttering blasphemies from his own world, Larson released Silme. He knew from past experience it was as unhealthy to ignore Gaelinar as a rearing cobra. For several seconds, the elf stood, touching only Silme's fingertips. "See you at breakfast?"

"Of course," she replied as if that had always been her habit. Hand in hand, they returned to camp.

Sunlight spilled through the clouds, coloring the river Sylg like gilt. But Larson was too preoccupied to notice. Feet soaked by dew, he followed Gaelinar's instructions with a renewed enthusiasm which pleased his teacher. "Good, Allerum. You've learned to treat your sword as a friend rather than an obstacle. Again."

Laughing inwardly at the unwitting double meaning of Gaelinar's praise, Larson repeated the maneuver. Valvitnir crashed solidly against the Kensei's notched wooden blade. Momentarily, Larson's attention strayed to Silme who watched his practice with approval.

"Enough." Gaelinar followed the direction of Larson's stare. "Work will make a swordsman of you. For now your interests are elsewhere."

Smiling, Larson sheathed his sword. Drying sweat intensified the late morning chill as he strode to Silme and took her arm. Returning to the campfire, they found Brendor sorting a sack of rations.

The four travelers breakfasted together for the first time in more than a week. Glad for company, Brendor prattled in an unending, childish banter. More attentive to Silme's hand, Larson heard little of the conversation until the sorceress spoke. "Yes. Brendor's done well. He's learned the spell I promised to teach him."

The child beamed as Silme continued. "I recognize this land. The town of Manivoll lies a half day ahead. I have friends there who would gladly watch Brendor while we complete our quest."

Brendor's smile vanished, replaced by a grimace of horror. "Watch . . . you can't leave me! You just can't, I . . ." His eyes pleaded with Larson.

Gaelinar nodded in tacit agreement with Silme's plan. Unable to meet Brendor's eyes, Larson took a sudden, inordinate interest in his meal.

Brendor leaped to his feet. His unfinished apple tumbled to the dirt. "I won't go! I won't go! I won't . . ." When this tactic gained no sympathy, the child changed to another. "Allerum." He knelt beside Larson and seized the elf's arm with grubby fists. "Please, Al. Pleeease."

Larson closed his eyes as the image of another child took vivid form in his memory. Ti Sun's voice rang clear as reality. "Candy, Joe?" A small hand tugged at his fatigues.

Larson heard himself reply, his voice stiff with feigned offense. "You know my name, Ti Sun."

The child amended. "Candy, Al. Please, Al. . . ."

"All right. Okay." Larson thrust a hand into his pocket and retrieved a packet wrapped in crisp, clean paper. Ti Sun watched with a bright-eyed excitement which made Larson smile. Slowly, he peeled away the wrapper to reveal a piece of chocolate melted nearly to liquid.

"Thanks! Thanks!" The child accepted the offering and soon coated his fingers and mouth with candy.

Gavin called from farther along the road. "Al, you coming?"

Larson turned. Light flashed through his thoughts like a warning. Suddenly, he realized he was caught in flashback as fully as a shallow sleeper knows when he is dreaming. Memory crowded him, solid as brick. Larson struggled against reexperiencing the catastrophe he could not bear a second time. He tried to force his mind from Ti Sun a dozen times with no success. Madness engulfed his conscious thought, pushing his mind back toward a village in Vietnam and the chocolate-stained child with the beatific smile.

Larson staggered. His hand cracked painfully against steel. Inadvertently, he seized Valvitnir's hilt, and another consciousness merged with his own. With Vidarr's aid, Larson escaped his flashback none the worse for his vision except for sweat-slicked palms and a shiver which wracked his entire body.

Brendor clung to Larson's shirt, his entreaties muffled by folds of cloth. Larson mentally communicated profuse gratitude to Vidarr, then turned his attention to the child at his chest. "Brendor, I like you very much."

The child tightened his grip.

"Enough so," Larson continued, "that I want to keep you as a son." The words sounded hollow to Larson's ears. Even nine months in Vietnam had not aged him enough to have a ten-year-old child. *Al Larson was only twenty, but I can't know the age of this elf body in which Freyr placed me. According to fairy tales, elves are immortal. If that holds true, the point becomes assuredly moot.* Larson forced his thoughts from this new distraction. "I won't have you killed because of my task. You stay in Manivoll, Brendor. I won't apologize for caring enough to keep you safe."

Brendor made no reply, but his mouth puckered to a scowl and he moved away with a tread sufficiently heavy to convey betrayal. Haunted by remembrances of a Vietnamese boy who became a casualty in the affairs of men, Larson paid the sorceress' apprentice no heed. He helped Silme and Gaelinar pack the horses, believing his decision a wise one.

The journey to the town of Manivoll convinced Larson of the soundness of his choice to side with Silme and Gaelinar. In an attempt to sway the lenient elf who had already proven himself a child's easy mark, Brendor became Larson's self-appointed servant. The boy volunteered to carry Larson's supplies on his own horse, dismounted to retrieve a cape pin the elf dropped, and offered to groom all the steeds at their next encampment. Larson supposed Brendor would have eaten, drunk, and pissed for him if given the opportunity. Since Gaelinar recognized the change in Larson's and Silme's relationship, he rode ahead on the pretext of scouting; but Brendor's constant presence made even simple exchanges of affection impossible. By the time the travelers reached the outskirts of Manivoll, Larson could scarcely wait to be free of the boy.

Brendor fell distressingly silent as they entered the town. Larson recalled the first time his mother had left him in the home of a strange babysitter. Then, he had clung to his mother, overwhelmed by the irrational fear she would never return. Sensing his discomfort, his mother had entrusted him with a necklace she wore every day. Though it was senseless to think she would abandon him and not her jewelry, the gesture consoled him. At the time, Larson had been considerably younger than Brendor; he knew a token far more valuable than a silver chain would be required to reassure the healer's nephew.

The moment Larson and his companions reached the town proper, peasants converged on Silme like groupies in the presence of a rock star. Disquieted by the gathering crowd, Larson, Gaelinar, and Brendor shied away from the sorceress' admirers. The Kensei explained in a whisper. "Years ago, Bramin sent a dragon after Silme. After a long and arduous battle, she defeated the wyrm near the town of Manivoll. Naturally, the citizenry was convinced she rescued them from the beast; and in all fairness, she probably did. Once Silme recovered from her confrontation, she hired me as bodyguard."

Larson nodded, only partially listening as he pondered a means to comfort Brendor. His only

item of value was Valvitnir, but he could not hand
the sword to the boy and still complete his quest.
Gaelinar's katana and shoto were surely off limits;
and Larson doubted Silme would surrender her
dragonstaff to a novice magician, though she often left it in Gaelinar's care.

A tarp-covered wagon creaked past Larson and
stopped before the throng which surrounded Silme.
A man reined in the horse while a plump woman
dragged a freckle-faced girl toward the sorceress
who was already engaged in an inordinate number of simultaneous conversations. A gust of wind
swirled a few dusty feathers from the wagon, and
the woeful clucks of its live cargo gave Larson an
idea. He placed an arm about Brendor's slumped
shoulders and addressed the Kensei. "How many
days of travel do we have left?"

Gaelinar kept his gaze on Silme, though she
surely had nothing to fear from her reverent crowd
of townsfolk. "A half day to the oracle and the
same back to the river. Then one more day to the
Valleys of Darkness and the Helspring."

"And another to return to Manivoll for Brendor,"
Larson finished. "How much food do we have?"

Gaelinar scratched his leg through the layers of
his wind-spread robes. "Four, maybe five days."

"Good," said Larson with surprisingly effective
finality. "Just enough to reach our goal and get us
back to Brendor. We won't buy any rations here."
He smiled at the child. Without supplies or a
nearby town, Larson and his companions would
be forced to return to Manivoll to secure food or
go hungry.

Gaelinar looked away from Silme to confront
Larson. His glower made it clear he understood
Larson's intentions, and equally apparent that they
displeased him. "We may be delayed."

Larson remained adamant. "Unless we're killed, we can make it back in five days."

Gaelinar rattled his fingers against the sheath of his katana impatiently. "I consider death a more extreme delay." He met Brendor's stricken stare and relented. "Fine, no rations. But I'm certain Brendor knows I could think of better ways to be rid of a young wizard than leaving him in a town, with my name and description, to wreak future vengeance." Gaelinar patted his sword pommel to make his pronouncement perfectly clear. Still staring at the boy, the Kensei pointed at the adoring peasants and changed the topic. "Brendor, Silme has many friends in Manivoll. If you ever wanted to become a silversmith or a baker or a cooper, let her know."

"I want to be a wizard." Brendor's pout was uncompromising.

"And?" Gaelinar asked as if the child had not finished.

"Just a wizard." Brendor jerked his head with resolution. "Wizards are the smartest people in the world."

Gaelinar laced his fingers on his chin as he pondered a situation which had grown more complex than he anticipated. Larson tried to help. "What's so special about wizards?"

Brendor answered without hesitation. "Wizards make magic, and they know more than anyone else."

"More than silversmiths and coopers?" Larson asked, though he was unfamiliar with the latter occupation and could only guess at its meaning.

Brendor nodded.

Larson winked at Gaelinar. "Then I guess you already know how to fashion jewelry and . . . um . . . shoe horses."

"Well . . . no."

Gaelinar chuckled at Larson's misinterpretation of a cooper's profession. "Did your Uncle Crullian know how to . . . um . . . shoe horses?"

Brendor bit his lip and nodded assent.

"As does Silme," Gaelinar finished. "Wizards are supposed to understand simple things like that." He cast a furtive glance toward Silme who had already begun working her way toward them through the crowd. The Kensei's voice dropped to a whisper as he addressed the child again. "Lucky for you Silme never discovered the gap in your education or she wouldn't have let you become her apprentice. You've only five days to correct your serious deficiency. But don't worry, we won't tell her." The swordmaster clamped a hand over his mouth in mock conspiracy as Silme dispersed the throng and returned to her companions.

"We won't have any problem finding a temporary home for Brendor." Silme jabbed the road dirt with the base of her dragonstaff. "I've found more than enough volunteers."

Gaelinar winked at no one in particular. "Brendor has requested a five-day apprenticeship with the blacksmith."

"Fine choice," she said to the boy. "I'm certain Sigurdhr would appreciate your company." She led her companions through a town smaller and poorer than Forste-Mar, stopping occasionally to exchange greetings and introductions. Larson met scores of blonds and redheads with names which required spelling out. He found that most had final pronounced e's or silent r's and promptly forgot all of them. For their part, the townsfolk spared Larson more than his share of stares, but he recognized none of the hostility against elves he had received in Silme's hometown. He wondered how much Silme's presence might have altered the events in Ura's tavern.

Larson heard the crash of hammer against anvil long before they rounded the corner of Sigurdhr's house. They found the blacksmith intent on a bent strip of steel, his honey-colored beard sweat-plastered to his chin. Back to the newcomers, a youngster a few years older than Brendor worked the bellows with an effort which grew sloppy with fatigue.

"Yo, Eirik!" Sigurdhr bellowed at the boy. He raised his head, caught sight of Silme, and stopped in mid-yell. "Silme!" He gestured her forward with an exaggerated wave. Sigurdhr examined his works briefly, dismayed to find only horseshoes, barrel hoops, and a wood-cutting axe, none of which seemed the proper gift for a lady. Eirik released the bellows with a relieved sigh and shook cramps from his arms.

While the blacksmith introduced his son, Eirik, and Silme presented her companions, Brendor clung to Larson despite the fact that the elf was every bit as inexperienced as himself. Eirik greeted Brendor with so much exuberance, the healer's nephew regained sufficient confidence and interest to release Larson and speak. "I'm a wizard!"

Eirik's features twisted in awe. Sigurdhr nodded encouragement. "Silme. You and your distinguished companions must stay for dinner and the night. Kelda's prepared lamb stew with goat's milk cheese. She always makes enough for a boat load of warriors. And we've plenty of room." He waved his guests toward the door of the cottage without waiting for confirmation.

For the first time, Larson noticed the streaks of

gray in the sky which heralded sunset. The gnawing in his gut which he had attributed to the anxiety of entering the town became a tense grumble of hunger. They had traveled right through without pausing for lunch. Eagerly, he followed Silme and Brendor through the cottage door, into the welcoming aroma of gravy and fresh-baked bread.

Gaelinar bowed politely to his hosts. "Forgive me, Sigurdhr Blacksmith. Lord Allerum and I cannot attend your meal. We've a sword lesson to complete."

Larson turned suddenly and reluctantly from the feast. "Now? But there's food on the table."

Gaelinar bowed again, but his words were without compromise. "Practice. Now."

"Excuse me," Larson mumbled to their host. He found abandoning dinner for swordplay painful, but he followed the Kensei across the brown grasses of the blacksmith's lawn to an open area beyond the forge. An edge of the sun had already slipped beneath the horizon, coloring the western sky as red as the blood in Vidarr's vision. Larson scowled as he reached for his sword. "You're one hell of a gung ho gook."

"Pardon me?" Gaelinar's hand paused on the brocade of his katana.

"Nothing." Larson sighed, enjoying the sound of English in this legendary Northern world. "But where I come from, it's impolite to refuse dinner with a host."

Gaelinar nodded once, his eyes dark as midnight. "Hero, if you miss a meal tonight, you will have another tomorrow." He paused as the air hummed with the first of the evening's mosquitoes. "If you skip practice, you may not. Begin."

Larson obeyed with reluctant annoyance. In two days, he would face the greatest challenge of his new life with nothing but the knowledge of a few dodges and strikes. Surely one lesson more or less would make little difference to his abilities. But Gaelinar seemed to think otherwise, and Larson found it impossible to argue with the swordmaster concerning his own trade.

Gaelinar worked Larson without mercy far into the moonless night. For each success, the Kensei presented a new challenge until Larson's annoyance folded beneath all-encompassing fatigue. More and more frequently, he relied on Vidarr's cues. By the time the practice concluded, without ceremony or praise, Larson no longer wanted food, just a place to lie down and a full night's rest.

Gaelinar and Larson returned to the cottage in a silence which pleased the elf. Condemning words or maxims would have rekindled the exasperation he struggled to suppress. Inside, Gaelinar joined the conversation of Silme, Sigurdhr, and Kelda who shared tea before a roaring fire. Larson excused himself with a yawn, and Kelda showed him to a bedroom with a straw pallet and a hand-knitted quilt. There, Larson promptly fell asleep.

The dream seized control of Larson during the shallow, twilight slumber near to awakening. It began as a pleasant vision of the extension of their journey. Gaelinar, Silme, and himself rode along a meandering path beside the river Sylg, which twisted like a silver serpent, widening to a torrent of ice-flecked waters. The trail forked many times. Always in the past they had taken the branch which most closely paralleled the river. But in the dream, Silme indicated a wooden sign corroded by fungus and started down a side path which led away from the stream.

As the dream-Larson turned to follow, panic seized him like an overdose of adrenalin. He dismounted and dropped to a crouch, heart hammering in his chest. His mouth dried to rawness. His vision blurred to haze. War memories pressed toward expression, but the being who inspired his nightmare wove barriers with the intricacy of a spider. In the vision, Larson shook his head with uncharacteristic violence and gestured toward the northern trail along the river Sylg.

There was no sound in Larson's dream, but when Silme cleared slime from the road sign, its writings became clear:

Temple to Odin
The Oracle of Hargatyr

With an air of exasperation, Silme and Gaelinar reined their horses down the eastward branch. Reluctantly, the dream-Larson remounted and followed, but with each hoof-fall his anxiety trebled. Rows of twisted juniper passed unnoticed. The scenery might have been painted backdrops for all the heed he paid it. Instead, his attention focused on the looming gray outline of the temple to Odin.

By the time Larson and his companions reached the temple dooryard, his clothing had adhered to his sweat-soaked torso. He paused, studying the squat structure with an aura of mistrust. Brown ivies swarmed its exterior in uneven clumps, making it seem to lean awkwardly to the left. Moss chinked the wall stones like green mortar. Larson almost expected to see lightning flare between nonexistent watchtowers. He shivered, wondering whether to blame the temple's eerie appearance or his heightened senses for the fear which coiled his muscles nearly to immobility. He felt like a traitor who had refused both cigarette and blindfold before the firing squad.

At Silme's knock, the ancient door swung open with a squeal of complaint. A half dozen drab-robed acolytes met Larson and his companions and escorted them past stained altars. Beyond, a dark curtain crisscrossed with glimmering silver threads spanned a doorway from ceiling to floor. Gaelinar and Silme passed through a slit in the fabric. Larson followed them into a room as gray as the moment before dawn. At its farthest end sat the oracle of Hargatyr, a young woman with a seemingly endless cascade of reddish hair. Though shadowed beyond recognition of detail, her face seemed not quite normal to Larson. Before her stood a marble slab which supported a clear, oblong diamond with a black central core rimmed green. Not unlike a giant eye, the stone winked and shone with an intensity which further shattered the dream-Larson's confidence.

Silme stepped forward and presented a request Larson could not hear in the frustratingly soundless world of his dream. The oracle passed a withered hand twice across the diamond. Mist swirled in the depths of the gemstone, floated upward in lines tenuous as heat haze. Abruptly the oracle burst to a conflagration of yellow flame. Larson reeled backward as a shapeless black form leaped from the fire and attacked the startled sorceress.

Claws rent Silme's flesh. Blood sprayed the room in arcs of red chaos. Gaelinar howled. His swords reflected highlights of scarlet and gold. Valvitnir rasped from its sheath. Larson and Gaelinar lunged together for the demon which savaged Silme. The beast's claws carved searing lines across Larson's arm, but steel also met its mark. Valvitnir plunged deep into the monster's gut. Even more swiftly, Gaelinar's swords went sticky green with demon blood. It fell, witch-screaming, across Silme's lifeless form.

The room was awash with color. No life remained in Silme's broken body. The sapphire in her dragonstaff shattered like glass on the cold stone floor. Grief struck Larson in a wave of mental anguish. As he stared at the wild waste of multiple hues, the scene swirled and blurred away to a single black face with glowing red eyes. *Bramin!* Rationality escaped in a rush of fear, and sound sundered silence in a rolling thunderclap of evil laughter. Bramin's misshapen mouth formed words which struck like daggers of ice. "Be forewarned, *Al Larson*. Should you choose to seek the oracle, you will pay with the lives of friends!"

Bramin's face winked out. His dark hand remained and scattered the carefully placed barriers in Larson's mind. Memories burst forth like a torrent through a broken dam. Rockets flared from every angle with roars which deafened Larson. Bullets whined in insect-like swarms where he cowered with no safe place to retreat. Screams formed a chorus of hell-born agonies, while ghosts of buddies and enemies alike sentenced Larson to an eternity of life.

Larson's mental flight from madness ran him headlong into a scene from the past. He crouched between the banks of a dried river, clutching an M-16 which grew surprisingly light in the moments before death. Surrounded by enemies, he charged from the banks with Freyr's name on his lips. But where the last time he had recalled nothing xcept awakening in a strange elf body and a

foreign world, now he recalled the torment of
bullets riddling his body, jerking his limbs like a
marionette. Horror held him screamless while a
river of his own blood washed between the banks.

Larson awoke with sinews knotted and no sense
of place or time. He was on his feet before he
could think, eyes searching the room for movement. He scuttled to a corner and pressed his
back to the wall. Sanity returned him to the blacksmith's cottage. Larson took several deep breaths,
rose, and paced until his muscles uncoiled and his
mood passed from panic to anxiety to crimson
fury against the half-breed hellion who sought
Silme's soul.

"Bramin!" Larson called with a courage he'd never
before known he possessed. "I don't fear your
threats, your dragons, your demons, or your . . ."
Short of insults, he ended lamely, ". . . your pid-
dling whangdoodles. Torment me as you wish, but
we will visit this oracle. If you could kill Gaelinar
or Silme, I think you would have done so already."

Larson believed his challenge was heard by no
one except himself. But a shadow fell across the
room, and the walls were suddenly suffused with
a faint white glow. Caught in the center of the
chamber, Larson spun like a fox between two packs
of dogs. A message burned through his mind.
"You underestimate me, Futurespawn." A long
black finger probed his thoughts for a painful
memory.

Prepared to fight though he saw no physical
threat, Larson freed Valvitnir. Instantly, a benev-
olent entity joined the intruder in his mind.
Bramin's mental presence hissed a shocked epi-
thet and departed. Vidarr's reassurances pervaded

Larson's consciousness. Then the god, too, disappeared to Larson's perception.

Before the startled elf could ponder the significance of the night's events, Gaelinar poked his head through the door to Larson's chamber. "Practicing, hero? Good. You should be ready for your lesson."

After the sword practice, Larson found his stomach too knotted for food despite his twenty-four hour fast. The conversations of his companions passed unheard as Larson made the decision not to describe his dream to Silme. Too proud to reverse his decision about the oracle, he saw no reason to trouble the sorceress with Bramin's untenable threats. Still, time passed in an interminable vacuum; Larson was glad when he exchanged his final farewells and promises with Brendor. In bleary silence, he passed through the remainder of the town with Silme and Gaelinar and continued along the pine-bordered banks of the river Sylg.

The path looked distressingly similar to Larson's nightmare. Discomforted, he unsheathed Valvitnir and balanced the blade across his knees. His stilted replies to Silme's attempts at conversation frustrated the sorceress and earned him a lonely trip. Still, midday came far too soon for Larson. The sun hovered overhead when Silme drew up her mount at the road sign to the oracle of Hargatyr.

Gaelinar reined his mount and addressed Larson for the first time since his lesson. "You must be hungry. Sorry to go against your wishes not to pack supplies, but Lady Kelda offered fresh meat for our journey. I couldn't refuse. Gather some kindling, and we'll have the best cooked lunch of our wanderings."

Glad for any distraction which differentiated events of reality from those of his nightmare, Larson clambered from his saddle, sheathed his sword, and wandered into the woods. Twigs were plentiful on the forest floor. Larson selectively collected only the driest ones of reasonable length. A mere hundred yards from the crossroads, he had managed to accumulate a thick handful of kindling, and he started back toward his waiting companions.

Brush crackled behind Larson. He whirled, sticks scattering from his grip, in time to watch a small, familiar figure scuttle behind a clump of trees. "Brendor!" Larson screamed. He charged after the retreating child.

Brendor crashed awkwardly through the weeds. Slower, Larson trailed with far more stealth. Ragweed and ferns gave way to a brushless clearing enclosed by intertwining pine. Larson stopped, afraid the chase might already have taken him dangerously far from camp. "Brendor! Come out now! I know you're here, and I'm not playing games." He added with a gentle sigh, "I promise not to hit you."

The child's blunderings transformed to softer rustlings. Within moments, Brendor emerged from the brush and stepped among the shadows of the clearing. His clothing was torn. Small scratches beneath dripped blood. He shuffled toward Larson like a disobedient dog, his head bent low in shame, his eyes oddly vacant.

At a subtle noise from behind, Larson looked around to see Silme who had followed his calls to the edge of the clearing. He conveyed his control of the situation with a nearly imperceptible nod and returned his attention to the approaching child.

Less than an arm's length separated Larson and Brendor when Silme screamed, "Allerum, wait!" Enchantments bright as a flare struck the child and rebounded to glowing streamers. Silme's magics appeared to have no effect on the boy, but its backlash sparked light from a jagged blade clenched in his fist. Even as Larson recoiled in shock, Brendor plunged his knife at the elf's chest.

Reflexively, Larson caught the tiny wrist. Brendor's other hand enwrapped Larson's free forearm with a power he had never demonstrated in the past. The child's strength was awesome, despite his size. Larson strained until sweat sprang from his face. The dagger shivered ever closer.

"No!" A beam of amber screamed past Larson's ear and struck Brendor full in the face. Impact jerked the child backward. Desperate, Larson planted his foot on Brendor's knee and rolled onto his back. Stone bit into his spine. The child flipped over Larson, but his viselike grip held. Brendor's fingers pinned Larson's wrist to the ground. The dagger sped for the elf's bared throat. "Brendor, no!" Larson struggled like a madman. He seized Brendor's knife hand, but all his effort scarcely slowed the blade's descent.

Enchantments whizzed over Larson's head, plastering Brendor with multiple barbs of energy. The child flinched. Pain blanked his features as the magics ripped through his body and pitched him backward in a mass of bloody tatters. Larson heaved aside the limp figure and sprang to his feet, staring at the gruesome lump of flesh which was once a beloved companion. Brendor's eyes seemed glazed as marbles, and his blood-flecked hair spread in an inky puddle. Memory slapped Larson, heavy and unforgiving as a migraine. To Larson's mind,

the clearing became a dirt road through a Vietnamese village; the bursts of sorcery transformed
to the cruel blatter of an M-16.

The child's face was no longer Brendor's. The
eyes slanted away from almond-colored irises. The
mouth gaped, smeared with melted chocolate. *Ti
Sun!* Larson's stomach lurched. His vision clouded
to red haze. He turned hollow, accusing eyes on
his buddy, Gavin, who still clutched his smoking
gun. Profanities spilled from Larson's throat in an
anguished sob. Blood fury raged like fever. He
threw himself upon Gavin, swinging his fists with
irrational, aimless outrage.

Many hands caught Larson. Men pinned him helplessly between uniformed bodies. Larson shrieked
as he struggled. The fingers which bruised his
arms caused a pain which only fueled his anger.
Several seconds went by while Gavin carefully
flipped Ti Sun's remains, and several more passed
before Larson recognized the significance of the
grenade which rolled from the child's limp hand.
"It was him or you, you stupid bastard," Gavin
explained with a wretched sob. "Him . . . or you."

The flashback broke to midday light. As Larson
passed from one world to another, he discovered
his fist poised to strike a figure already grounded
by his blows. From nowhere, Gaelinar's hand seized
his wrist and whipped his body to the ground with
surprising speed. The Kensei's grip barred Larson's arm at an awkward angle. His other hand
neatly caged Larson's throat. Larson knew Gaelinar
could fracture arm or windpipe with a simple
strike.

Larson lay perfectly still. His knuckles felt raw,

and his wrist was bruised from Brendor's attack. "I'm sorry," he whispered hoarsely.

Gaelinar's grip eased slightly. Silme knelt at Larson's side. Blood trickled from the side of her mouth, and Larson realized with a sudden rush of horror that she was the victim of his own crazed assault. "Oh my god. What have I done?"

Gaelinar released Larson. The elf staggered to his feet. He caught Silme in an embrace strengthened nearly to violence by the need for apology. "I'm sorry . . . I'm sorry . . ." Larson repeated it twenty times before humiliation broke his grip, and he turned away with self-loathing.

"Finish the quest without me." Larson unhooked Valvitnir and let the sword drop to the ground. "I could have killed her."

"I assure you, you couldn't have." Gaelinar drew to Larson's side. "Hero . . ."

"I'm not a hero!" Larson's screamed reply echoed between gangling pines and warped juniper. "I'm a raving lunatic, a madman, a paranoid maniac with delusions of . . . of . . . sanity . . ." When he ran out of Norse descriptions, he switched to English slang.

Gaelinar waited until the tirade passed and spoke with the sincerity he usually reserved for sword practice. "All heroes are flawed."

Larson whirled abruptly. "Heroes? Flawed?"

"All heroes," Gaelinar repeated. "To have courage, a man must know fear. Good cannot exist without evil. And a man becomes a hero when he excels despite his flaws."

Larson hesitated, mentally drained of emotion. Silme took his hands gently. "Hero, you are forgiven. I can't blame you for avenging the child, even against me. You couldn't know he was not

the same Brendor we loved. Only my training as
enchantress enabled me to recognize Bramin's influence when I reached the clearing."

"Then Brendor. . . ?" Larson's voice quivered
with hope.

Silme turned her gaze to her feet. "He's dead,
Allerum. Bramin would need to destroy him completely to gain control of his body. I'm as sorry as
you."

Larson hugged Silme again, grieved by the loss
of a friend who was as a son and scarcely daring
to believe the sorceress' unbounding compassion.

While Larson recovered his poise, Gaelinar set
Brendor's body to pyre. It was only a formality.
Bramin's automaton was a soulless shell no more
worthy of dignity than a fallen sapling. Even so,
Brendor's corpse left the world with a whispered
eulogy and the Kensei's priceless respect.

As the three companions solemnly mounted
horses and reined toward the oracle of Hargatyr,
Larson confronted Gaelinar with a question. "Kensei, what's your flaw?"

Gaelinar's lips bent to a slight smile. "I, Lord
Allerum, am no hero."

CHAPTER 6

Mageslayer

"The haft of the arrow had been feathered with one of the eagle's own plumes. We often give our enemies the means of our own destruction."
—*Aesop,* The Eagle and the Arrow

The temple to Odin appeared far more benign in reality than it had in Larson's dream. The ivy which covered its walls was shaped and tended, though cruel northern winds battered the vines flatter on one side than the other. Age claimed its toll in cracks, discolorations, and grime. Yet someone had taken the time to nurture bluebells at its foundation, despite soil so solidly frozen it scarcely supported the scraggly vegetables which were the sustenance of oracle and acolytes.

Larson paced fretfully between Gaelinar and Silme. The shock of Brendor's death had faded, replaced by memories of the demon in his nightmare. Repeatedly, he replayed the scene in his mind. Each time, the shapeless shadowform sprang from the oracle's swirling mass of flame, shredding Silme's body with talons sharp as steel. And always Larson's defense came too late to save his beloved.

Silme knocked on the temple door. The heavy, wooden panel muffled sound nearly to silence. It was opened almost instantly by a young man who ushered Larson and his companions inside. He wore a clean gray cloak. Lines of hardship marred his features, but his lips curled in an amiable smile. He flicked away his hood, and hair the color of goldenrod fell to his shoulders. "Have you come to pay homage?"

Silme tapped the base of her dragonstaff against the earthen floor. "We wish to see the oracle."

The acolyte's expression grew grave. He led his new charges past groups of priests engaged in ritual. Light spilled through numerous windows, muted to gray haze by crudely thickset glass. Other acolytes nodded pleasantly as they passed, and Larson found nothing inherently threatening about the temple to Odin. Still, the memory of his nightmare wracked his spine with shivers, and anxiety closed him in an icy grip.

The acolyte led Larson and his companions past a row of three stone altars. The elf paused by the last, attracted by a stain dark as spilled wine. Closer inspection revealed the faint odor of death. Larson flinched back with a small cry and crashed against Gaelinar.

The Kensei turned swiftly and followed Larson's horrified gaze. He answered the unspoken question in a whisper. "War casualties, Allerum. Calm down. You've seen blood before." He caught the elf by a cloak sleeve and hauled him through a silver-threaded curtain identical to the one in the dream inspired by Bramin.

In the adjoining room, the oracle sat before her

marble table. As Larson, Silme, and Gaelinar stepped through the curtain, she raised her red-maned head. One blue eye examined her visitors with withering disdain. Beside it, a scarred socket gave mute testimony to the traumatic loss of her other eye. Leery of the oracle's disfigured and condemning features, Larson stared at the viewing stone before her. In the dream, he had thought the gemstone a diamond. Closer, he recognized it as a nearly transparent, oval-shaped block of quartz. Yet some work of nature or magic gave it the strange, eye-like configuration of green-irised black.

The oracle laced her long fingers on the table. Red hair streaked her knuckles like blood. "Welcome, Lady Silme, Sapphirerank." Her eye met Larson and Gaelinar in turn, but she extended them no greeting. "You have a question for my divination? Come forward."

Larson drew his sword and stepped forward with Silme. He poised a half stride before and to the right of the sorceress. His hand shook against Valvitnir's hilt. His tongue went dry as cotton. Hyperalert, Larson recognized Silme's drooping eyelids and shoulders and knew the enchantments she had channeled against Brendor had heavily tapped her physical energy.

The oracle's face went pale with a strange combination of anger and fear. "I'll not be threatened," she said softly. "There shall be no bare steel in my chamber."

Gaelinar gripped Larson's sword arm. "What's the matter with you?" he asked in a chastening whisper. "You've been acting strangely since we entered the temple."

Larson sheathed Valvitnir reluctantly. His reply was an anxious plea. "Just watch Silme. Please?"

Kensei Gaelinar scowled in offense, but he held his tongue with the subtlety of a master. "I always do," he answered after a moment. To Larson's relief, his instructor paced to Silme's other side.

The oracle waited until the men completed their exchange, then continued as if the disturbance had never occurred. "Your query, Dragonmage?"

Silme's words slurred slightly, as if the mere effort of gathering breath taxed her remaining strength. "Please, lady. My question concerns Allerum's sword, a quest, and the tranquillity of Midgard. Will hurling Valvitnir in the Helspring of Hvergelmir bring rescue or ruin to the gods of law and men?"

The oracle bent her head over the crystal, and her endless sea of hair covered the scrying stone like a curtain. Larson watched in horror as her wrinkled hand passed twice above the gemstone. He tried to loosen muscles coiled to pain by tension.

Silme yawned and rubbed fatigue from her eyes. Larson voiced a staccato grunt and edged closer to the sorceress. The oracle sat as still as death. Minutes dragged like hours. By the time the oracle looked up from her device, Larson had nervously worked his way directly in front of Silme.

The oracle's lips framed a smug smile which disappeared as she addressed Silme. "Have no fear, sorceress. Your quest is sanctioned. But quickly now; time runs short."

Silme looked around Larson with newfound energy, as if suddenly freed of some grave responsibility. "Thank you, lady. Your efforts may have saved our world from Chaos. May Odin continue to grace you with his favor."

"And Vidarr, you." The oracle returned the compliment in kind.

Irony made Silme wince. She turned, strode across the chamber, and passed through the shimmering curtain with Gaelinar at her heels. Larson retreated with more caution, gaze locked mistrustfully on the oracle whose lips pursed in antagonizing confidence. Wired, and eager to desert the red-haired seer who had become so abruptly lethal in his nightmare, Larson scrambled through the cloth slit. He jostled against Gaelinar in his haste.

The Kensei rolled his eyes with fading indulgence, and followed Silme around the milling acolytes. His glares grew less tolerant when Larson twice trod on his heels in his rush to vacate the temple to Odin. Once they stepped from the grayed interior of the building to the pleasure of afternoon, Larson loosed a shuddering sigh of relief. Even the biting winds seemed preferable to another moment of emotional agitation, especially to an elf impervious to winter's chill.

Larson and his companions mounted their horses. Ten minutes into their journey back toward the river Sylg, Larson shed the last of his apprehension and muttered to himself in triumph, "The half-breed ain't as all powerful as he thought."

Silme caught his arm. "Did you say something?"

Larson shook his head in denial. Then, seeing no reason to hide the truth from Silme any longer, he explained. "Bramin came to me in a dream and promised violence if we contacted the oracle. Idle threats, I'm certain, but just scary enough that I . . ." He broke off as Silme reined with an abruptness which sent her horse into a startled half rear.

"I thought I sensed his presence." Silme shaped her words with a self-accusatory anger. "But I blamed it on paranoia and weakness. Quickly now.

The oracle may be endangered." She turned her steed and kicked it to a gallop back toward Odin's temple.

Gaelinar whipped his horse about and reined after Silme. More accustomed to cars than horses, Larson clung to saddle and mane as his mount wheeled and followed its fellows at a run. They covered lost ground in minutes. Stopping only to tether the horses, Silme rushed to the dooryard, her companions close behind. Without troubling to knock, she pushed open the temple door. Priests looked up in alarm, but the sorceress paid them no heed. At a trot, she led Gaelinar and Larson through the slit in the silver-threaded curtain.

The oracle's chamber was as Larson remembered it from both dream and reality. Its dim, dank interior supported a marble block on which the eye-like crystal lay balanced on an edge. Gray cloth drapes covered the room's three walls. Conspicuously absent was the oracle of Hargatyr.

Larson waited by the slitted entrance, prepared for violence. Gaelinar stood in the center of the chamber, and his eyes followed Silme's anxious path. The sorceress peered behind the marble, paused a moment in confusion, then trotted to a far corner. She peeled aside a corner of the curtain which hid the back wall. Matched, gold-tasseled cords fell into her hand. When she pulled one, the cloth parted. Beyond, Larson and his companions saw a smaller chamber.

Gaelinar strode around Silme and entered the room first. Larson crossed the scrying chamber in time to step around the curtain with Silme. Behind a writing desk and before a simple cot, a pallid body sprawled, face downward, on the floor.

Red hair spread about the narrow shoulders and waist in a mass of tangles.

"No," said Silme softly.

Gaelinar eased the corpse to its back. The oracle's single eye was closed tight beside the massively scarred empty socket. Her breasts, thighs, and torso were violet with pooled blood. Though more familiar with rapid decomposition in the heat of Vietnam, Larson knew the oracle had been dead for several hours at least. The thought left him with a head-pounding certainty. *The woman who had answered Silme's question and sanctioned their quest was not the oracle of Hargatyr.*

Gaelinar ushered his grieving companions back into the scrying room and pulled the curtain closed, leaving the oracle what little decency remained in death. Silme pressed her back to the marble table, laid her staff at her feet, and buried her face in her palms. Exhaustion from wasted enchantments and frustration preyed heavily on her remaining strength. She looked as vulnerable as a child.

Larson lowered himself beside Silme and rested his arm across her sagging shoulders. "What now?"

Silme sighed. "All I dare believe of the false oracle's prophecy is the value of time. We still don't know how to free Vidarr. I'm certain only that we mustn't surrender him to the Helspring." She fell silent and still. Just as Larson convinced himself she had fallen asleep, she rallied internal energy and leaped to her feet.

Silme knocked Larson aside and paced with the steady tred of a caged tiger. "If Fates or gods know the method of breaking Loki's spell, the answer lies in the stone of Hargatyr." She indicated the crystal. "Anyone who understands its enchantments can tap its knowledge."

"And you?" asked Larson hopefully.

Silme paused, hands against the marble. She shook her head. "Dragonrank magic taps its caster's life energy. That's what makes it so powerful and desirable, and also dangerous. Devices like the gemstone are of no more use to me than crossbow bolts to a longbowman. I have the basic knowledge, but too many gaps exist to correctly glean information."

"Try, at least." Larson rose.

Silme caught his hands. Her palms left sweaty prints on the edge of the marble table. "I can do better than try. Another in this room may have some of the knowledge I need. Allerum, did Vidarr tell you why he can communicate only with you?"

Larson tried to recall. "He said people from my world lack mind barriers."

Silme dropped his hands, eyes widening incredulously. "None?"

Larson shrugged. "I suppose. I don't even know what it means."

"For now, it means a way to link myself with Vidarr." Silme's gaze dropped to the sword at Larson's hip. "Together, we may fathom the workings of the oracle's stone." Her cheeks colored slightly, but she continued eagerly. "Allerum, can you hold your mind blank?"

"My mind? Blank? No!" He flinched back as the sorceress' request became clear. The thought that Silme might access his memories of murder made him light-headed. "My mind runs and lapses without my control. From moment to moment, I don't know if I'll find myself here or home, whether I'm experiencing reality, memory, or the inspired illusions of trapped gods and vicious warlocks. For me, Silme, blank is not a state of mind."

Larson had quite forgotten Gaelinar stood behind him. The Kensei's husky voice made him jump. "It is now, hero. Would you have us damn the world for your reluctance?"

Silme finished the appeal more gently. "I require only that you keep people and places from your consciousness. Concentrate on naming foods or counting twigs, anything repetitive which requires channeling thought. Will you try it?"

"I've no choice." Larson swallowed around a lump which grew in his throat. "What do I have to do?"

"Sit." Silme waved him to the floor.

Larson sat, knees pressed to his chest. His hands trembled as he watched Silme reach for the crystal of Hargatyr. "Wait!"

Silme paused.

"How do you know Bramin hasn't tampered with the stone or replaced it with something evil?"

Silme seized the eye-like gem with an impatient toss of her head. "This is Odin's temple. The oracle's scrying stone must be warded by Law. A simple touch would maim or even kill Bramin. It would reflect his destructive magics. Any other attempt to remove it from the temple would require him to work it past a room full of priests." Silme lowered herself to the floor before Larson and placed the stone between them. "Lay the sword across your legs."

Larson complied reluctantly. Valvitnir buzzed slightly against him, glowing with blue light. "Silme. Shouldn't we wait until you've had some rest."

Silme locked her fingers between Larson's. Her voice became a low drone. "No time. Bramin can trace us through the gaps in your mind. We don't want him to know we discovered his treachery."

Silme let her eyes fall shut. Her head lolled forward.

"Silme?"

"What!" Impatience made her curt.

"What if I can't control my thoughts?"

Her voice assumed a hiss of dry warning. "Let's just hope you can."

Her reply did nothing to reassure Larson. Near panic, he chose to conjugate verbs from his high school French lessons. *Je suis, tu es, il est. . . .* Twin presences pressed against his mind with the banding grip of a headache. Vidarr and Silme scuttled without direction, silent as mice in the jarring loops of Larson's flawed thought pattern. God and sorceress probed blindly for one another, and Larson felt all too aware of their locations.

Nous sommes, vous etes, ils . . . ils sont. . . . Gradually, Silme and Vidarr closed the distance between their mental presences. Their union broke to a dazzling explosion of light, sparking one of Larson's frayed memories like a dried piece of kindling. Hurled into flashback, Larson stared at a mine crater the size of his bedroom back in the States. Then a barrier snapped into place with a force which broke the illusion. Threat carved into focus. *Hold your thoughts! I've no power to rescue you again.*

J'ai, tu as, il a, nous avons. . . . Larson plunged into his studies with desperate passion. The combined essence of Vidarr and Silme wove drunkenly through his brain. A flurry of enchantments battered through consciousness unsteady as fever. *VOUS AVEZ. . . . Will hurling Valvitnir in the Hel spring of Hvergelmir bring rescue or ruin to the gods of law and men?* Silme's question echoed through

Larson's mind, pulling him from his furious attempts at conjugations.

Smoke eddied like car exhaust. The fused presence gasped in triumph, then hissed in fury as the haze peeled away, like scalded wax, without answer. *Je vais, tu.* . . . Frustration settled in Larson's mind, dimmed to resolution. Silme/Vidarr gathered energy, unwittingly tapping him in the process.

Reference folded in nightmare as magics enwrapped him in drugged awareness. Fog thick as earth warped vision. Another alien presence winked to life in Larson's already overcrowded mind. *Destroying the sword heralds Vidarr's death. Beware! Such an action will doom the world to Chaos.*

Sanity flickered. *Tu vas, il va, nous allons, vous allez, ils allont!* Emotion pervaded him in a perfect mixture of outrage and concern. Silme/Vidarr coiled like a cat prepared to spring. Magic formed a tense ball in Larson's mind, crushing aside fragile circuits of memory. Pain blurred thought to blackness. *Je fais, tu fais, il fait.* . . . Rationality exploded to madness.

A painted forest replaced the emptiness of Larson's eye-closed world. He walked between Silme and Vidarr beneath a mercilessly hot sun. Blue haze ringed the sorceress, and the god shone with a golden glory. *Where the hell?* thought Larson. *Oh . . . a . . . nous faisons.* The syllables warped to nonsense. Suddenly, a woman tall as a watchtower stepped from the brush, directly in his path.

Larson recoiled. The life auras of god and sorceress fused to glaring green. "Who are you?" demanded Silme boldly.

"I am Skuld, *Future.*" The giantess' voice rattled trees. "In what cause have you summoned me, Silme Sapphirerank?"

"The cause of men and gods." Silme replied nearly as loud. "Should Chaos claim this world, there shall be no Law nor time nor knowledge. You and your sister Fates would perish." Her entreaty rolled like thunder through the silence of the forest. "How must we free Vidarr from imprisonment?"

A breeze rose and fell, rose and fell again. Several seconds passed before Larson recognized the wind as the breath of the giantess Skuld. "Your fears are founded, Lady Silme. Your quest is honorable, though it brings doom upon others, men and women of my domain, those ruled by one of your companions and beloved by the other. It is not my place to judge your task nor prevent it. The answer to your question lies with my sisters." Skuld marched back into the forest, trampling trees like matchsticks.

The giantess' prophecy sounded strange to Larson's numbed mind. *How could rescuing men from Chaos doom them for the future?* Before he found time to ponder the question, another woman shouldered between the trees. She looked sufficiently like Skuld to be her sister, yet not similar enough to be a twin.

"I am Verdandi," the giantess said, though no one asked her name. "I hold title to the present. Your query has gone beyond my realm to the past. I can tell you only that your quest stands contested by a god and a half-breed with the power to destroy you." Swiftly, she returned to the forest.

Cold sweat ran down Larson's back, and he shook with chills despite the heat. The third sister of Fate glided from the tangled brush. Vertigo transformed her to a blur which sharpened slowly to detail. She was obviously the eldest of the giantesses, smaller, withered, face puckered with burdens transferred from her sisters by time.

"I am Urdr, keeper of the past and the understanding of Odin. It was I who added the final provision to Loki's spell, and I who shall reveal that knowledge to you. To free my lord, Vidarr, the elf must claim Loki's life with the blade Valvitnir."

Shock battered Larson, obscured Urdr in glare. Silme's scream pierced his mind like a spear, jarring loose a wild memory. The sound transformed to the shrill whine of jets. Even as Larson located the blood-red afterburners of the paired phantoms, he recognized his surroundings. He traveled a familiar road in the Mekong Delta. Some distance ahead, a dozen buddies in cammie paused in horror as they discovered the jets' target was the same village which had, moments before, been their destination.

The lead jet passed over the village. A raging column of flame consumed grass huts and villagers without mercy. Panicked screams made Larson cringe. Even as the gasoline fumes pinched his nose, he realized he was neither in flashback nor alone. The dry crackle of gathering magics made him whirl toward Silme and Vidarr. "Oh my god! Silme, no!"

His warning came too late. Sorceries howled past his ear with all the inhuman speed of the phantoms. Bluish magics impacted the trailing jet and broke to a savage explosion of emerald. Shards of twisted steel rained to earth. Larson's sinews went taut with shock. He could only suppose Silme saw the jets as dragons swooping upon an innocent town. Ahead on the road, the camouflaged men dropped, as one, to the ground. Suddenly,

Larson knew he and his otherworld companions had become the enemy.

"Down!" hollered Larson. He dove into the roadside ditch. Gunfire popped and sputtered around him, sounding oddly impotent after the scourge of napalm and the thunderclap of Silme's spell. With no means or desire to return fire on his buddies, Larson flattened to the dirt without recourse. *What have I done?* Worried over the ignorance of his alien companions, he forced his gaze toward the road. Vidarr and Silme stood behind a shimmering curtain which reflected bullets like a wall.

The oddity of their magical defense was not lost on the Americans. One yelled. "Holy fucking god!" Silme began a new incantation. Dark mists broiled from her fingertips. A graying glow flickered around the enchantress and winked out like a spent candle. As Silme drained her life energy, she fell in a soundless faint.

"Silme!" screamed Larson. The sorceress lay still within her magical shield, but her final spell was cast, Wizardry rolled along the road like a living ball of fire. The men in cammie dodged from the path of the sorceries with startled cries. And, from over the burning village, Larson caught sight of the returning phantom. Faster than its own report, the jet glided toward them in vengeful silence.

"No!" Larson hollered. Smoke from the smoldering village swirled like ghosts into the phantom's twin intakes. Larson lay frozen in terror. A rocket dropped from beneath the jet, plummeted, then shot forward with a speed which outdistanced the plane. Before Larson could scream, the missile crashed to ground with a blast of red-orange. Its explosion seemed to shatter earth. Though the magical shield contained most of its impact, force crashed against Larson's head and knocked him to oblivion.

Larson awakened to utter darkness. Screams of terror ripped from his lungs and reverberated like distant answers. Throat raw, he fell to silence and recognized the slosh of running water. The rasp of a sword scraping from its sheath restored his rationality. Larson struggled to legs stiff with disuse. His hand closed about Valvitnir's hilt. "Gaelinar?" he whispered hopefully.

Gaelinar's gruff reply had never seemed so welcome. "I should have known it was you, hero. How do you feel?"

"Shaky," Larson admitted. "And blind." A scene threaded through his mind, the memory of Silme lying still as death on a road in the Mekong Delta. "Where's Silme?"

The sorceress called over the bubbling of the river Sylg. "Here. The real question, Allerum, is where *was* Silme."

Larson groped toward Silme's voice. "My world. I'm sorry. I tried to control my memories, I swear I did, but . . ." Silme caught his arm. It occurred to Larson with frightening abruptness that the surrounding darkness was too complete for night. He finished with an anxious whine. "Dammit, why can't I see?"

Gaelinar replied. "We're in the Valley of Darkness."

"H-how?"

"We carried you," Silme explained. "Bramin can only track us through your mind. With you unconscious, we traveled as quickly as we could."

Larson pulled Silme closer. "Why are we still headed toward Hvergelmir?"

Gaelinar sounded nearer. "Because Loki expects us there. He wants your sword destroyed in the Helspring, and for all he knows we plan to complete that quest. He'll be there to make certain it gets done."

"Please, Allerum" Silme spoke with concern. "Talk with Vidarr. Make certain he's all right after . . . what happened."

Reluctantly, Larson released Silme and drew Valvitnir. The sword quivered mournfully in his grip. Vidarr's mental presence wound cautiously through the fragile tangles of his mind. *I pity your people. The men of your world removed all the glory from war and left only killing.*

Larson jammed the sword into its sheath and broke his link with Vidarr. "He's fine," Larson grumbled. But the god's assessment echoed through his mind, awakening a terrifying thought. *When we complete this quest and the gods of Asgard no longer need me, what becomes of me? Will Freyr return me to the skill-less death machine of the Vietnam war?*

With a strength born of imagined injustice, he jerked the sword free again. *Vidarr. . . ?*

The god answered defensively before Larson finished the question. *I don't know what Freyr plans! My own fate is tenuous enough. Since my imprisonment, I know only what I see through your eyes.*

Damn! Larson dashed the sword to the ground. Its blue flare faded darkness in a circle of purple. Larson crushed Silme to his chest in frustration, and her dragonstaff cracked painfully against his shoulder. His lips brushed her face, found her mouth, and pressed into a passionate kiss. Desire burned him like fire, but he loosened his grip and fought bitterness. "Silme, the success of this quest may doom us to separate worlds." Grief caught the words in his throat. "There is a link between our worlds, even if it's only in my mind. We passed through it once. I swear, if Freyr sends me back to Nam, I'll find a way to return to you."

Larson heard the scrape of metal against sand as Silme hefted Valvitnir and returned the sword to its sheath. "Or if necessary, I'll find you," she told him gently. "It's not often I meet a hero like you."

Gaelinar shuffled his feet, and sand showered against Larson's ankles. "Forgive me. If we don't move along soon, we forfeit whatever advantage we gained. Allerum?"

Larson felt a slight breeze of movement. A ration sack thumped into his side. He accepted the pouch and slung it across his shoulder. "Where are the horses?"

"They refused to enter the valley." Gaelinar's voice came from some distance ahead. "Animals can sense evil."

Larson caught Silme's hand and trotted after the Kensei. Two days had passed since his last meal, but Larson felt no hunger. His stomach balled in an aching knot of tension. Soon he would face the greatest challenge of any life. He would become a godslayer or damn his soul and Silme's to an eternity of torture.

A victim of his own doubts, Larson did not notice as darkness diffused to gray. But another in the party was more wary. Gaelinar stopped, silent in the mist, and caught his companions as they passed. "Caution," he warned. "We're approaching the Helspring. I hear the falling waters."

Larson released Silme's hand and wiped slick

palms on his cape. Beyond the gurglings of the river Sylg, Larson heard a sound like a roomful of serpents. The air felt suddenly chill. For the first time since his recovery, Larson discerned huddled cliffs which hemmed the Valley of Darkness. The river Sylg spanned nearly four times its earlier width, and ice blocks as large as a man's head bobbed in its current.

Gaelinar drew his katana and tested its edge with his thumbnail. "Ready?"

"Ready?" repeated Larson incredulously. "Ready! Loki's a god. Shouldn't we make a plan of some sort?" His own words struck with mind-jarring force. *We're fighting a god. Like Christ or something. What chance do we have?*

Gaelinar sheathed the katana, trading it for his companion sword. His hand slid along the blade, but Larson could not perceive the Kensei's expression in the semidarkness. "I cut him. Silme throws spells. And you . . ." Gaelinar paused thoughtfully, ". . . bested the guard captain of Forste-Mar before your first sword lesson. So, I guess you hit people, too."

Larson paced to hide his trembling hands. "Loki's not people. He's a . . . a god."

Gaelinar walked toward the palisades, and his figure was lost to the hovering shadows of the Valley of Darkness. "He can die just like we can."

Silme caught for Larson's arm, but her hand slipped free in the sweat which slicked his limbs like grease. "Loki's both a wizard and a swordsman, which gives him a large repertoire for attack. Plans become worthless against a god as unpredictable as his Chaos, especially when one of the parties privy to the strategy can't hide his knowledge from the enemy."

Larson nodded his understanding. Silme and Gaelinar might have plotted while he recovered from the phantom's rocket, but anything they told him could become accessible to Loki through the flaws in his mind. Doubt rushed down upon Larson, merciless as a volley of gunfire. "I'm not prepared to war with gods. I may never be." *A private in one of the bloodiest wars in history, and I've never even killed a man with my own hands. The murders on my conscience were all the impersonal and distant victims of an M-16.* Yet the gun he had wielded lay without guilt between the banks of a dried river in a body-littered jungle, while the screams of the dying haunted the memory of Al Larson. Larson stopped pacing and deliberately avoided touching Valvitnir.

"Allerum!" Threat colored Gaelinar's words. "Freyr brought you to complete this quest at a price a mere mortal cannot comprehend. You will fight gods, I promise. Need I remind you there are three gods of Chaos and fifteen of Law? Choose your enemies with care."

Larson fixed on the first numerical fact. "*Three* gods!" he screamed, nearly hysterical.

Silme clarified quickly. "Loki's daughter, Hel, can't cross the bridge from her citadel. As for Helblindi . . ."

"He's trapped in a sword, too," Larson interrupted as he recalled Vidarr's vision. "Loki's sword." His hand dropped unconsciously to Valvitnir.

Vidarr's mental presence filled his mind like storm wind. *Bramin's sword,* he corrected. *And you should know something. Freyr brought you here with full knowledge that the choice to face Loki must remain your own. I want freedom, but it's your right to know the gods of Law are not vindictive. Slay Loki or not as your conscience sanctions. A moral decision will not be held against you.* Vidarr ended contact with Larson, though not quickly enough to hide the grief which lapped Larson's mind like a tide.

"Ready," said Larson softly. Resolved, he filled his lungs with air and exhaled through clenched teeth. "Let's go."

Silme followed Larson through the lightening mists of the valley. The cliffs ended abruptly. The river washed across a plain of dying grasses, then plummeted through a pit as large as a mine crater. Larson strode from the valley; wind bitter as hoarfrost whipped hair into his eyes. Anyone but a native to the climate would have found it unbearably cold, but as a creature of faery, Larson was impervious. The rapid change from darkness to daylight made him blink, though clouds obscured the sun with gloom.

Larson's eyes adjusted quickly. He recognized ten similar valleys radiating from the central chasm like the spokes of a giant wheel. Curious, he trotted forward; weeds crushed to powder beneath his feet. The rush of waters through the pit grew loud as a lion's roar, and then faded as Larson's ears adjusted to the noise. As he neared the edge of the cliff, he found a narrow path which threaded into the abyss. Poised at its lip, he saw a sight more breathtaking than the falls of Niagara.

Eleven rivers plunged as one through the rounded crater, their waters wound in a shimmering braid. The pittance of light which pierced the clouds drew glittering lines through the torrent crashing into the Helspring. Droplets bounced upward in a frozen mist and pelted Larson's face like hail. Entranced, he took a step forward. A stone broke loose beneath his foot. He went giddy as he imagined himself tumbling with it, weaving through the cascade, smashed to lifeless, soulless waste beneath Hvergelmir's current.

A shiver traversed Larson. He shielded his eyes and shied away just as Silme bellowed. "Loki!" Her voice echoed about the many valleys. "We know you're here. If you want Valvitnir in Hvergelmir, come get him."

Larson whirled and freed his sword, edging nervously from the Helspring. Gaelinar waited near the valley. Silme stood, ready, in the center of the plain. Her challenge went unanswered.

"Loki!" Silme started again.

Bramin glided from the waning fog of Sylg's valley, black as oblivion. The winds of the waterfalls swirled iron gray robes about his torso. His eyes flashed red threat from shadowed sockets. The diamond in his staff glowed bright as a street lamp. "Did you think Loki would waste energy on you?" As he spoke, a sunburst of sorceries blossomed in his hand. "You're scarcely worth my time."

Gaelinar moved first. Fast as thought, his fingers freed a shuriken. Even as he tensed his arm to throw, Bramin's enchantments sheeted through the air. A raw blaze of magic enwrapped the Kensei in a glimmering net which held him still as stone.

"No!" screamed Silme. Light pulsed across the plain as wizard and sorceress howled spell words forceful as explosions. Bramin's diamond blazed through a chaotic spectrum of color. His raging red eyes locked suddenly on Larson, and Silme loosed a short scream. Her tone changed abruptly. A beam of ruddy light leaped from Bramin's fingers. Silme's magical parry pinwheeled protectively before Larson.

Bramin cursed, then laughed as his spell shattered to colored highlights. Sunbright sorceries surrounded both Dragonrank mages in a wave which blinded Larson. Light blazed and died; magics fizzled. Silme dropped to her knees as Larson lunged at Bramin. Valvitnir arced over Larson's head and sliced toward the half-breed.

In a single motion, Bramin dropped his staff, drew his sword and blocked. Six inches of air separated the swords when they stopped abruptly. The motion jarred both wielders. The half-breed riposted. Larson jerked his blade upward in instinctive defense. Bramin's sword shied awkwardly from Valvitnir, as if of its own accord.

Larson and Bramin recovered together. In the brief respite, Vidarr's presence imparted a panicked message. *Helblindi and I are prisoners of the same spell. A touch will destroy us both!*

Conditioned, Larson repeated the first maneuver Gaelinar had taught him. Valvitnir whistled reluctantly around him and lanced toward Bramin. Bramin sprang forward as he blocked. The swords quivered, desperate inches apart. Too close for an adequate sweep, the half-breed retreated.

Drop me, damn you! Vidarr's command pierced Larson's mind with painful force.

Larson responded with a desperate thought. *Drop you and die! I can't face Bramin weaponless!*

Bramin thrust. Larson waved Valvitnir before his body, and Helblindi sprang aside. Bramin swung low. Larson withdrew his front foot, but the Helblade scraped skin from his calf.

Larson swore, deaf to Vidarr's pleas. Again, he sprang at Bramin and skipped back as the half-breed returned his strike. Apology rolled through his mind in waves. Vidarr gathered mental strength, dragged Larson's consciousness with him in a short conspiracy with Helblindi.

Larson's breath came in wild sobs. He repositioned his sword, just in time to block a sweep for his neck. Vidarr tore free of his grip and tumbled through the air like a wounded bird. To Larson's relief, Helblindi also pitched from its wielder's hand.

Bramin paused a moment in shock, then retreated across the plain. Larson noticed the sharp sting of ice pellets on the back of his neck, and only just realized how close Bramin had maneuvered him to a fatal plunge into the Helspring. Cautiously, he came forward to face the sorcerer in the dying grasses. Over Bramin's wide, black shoulders, he saw Silme watching with wide-eyed helplessness. She mouthed a silent message: I love you. Beyond her, Gaelinar stood motionless as a painting.

Bramin lashed, backhanded, at Larson's face. The elf blocked with his left arm. Before he could return the strike, Bramin closed. The half-breed's foot kicked painfully against the back of Larson's knee, and his elbow crashed against Larson's chin. Larson staggered, recovered. As Bramin realigned, Larson sprang and punched. Bramin blocked effortlessly. His dark fist smashed Larson's nose.

Larson lurched as sparks danced before his eyes. Dizzied with nausea, he tried to think. Bramin's maneuvers came with practiced speed and machinelike efficiency. Larson knew he could never avoid the blows. He could only hope to endure.

Resolved, he jabbed at Bramin's face. Again, the half-breed blocked and returned the strike. This time, Larson took the punch. Pain exploded across his jaw, but he bore in on his enemy. His knee crashed into Bramin's groin. The half-breed gasped. Silme screamed. Larson's elbow thrust toward Bramin's head. The half-elf ducked, using Larson's own momentum to hurl him to the ground. Bramin's foot lashed out, passing over Larson's head as the elf rolled to his feet.

Several yards away, Silme rolled in the grass as if in pain. Bramin's features twisted in a savage smile. His hands rested peacefully at his sides as he raised his face to Larson. "Go ahead, hero." He spat the last word in contempt. "Hit me."

Larson did not need prompting. Bramin made no attempt at defense. Larson's fist smashed into his face, and Silme shrieked in agony. Stunned, Larson did not press his advantage.

Blood trickled from Bramin's nose, but his mouth parted in silent laughter. "Hit me again, elf coward." Malice danced in his feral eyes. "Hurt Silme!"

With a cry of anger, Larson struck. Cartilage snapped beneath his knuckles, jarring Bramin to his knees. Silme howled in torment. Her body writhed in the dirt.

Alarmed, Larson started toward her. "Silme?" As Bramin rose and advanced, Larson turned back to the fight. "What have you done to her?" he demanded. Hysteria raised his voice an octave.

Blood colored Bramin's mouth scarlet. "I did nothing," he replied triumphantly. He flicked blood from his cheek. "But every time you mar this pretty face, you injure hers as well."

Larson retreated defensively, afraid to strike. Bramin swept forward. His left foot drove into Larson's gut with a force which doubled him over. As Bramin completed his spin, his right foot jolted against Larson's head. Larson rolled clumsily, awaiting a death stroke which never fell. Confidence made Bramin patient as a cat. He explained while Larson struggled dizzily to his feet. "To save you from my sorceries, Silme linked her life aura to mine. She holds our magic inoperative, but our souls are fused. Her fate and mine have become one."

Bramin faked a foot strike. As Larson dodged, Bramin delivered a brazenly high kick. His heel slammed against Larson's forehead. Impact snapped Larson's neck rearward. The back side of his skull struck the ground first. Darkness swam down on him. Larson shook his throbbing head, watching Bramin's retreating back through a veil of colored mist.

Fury gave Larson renewed strength. He charged Bramin's back, just as the sorcerer bent for his Helsword. Larson punched. Bramin wheeled. His elbow caught Larson in the gut. The half-breed seized Larson's outstretched arm and hurled the elf over his shoulder.

Accustomed to wrestling, Larson struck the ground, unhurt. Bramin knelt beside him, pinning his right wrist to the ground. Larson rocked toward the half-breed, wrapped his left arm about one dark leg, and rolled. Bramin flipped to the ground. Even as he landed, Larson reversed direction. The force pitched Bramin to his stomach, hands trapped beneath his chest. Larson pressed his full weight against the half-breed. His one hand clutched a swarthy wrist. His forearm thrust Bramin's face in the dirt.

Silme screamed between panting gasps. "Kill him, Allerum! Forget me. Kill him!"

Larson jolted his fist against the back of Bramin's skull, cursing himself for Silme's pained whimper. He released Bramin and seized Helblindi's hilt before the half-breed could do anything more than roll to his back. Larson spun and pressed the blade to Bramin's throat. The sorcerer went still. His face drained of color; his chest heaved. "If you kill me, you kill Silme, too." Bramin warned in a reedy whine.

Larson's hand shook. Sick with worry, he called over his shoulder. "*Is it true?*"

Silme made no reply.

Larson twisted toward the sorceress. "Damn you, is it true?"

"Yes," she whispered. "It's true, but . . ."

Bramin clawed to his feet and ran. Gaelinar's training resurfaced mechanically. Larson struck. Helblindi's blade carved through Bramin's hamstring. The muscle curled into a ball. Bramin collapsed. Larson finished the strike from habit gained from hours of practice. He thrust the blade through Bramin's chest. The half-breed quivered, then fell limp, and Silme's dying scream reverberated in accusation.

Anguish tore denial from Larson's throat. "No! No!" He ripped Helblindi free and cast it aside in wild sorrow. Blood splashed as the blade tumbled awkwardly to the ground, and Larson fell with it. Grief-mad, he howled like a wounded animal and crawled to Silme's prone form. She lay like a marble carving beside the blade which imprisoned her god. Larson dropped to her side. She was cold as ice and every bit as still. Tears burned his eyes like poison, cleaning tracks through the blood which stained his chin. His gaze fell upon the motionless Kensei, and he howled anguished curses at the swordmaster who had drilled him until the sword figure which killed Silme became reflex.

Larson's sanity crumbled to a muddle of thought.

His fist struck the ground with a force which jarred his arm to the shoulder. His second blow landed against Valvitnir's blade; its sharpened edge slit the side of his hand. Oblivious to physical pain, Larson caught the sword by its hilt. Vidarr filled his mind with warning. *Allerum, behind you!*

CHAPTER 7

Godslayer

*"Death closes all: but something ere the
    end,
Some work of noble note, may yet be done,
Not unbecoming men that strove with
    gods."*
    —*Alfred Lord Tennyson*, Ulysses

Larson whirled. Light lanced toward him from
the direction of the valleys. He cringed defensively. The magics struck Valvitnir and broke to
streamers vivid as rockets. "Yow!" Larson dropped
flat to the ground. The valleys seemed to mock
him, black as moonless night, yet somewhere in
the gloom stalked a sorcerer more dangerous than
any sniper. *Is it Loki?*

Yes, Vidarr confirmed. *Look up. And lift your
sword, or I won't be able to shield you from his spells*

Pressed tight to the dirt out of habit, Larson
raised his eyes. Reddish light hovered on a crag
above Sylg's valley. In its center, Loki gestured,
menacing as a demon in a fire pit. His sorceries
streaked toward Larson with a roar like thunder.
Larson rolled aside. Enchantments swirled into a

fizzling whirlwind and funneled into Valvitnir's blade. *How?*

Vidarr's presence seemed weak in Larson's mind. *Not certain. Some aspect of Loki's imprisonment spell renders me capable of negating his other magics.* Vidarr's reply came, labored as a winded asthmatic. *But it requires concentration. . . .*

Larson rose to a crouch, seeking cover. On the cliff face, light flared around Loki, brief and glorious as a dying star. Larson squinted against its brilliance. Red and green shadows winked on the inside of his eyelids. When he recovered his vision, Loki was gone.

Where is he? Dammit, where is he? Larson spun like a dancer, sword pressed to his chest in a position more appropriate for a gun.

Be still! Vidarr chastised, but his tone betrayed fear.

Between Sylg's valley and Larson, sorceries blazed. He raised Valvitnir offensively, shielding his eyes as light billowed to agonizing intensity, a mocking column of white flame. The enchantments broke suddenly to traces. Ahead, Loki appeared, sword readied, beneath his fading magics.

Larson felt Vidarr poised to fight enchantments. Loki lunged forward. Larson blocked. The blades met in a shower of glittering sparks. Impact jarred Larson to the elbow. He staggered backward, recovering just in time to block a second strike. The force of Loki's blow drove Larson nearly to his knees.

Loki's assault seemed ceaseless. His strokes came fast and were rhythmically competent. They left Larson no opening for anything but awkward blocks and retreat. The god's face pinched in concentration. Yet, despite Larson's obvious inexperience,

Loki treated his opponent like a worthy threat. He displayed none of Bramin's assuredness. Loki knew overconfidence contrives incompetence.

Larson defended as well as he could, but his efforts seemed woefully inadequate. Loki's sword bit rents in his tunic and skin. Any one of the god's maneuvers could easily have taken Larson's life. But Loki's strategy soon became obvious. He would drive wielder and godsword into the Helspring together, obviating the need to handle Valvitnir himself. And Larson was helpless to prevent him.

Loki's sword wove a wall of steel, herding Larson toward Hvergelmir as a shepherd does an errant sheep. The sharp nicks of his enemy's blade reawakened the throbbing pains left from Larson's fight with Bramin. Tortured sinews screamed with every movement. His face felt as if it were on fire. He tried to stand firm against Loki's hammering blows, but his body could no longer obey.

Blow after blow rang against Valvitnir. Larson's ears buzzed, then roared. Ice shards prickled the back of his neck. The cold made him realize, with sudden terror, that the noises in his head did not come from within; Loki had driven him to the verge of Hvergelmir's pit.

"Christ!" Larson dredged deep for reserves of energy. Strength flowed back into his limbs. But the effort of blocking Loki's strokes drained his second wind almost instantly. Fatigue obscured Larson's vision to a blur. Sweat stung the many scratches inflicted by Loki. Scarcely able to lift his arms, Larson could only retreat and let Valvitnir tend defense.

Loki bore in. Larson recoiled. The ground fell out beneath his heel. Near panic, he staggered away from the ledge and nearly impaled himself on Loki's blade. Hope shattered beneath a wild explosion of despair. *What the hell am I fighting for anyway?*

Vidarr's reply seemed weak, as if the efforts of defense cost him as much as Larson. *Loved ones, Allerum. The future, my freedom . . .*

And liberty and justice for all. . . .

Loki's eyes glittered, violet-blue as gemstones. He drew back his arm for the final lunge.

Loved ones, Vidarr? Larson's thoughts grew bitter. *Silme's dead. She's dead by my own hand. Silme is DEAD! Whose cause . . .*

Vidarr jerked upward to block. *Her cause! And the cause of all men in the future.*

Larson stood, ready to accept the death promised by Loki's descending sword. *The Fate giantess, Skuld, claimed freeing you would doom my people.*

Vidarr's mental presence went oddly silent. Loki lanced forward.

Larson demanded an answer. *Vidarr!*

Gaelinar! Vidarr's cry echoed through Larson's consciousness. Hope displaced futility in a corner of his mind. A shuriken skimmed through the air, visible only as a glint from a sun ray. It embedded in Loki's sword hand with a nearly inaudible thunk.

Loki uttered a startled oath. Rather than drop his sword, he pulled his thrust. Holding his blade between Larson and himself, Loki twisted toward his new antagonist. Magics crackled from his outstretched left hand and sheeted toward Kensei Gaelinar.

"No!" Concerned for Gaelinar's life, Larson struck. His upstroke crashed into Loki's armpit, and bit through muscle. Loki screamed. The shuriken dislodged from his hand, flicking blood across Larson's foot. Of itself, Valvitnir jerked downward, severing the tendon behind Loki's knee.

Loki fell. Unable to use his right arm to catch himself, he dropped, face first, to the mud. Larson pressed Valvitnir's point to the back of his neck. The Trickster howled his frustration.

"Wait!" Loki's high-pitched voice betrayed fear.

Hatred, exhaustion, and grief warred within Larson, warping intellect in a gray haze of confusion. Despite its frightened quality, Loki's command held an inviolate authority. Larson paused.

Loki continued quickly. "If you kill me, you destroy your own world."

Loki's voice inspired violent hatred in Larson for this god who had twisted Silme's half brother into a vindictive demon and designed the ruin of gods and men. Abhorrence flared toward the god whose ugly daughter possessed Silme's soul. "Die, you scum!" He arched Valvitnir to gain momentum. The blade leaped hungrily for Loki's neck.

Loki loosed a cry, half sob and half scream. "Your mother's blood is on your hands!"

Inches from Loki, Larson pulled his blow. The accusation seared like a hot knife, but he dared not display weakness before the Trickster. "Explain," was all he trusted himself to say.

Vidarr's presence intervened, weaker than a whisper. *Caution, Allerum. He'll trap you, too.*

Larson pressed Valvitnir tighter to Loki's neck. Though the sword fought Larson's restraint, he forced it steady. A second mental being poked gently into Larson's mind, more powerful than the first and as beautiful as the god at his mercy. *If you slay me, no one will contest Odin. The Norse pantheon will endure, supreme through eternity. Christianity can never reign. Al Larson, if you kill me, your world, your family, and the people you loved will never exist!*

Never exist . . . never exist. . . . The last phrase reverberated through Larson's mind and no original thought replaced it. Loki's mental essence reached for a memory.

No! Vidarr blocked Loki like a physical entity. *You can't . . .*

Stop me! Loki's far stronger presence thrust Vidarr aside effortlessly. Larson remained motionless, his eyes fixed on Gaelinar, who struggled to his feet, still dazed by Loki's magics.

The sky seemed to open. Sunlight streamed through the clouds, accompanied by the moist heat of a New Hampshire summer. Hvergelmir's roar became the crackle of a campfire. The mingled reek of mold and death transformed to the lighter aroma of pine. Larson watched himself with the detachment of a movie. He was twelve years old.

"Al!" The familiar voice of his father rose over the rustle of grasses in the wind. "Let your sister tend the fire. You've got more important things to do. I promised you'd teach your brother to fly his kite."

Larson felt his heart quicken at the sound of his father's voice. He watched himself trot across a plain of weeds to where his father stood beside his little brother, Timmy. Spectator to his own memory, Larson examined his father with a stranger's eye. Carl Larson was a large man, powerful yet gentle. His close-cropped, blond hair had a tendency to stand on end, giving him an air of harshness. But his soft, blue eyes betrayed him. The vivid vision of the dead father he loved brought tears to Larson's eyes. Instantly, the scene changed. Larson saw his mother kneeling beside the dented fender of his father's brand new Plymouth. Tears blurred her pale eyes and drew crooked lines through the blush on her cheeks. It took Larson several seconds to recognize the child at her side, himself at age five, torn by his mother's sorrow.

He remembered the scene well. Planning to take the Plymouth for its first test drive, Cindy Larson had backed the car into the garage wall. "Tell him I did it," Al Larson told his frightened mother. The ridiculousness of his suggestion made her laugh through her tears. She hugged him to her chest, and Larson reveled in the memory of her warmth and the touch of her lips against his forehead.

"Mom!" Images dimmed, crumbled, and re-formed in a different sequence. He heard his father's cheers, mixed with the goading cries of other parents. A soccer ball whuffed toward Larson's knee. Twisting sideways, he stopped the ball's momentum with his calf, dribbled several paces forward, and kicked a pass to the right wing. A crowd of players overran Larson's position at fullback. As the ball reversed direction, they turned and raced after it.

The shrill of a whistle called the first half to its conclusion. Larson took his turn at the water bottle and sat on the bench. His closest friend, soccer hero Tom Jeffers, dropped to the seat at his side. "Nice block, Larson."

Larson combed hair from his eyes with his fingers. "Thanks, T.J. You're doing pretty good yourself. Think we'll catch them in the second half?"

"Think?" Jeffers winked at a girl on the sidelines. "I know it, man. I'll put in a couple shots. You just keep them scoreless."

Larson watched the girl blush and turn away, slightly jealous of his friend's rugged good looks. "Talk to the goalie. I can't make a promise like that."

Jeffers met Larson's stare, and the center forward's face waxed pensive. "I got a promise for you. Keep them scoreless next half, and I'll get you a date for the prom with my sister."

"Terry?" Larson's voice rose in surprise and excitement. He cleared his throat and continued at his normal octave. "You serious?"

Jeffers laughed. "Yeah. Sure. Just play that defense. I want to win this one."

"Yeah. Sure." Larson's mind turned from the game to a picture of Terry Jeffers. Long-legged, dark-haired, blue-eyed, Terry Jeffers could find her own share of dates. And he never possessed the courage to ask her.

Jeffer's voice and his heavy hand clamped to Larson's shoulder pulled the fullback from his reverie. "So what are you doing after graduation?"

"I don't know. College, I think. What about you?"

Jeffer's started toward center field. "I'm joining the army. *Going to Vietnam to become a war hero . . .*"

Larson's memory broke with jarring abruptness. He felt his consciousness jolted to the path of a different recollection. It was the summer after his high school graduation. Seeking spending money for college, he found a job working as a day camp counselor. The pay was comparatively high for employment of its type, and the benefits undeniable. Camp Collinswood had two pools, four athletic fields, sixteen tennis courts, and fifty wooded acres. Yet despite the many facilities, the boys in Larson's group preferred a game which required no special equipment.

Standing with his assistant before a dozen rowdy seven- and eight-year-old boys, Larson heard himself ask. "What do you guys want to do now?"

"Kill the counselor!" they chanted, nearly in unison. A wave of small bodies converged on Larson and his assistant. Resigned to the punches and prods of children too young to inflict significant pain, Larson alternated between feigned defenselessness and throws which sprawled the campers in giggling heaps. He passed off wrestling moves as karate throws, or tricks from his days of "alligator tussling" and "dinosaur hunting."

"Al's got a girlfriend. Al's got a girlfriend," one of the youngsters chanted teasingly. Larson rose, dumping two boys from his back. Terry Jeffers stood several feet from the game. Her drab-colored dress was rumpled, and her hands knotted together at her waist. As he drew closer, Larson noticed her eyes, red and swollen, hollowed by anguish.

"Terry. . . ?" he started uncertainly.

"Al." Her voice was a tenuous quaver. "It's . . ."

The scene shattered with Loki's muttered curse. Larson's thoughts jumped to his prom with the disquieting transition of a scratched record.

Terry wore a gown of blue satin. Dark hair haloed her face in burnished waves. Eye shadow and mascara focused attention on the sapphire depths of her eyes. Breathless, Larson stared. But his thoughts drifted back toward the unfinished sentence of his previous memory. Somehow, Larson knew Terry's message was extremely important.

Loki's presence nudged Larson back toward his

vision of Terry Jeffers before the prom. Each line
in the petals of her corsage blossomed into vivid
focus. Satin swirled about her slender hips. . . .

Damn you, Trickster! Vidarr shoved Larson's memories askew as the gods circled the flawed and
tangled circuitry of his mind with the caution of
dancers on a bed of needles.

. . . Terry's dress went black as death; her head
buried in her hands.

Loki snarled. Larson felt sanity slide beneath a
wash of terror.

. . . He danced to a slow ballad. Terry's head
rested against his shoulder. His sweating palms left
marks in the fine, blue satin of her dress. . . .

. . . But the feeling was all wrong. The music
muted to the heavy toll of bells, chilling harmony
to the anguished sobs of Mrs. Jeffers. Terry stared
at a closed coffin. And Larson remembered. *T.J.
died in Vietnam!*

Rationality broke beyond control of the spar-
ring gods. Thoughts merged in a disharmonic
orchestra of memory. Lights flashed as one: the
cold yellow of porchlight, the glaring red-orange
of mortars, the multi-hued explosions of sorceries.
Larson felt alternately hot as fire and cold as death.
Grief and hatred, sorrow and vengeance, self-pity
and empathy swirled to a numbing, incomprehensible mix of emotion which tore screams from his
throat.

Larson froze, listening to the echoes of his own
pained cries. Gradually, sanity drew his crumbled
thoughts together like pieces of a puzzle. *It was all
a lie, a world of men who sought honesty in falsehoods
and war in the name of peace. They preached "turn the
other cheek" and practiced "kill or be killed." We believed in death for freedom, and honor, yet dismembered*

the dead without respect. I've seen too much fear and not enough glory, a single God who promised forgiveness and banished his children to hellish tortures for their doubts and uncertainties. My country trained its babies to kill, then condemned them as murderers.

"Larson!" Loki's plea jerked Larson back to the present. Gaelinar stood watching, his eyes dark with concern. Again, Larson raised Valvitnir, its steel a dull, gray shadow in the mist. His arm rose and fell. The blade sheared through Loki's back, the god's death justified by the lives of the innocent, the unborn casualties of future wars. And Larson wept for the other casualties, men and women whose existence became nothing more substantial than his memories of them. His own existence became a paradox, a life from a future which was no longer reality.

Vidarr's mental presence whispered softer than wind. *I'm sorry.*

The words struck Larson like a physical blow. He stared at the sword in his fist; fresh blood trickled from its haft to stain his fingers scarlet. *It was all another lie.* Despite the utter destruction Larson wreaked upon his own world, Vidarr remained imprisoned in the sword.

"Damn your evil heart!" Larson jumped to his feet and hurled Valvitnir. The sword flipped end over end, glittering as it passed beneath tears in the clouds. "Damn all gods and men! You forced my hand against everyone I loved in both worlds." Turning his back on the sword which had served as his companion for weeks in a strange land, Larson staggered several paces. He collapsed at Silme's side. Her flesh was cold to his touch. Her lids remained closed, as if in sleep. Tears poured from Larson's eyes like a miniature replica of Hvergelmir's falls.

Larson watched Gaelinar move through a grief-inspired haze which gave all reality the consistency of dream. Respectfully, the Kensei averted his eyes from Larson's tears. He trotted forward and seized the blooded Helsword which still lay beside Bramin's soulless body.

"You stand for everything I despise and against everything I believe." Gaelinar's voice sounded strangely solid in the lingering silence which followed Larson's mental battle. Several seconds passed before Larson realized his teacher addressed the sword.

Larson heard no reply, but the sword shimmered in Gaelinar's hand and its form blurred. Numbly, he watched the Kensei carry the blade to Hvergelmir's chasm and set it, point first, at the edge of the falls.

Sound rose from the warped swordshape, scarcely loud enough to rise above the water's roar. "Back, mortal fool. You've no right to challenge gods."

The shifting mists before Gaelinar revealed a vague man form. Shock weakened Larson's grasp, and Silme's body slipped to the ground. Kensei Gaelinar cleared his throat. "God or man, Helblindi, you've no right to take glory from a warrior's battles. You're a tool of chaos and evil, a being with no reason to live."

Helblindi's figure sharpened to clarity. Though golden-haired and fair-skinned as Loki, Helblindi displayed none of his brother's beauty. "Men, not gods, are tools, mortal. Your weaknesses shall become my strengths. You're a toy, swordsman. I'll crush you with your own flaws."

The bitterness and power in the god's voice

made Larson flinch. But Gaelinar stood steady as the land itself. "I have no flaws. Ask Allerum." Gaelinar's foot lanced toward the god, faster than thought. The blow crashed into Helblindi's gut. Off-balanced, the god fell, twisting and screaming, into the cascade. Gaelinar completed his statement in a triumphant whisper. "I'm no hero."

Awe nearly deafened Larson to a noise from behind. Even as he whirled, he knew what he would find. The spell which had imprisoned Helblindi in a sword was the same which held Vidarr. As promised by the Fates, Loki's death did break his enchantments; they just took time to fade. Larson recognized Vidarr from mental images and the broken reality of Vietnam. Though freed, the god still addressed him telepathically, but now Vidarr's actual presence was undetectable in his mind. *I owe you, Allerum. Ask what you wish. If it is within my power, it is yours.*

Larson did not hesitate for consideration. "Silme . . ."

Vidarr's face looked stricken. *Allerum, I'm sorry. I want her back as much as you do. If you had used any other sword . . .*

What little strength remained to Larson dispersed. He turned away.

There is something I can do.

Larson heard nothing. He cradled Silme's body like a doll. Both his lost world and the one he had come to save seemed faded and distant as childhood dreams. Vidarr's presence materialized in his mind. The god enfolded his charge, flicking consciousness to peace, and Larson dropped into a twilight sleep.

While Larson lay, anesthetized by Vidarr's powers, the god set to his task. Larson's mind patterns stretched before him like a road map designed by a maniac. Vidarr sighed without bitterness. With the tenderness of a father with his child, he sliced blind loops and alleys. His will forced coiled paths straight, broke unrelated connections, reaffixed the frayed thought waves which allowed Bramin and Loki to torture Larson with memory.

Vidarr's work continued well into the afternoon. The god mended all the flaws his capabilities allowed, deleting only those ideas which Larson found intolerable. He left the recollections of Vietnam, T.J.'s funeral, and Larson's own death along with happier ones of his parents and Terry in her prom dress. Though painful, they belonged to Larson and had their role in shaping his personality. Vidarr had no wish to change his savior, only to restore the sanity which was his by right of birth.

As the last of the tortuous pathways assumed its proper place, Vidarr withdrew to assess his work with pride. He retreated from Larson's mind, leaving a final message of hope and peace, a promise of future happiness and pain in a world with elves, dwarves, gods, and magic. Then Vidarr disappeared for Asgard, mentally and physically, leaving Larson with little or no understanding of his reward. *Farewell, Allerum.*

EPILOGUE

"Every man takes the limits of his own field of vision for the limits of the world."
—*Arthur Schopenhauer,*
Studies in Pessimism

Still dazed, Larson watched Gaelinar examine the long row of weapons spread before him on the dirt. A half dozen steel shurikens weathered the Kensei's gaze. Each sharpened corner underwent and passed the test of Gaelinar's thumbnail, and he dropped the shurikens in the grass. Next, the swordmaster turned his attention to a silver chain, tipped at both ends by a five-inch spike. Every link met Gaelinar's intense scrutiny before the Kensei set the manrikigusari aside with the same satisfaction.

Stung by Gaelinar's insensitive disregard for the three corpses and for his own sorrow, Larson abandoned Silme's body and moved toward the Kensei.

Gaelinar looked up briefly, smiled a greeting, and returned his attention to an instrument which resembled a large tuning fork with unequal blades. This, too, the Kensei set aside. He reached for a dagger, unsheathed it, frowned, and wiped a spot on the blade with his cloak. With a toss of his head, he set the edge of the steel to his whetstone and scraped.

Annoyance rose in Larson. He waited for his teacher to speak.

Gaelinar said nothing. He nodded approval at the knife, sheathed it, and placed it with his other weapons. Katana and shoto soon joined his arsenal, along with a small knife which slid from a position in the katana's sheath. Larson had not previously noticed it.

Gaelinar hefted a short metal band and flared it into a fan with recklessly sharp edges. Larson's discomfort exploded into anger. "You inhuman bastard!"

Gaelinar looked up.

Larson paced furiously. "How can you sit there prissing and preening while Silme lies there dead? You're wrong! You do have flaws. You're not a man, you're an insensitive beast, a stone without feelings. Silme is dead! Can't you understand that? Can't you even cry?" Grief crushed wrath, and Larson was overcome by a fresh bout of tears. "Damn you!"

Gaelinar made no reply. A deft flick of his wrist closed the fan. Slowly, he reached for his arsenal. He tied the manrikigusari around his waist, beneath the wide sash. The swords and dagger regained their places at his sides. He stuffed the hachiwari in his belt, behind the katana. The metal fan disappeared beneath his cloak. Carefully, Kensei Gaelinar set to work, arranging each shuriken in its proper position in its arm sheath.

Each moment of silence jabbed Larson like a knife. He cursed the Kensei in Old Norse, switched to English as he expended his repertoire of insults, then finished in the Vietnamese version of American.

Gaelinar seemed to take no notice. He finished his housekeeping efficiently, patted the hilt of his katana, and finally turned his attention to his raving companion. "You coming?"

Larson bit his lip, having exhausted his supply of oaths, blasphemies, and affronts. "Where?" was all he managed to say.

Gaelinar studied the foaming hybrid of waters which formed the falls of Hvergelmir. "To Hel. I'm bringing Silme back."

Larson's eyes widened. His nostrils flared. He found himself utterly incapable of speech.

Gaelinar continued. "In the chasm, beyond the Helspring, is a bridge which leads to Hel."

Larson found his tongue. "You're crazy! Vidarr said he couldn't . . ."

Gaelinar interrupted, his stare distant. "Vidarr's only a god. Together, we've already killed two, Helblindi without even a weapon. There's only one left." His gaze met Larson's, and the elf looked away. Gaelinar's tone went grim. "Allerum, you made a promise to Silme. You vowed that if this quest doomed the two of you to separate worlds, you would find her."

"But that was when I thought . . ." began Larson in defense.

Gaelinar waved him silent. "You think too much. I'm going after her. Are you coming?"

Larson chewed his lower lip and turned away. He heard the rustle of grasses as Gaelinar walked toward the narrow path into Hvergelmir's valley.

Gods. Larson approached Loki's body, examining the dark blood which had clotted around his fatal stroke *Even for the remote possibility of retrieving Silme's soul, I can't face another god.*

Can I?

The rush of cascading rivers and the howl of wind were his only answers. Gaelinar's golden figure marched on toward Hel's pathway. Gritting his teeth against what he might see, Larson rolled Loki's body to its back. The god's face seemed as handsome in death as in life. His oddly-colored eyes still glimmered. "Good-bye, noble foe," said Larson softly. He caught Loki's rigid arm and flipped the body into the Helspring.

Loki tumbled limply through the surge of intertwined rivers and was soon lost beneath the boiling current of white water. Larson caught up Loki's sword and scrambled after the Kensei.

Gaelinar stopped as Larson approached. He waited until the elf drew to his side. "Yeah," Larson said softly. "I'm coming." They turned toward the narrow pathway together.

For some distance, man and elf picked their way down the incline in silence. Larson paused a moment in thought, then confronted his companion. "Gaelinar?"

"Hmmm?"

"While we're at it, can we free Brendor, too?"

Kensei Gaelinar's smile was slight, but unmistakable. His arm pressed to Larson's shoulder. "Sure, hero. You can only die once."

Mickey Zucker Reichert

☐ **THE LEGEND OF NIGHTFALL**   UE2587—$5.99

THE RENSHAI TRILOGY

☐ **THE LAST OF THE RENSHAI: Book 1**   UE2503—$5.99
☐ **THE WESTERN WIZARD: Book 2**   UE2520—$5.99
☐ **CHILD OF THUNDER: Book 3**   UE2549—$5.99

THE BIFROST GUARDIANS

☐ **GODSLAYER: Book 1**   UE2372—$4.50
☐ **SHADOW CLIMBER: Book 2**   UE2284—$3.99
☐ **DRAGONRANK MASTER: Book 3**   UE2366—$4.50
☐ **SHADOW'S REALM: Book 4**   UE2419—$4.50
☐ **BY CHAOS CURSED: Book 5**   UE2474—$4.50

DAW

Tad Williams

Memory, Sorrow and Thorn

THE DRAGONBONE CHAIR: Book 1
☐ **Hardcover Edition**   0-8099-003-3—$19.50
☐ **Paperback Edition**   UE2384—$5.99

A war fueled by the dark powers of sorcery is about to engulf the long-peaceful land of Osten Ard—as the Storm King, undead ruler of the elvishlike Sithi, seeks to regain his lost realm. And to Simon, a former castle scullion, will go the task of spearheading the quest that offers the only hope of salvation . . .

STONE OF FAREWELL: Book 2
☐ **Hardcover Edition**   UE2435—$21.95
☐ **Paperback Edition**   UE2480—$5.99

As the dark magic and dread forces of the Storm King spread their evil across the land, the tattered remnants of a once-proud human army flee in search of a last sanctuary and rallying point, and the last survivors of the League of the Scroll undertake missions which will take them from the fallen citadels to the secret heartland of the Sithi.

TO GREEN ANGEL TOWER: Book 3
☐ **Hardcover Edition**   UE2521—$25.00
☐ **Paperback Edition, Part I**   UE2598—$5.99
☐ **Paperback Edition, Part II** *(July '94)*   UE2606—$5.99

In this conclusion of the best-selling trilogy, the forces of Prince Josua march toward their final confrontation with the dread minions of the undead Storm King, while Simon, Miriamele, and Binabek embark on a desperate mission into evil's stronghold.

The Ancient Hatreds

Astride the Wind expected the man's eyes to bulge in surprise or even fear. He expected the man to have some reaction to the sight of six kenku in a sharp dive in the direction of the top of his head, but there was nothing. The man with the green eyes took note of them and drew his black sword. He opened his mouth to say something and pulled his sword back to strike, but Astride the Wind was there. The kenku felt his blade take the man's head off and there was a spray of red as Astride the Wind swished past and down.

The Assassin's Prize

The door to the room opened then, and Jarlaxle fell back toward the window. Entreri stayed to his left, over by the bed. In stepped a muscular, dark-skinned man dressed in long and ragged-edged black robes, a many-crested helm on his head. Behind him loomed a horde of huge gray and black dogs, blending in and out of the shadows in the hallway as if they were made of the same indistinct stuff as those patches of blackness.

Entreri felt a pull from Charon's Claw, his magnificent sword. It didn't feel to him as if the sword was relating its eagerness for battle, though, as it usually did, but rather, almost as if it was greeting an old friend.

The Northman's Debt

An ox bellowed in alarm, then there was a huge glugging sound followed by the crackle of splintering wood and the shrieks of terrified women and children.

"T-t-traveler?" called Bodvar, sounding weaker and colder than before. "H-have you left us?"

"Stay quiet, Vaasan, or there will be no reason for me to stay," Melegaunt shouted back. "I am working as fast as I can."

RETURN OF THE ARCHWIZARDS

Book I
The Summoning
TROY DENNING

Book II
The Siege
TROY DENNING

Realms of Shadow
EDITED BY LIZZ BALDWIN

Book III
The Sorcerer
TROY DENNING
November 2002

REALMS OF SHADOW

Return of the Archwizards

ANTHOLOGY

Edited by
LIZZ BALDWIN

REALMS OF SHADOW
Return of the Archwizards, Anthology

©2002 Wizards of the Coast, Inc.

Distributed in the United States by Holtzbrinck Publishing. Distributed in Canada by Fenn Ltd.

Distributed to the hobby, toy, and comic trade in the United States and Canada by regional distributors.

Distributed worldwide by Wizards of the Coast, Inc., and regional distributors.

Cover art by Jon Sullivan
First Printing: April 2002
Library of Congress Catalog Card Number: 2001089473

9 8 7 6 5 4 3 2 1

US ISBN: 0-7869-2716-X
UK ISBN: 0-7869-2734-8
620-88555-001-EN

U.S., CANADA, ASIA, PACIFIC, & LATIN AMERICA Wizards of the Coast, Inc. P.O. Box 707 Renton, WA 98057-0707 +1-800-324-6496	EUROPEAN HEADQUARTERS Wizards of the Coast, Belgium P.B. 2031 2600 Berchem Belgium +32-70-23-32-77

Visit our web site at **www.wizards.com/forgottenrealms**

CONTENTS

TRIAL BY ORDEAL

Lisa Smedman

Netheril Year 3389
(The Year of Perdition's Flame, –470 DR)

Hands clasped behind his back, Andoris Derathar stared out the warded window at the drifting clouds that veiled the farmland so far below. The city was currently floating over a lush checkerboard of leaf-greens, wheat-yellows and loamy browns, but in the distance he could see a ridge of sun-bleached white that should not have been there: the low dunes of the encroaching desert.

He had just come from the Hall of Judgment and was still wearing his robes of office: a starched and pleated black kilt that hung to the floor and a long-sleeved black shirt with a pair of scales, embroidered in gold thread, on its left breast. A gold cord was knotted around his waist. Suspended from it was a mask—a smooth circle of ivory with holes for eyes and nostrils, and a slit for the mouth. Its color matched that of Andoris's white-blond hair, which was receding on either side of a high-swept forehead. The face of the mask was as bland as Andoris's own; his beardless cheeks were smooth—unmarred by lines of age or worry.

Turning away from the window, Andoris regarded the gem he had been holding behind his back: an enormous blood-red ruby, faceted at such odd angles that the sides of the gem seemed to turn in upon themselves. Drifting at the center of it was a ghostlike essence that twisted slightly—the soul of the man Andoris had just found guilty of murder. Two holes that might have been eyes stared mournfully out through the walls of the crystal prison.

"Death," Andoris said, repeating the sentence he had just imposed, "without possibility of resurrection for fifty years."

He placed the ruby in a niche on the wall beside a dozen others.

Behind Andoris, a homunculus—a vaguely humanlike creature with green, leathery skin, enormous batlike ears, and glistening black eyes—gave a faint snort. Folding its leathery wings around itself like a cloak, it made a disdainful gesture with webbed fingers.

Horbal was a cruel bastard, it said in a voice that was part squeak, part croak—a voice that only Andoris could hear. *He killed that cat slowly—and enjoyed watching it suffer. You should have given him five hundred years, not fifty.*

Andoris stared down at the homunculus. Even standing fully upright, the creature was no taller than his knee. Created through an alchemical process with a pint of Andoris's own blood, it was in constant telepathic contact with its master. In the years since its creation, it had served as an invaluable tool in Andoris's climb up the ranks of the judiciary.

"Fifty years is the punishment proscribed by law for the killing of a familiar," Andoris told it.

He spoke the words aloud—something he only did when he and the homunculus were alone.

It isn't fair! the homunculus whined. *That bastard Horbal will be free in fifty years, while poor Jelal—*

The homunculus had been reaching for the ruby, intending to give it a furious shake. Even though this wouldn't damage the gem or its contents, decorum had to be maintained. Andoris forced his will into the homunculus's mind and wrenched its arm down. Sulking, the creature huddled into itself, nursing a dislocated shoulder.

Andoris, his mind shielded from the pain, stared down at the homunculus with a face as dispassionate as the mask that hung at his belt. With a flick of his fingers, he cast a healing spell.

A moment later, he heard sharp raps at the door. His finger pointed in silent command, and the homunculus stiffened, then scurried under a table. It watched with large, luminous eyes as Andoris first cast an illusion spell to mask its presence, then flicked a sparkle of magical energy in the door's direction, unlocking it.

"Enter."

The door swung open, revealing Justice Vlourir, a woman with long black hair and deep frown lines across her forehead. She wore a judge's black kilt and shirt, with an ivory mask at her belt.

"Lord High Justice Derathar," she said, "I am sorry to trouble you so soon after your sentencing, but there is a case requiring your judgment."

A small fist thumped in irritation under the table, but went unheard.

"What is the charge?" Andoris asked in an expressionless voice.

"Espionage—specifically, the theft of state secrets. The arcanist Algar Ptack was, under direct commission from

Lord Karsus, researching a way to reverse one of his spells. Lord Karsus hoped the reversed spell might be used to further decipher the Nether Scrolls. Ptack's research notes from that project, however, were stolen."

Andoris nodded. Lord Karsus had confided in him, some time ago, the details of this particular research project. Ptack was trying to reverse his secret script spell, an incantation that made even magical text indecipherable to anyone who didn't know the command word that would negate the encryption. If he succeeded in reversing the spell—assuming the Nether Scrolls were ever found again—the enclave that possessed that spell would be the first to read the scrolls' secrets and would become the most powerful in all the land. The case was certainly an important one, but did that mean Andoris had to hear it?

From under the table came a small sigh, audible only to Andoris.

"High Justice Emilus Wentar is qualified to hear evidence in capital cases," he said.

The frown lines on Justice Vlourir's face deepened. "He has heard the case, but he finds it impossible to reach a judgment. He says the trial invokes questions about legal procedure that only the Lord High Justice can answer—and that the testimony itself presents an insoluble puzzle."

Visible only to Andoris, the homunculus sat up, ears erect and a gleam in its eye. *A puzzle?*

As if she had heard the echoed question, Justice Vlourir continued, "There are two defendants. High Justice Wentar said deciding which is guilty is like trying to choose between a reflection and a mirror."

What do we suppose he meant by that?

Andoris merely inclined his head. "Where is the case being heard?"

"In the Spiral Court. It has been adjourned temporarily, and High Justice Wentar awaits you there."

Andoris nodded. "Inform High Justice Wentar that I'll join him at once."

The Spiral Court had been named for its dominant feature: a flat inlay of white ivory, about two paces wide, that spiraled up the wall of the circular chamber. As voices echoed up from the floor of the deep, well-like chamber, ebony-black letters flowed up the spiral: a transcription of the testimony being given below.

The force of gravity had been twisted during the construction of the Spiral Court, allowing its walls to serve as floors, and these walls were crowded with the citizens of Karsus Enclave—arcanists and lay casters alike—who stood at a right angle to the floor below, affording them an excellent view of both the proceedings and the transcription that flowed past their feet.

At the bottom of the Spiral Court, Andoris sat on an ornately carved chair of solid silver that floated a handspan above the floor. He wore his judge's mask—but pushed up onto his head, leaving his face bare. A few paces behind him, High Justice Wentar sat in a similar chair, listening quietly as portions of the testimony given earlier were repeated, his face hidden behind his judge's mask. His body appeared young and trim and his hair was still thick and dark, thanks to age-resisting magic, but his shoulders slumped with the heaviness of decades of difficult decisions, betraying his true age.

On the opposite side of the room, the stone floor had been marked with two intricate circles, painted with a brush made from three braided hairs from a minotaur's tail. Each maze-circle was perhaps two paces wide, and inside each stood a woman with a proud, narrow face and long red hair. One woman had pulled her hair back with a gold cord and dusted her lips and eyelids with powdered ruby and was dressed in a silver-gray gown dotted with tiny flecks of black that whorled across its surface like shifting smoke. The other wore her hair loose over her shoulders and was dressed in gray tights, a loose gray shirt, and thigh-high boots that were scuffed at the heel and knee.

Though the two women had chosen dramatically different clothes in which to appear before the court—one looking as though she were ready for a celebration at Lord Karsus's tower, the other as if she were about to set out on an adventure—their faces were as identical as those of twins. Even their expressions were the same. Each stood rigidly, glaring haughtily out at the other through the shimmering circle of latent magic that would cause her to become lost inside the maze-circle were she to try to cross it, either bodily or with magic. The two women even expressed their tension in the same way: a narrowing of her pale green eyes and the occasional restless drumming of the fingers of her right hand against her thigh.

One of the women, according to the testimony, was a shadow double—but so cunning was the magic that had brought it into being that it was impossible to tell which was the arcanist and which the magical construct. High Justice Wentar had already tried all of the standard tests, but none had shed any light on the question. Each of the women had a heavy aura of magical dweomer surrounding her—but it was well known that Blamira, like most arcanists, had prolonged her life span using powerful magic. Wentar had exhausted himself trying to determine precisely which spells had created this aura, and he failed. Blamira's magic was too powerful.

He had next ordered the women stripped of all clothing and possessions and had analyzed each of these objects for any traces of nonfunctionality. Had they been created at the same time as the double, as part of

Blamira's spell, that magic should have been unable to fully sustain them, once they were no longer in contact with the double. But all of the objects proved to be completely devoid of dweomer—mundane items acquired by the shadow double after its creation.

In his final test, Wentar had teleported one of the women briefly to another plane, in the hope that the other would dissipate—something that normally happened when the magical bind between alchemist and construct was severed by such a distance. Like the other tests, it hadn't worked.

Staring at the women now, Andoris noted that each of them moved independently of the other and appeared to be fully in control of her own actions. There were none of the usual signs of a shadow double being commanded by its creator: no hesitancy of speech, no mirroring of movement.

The magic that was sustaining the shadow double was durable. Wentar had already spent the better part of a day hearing testimony, and the shadow double had not faded in the slightest. Its creator appeared to have cast a permanency spell upon it.

From Andoris's bedchamber—where the homunculus was safely locked away—came a nervous, worried voice.

We don't like this case, it said, wringing its hands. *It reminds us of—*

The similarities are superficial, Andoris told it. *Be quiet.*

He stared expressionlessly at the arcanist who was giving testimony. Algar Ptack, a man with a high forehead and thinning blond hair that hung to his shoulders, was pacing back and forth in front of the chairs in which the two judges sat. He wore an alchemist's leather apron over his trousers and a loose white shirt. The cuffs of his sleeves were dusted with yellow, and the smell of burned sulfur clung to his clothes, suggesting he'd come straight from his laboratory to give testimony. His eyes were enormous behind clear glass lenses that floated just in front of his face. As he gave his testimony, he peered nervously at the two women held inside the magic circles.

Every now and then he glanced to the judges, as if for encouragement, but failed to find it in Wentar's blank mask or Andoris's emotionless expression. The mantle Ptack had been ordered to wear while giving testimony—a cape of fine-spun gold—billowed out behind him as he paced, humming like the strings of a melodious harp with each word he spoke.

"You know I can't lie—not with this thing on," Ptack groused. "I'm telling you the truth. Shiris Blamira is the thief. I'd engaged her as a consultant for my, ah . . . my latest research. I needed her expertise on magic that reaches into other planes and demiplanes. She guessed what my research notes contained and figured out how I'd . . . where I'd hidden them." He grimaced. "To think I trusted her! I'll never work with another wizard again—especially one from the Shadow Consortium."

From the walls above came a rustle of subdued voices as Ptack's words spiraled up the ivory inlay. The crowd of spectators had been growing throughout the day, as whispers spread that a disciple of Shadow was on trial for stealing state secrets.

Into Andoris's head came a malicious giggle: *Shadow had better tread carefully! If his disciple is found guilty, Karsus may withdraw his favor.*

Andoris ignored the homunculus's tittering. "This is a serious matter," he cautioned Ptack. "You're accusing a fellow arcanist—a member of the Shadow Consortium—of a capital offence, and yet you have provided no proof, other than your own testimony, that magical research was stolen from you late yesterday afternoon, or that it was Shiris Blamira who committed the theft."

Ptack's eyes gleamed behind the floating lenses of his spectacles. "There was a witness," he said. "One of my servants. It saw the whole thing—but High Justice Wentar refused to hear its testimony."

Wentar, who had been listening quietly, sat up sharply. His blank white mask hid his expression, but the tone of his voice gave away his irritation.

"He wanted to summon an elemental!" Wentar protested. "It's too dangerous. This court doesn't have the proper magical containment to—"

Andoris motioned his fellow judge to silence and said, "If there is a witness, its testimony must be heard."

"If Ptack loses control of it, the elemental could kill us all!" Wentar sputtered.

Back in Andoris's bedchamber, the homunculus rocked back and forth nervously, chewing one of its finger talons.

What if it does get free? What if it kills someone? We could be blamed. Are we sure we want to risk—

"This court will hear the testimony," Andoris announced.

Above him, the crowd began to thin as the spectators looked at one another, shook their heads, and teleported away.

Andoris turned to Ptack and said, "Summon your witness."

Nodding, Ptack reached into a pocket of his trousers and pulled out a lump of wet clay. Dropping to his knees, he used it to smear thick gray lines on the floor. When he was done, he rubbed the remainder of the clay on his palms, then stepped back and curled his hands over the patterns on the floor, making digging motions as he chanted.

After a moment, the stone at his feet began to bulge. A moment more, and the bulges took on the shape of a face. Eyes slowly turned in Ptack's direction with a sound like boulders being dragged across hard ground, and a crack formed and ruptured into a mouth, emitting a dank, earthen smell. The floor trembled underfoot as the lips slowly began to move.

When the words at last came they were as heavy and slow as a grindstone. *"Maaasterrr."*

A ripple of relief came from the walls as those spectators who had been brave enough to remain realized the elemental had indeed successfully been held in thrall. Some of them teleported out to spread the news, and the hall gradually began to fill again. An excited buzz of voices grew as they realized what they were seeing.

Ptack had just summoned an earth elemental—a creature that none had suspected existed within Karsus Enclave. When Lord Karsus had sheared the top off a mountain and used it as the foundation for his floating city, he must have inadvertently taken the elemental up with it, condemning the creature to an existence forever severed from the ground below. And yet the thing still lived—and was under Ptack's control. Equally amazing was the fact that the normally secretive Ptack had revealed this fact.

Ptack concentrated on his spell, his palms pressing down with invisible force, holding the earth elemental in place.

"Tell the Lord High Justice what you saw," he commanded. "Describe the thief who stole my scrolls."

"Humaaan. With . . . great . . . maaagic. She . . . waaalks . . . in . . . shaaadows."

Andoris nodded. A shadow-walk spell would explain how the thief—if it was indeed Blamira—was able to enter Ptack's laboratory, protected as it was by numerous magical locks and wards.

"Was it one of these two humans?" he asked, pointing simultaneously at both of the accused.

The elemental's unblinking eyes rolled in their sockets to stare at the closest of the red-haired women. The ground under her feet bulged then subsided.

"Thaaat . . . one."

Slowly, the eyes ground in the other direction, and the ground bulged under the second imprisoned woman.

"And . . . thaaat . . . one."

"Just as I said!" Ptack exclaimed.

Behind the floating lenses, his eyes swiveled briefly to gauge Andoris's reaction to the testimony—but only briefly. Sweat was running down his temples from the strain of holding the massive elemental inside the earth.

Andoris leaned forward on his chair. The elemental's eyes were slowly rolling back and forth, grinding softly in their sockets.

"Which one is the thief?" he asked.

A heat haze shimmered in the air above the elemental's mouth as it licked its lips with a tongue of molten lava.

"They . . . taste . . . saaame."

"Did both of them enter your master's laboratory?"

The floor trembled, forcing Ptack to catch his balance, as the elemental slowly shook its head. On the walls above, some of the spectators who had been drawn back by curiosity disappeared again.

"Juuust . . . one."

"Can you tell which one?" Andoris asked.

"Nooo."

Ptack, sweating more profusely now, shrugged a shoulder to wipe a trickle of sweat from his temple, but kept his palms motionless over the elemental.

"Blamira knew about the elemental," he said, "yet she had the audacity to steal my notes, despite the fact that she was being watched. She must have counted on Went— on this court being too timid to hear its testimony."

"When did the elemental alert you to the theft?" Andoris asked.

"Immediately," Ptack said. "Unfortunately, Blamira had already fled with my notes."

Andoris glanced at the two accused—both of whom

were watching the elemental with rapt, silent frowns—
then sat back in his chair, considering. It was possible the
elemental was lying, but unlikely. Ptack could control it
and force it to carry out his orders, but he couldn't control
its thoughts. It was an independent creature, with a mind
of its own—a mind filled with fury at being forced to
serve a mere human. If the elemental did lie, it would do
so out of malice, to damage Ptack's testimony.

*We would never do anything like that. We would never,
ever tell a lie about our master if we were ever called to
testify. But we wouldn't ever be called to testify, would we?
If people knew the truth about us, it would ruin our reputation.*

Andoris ignored the homunculus's words, which were
sent in a fawning tone, but with a slight edge.

"The testimony of the witness is deemed valid," he
announced. "The witness may be dismissed."

Taking a deep breath, Ptack leaned forward, forcing
his hands ever closer to the floor. The elemental grimaced, causing the floor and walls to tremble violently. It
slowly sank back into the floor. Ptack moved his hands
back and forth, as if erasing a picture. A heartbeat later,
the floor was smooth, flat, and featureless, as if the elemental had never been.

As High Justice Wentar let out an audible sigh of
relief, Andoris turned to the two accused and said, "You
have heard the testimony given against you. You now
have an opportunity to plead guilty or to—"

Both interrupted at once.

"But I'm innocent!" they cried. Each pointed at the
other and spoke, their words fitting together like heartbeats. "She must be—" "She's the one who's—" and came
together on the final word, "guilty!"

They continued to protest, each trying to shout the
other down. Andoris, noting that the testimony was
becoming jumbled on the ivory spiral—even the Spiral

Court was having a hard time telling the two apart—forked the fingers of his right hand, simultaneously casting a holding spell upon them both. Each woman froze in place, unable to do more than breathe or blink, but still capable of hearing any testimony given against her.

"They're both guilty," Ptack muttered, peering back and forth at the frozen figures. "One's the arcanist, and the other's her shadow double. One directed the crime, the other committed it. Execute them both—but force them to say what they've done with my research notes, first."

Andoris crooked his finger. "The mantle."

Ptack plucked it from his shoulders with a grateful shudder, as if removing a leech. Andoris gestured, and the mantle floated across the circle that held the Blamira claimant with the gown and gem-dusted face. As soon as she was released from her spell she flung the mantle across her shoulders with a haughty expression and stood poised and expectant, waiting for Andoris's questions.

"Are you Shiris Blamira?" he asked.

"I am," she began, then winced as the mantle struck a slightly sour note. "That is, I believe that I am. There is a chance, of course, that I am wrong. If I am the shadow double, I wouldn't know it. I have all of Shiris Blamira's physical and mental attributes, including her spellcasting abilities—even the same memories."

"And the same motivations to commit theft?" Wentar asked.

Ha! Got her!

Andoris held up a hand. "The accused is not required to speculate on whether she *might* have committed the crime," he cautioned. "Only to testify as to whether or not she *did* commit the crime."

Wentar considered a moment, then said, "Assume, for now, that you are the original Shiris Blamira, and answer my questions accordingly." He pointed at the woman in the other maze-circle. "Did you create this shadow double?"

"I must have. It wouldn't be possible for another arcanist to have created so exact a duplicate."

"Do you remember casting the spell?"

"No. I know only that the shadow double must have been created yesterday—and that somehow, my memory of yesterday has vanished."

"What do you remember?" Andoris asked.

"One moment I was sitting in the library of the Shadow Consortium, reading and enjoying my morning tea, and the next, I found myself in my laboratory, face-to-face with this . . . creature. I thought it was a doppelganger at first, and only realized what it must be after I tried to magically bind it—and it dismissed the binding as if it had cast the spell itself. That's when I realized it must be a shadow double."

"Did you try to command it?"

Blamira nodded vigorously. "Immediately—but it didn't work. Somehow, the thing must have become free willed."

Free willed?

Back in the bedchamber, the homunculus was sitting on the edge of Andoris's four-poster bed, riveted by the testimony.

"Did you try to dismiss the shadow double?" Andoris asked.

Blamira nodded. "That didn't work either."

"Did you try dispelling the magic that sustained it?"

"Of course I did," Blamira said, curling her lip disdainfully. "I'm not some newly initiated apprentice, you know."

Andoris thought for a moment, then asked, "When did the constabulary arrest you?"

"At shadowfall—dusk," Blamira answered. "That was the first I heard of the missing research notes."

"Did you steal Ptack's research?" Andoris asked bluntly.

Blamira looked pointedly at her double and said, "One of us did. It may or may not have been me."

"Do you know where the stolen research notes are now?"

"No."

Throughout Blamira's testimony, the mantle of truth echoed her words with a continuous harmony, without striking a single off note. Blamira was telling the truth.

Andoris tried a different line of questioning. "When your memory returned, what was the shadow double doing?"

"What do you mean?" Blamira asked, frowning.

"Did it appear to be casting a spell?"

"No. It was just standing there, staring at me."

Andoris sat quietly a moment, considering. "Shadow doubles normally have only a limited duration, yet this one appears to have been made permanent. A simple permanency spell should have collapsed under the dispellation spells High Justice Wentar subjected you both to, but this one did not. How do you explain that?"

"How can I explain anything?" Blamira cried, throwing her hands in the air. "You obviously weren't listening to what I just said. I have no memory of anything that happened yesterday—including casting the spell that created the shadow double."

Bitch! Of course we were listening.

Andoris sat on his silver chair, motionless and impassive. He would not allow his judgment to be swayed by the expression or tone of voice of the accused.

"The court will hear the defense of the second accused," he announced. He pointed at the mantle on Blamira's shoulder. "Remove the mantle of truth."

As soon as she complied, Andoris froze her in place and floated it to the second woman, dispelling the magic that prevented her from moving. He posed the same questions—and received almost identical replies. The second Blamira also swore she had no memory of the shadow double's creation and said her first clear recollection after the gap in her memories was of she and the shadow double standing in her laboratory, blinking at each other in confusion. All the while, the mantle hummed in perfect harmony with her words.

Wentar leaned toward Andoris, his eyes troubled behind his ivory mask. He spoke in a low voice, but even so, the spiral of ivory picked up his words.

"By law, an arcanist is legally responsible for the actions of any creatures created by his or her magic," he began, "but in this case . . ."

"In this case, it's obviously not an ordinary shadow double," Blamira interjected, tossing her long red hair. "It's free willed, with a mind of its own. It could have committed the crime entirely of its own accord, using my spells and my knowledge of Ptack's research to steal his notes. If that's what happened—and if you find us both guilty and sentence both of us to die—you'll be killing an innocent woman. You have no other option but to find us both innocent, and let us go."

Found innocent. If only we'd had that option with Jelal.

Choking back a sob, the homunculus sank needle-sharp teeth into one of its fingers.

Andoris ignored the mental image of blood dripping from the homunculus's punctured finger. He sat in silent contemplation as a murmur of voices drifted down from the spectators. Now that the defense of the two accused—slight though it was—had been heard, all attention was focused on the judges. On Andoris, in particular. The spectators, the two accused, Ptack, and Wentar all watched his face closely, looking for the slightest of frowns or the twitch of a smile, hoping to interpret it in their favor. As usual, he disappointed them.

"This court will temporarily adjourn," he announced. "High Justice Wentar and I need to discuss this case in chambers." He glanced at his fellow judge. "Shall we retire to the Crystal Chamber?"

Wentar nodded behind his mask and spoke the words of the spell that would take them there.

An instant later, both men were standing in a room whose oddly angled walls and ceiling were made of a clear, glasslike material. Perched on one of the enclave's highest towers, with nothing but air surrounding it on all sides, the chamber caught the light from all angles. Beams of sunlight slanted in through walls and ceiling, erupting into thousands of tiny blue and red sparkles, revealing the chamber to be an enormous, hollow diamond. Wards etched by magic into each facet of the gem prevented those outside from scrying on those within.

Far below the tower that supported the Crystal Chamber, the rooftops and spires of Karsus Enclave could be seen, clustered like barnacles on the inverted mountaintop from which the enclave had been formed. Two buildings stood out from the rest: the cagelike enclosures that housed the enclave's two mythallars—enormous spheres, more than one hundred and fifty paces in diameter, that channeled raw magical energy from the Weave. Energy pulsed out of each mythallar, sustaining the magic that kept the enclave afloat, and powering all quasimagical devices within the energy field's one-mile radius. That energy was visible to the eye as a light colder than ice and brighter than the hottest flame—and like a flame, it drew its moths. Those bent upon self-destruction had only to touch one of those brightly glowing spheres to be instantly killed, without any possibility of resurrection.

Back in the bedchamber, the homunculus shuddered.

Horrible, it moaned. *A horrible way to die.*

Andoris, however, merely turned away from the view. He snapped his fingers, causing a decanter and two tiny glasses to hover in the air in front of him. He glanced at Wentar, who nodded, then caused the decanter to tip, filling one glass with a yellow liquid, then nudged it through the air to Wentar. He then filled the second glass and took a sip. The honey wine was delicious, warm and sweet.

"I'd like to hear your thoughts on the case," Andoris said.

Wentar pushed his mask onto the top of his head and took a sip of wine. He gently swirled the liquid in his glass, considering it with a slight frown.

"The accused has a point," he began. "If the shadow double was an independent creature that committed the theft of its own volition—even if the original motivation sprang from its creator's psyche—then Blamira must be found innocent. Whichever one she is."

"Quite so," Andoris agreed.

"It all comes down to the question of when the thing gained free will," Wentar continued. "If the shadow double was commanded by Blamira at the time of the theft, and only gained or was granted free will afterward, then Blamira is guilty—and only Blamira. Enclave law states quite clearly that any 'person or creature' that is magically compelled to commit a crime is innocent of that crime. This shadow double can indeed be classed as a 'person or creature.' Since it displays permanence combined with independent thought, it is no longer a 'spell effect' in the eyes of the law. That entitles it to be judged an independent, sentient being."

Am I a spell effect?

Of course you are, Andoris answered.

"I wish we had some way of telling arcanist and shadow double apart," Wentar continued, "but even that

Blamira's magical capabilities—and her cunning. There is a possibility that it got the better of her—that it really did act of its own accord to steal the research notes. The shadow double could have been the one who cast the forgetfulness spell on Blamira—and on itself—to ensure its own alibi."

Wentar's shoulders sagged. "So we're back where we started," he groaned.

Back in his bedchamber, the homunculus was pacing, its clawed toes clicking against the hardwood floor, but Andoris remained calm, in complete self-control. He knew that logic wouldn't fail him—it never had.

Wentar drained his glass, then released it and snapped his fingers, teleporting it away.

"I'm glad you're judging this one, Andoris. This case just gets more and more confusing the more I try to decipher it. We may just as well be trying to read one of the Nether Scrolls with Ptack's half-completed spell notes."

The homunculus halted abruptly, atremble with excitement.

That's it! How could we have been so stupid? If Blamira was helping Ptack reverse his secret script spell, he must have taught her how to cast it.

Andoris, however, merely turned to his fellow judge, and said, in a quiet voice, "Did the constabulary search Blamira's laboratory when they arrested her?"

"They did, and I supervised," Wentar said. Then he added, "I can see where you're going with this one. You think we overlooked some innocent looking scroll that might really have been Ptack's notes, but I know he protected those notes. They could have looked like anything, from an accountant's ledger to a page of poetry. That's why I insisted he be present during the search. Ptack spoke the word that negated his secret script spell and looked over the books, scrolls, and pages himself, but though some of the written materials on Blamira's desk had been disguised with a secret script spell, Ptack's research notes weren't among them."

"There may still have been clues to be found," Andoris mused.

"What do you mean?"

"I think a second search of Blamira's laboratory is in order."

The Shadow Consortium was noted for its gloom-filled corridors and tiny, claustrophobic rooms. Blamira's laboratory was no exception. Though the tower it was situated in had numerous windows—all of them ensorcelled against teleportation and scrying—they were long and narrow, filled with gray glass. The beams of sunlight that did penetrate the crowded, stuffy room seemed more like questing fingers of lighter shadow.

Wentar and Andoris were sifting through the books, scrolls, and loose sheets of vellum on Blamira's workbench. They'd shifted each pile from one end of the workbench to the other at least three times but weren't any closer to finding anything.

"It's hopeless," Wentar moaned. "I can't remember which of these changed when Ptack negated his spell."

Idiot! You should have paid more attention.

"Keep looking," Andoris said.

"What are we looking for?" Wentar asked.

Andoris was no longer listening. His attention was wholly focused on the book he had just opened. Reading it, he saw something he would have thought impossible: notes on the creation of a mythallar that drew not from the Weave but from the spaces between it. From the Shadow Weave.

Back in Andoris's bedchamber, the homunculus trembled with excitement.

So that's how she did it!

Andoris pointed to the page in the book that lay open in front of him and said, "According to these notes, Shadow and his disciples have succeeded in creating a shadow mythallar."

Wentar shook his head in puzzlement. "A shadow mythallar? Incredible! But what does it have to do with—"

"If the mythallar is sustaining the shadow double," Andoris explained, "that means the shadow double is quasimagical, rather than permanent. It's a spell effect, rather than a sentient being."

"Ah," said Wentar, a smile of relief spreading across his face. "I see. Our case is solved. We can find Blamira guilty—"

Even if she isn't?

"And hold the shadow double inside the maze-circle until we find some way to dispel it," Wentar continued. "But how are we to tell which is which?"

"Wentar," Andoris began thoughtfully, "when you teleported one of the accused to a different plane to see if the shadow double would dissipate, which one did you choose?"

When the trial resumed, the Spiral Court was even more crowded than it had been before. Word had gotten out that a decision was about to be rendered in the case, and the walls were so crowded with spectators that it was impossible to see the testimony that scrolled up the ivory spiral. Even Shadow had come to watch the proceedings—albeit surrounded by a protective bodyguard of his disciples.

On the floor below, all was in readiness. Andoris sat on one of the silver chairs. The second was empty. Wentar had explained the legal technicalities of permanence versus quasimagical non-permanence as it related to the issue of the shadow double being a person or creature. The crowd had listened in mystified silence, understanding the legal explanation but uncertain why it was being given, then Wentar had disappeared. Now it was up to Andoris.

Raising a hand to hush the crowd, Andoris spoke. "Earlier today, High Justice Wentar and I discovered the source of the magic that is sustaining the shadow double. There is a third mythallar on Karsus Enclave."

A buzz of excited voices rushed up through the Spiral Court. Andoris waited for it to subside, watching the faces of the two accused. They seemed wary but puzzled—as though they knew which mythallar Andoris was referring to but were unaware of its significance. This was perfectly logical. All knowledge of having used the mythallar to create and sustain the shadow double must have been erased, together with Blamira's other memories.

"One of these women is a quasi-magical spell effect, and thus is not responsible for its actions, according to enclave law. Therefore, Blamira must be found guilty of the crime with which she has been charged and dealt with accordingly."

The homunculus's voice was nearly lost to Andoris in the excited crush of voices that followed this pronouncement.

Even if the law's not fair?

Andoris held up a hand for silence. "As for the shadow double," he continued, "since it is no more than a spell effect, it can be dispensed with."

Just a spell effect. . . .

"In a few moments, I will conduct a trial by ordeal," he announced. "I will teleport both of the accused to a spot more than one mile distant from the enclave, where High Justice Wentar is waiting. Whichever one is the shadow double will be too far removed from the sustaining magic of the mythallar and will cease to exist."

She'll die.

"Whichever one is Blamira will survive the journey. High Justice Wentar will immediately teleport her back here, to face sentencing."

He turned to the two women, a distant corner of his mind feeling the homunculus tremble.

"Have you anything to say before your ordeal?"

The two women squared their shoulders then, a heartbeat behind one another, they shook their heads. From the grim look in their eyes, Andoris could see that both women knew what the end result would be: in a few seconds one of them would cease to exist—and the other would be facing a death sentence. All of the haughtiness they'd displayed earlier was gone.

"Do it," the woman in the gown said grimly, the fingers of her hand drumming nervously against her thigh.

"I'm ready," the second said, her face pale.

Andoris nodded and chanted the words that would fuel his spell. As he spoke, he pulled two pinches of fine-ground amber from the pouch at his belt. Feeling the magic build within him, he concentrated, sending it down into his fingertips. He flicked the dust into the two maze-circles.

Both women vanished. In the crowd above, Shadow tensed and leaned forward expectantly. For the space of several heartbeats, the Spiral Court was utterly still then the woman in the gown reappeared, a look of relief—and dread—on her face. Andoris nodded, having seen what he'd expected. He was turning to sit down again when he heard excited shouts from the spectators above. He whirled—and saw that the second woman had also reappeared. Both stood, gaping at the other.

An instant later Wentar returned to the Spiral Court, teleporting in beside Andoris with a soft popping noise that was lost in the uproar.

"What happened?" Andoris asked. Distantly, he could feel the heart of the homunculus thudding in its chest.

Wentar gave him an exasperated look and said, "We must have been wrong about the mythallar. The shadow double really is permanent. Now we're back at the beginning again."

Wrong? How could we have been wrong? the homunculus raged. In a fury, it snatched a pillow from the bed and tore it to pieces. *We've never been wrong before. Never. We can't have been!*

Andoris ignored the distant commotion—venting his emotions was what the creature was for, after all, and he'd taken care to ensure that emotion and pain only flowed in one direction: from arcanist to homunculus. Strangely, though, he found that his fingers were starting to curl. Only by concentrating was he able straighten them.

Vaguely disquieting thoughts began to surface. Was he losing control? Firmly, Andoris pushed these doubts away—only to find they had nowhere to go. The homunculus, already filled to the brim with a stronger emotion, was unable to accommodate more. It continued its furious assault upon the pillow, tearing it to shreds.

What if . . . rip . . . we were wrong about . . . rip . . . Jelal, too?

Like an incoming tide, memories from more than twenty years before rushed back at Andoris. Dizzy, he gripped the edge of his chair.

The accused was a young man with an athletic bearing, his chest bare above baggy, striped silken pants that were tucked into knee-high leather boots. Blond hair hung in a braid over the mantle of truth that draped his shoulders. His wrists were heavy with gold and silver bracelets, and a multitude of rings sparkled on fingers and thumbs. He stood in the Columned Court, ringed by pillars and gawking spectators, staring up with a confident, almost cocky expression at the judge who stood on the dais with hands clasped behind his back and an ivory mask pushed up on top of his head. The younger man gave a quick, graceful bow.

"It's good to see you again, even under these circumstances," Jelal told Andoris softly. Then, with a slight tilt of his head, "Tell me—am I still your favorite?"

Andoris nodded slightly. "You are."

At this answer, Jelal's face broke into a relieved smile.

Back in Andoris's bedchamber, the homunculus let out a soft sigh.

Even though the words had been spoken too quietly for the crowd to hear, the transcription crackled into glowing life in the air between the columns. As the spectators read it, a murmur swept through the crowd. Andoris realized what they were eagerly anticipating: that the emotionless, infallible Andoris would abandon both logic and the law.

Back in the bedchamber, the homunculus growled softly, *We'll show them.*

"I understand you've reached a verdict," the accused said.

"I have," Andoris said in a clear, carefully measured tone. "Have you chosen a method of execution?"

"I have." Jelal glanced across the city toward the spot where the mythallar pulsed blue energy into the sky. "If you really *must* find me guilty of murder, I choose to die by touching a mythallar."

He looked up expectantly, as if waiting for a reaction.

Though the crowd whispered urgently, Andoris remained utterly impassive.

The young man's smile slipped, just a little.

No! the homunculus wailed. *Tell him to choose a death that will allow him to be resurrected!*

Andoris brought his hands in front of him, revealing the object he'd been clasping behind his back. With a flick of his fingers, he teleported away the enormous red ruby. Jelal had made his decision.

No! Make him change his mind!

Andoris waited until the crowd fell once more into an anticipatory silence, then gave his judgment.

"Jelal Derathar, I find you guilty of murder, in that you did maliciously and with forethought cause the death of a toad belonging to Quinar Redux, a creature that was a familiar to this arcanist. The sentence I impose upon you is death."

The young man recoiled.

"No!" he cried. "I thought you'd give me a fair trial."

"I did. Your own testimony confirmed your guilt."

"Didn't you *listen* to my testimony?" Jelal asked in a frantic voice. "I'm guilty of property damage—even involuntary slaughter—but not murder, and certainly not with malice aforethought. When I projected the duplicate of myself into Quinar's laboratory, I ordered it to smash all of his magical apparatus and spell components. It was a spur-of-the-moment impulse, a crazy, stupid act of retaliation for him having seduced my lover with that potion He forced her to . . . to . . . Doesn't that make him the guilty one?"

Jelal looked wildly around, but though some of the spectators were nodding in agreement, Andoris's face remained as devoid of expression as his mask. He swallowed, like a man feeling the noose around his neck.

"I was seeing red," said Jelal. "I didn't even realize the toad was in the laboratory at first. As soon as I realized what it was—Quinar's familiar—I tried to stop my double. I couldn't. It was as if it had a mind of its own. It just kept smashing, smashing . . ."

Back in Andoris's bedchamber, the homunculus worried its lip with sharp teeth.

See? He didn't mean to do it!

Andoris ignored the taste of blood. "Do you have anything more to say before sentence is carried out?"

"It was just a bloody frog! For all we know he's already resurrected it. Surely the life of a frog—even if it is an arcanist's familiar—isn't equal to the life of a man."

"Death is the sentence the law proscribes."

"But I am your son!"

His face devoid of expression, the judge began the spell that would teleport Jelal into contact with the mythallar. Already the crowd in the Columned Court was thinning. In the distance, Andoris could see them clustered around the building that housed the mythallar, peering expectantly in through its barred walls. Magical energy crackled down his arm, toward the pointing finger. As it coalesced to a hot, white point, the young man's lips curved into a sneer.

"Tell me, Lord High Justice Derathar, what's it like to be right all the time? Are you going to enjoy watching your own son d—"

Nooooo!

Andoris clung to the silver chair, breathing heavily. For the first time in decades an unfamiliar emotion filled him: pain. He shoved most of it away, and shuddered with relief as it was forced into the homunculus, but a tiny shard of the emotion remained. It felt like an icy sliver in his heart.

Back in his chamber, the homunculus sat on the floor with its knees drawn up against its bony chest, and its wings folded tightly against its back. It rocked back and forth like a wounded child, alternately moaning and sobbing, fresh tears sliding from its eyes each time it squeezed them shut.

Jelal was telling the truth—the mantle said so.

I know, Andoris replied.

The sentence wasn't fair.

I know, but it was . . . the law.

But he's dead!

The homunculus flailed out of its fetal position, seizing a portrait of Jelal from the wall and hurling it onto the floor. When this gave it no satisfaction, it smashed an inkwell on top of the picture. Black ink exploded in all directions, obliterating Jelal's smiling face.

How could we have murdered our favorite son? We hate ourselves!

A part of Andoris's mind held onto the here and now. He was standing in the Spiral Court, hearing but not really hearing the murmurs of the crowd and the anxious questions High Justice Wentar was softly asking him. Another part of him was staring through the homunculus's eyes at the destruction that had just been wrought—at the spreading pool of black ink, surrounded by a fine spray of dots.

Staring at them, Andoris was struck by how tiny they were, how small a space they occupied. A realization came to him then—one so startling that he didn't even notice he was sharing the homunculus's pain when it slammed its hands down onto the broken glass of the inkwell, cutting them in several places.

His realization was that an ordinary mythallar was absolutely enormous—it had to be, because of the material that went into its construction: long strands of the Weave itself—but a mythallar made of shadowstuff, made from the spaces between the Weave didn't need to be so large. It could be compressed, tiny. Small enough to place *inside* a shadow double.

This would explain why Blamira found herself unable to command or dispel the double after erasing her own memories. Fueled by a self-contained source of magic that came directly from the Shadow Weave, the shadow double was independent of her. It had been all along. Incapable of being under her control from the start, it had to be innocent—created solely to provide her with an alibi, probably after the crime itself.

For the briefest of moments, Andoris felt his lips twitch. In any other man, it would have been a smile, but Andoris pushed the emotion securely back into place—back into the homunculus.

Only to have it shoved back at him again.

Your hypothesis is very clever, said a mocking voice, *but what makes you so sure you're right?*

Seizing a piece of glass off the floor, the homunculus held it above its arm.

Were you right about me?

The shard slashed down, and bright red blood joined the black ink on the floor. Andoris tried to force the homunculus to stop but found he could not.

"Of course I'm right!" he shouted. "I can prove—"

In mid-sentence, he realized that he'd spoken aloud, and not only spoken but shouted, his voice loud with anger.

Wentar gaped at him through the eyes of his mask.

"Andoris," he said softly. "You look so . . . strange. Are you unwell? Should we adjourn?"

For the first time in many years, Andoris felt uncertain, like a man who suddenly finds that the solid ground beneath his feet has turned to thin river ice. He glanced wildly around the Spiral Court. It wasn't just Wentar who was staring at him.

Sometimes it isn't good to be right all the time, a small voice whispered as the homunculus lay down on the floor in a spreading pool of blood. *Sometimes doubt brings . . . justice.*

Then it was gone.

With a soft sob, Andoris lurched forward and found himself plunging down into the icy waters of guilt. As he struggled to surface, he realized something. The finer points of law and being right didn't matter. Justice did.

Had the first trial by ordeal been successful, he would have been condemning an innocent creature to die.

Just as he had condemned his own son.

Still shaking, he raised a hand and waited until the Spiral Court was quiet. Then, with a confidence he had not truly felt in many years, he gave his verdict.

"On the charge of espionage, I find Shiris Blamira guilty, and sentence her to death without possibility of resurrection. I find the shadow double she created innocent. I also find it to be entitled to all of the rights and privileges enjoyed by a 'person or creature' even though it is sustained by a mythallar. I realize that this sets a precedent, but it is my prerogative, as Lord High Justice of Karsus Enclave, to do so.

"Finally, I am taking the unusual step of choosing the means by which Shiri Blamira will be executed. There will be a second trial by ordeal. Each of the accused shall be taken to the Shadow Consortium, where she will place her hand upon a shadow mythallar. The shadow double, since it is already in contact with a mythallar, will be immune. The arcanist Blamira will not. By touching it, she will be utterly destroyed."

As the two Blamiras braced themselves for this second ordeal, the crowd above broke into an excited tumult. Ignoring it, Andoris pulled his mask from his head and stared at it. Tears poured down his cheeks, dripping onto the cold ivory and running down its blank cheeks. His fingers trembling, Andoris released the mask. It fell onto the stone at his feet, and split with a loud crack.

He wouldn't be needing it anymore.

ASSASSIN'S SHADOW

Jess Lebow

Netheril Year 3392
(The Year of Emerald Groves, −467 DR)

The wet stink of mud hung in the air.

Olostin lowered his foot to the floor at the bottom of a long flight of stairs. The cellar was dark and wet, and rats splashed, unseen, in the far corners of the room.

"You have come," said a voice from out of the darkness.

"As I was directed," replied Olostin.

"You have served us well," came another voice.

"Thank you," replied Olostin.

"And you have prospered from the knowledge and power we have granted to you," continued the first. "Your raiders wreak havoc all over the countryside, and your name strikes fear in the hearts of the common man. Indeed, even the archwizards take notice."

"Your friendship has indeed benefited me greatly. One day I shall bring about the end of the archwizards' rule, and thus I am forever in your debt." Olostin bowed toward the sound of the voices.

"Then we have a task for you."

"One that will no doubt be fueled by your hatred of the ruling wizard class," added the second voice.

"Of course," replied Olostin, still bowed. "Tell me only what you require, and consider it done."

"An archwizard by the name of Shadow has been experimenting with a new type of magic," explained the first voice.

"He calls his new source of power the Shadow Weave," interjected the second.

"This Shadow Weave could be the very thing the archwizards need to destroy us."

"How is it that I may serve you?" asked Olostin.

"Kill Shadow before he uncovers too much," affirmed the first voice.

"As you have directed," replied Olostin. He stood and headed back up the stairs.

"In the name of Olostin, submit or meet your doom!"

Cy hurled his torch at a thatch-roofed house and spurred his horse on through the village of Kath. Night had fallen hours before, and the moon was just visible over the high cliffs that outlined one edge of the valley. The sound of almost one hundred horse hooves beat on into the slowly brightening night as the southern border of Kath went up in flames.

The door of a house just in front of Cy burst open, and a man in a nightshift ran into the street, away from the flames and the contents of his house. The side shutters of the same house creaked open and smoke billowed out as a coughing woman, dark streaks of ash lining her face, climbed out with a small child under her arm. The child's head lolled to one side and back in wide flopping arcs with the rhythm of the mother's frantic escape.

Cy rode on, herding the villagers toward the north end of the settlement. There, Kath butted up against a heavily wooded forest, and nearly half of the raiding party waited there for the fleeing villagers.

We'll round 'em up and rob 'em blind, thought Cy.

He smiled. Rich was definitely going to be a good way to go through life.

Someone screamed ahead. Cy reigned in his horse and stopped in front of a dead-end alleyway. Two other raiders had gotten off their horses and had cornered a village woman. She was dressed in only a light white dress, and she held a tightly bunched section against her chest with one hand. With the other, she was feeling behind her for the wall of the alley, not letting her eyes stray from the men in front of her. Her hair was disheveled, and streaks of dirt or dried blood outlined the curve of her jaw.

"Hey," hollered Cy, getting their attention. "Take your pleasures another time. You heard Lume! Force the villagers to the woods. We don't have time for these games."

The two dismounted men grumbled at Cy and spit toward his horse. They turned their attention back to the woman. She had backed into the corner as far as she could and was pounding on the stone behind her in desperation.

Damn fools, thought Cy, and he spurred his horse down the road.

The village was no more than thirty houses deep from the southern border to the edge of the forest. In the confusion of the raid—the unrelenting thunder of horses, the burning roofs, and the hollering of the bandits—the villagers scattered and quickly fell into the raiders' trap. Cy spurred his horse toward the forest, and in the next moment, he found himself on the ground, his horse barreling away from him. His tailbone and back hurt from the fall, and his chest burned in a line right across the middle. He shook his head and tried to clear his vision. A large hulking form loomed up out of the night in front of him. The figure raised its arm, and Cy instinctively rolled to one side. A heavy chain impacted the ground. Cy rolled back onto his feet and stood up, pulling his scimitar out of its scabbard as he did.

The man with the chain raised his arms over his head, swinging the heavy links around in a circle, gaining momentum with both hands. Cy's vision cleared somewhat, and he got a better look at his attacker. The man had long, ragged blond hair and was wearing only black robes, tied at the waist with a length of rope. He was wearing no shoes. Scars crisscrossed his face and forearms. One near his ear was still covered by a dark scab. His shoulders were knotted with lumps of muscle, and his arms easily suspended the weight of the chain. He moved with a quick, considered motion, passing the chain back and forth between his hands, making arcs in the air around his body.

Cy turned his blade in his hand, the metal casting reflected light from the fires on the dark ground. He lunged. Metal clanged, and the tip of his scimitar hit the ground. He just managed to keep his grip on the hilt, but the chain was still moving in quick circles. A crunching thud rang through his ears, and Cy saw stars. His jaw was numb, and he could taste blood. The chain-wielder seemed to grow much, much taller, then Cy realized he was on the ground again. He threw himself flat as the chain whistled by his ear.

Lifting himself up on his hands and feet, Cy crabbed backward, growing the space between himself and the blond man. The chain hit the ground again, throwing dirt in Cy's face. Rolling backward, the raider came up on his feet, sword in front of him. The dark-robed man nodded and closed in, moving the chain back and forth, letting it gain momentum as he changed hands again and again.

This time the chain came in low. Cy jumped and slashed in a flat arc while he was in midair. The tip of his blade tore through the dark robes and cut a deep wound in the blond man's chest. Landing on both feet, Cy leaped backward, narrowly avoiding a blow to his head. The chain was moving faster now. It looked almost like a solid wall of metal as it careened through the air.

Cy pulled his dagger from its sheath. It was the only enchanted weapon he owned. Flipping it over in his left hand, he clutched the tip of the blade between two fingers, then he feigned a lunge with his scimitar. The blond man brought the chain up in a defensive arc, striking at the hilt of the sword. Cy lowered the blade under the flailing chain and brought the dagger up to throw. The chain-wielder was too fast, and he changed directions, throwing Cy off balance. Just barely able to keep to his feet, the raider held onto the dagger but had to lower his arm to keep from falling.

The chain whistled as it came down in an overhead strike. Cy leaped forward, pressing his body as close to his attacker's as possible. Blood spattered his boots as his scimitar cut a deep wound into the blond man's leg. The chain changed directions and hit Cy hard in the back, knocking him straight into the black-robed man. The raider lost his grip on the curved sword as he bounced off a human wall of muscles. The ground came up, and Cy found himself once more on the rocky, hard-packed dirt in the streets of Kath.

This is starting to annoy me, he thought as he got to his feet.

He didn't have time for much more as the chain hit him again right around his midsection. The cold, heavy links wrapped themselves around his body and tangled with the rest of the chain as they made one full circle around Cy's stomach. Just as the dark metal clanked into itself, the raider felt himself lift off the ground. The blond man pulled him clear off his feet, and Cy grunted as all the air left his lungs. Coming down in a heap at the foot of the chain-wielder, Cy struggled to stay conscious. He felt the chain tug and begin to unravel itself from his body. The force of the larger man pulling caused Cy to roll over onto his back as the chain uncoiled. He looked up. The blond man glared back, a crease in his brow, his lips pursed and hatred in his eyes.

Flinging his arm forward with all of his might, Cy hurled his enchanted dagger at the chain-wielder. The magical metal blade sunk easily into the soft flesh of the neck, and the hilt moved up and down as the man tried to swallow. Blood seeped out around the edges of the wound.

The blond man staggered backward a step and raised his hands to his throat. The look of anger and spite had left his eyes, only to be replaced by a distinct note of fear and uncertainty. Grabbing the hilt of the dagger, the blond man pulled the blade from his neck. Blood poured out in spurting gouts.

Cy slid away, getting slowly to his feet. The raider looked around for his scimitar. It was lying in the dirt a few yards away. As he moved to retrieve it, the chain-wielder fell to his knees, bright red blood covering his hands, and a look of complete disbelief filled his eyes. Before Cy had retrieved his blade, the man was facedown on the dirt.

Cy took a deep breath and looked around. The houses were completely consumed by flames. The screaming and chaotic sounds of the raiders riding through the village had stopped. His own horse was nowhere in sight, and he cursed his bad luck for having ridden past this chain-swinging baboon. He felt around his own body to assess the damage. The bruise on his chest where the chain had taken him off his horse had already turned deep purple. His tailbone and back were sore but functional. He had lost a couple of teeth, but his jaw worked well enough for him to be able to enjoy supper around the campfire that night, and that was all he needed to know.

Sheathing his sword, Cy walked over to the blond man. His enchanted dagger lay just past the man's fallen fingertips. The chain-wielder lay facedown in a good-sized puddle of his own cooling blood. Cy wiped the dagger off on the back of the fallen man's dark robes.

The sound of horse hooves lifted over the crackling of the burning thatch roofs. Cy spun around, his dagger in hand.

"That was a nice bit of fighting, if I do say so myself."

Cy recognized the speaker—Lume, the captain of the raiding party. He rode up on his horse and stopped just in front of the fallen man.

"Sir?" Cy looked down at his bruises and bleeding wounds.

"I saw the whole thing. Most of the rest of this scum—" He waved his arm over his shoulder toward the forest and the raiding party—"would be dead after fighting a man like that."

"Thank you, sir."

Cy looked down at the blade of his dagger and twirled it absently.

"If all my men could fight like that, we'd be able to take Karsus without the rest of Olostin's raiders."

Lume dismounted and walked over to the dead man. He kicked him once in the ribs, then rolled him over with his boot.

The man's eyes were open but unfocused. His mouth hung wide as if he were trying to catch a last breath, and blood still trickled down his neck, but it was already starting to harden into scabs.

Lume regarded the dead man for a moment then said, "You know, Cy, I think I might just have a job for you. Stop by my tent in the morning, and we'll discuss the details."

Lume put one foot in a stirrup and swung his weight into his saddle.

"In the meantime," the captain said, "head back to camp. The rest of the party has the villagers well in hand."

Lume turned his horse back toward the village.

"And one more thing, Cy," he said over his shoulder.

"Yes, sir?"

"Enjoy yourself around the campfire tonight, and don't forget to get your share of the booty. We made a good haul this time."

"Thank you, sir, I will."

The evening's festivities were grand. The raiders had made their biggest haul ever. One of the men had ransacked Kath's stock of supplies and come up with several kegs of good red wine and a large cask of mead. There was more than enough in those barrels to make the fifty or so raiders in Cy's party jolly as monks in a vineyard.

The campfire raged. The wine flowed freely. Men told stories of their conquests during the raids. The men they had fought grew larger and more fearsome as the evening wore on. The riches they had stolen became fortunes even the most powerful kings would envy. They laughed and danced and lied to each other until they had all passed out. Then they slept. They would be allowed their excesses for the evening since their booty had been so large. Captain Lume didn't participate in the campfires, but he didn't wake the men early after a good night's haul.

Yes, life as one of Olostin's raiders was very fulfilling for someone like Cy. He had the freedom to do what he wanted, so long as it didn't directly contradict the orders he had been given, and he had the camaraderie of the other raiders. He had riches and wine, and from time to time he even had the affections of a lady or two. All in all, life was good.

"You're quite fast, Cy," complimented Lume.

Cy had woken just before midday, and after he had dunked his head in a rain barrel and re-bandaged his wounds from the fight the night before, he went to see his captain.

"Thank you, sir."

Cy didn't have a military background, but he believed in giving respect to his elders. Lume was the captain of the raiding party and at least ten years older than Cy, so he figured the man deserved the title of "sir."

"Sit down, please." Lume pointed to a simple chair in the corner of his tent.

Cy nodded and did as he was told.

For a tent, Lume's place was comfortable and well appointed. A hammock stretched from a pole holding up the center of the roof in the middle of the tent to another support forming the corner. A desk sat in the opposite corner with a chair behind it and a large chest beside. Papers were stacked in neat piles on the desk, and a large water pipe sat near them. It was lit, and Lume took a few puffs on it while Cy got comfortable.

The captain leaned forward in his chair, bracing himself against the desk.

"How long have you been with this raiding party, Cy?"

"About a year now, sir."

"Is that all?" he asked.

Cy nodded.

"You know, I hate to admit it, but I've been working for Olostin for fifteen years. I've been leading raiding parties for almost five years now." He leaned back in his chair. "I'm afraid I lose track of all of the young men whom I've seen come and go. I would have thought you'd been with this group longer, but I guess I'm just remembering someone else."

Lume looked at the palm of his hand for a moment.

Cy shifted in his chair.

"Cy, I make no apologies for the mistakes of other men. If a man in my party gets himself killed, then it's his own fault."

He looked the younger man up and down then stared him right in the eyes. Cy held his gaze for a moment, then let it fall.

"If I can't remember how long you've been with this group it's only because I've seen hundreds of others just like you get killed. To tell the honest truth, I can't even remember any of their names. To me, they could have all been named Cy."

Lume chuckled at this. Cy did not.

The captain became serious and once again looked Cy over. "I'll come to the point, Cy. I have a job for you."

"Sir," he said, not sure what else he could say.

"You're as good with that dagger as I've seen in a long while, and you managed to keep yourself alive last night. I'm hoping," continued Lume, "that you'll manage to get yourself out of this little project alive as well. Tell me, what do you know about our illustrious leader Olostin?"

"Sir, I know he fights to stop the tyranny of the arch-wizards, sir."

"That's a good practiced answer if I've ever heard one."

Cy was startled and began to stand to defend himself.

Lume raised his hand and started to laugh. "It's all right, son," he said. "You've got the basic idea."

Cy settled back down into the chair. He felt as if he has been scolded by his father.

"Do you want to stop the . . . tyranny of the arch-wizards?"

Cy just looked at the captain, wondering where all of this was leading. For a man who said he was going to get to the point, he sure had a round about way of getting there, Cy thought, and all of this questioning of his loyalty and teasing about his age was starting to make him angry.

"Well, Cy?" The captain raised his voice. "Do you believe in what we're fighting for?"

"Yes, sir, I do."

Cy gritted his teeth. He didn't think his performance the previous evening had been as spectacular as the captain seemed to believe, but as Lume himself had said, he was still alive. Surely he didn't deserve a reprimand for killing a skilled fighter in the middle of a raid. This meeting had started so well, and now it seemed as if the captain was accusing him of being a spy or something.

"Well, then, son," Lume said, his voice calm, "I need you to assassinate the archwizard Shadow."

The journey to the floating city had taken Cy two days on griffonback. The archwizard Shadow lived in Karsus, a city unlike any Cy had ever seen before. It floated, for one thing, but that was the least of the oddities this bustling town had in store.

The streets were lined with small gutters of running water. Brooms moved purposefully along on their own, sweeping dust and debris into the moving water as they went. Bridges lifted streets up over wider rivers, and passersby walked not only on top of the curved stone structures but on the underside as well. Wizards, carefully carrying parcels of food or armloads of books, passed each other and waved as they casually walked upside down. In a city park, four elderly, robed mages rotated freely through the air, their attention focused on a globe the size of a maidensthigh melon that floated between them. Each took turns moving intricately carved gems across the globe and laughing as the result of their moves changed the pitch, angle, or speed of rotation of one of the other wizards playing the game.

It seemed everyone in Karsus used magic, for everything they did defied what little Cy knew about the world and how it was supposed to work. Children played games on the sides of buildings instead of on the ground or in a park. Water flowed uphill and in some places through thin air. The strange canals that lined the streets didn't start or end anywhere; they just simply continued to flush fresh, clean water through the entire city. People walked adolescent pet dragons through the busy city streets, waving and smiling as they went. Groups of wizards appeared—as if from nowhere—in mid-conversation, apparently unaware that their surroundings had changed. Bags and boxes floated through the air, suspended by nothing, but bound intently for some destination or another.

Cy tried not to gawk as he made his way through the city. Across one bridge and down several blocks, he found a tall, narrow building with dozens of doors stacked one on top of the other all the way up the building's entire facade. A carved wooden sign on street level read: "The Charlesgate Inn," and robed mages floated casually out of the doors on the higher levels, turning around, suspended in midair, to lock the doors behind them.

Cy entered the bottom floor of the inn and rented a room for a few days. He wanted to learn as much about his target as he could before he had to face the man.

Hopefully, Cy thought, Shadow will be so engrossed in his research that he won't see me coming.

It was the young assassin's only hope. In open combat, Cy may have been able to defeat that skilled fighter in Kath, but an archwizard was an entirely different story. If he didn't get a quick, clean, surprise kill, he'd be done for. As he settled into his room, he realized he'd get only one chance at this assassination. He intended to make the most of that chance.

Before Cy had left for Karsus, Lume had opened the raiding party's store of materials and weapons to allow Cy his pick of equipment. They had racks and racks of swords, armor, and bows, and even some things Cy had never seen used before. The job he had been tasked with would be difficult for sure, but extra gear wasn't going to make it any easier. In the end he simply took with him a small crossbow, some magical leather armor, and his own enchanted dagger. Better to travel light, he decided.

The ornately carved brick tower that Shadow lived in was easy enough for Cy to break into. In fact, there wasn't even a lock on the door. Not wanting to fall prey to overconfidence, the assassin moved through the entry hall very carefully, checking every few feet for traps or magical glyphs. It took him almost an hour to creep slowly down the hall and around the corner.

For all of his caution, there were no traps in the long hallway. At least I wasn't blown to bits, he thought. Rounding one corner, he entered a very large, grossly wealthy sitting room. The raider in Cy was in awe. Perhaps Lume should have sent him to simply rob the archwizard. The riches held in this one room could have paid for a hundred assassins ten times over. High-backed chairs sat around ornately carved wooden tables. Silver sconces with mage-lit stones in them were stationed around the windows, and jeweled candelabras rested on desks, tables, and windowsills. Leather-bound books sat in hundreds of neat rows, arrayed over several dozen large bookshelves lining the walls.

A door swung open on the opposite side of the room. Cy crouched and somersaulted behind one of the high-backed chairs. He pressed himself close to the furniture and held his breath. Heavy footsteps echoed across the hardwood floor. Cy clutched his dagger. So much for surprise.

The footsteps got closer then passed the chair. Cy felt a light breeze pass his cheek, and his vision filled with vivid, swirling colors of magenta, yellow, and silver. The young man blinked, trying to rid his head of the befuddling magic, and the colors passed—but they weren't magic. Cy's vision cleared, and he recognized the hem of a lady's skirts. A young blonde woman, wearing heavy, embroidered linens and carrying a silver tray had passed Cy's hiding place. She walked swiftly past the chair and out into the hall. Her heavy footsteps receded.

Cy stood up, and the door swung open again. Ducking his head behind the furniture, he was certain he'd been seen this time. Once again, heavy footsteps traveled across the floor. Cy dodged behind the chair, rolling across the floor, around a table, to pop up behind whoever had entered the room. Bringing his dagger down in a broad arc, the young assassin stopped cold. The same blonde, brightly dressed woman who had just passed, only a moment before, was again standing in the middle of the room, only this time she was carrying a large silver jug. The woman's skirts rustled as she continued across the floor, unflinching and unfazed by Cy.

The door opened again. Cy spun around, his dagger out in front of him. The blonde woman was coming out into the sitting room for the third time, but now she had a large box in her hands. Her brilliant blue eyes stared straight ahead as she continued to move toward the young assassin. Two sets of heavy footsteps echoed on the hardwood, one in front and one behind. Shaking his head, certain that he was under magical assault, Cy leaped out of the woman's path, landing hard on a plush leather chair and letting it break his fall as he clattered to the floor.

Spinning around and backing into the corner, Cy scanned the room for any way to escape. Two blonde women—both wearing identical magenta, yellow, and silver linen skirts, one carrying a jug, one a box—continued across the hardwood floor. Neither seemed the least bit interested in Cy. They moved through the room and out into the hallway, intent on carrying their packages to their final destination. The young man watched them as he stood in the corner catching his breath.

The door opened again. Two more blonde, brightly dressed women—the *same* woman Cy had seen three times already—entered the sitting room and proceeded across the hardwood, their footsteps echoing heavily as they crossed. Cy made no attempt to hide this time, and the women ignored him completely. Picking up a book, the young assassin hurled it at one of the women. It struck with a thud and fell to the floor. Still, the women ignored him.

If they aren't illusions, thought Cy, then they must be constructs.

Convinced that he wasn't under a spell, he continued on his mission.

A set of stairs led down one side of the room. Cy crossed and headed down, avoiding the female golems as he went. The stairway was long, and the air grew cooler as he continued down. The old wooden steps were warped in places, so Cy was careful to transfer all of his weight onto each step slowly, so as to avoid creaking. At the bottom, another hallway continued on. A doorway near the end was partly open, and light spilled out into the hall from the opening. Another of the magenta-skirted women came out of the room and walked down the hall.

Slipping past the unobservant construct, Cy looked through the opening. He could see a bed and a night stand in half of a nice, if messy, bed chamber. Someone was shuffling around with a drawer and some papers outside of his field of view. Cy pulled his dagger from his sheath, pressed himself up against the wall, and waited. Several moments passed. Sweat started to bead on Cy's forehead. The shuffling inside the room continued.

A drawer slammed shut, and a figure came into view and sat on the bed. Square jaw, sandy-brown hair, green eyes, small wire-rimmed glasses, and a tell-tale scar on his left cheek—this was Shadow. Though younger-looking than Cy had expected, this man matched the descriptions Lume had given him. The archwizard's attention was focused on a large stack of papers he had in his hands, and he was making marks on them with a piece of charcoal.

Cy took a deep breath and held it. Raising his dagger up to his shoulder, he burst into the room, hurling the enchanted blade at Shadow as he did so. The wizard didn't even look up from his papers. He simply waved his hand, and the dagger stopped in midair. Worse, Cy stood frozen as well, unable to blink or even wipe the ever-increasing sweat from his forehead.

For quite some time, Shadow simply continued to read his papers, leafing through them casually as if he didn't have an assassin magically suspended in his bedroom. Eventually, he finished with his work, straightened the papers, and turned his attention to Cy.

"Aren't you a little young to be an assassin?" he asked.

Cy didn't answer. This had been his first assassination, so he really didn't know how the industry worked. He supposed he'd never get the opportunity to find out now.

"No matter," reassured the archwizard. "Your age isn't important. What is, however, is the fact that you tried to kill me. So?" He looked Cy right in the eye. "What do you suppose we should do about that?"

Cy tried to spit at the man, to show his indignation and contempt for the wizards who mucked around with the powerful, otherworldly magic that he felt certain would be the doom of all the world, but he was stuck. He couldn't move his lips or even his tongue.

"Well?" asked the archwizard. "Aren't you going to answer me?"

The man chuckled, then he put his hands on his knees and stood up from the bed. He plucked the enchanted blade from where it was suspended in the air.

"Very nice, very nice indeed," he commented. "Don't have much use for these sorts of toys." He walked over to a chest of drawers and placed the dagger on top of it. "I have a few I keep around as souvenirs of the assassins who have most interested me, but I generally don't like to use them. All that blood and such." Shadow wrinkled his nose. "No, magic is much cleaner."

He picked up a wand with a clear stone attached to the end of it by a leather band.

"And," he added, walking back toward Cy, "far more entertaining and punitive. Just think, if I simply poked you with your blade a few times, sure it would hurt, but in short order you'd die, and the agony you'd feel would be over. With magic—" he brandished the wand—"I can trap you inside this crystal. There you will die slowly as your predecessors sap your strength and tear at your skin."

He smiled warmly at Cy who was still unable to move.

"The best part, however, is that once you've died, your punishment hasn't ended. You will awaken as a shadow, and you'll live out the rest of eternity as an ethereal creature, unable to affect the solid world around you. Doesn't that sound far more horrifying?"

Cy grunted, trying everything in his power to simply move his fingers.

"Yes, I'm sure you'd agree, imprisonment is far worse than simple death."

Shadow turned away from the doorway and started tidying up the room.

"Though I don't want you to think my trapping you in this wand is at all an easy feat."

Cy continued to struggle, gaining a modicum of hope from the fact that he could now wiggle his toes and clench the muscles in his jaw.

"It's taken me years to be able to perfect this wand," continued the archwizard. "True, the imprisonment spells are simple enough, as you are now, I'm sure, painfully aware."

Shadow continued to fiddle in the room.

"No, it's the transformation from human flesh to the insubstantial that has proven tricky, though not impossible."

Cy could feel warmth spreading through his arms and chest, and he was able to shuffle his feet a little.

Shadow looked at the wand with reverent awe.

"This little device right here represents most of my life's work. You know," he said, speaking not really to Cy but rather to himself, "I've lived a long time, and it seems to me that as we've grown, things just keep getting smaller and smaller." He chuckled. "I guess that's what we call progress."

Cy almost had control of his body back. If Shadow continued to amuse himself for just a few more minutes, he might be able to make a break for it, and he'd much rather get killed fleeing than just standing there like a stupid jackass.

"Anyway, enough with the chit chat." The archmage turned his attention back to the young assassin and leveled the wand at him. "I suppose I should figure out who hired you to kill me before I dispose of you. I don't suppose you came of your own accord. You're too young for that."

The wall behind Shadow exploded outward into the room. What had appeared to be solid stone was actually a secret door made of wood, and the splinters of stone-colored door sprayed out at the two men. Two gigantic ogres stood at the top of a set of stairs in the space where the door used to be.

Cy was thrown to the floor next to the bed. Shadow, too distracted with the first assassin to protect himself from the two new ones, was also knocked face-first to the floor. The ogres didn't waste any time, and they rushed into the room to clobber the fallen archwizard. Ham-sized fists began to beat the mage. The two beasts worked together, pummeling the man simultaneously with opposing blows. Then one stopped pounding the wizard and unsheathed a large sword off its back. The blade slid out of the scabbard with an oily grind.

Cy had regained control of his body, and he got to his feet, pulling the larger splinters from his skin. The ogres were completely ignoring him, but they were pounding Shadow into a bloody pulp right in the middle of the doorway. He glanced over toward the passageway.

If the ogres got in that way, then there must be a way out, he thought.

He took a deep breath and steadied himself. In the moment he took to compose his thoughts, his mind reeled. What if there were more ogres down there? What if they had used magic to get into the lower chamber? If he went down there, would he be trapped?

"Lift him up," shouted the ogre with the sword.

The other grunted and stopped beating the archwizard long enough to bend down and grab the man by the robes.

Cy turned back toward the doorway, deciding to take his chances with the ogres he knew of rather than whatever could be dwelling down the stairs. While they prepared to behead Shadow, the young assassin charged the door, hoping to slip behind the busy brutes and the doomed archwizard on his way to freedom.

He took two large steps and dropped into a crouch, trying to ram right through. The ogre holding Shadow took a half step back at that precise moment, crashing into the charging human as he barreled across the room. The two assassins got tangled in each other's limbs, and they both hit the floor with a crash—Cy tumbling head over feet into the hallway, and the ogre against the doorframe. Shadow came to his feet, being pulled from the floor by the ogre and gaining momentum from the great brute's fall.

Wand still in his hand, he shouted, "*Shadominia-ropalazitsi*" and leveled the crystal end at the standing ogre.

A dark gray stream fired out of the wand in a direct line at the ogre assassin. As it approached the ogre's upright form, the stream spread out and began to curve and split. It formed a whirlwind of darkness around the beast, and the gray areas started to separate and take on individual, humanlike shapes. The shadows had narrow, elongated heads, and spindly, malformed limbs, and they flew in ever-quickening circles around the ogre. For his part, the assassin stood, his sword poised over his head, and gawked in awe and horror.

The shadows attacked, diving toward the armed figure and tearing at him with claws that seemed to form out of thin air. Cy could hear the beast howl as if he were in great pain, but no blood issued forth. Instead, the ogre dropped his sword and slowly sank to the floor, landing on the ground with a thud like a sack of horse manure.

Cy gained his feet and turned up the steps. He'd seen enough. As fast as he'd ever felt himself move, he was up the stairs, dodging brightly dressed constructs as he fled out the front door. Never did he turn around and it wasn't until he was on his griffin on the way back to report to Lume that he realized he no longer had his enchanted dagger.

Arriving in camp by sunup the second day, Cy entered Lume's tent at a run.

"Sir, I have terrible, urgent news."

Lume was sitting at his desk eating his morning meal, and the young man's frantic entrance startled the captain, causing him to cough up a mouthful of food.

"In the name of all the gods, what do you think you're doing," he screamed. Then, abruptly, his tone changed. "Oh, Cy!" Lume stood up. "What is it, lad? Did you kill the archwizard?"

"No, sir, I did not."

Lume slammed his hand on the desk. "Then what are you doing here?"

Cy proceeded to intone to Lume all the details of his assassination attempt. He left out nothing, and the captain listened intently to the entire story. Then it was Lume's turn to talk.

"Are you certain they were shadows that came out of the wand?" he asked.

"Yes, sir, I'm absolutely positive."

"Gods. A wand with that kind of power could . . ."

Turning around and placing his hands to the sides of his head, he paced out from behind the desk and moved around the tent. After a few moments, he came out of his reverie. He looked at Cy and shook his head.

"But you failed. I should have known that chain-wielder wasn't an adequate challenge to determine if you could kill an archwizard."

"Sir?"

Lume whirled, blurting out his words. "The chain-wielder, son! I sent him to test you. How else do you think a man of that skill ended up in such a backwater village as Kath?"

"*You* sent the blond man after me, sir? But, I . . . I don't understand."

"Are you stupid, boy? I planted the man in Kath and paid him to attack you," replied Lume.

"But . . . but why? That man almost killed me."

"To see if you were up to this assassination," he explained, "but obviously it was a poor test."

Cy stood with his arms limp and his mouth open wide.

Lume paced back and forth for a while longer, then he caught sight of Cy. "Child, stop your bemoaning. You lived. All that matters now is that we go back to kill Shadow and get that wand." Lume walked over to the young man and put his hand on his shoulder. "Despite the fact that you failed, you've provided us—provided our great leader Olostin himself—with a real opportunity to reclaim our world from the haughty archwizards."

Cy just stared, fuming at Lume.

"Son, if we get that wand," explained the captain, "we could use it against Shadow and all of his kind. We've been trying to kill that man for years, and now we might finally have an opportunity to use his own research against him. Wouldn't that be beautiful?" He smiled and slapped Cy on the shoulder. "You know something, Cy, I've sent a count-less number of assassins after Shadow over the years, and you're the first to come back alive. You should take pride in that. You're one in perhaps a thousand, and now you'll get another chance to complete your mission."

Cy pulled away from the captain. "You do what you want, but I'll have no part of it."

Lume narrowed his gaze. "You'll do what I tell you, or you'll be dead." He stepped toward Cy and lowered his hand to his saber.

Cy stood his ground. "You sent me to die once already. I'm not going back."

The captain brought his sword up in a quick arc, hitting Cy squarely under the jaw with the pommel as the blade scraped out of its scabbard.

The young assassin fell back, and he held his hand to his face, trying to stop the flow of blood as he stared up at his captain from the floor. Two armed guards came through the tent flap, their swords drawn.

"Take him back to his tent," Lume instructed the men, "and make sure he doesn't go anywhere." He turned back to the young man on the floor. "He'll be needed shortly— to finish his failed duties."

❧ ❧ ❧ ❧ ❧

Two days later, Lume sent a group of guards to escort Cy to the party's armory. The captain was there briefing a small group of men on the coming assassination.

"I will personally accompany you men to make sure that this time we succeed where Cy failed," intoned Lume. He smiled at Cy as the guards untied the younger man's bonds. "Cy will go along, under my personal supervision, to provide the necessary details about Shadow's home and habits." He looked out at the crowd of assembled assassins. "If this man—" he pointed to Cy—"attempts to escape or in any other way avoid his duty to this group, he is to be executed. Do I make myself clear?"

Every head in the group nodded assent.

Each of the assassins was given special boots that masked the sound of their footsteps and special cloaks that made them more difficult to see, and each was issued an amulet that made them less susceptible to the effects of Shadow's magic.

"These won't protect you from the shadows," explained

Lume, "but they will make you less of a target for the archwizard."

Cy gritted his teeth. This whole mission might not be necessary had he had one of those amulets on the first attempt.

Then Lume gave each of the men a light crossbow with a single bolt, and a small dagger, and they left for Karsus. The plan was for Cy to lead the other assassins into Shadow's bedchamber where they would overwhelm him with sheer numbers.

"The archwizard won't try to use anything too deadly inside the small confines of that room," strategized the captain. "He'll more likely try to subdue us as he did Cy, or enspell the whole group to make us think he is our ally and deal with us individually at his leisure. We're not going to let that happen. As soon as we get in sight, we unload with the crossbows. The bolts I gave you are magically enhanced to ensure a perfect strike. You only have one, because if you fail, there won't be an opportunity for another shot. Keep him distracted, so he can't use his magic, and we should all live through this." Lume looked at each of the assassins in turn. "Once Shadow is dead, we find his wand, and we get out of there and celebrate."

The other raiders let out a loud whoop at their captain's confidence. Cy kept his mouth shut. It wasn't going to be that easy, and he knew most of these men, himself included, weren't coming back. He just hoped that one of those who wasn't going back to camp would be Captain Lume.

At the entry to Shadow's opulent home, Lume jabbed the end of his saber into Cy's ribs. "Now, be a good lad and show us in."

Cy led the silent, nearly invisible band of assassins down the long hallway into the decadent siting room. In complete silence, the entire troop weaved through the blonde constructs and marched down toward the bed-chamber.

Just as before, the door at the end of the hall was ajar and a light was on inside the room. Cy beckoned the other assassins ahead of him and pressed himself against the wall. The raiders complied and moved around him, taking up positions on either side of the door. Lume came up behind Cy, and he nodded to the waiting troops. One of them held his hand out and silently counted to three with his fingers, then he charged through the door, the others following him in.

From where he was standing, Cy could only see the men leave the hall. With the boots they were wearing, he couldn't even hear them move. He and Captain Lume waited for the sounds of a scuffle or of magic being cast, but they never came. After several moments of silence, one of the men came back into the hall and waved the two men in. Lume pushed Cy by the shoulder, and he moved around the door in front of his captain.

The bedchamber was still in a shambles, but the wall was once more intact where the ogres had burst into the room. The other assassins stood around, casting nervous glances back and forth as if something invisible might sneak up on them. Cy moved over toward the wall, stopping briefly at the chest of drawers where his enchanted dagger was still resting.

I'd rather die with this in my hand, he thought. He picked up the blade.

When he reached the section of wall where the secret door had been, he placed his hand where he thought the doorframe might begin. His fingers slipped through the wall. The archwizard hadn't fixed the broken section, he had simply cast a spell over the opening. It would be a simple matter of stepping through the illusion to get to the stairs beyond.

Cy straightened up and headed out into the hall, motioning to Lume as he did.

The captain glared at Cy and asked, "What's going on?"

"Shadow has a laboratory in the basement behind that wall. He's cast an illusion over the opening to make us think the wall is solid, but if I were him, I'd have other defenses in place as well. I think we're better off hiding out here and waiting for him to come out."

Lume nodded and pushed Cy back through the door. The captain arranged the assassins in strategic positions around the room, then he went back into the hallway, dragging Cy with him, waiting from relative safety.

Hours passed. The assassins waited. Finally, the wall wobbled as the illusion allowed someone to pass through. Shadow was looking down at a contraption in his hands and not at all paying attention to his surroundings. The wand was stuck in the belt of his robe, and he didn't appear to have any of the bruises or scars that a man who had been brutally beaten by two ogres should have.

Two steps into the bedroom, the archwizard realized that something was wrong, and he began to cast a spell. The assassins unloaded their crossbows, and the man screamed, dropping the gadget in his hands and stumbling toward the bed, his spell lost on his lips.

Cy watched as the wizard fell to his knees, and Lume let out an excited yelp and bolted into the room, his dagger in hand. Shadow was holding his hands against his chest and looking at the ground. He was bleeding quite heavily.

"Well, well, well," intoned Lume. He was standing a few feet away from the archwizard with a large smile on his face. "If it isn't the mighty archwizard Shadow. Do you have any idea how long I've been trying to kill you?"

The man looked up from his position on the floor, and he finished mouthing the lasts words of another spell. He glared up at the captain as the magical bolts jutting from his body shot back out, sailing across the room and striking the assassins who had shot them. Every one of them fell to the floor, dead with a bolt buried in his forehead. Shadow continued to bleed, and he put his hand out to steady himself. His skin turned quite pale.

"No. Frankly," said the wizard, "you have a lot of competition when it comes to assassinating me."

Lume didn't waste any time. He crossed to the wizard and pushed him to the floor, taking the wand from his belt with one hand and placing the edge of his dagger to Shadow's throat with the other.

"Well allow me to introduce myself. My name is Lume, and I work for Olostin."

"Yes." Shadow coughed hard. "Yes, I recognize the name. Pleasure to make your acquaintance."

"Believe me, the pleasure is all mine." He turned to Cy. "Is this the wand you spoke of," he asked, holding up the crystal-tipped rod.

"It appears to be, yes."

The captain took a step back and turned again to the archwizard.

No longer under the watchful eyes of a band of assassins, Cy lunged at Lume with his dagger. "Die, you pig!"

The captain sidestepped the blow, but he stumble-stepped to one side.

Cy swung again at the older man's back. The enchanted blade sliced through Lume's leather armor, opening a long, bloody gash in the captain's side.

"You stupid fool," Lume hissed.

Pulling his saber in a flash, the captain made two quick slashing attacks.

Cy parried the first blow, but the second landed just below his wrist, knocking his dagger from his hand.

Lume swung again, and Cy struggled backward, avoiding the blade but falling back over the bed. Cy landed on the floor against Shadow, cradling his wrist where Lume had cut him.

The captain leveled the wand at the two men on the floor.

The archwizard struggled to breathe, but he laughed anyway. "You can't use that. You don't know the command word."

"You're wrong, wizard, and now I'm going to destroy you with your own toy." Lume smiled down at Shadow. "Ironic that you could spend so much of your life perfecting a tool such as this—" he shook the wand—"only to be killed by it in the end."

"You don't know what sort of forces you are messing with." He coughed, blood trickling down the corner of his mouth.

"Neither did you." Lume straightened his arm and spoke the word Cy had repeated for him back at camp. "*Shadominiaropalazitsi.*"

Once again a column of rushing dark gray plasma flowed out of the wand. It headed straight for the prone archwizard, coalescing into humanlike forms along the way. As it jetted forward, the stream of shadows split into a curling mass. Shadow raised his hand instinctively to protect his face, but this time, the shadows broke into individual swirls, and twisted, wavering forms spread out all over the room. They filled every corner and place of darkness.

Now spread out, the shadows began to collect again, forming a cyclone around Captain Lume.

Lume screamed, "What's happening? What's going on?"

"Don't you see, you fool?" explained the archwizard. "Don't you recognize any of those shadows?"

"No, no, I don't." He swung his dagger in wide, swooping arcs. "Stay away from me," he screamed. "Stay away, you hear."

Shadow lifted himself off the floor. "Is that any way to treat your previous assassins?" asked the archwizard.

Lume's face dropped, and his swinging momentarily slowed.

"That's right." Shadow smiled. "I punished your assassins by turning them into shadows and trapping them in that wand, and you just released them to seek vengeance on you for earning them an eternity of suffering."

The shadows wasted no time, diving in to touch the stunned captain while he listened to the archwizard.

Lume's knees went weak, and he began his frantic swinging again. "But you were the one who sent them to their deaths," he screamed.

"They don't blame me for defending myself from assassination. They blame you for sending them to kill an archwizard. You should learn to not mess with forces beyond your control."

Lume was getting tired, and his defense was weakening. His wild arcs with his dagger were slowing, and the shadows were touching him repeatedly. He dropped to the ground, lifting his head to speak again to Shadow.

"Those are fine words, coming from the likes of you."

Lume collapsed, his head hitting the wooden planks of the floor with a decided thud.

The shadows spun around in a pack over the limp body on the floor. A dark shape formed around the captain's corpse, then it coalesced into a humanlike shadow and lifted into the air, joining the swirling mass above. As a group, they dived toward the wand still gripped in Lume's dead hand. The dark gray stream narrowed as it approached the crystal, and as quickly as they had come forth, the shadows disappeared.

The archwizard reached into the sleeve of his robes and pulled forth a large purple bottle. Uncorking the vial, he swiftly drank down the contents. A strange white glow surrounded his skin, and the bleeding stopped. He appeared much better, though not quite whole and hardy.

He looked at Cy, who was still on the floor cradling his bleeding wrist, and said, "As I said before, you are entirely too young to be an assassin. I suggest you find another line of work." With that, he turned around and went back through the illusionary wall.

Cy looked down at the dead body of Captain Lume and nodded, then he turned around and headed back up the stairs, dodging a pretty blonde golem on his way out.

TOO LONG IN THE DARK

Paul S. Kemp

Netheril Year 3520
(The Year of the Sundered Webs, −339 DR)

Zossimus watched with appreciation as a vight hawk broke off its predatory circling and dived silently earthward through the perpetually twilit sky of Shade. A squirrel scampering across the lush lawn of the villa's interior courtyard sensed its danger a heartbeat too late. The unfortunate rodent gave an agonized squeak as the raptor's claws impaled its small body. Death was quick but no doubt painful.

Zossimus, seated on his favorite bench beside the courtyard's reflecting pool, nodded appreciatively as the hawk began to feed.

"Well done, little hunter."

Death to prey—and to enemies—should always come unexpectedly to the victim. Zossimus had learned that lesson well over the years. So too had the other leading arcanists of Shade. Indeed, the city's rivalry with its floating Netherese sister-cities had led Shade's arcanists to seek ever more obscure sources of magical power and ever more unexpected magical weapons. Recently, after long study of the writings of the arch-arcanist Shadow, they had learned of and begun to tap a new source of magic, a source that derived its power not from the Weave, but from a heretofore unknown source of power that the arcanists had named the Shadow Weave. None of Shade's arcanists yet knew the full potential of this alternate energy source. They knew only that it drew on the often unpredictable energies of Plane of Shadow.

To better tap those energies, and to further their research into the Shadow Weave, Shade's Twelve Princes had caused the city to straddle the border between Faerûn and the Plane of Shadow, between light and twilight. Now cloaked always in muted grays, the city had not seen the unadulterated light of Faerûn's sun in years. It bothered Zossimus little to live always in the dark; he deemed it a small price to pay in exchange for the city's magical preeminence. Jennah, of course, thought otherwise.

His love hated the city's darkness and would have left long ago but for Zossimus. At every opportunity, she begged him to transport them magically from the city to the sun-drenched plains below, where she ran through the waving grass and fragrant purplesnaps, laughing. He smiled at the thought of her long hair shining in the sun—

Without warning, the familiar presence of the Weave was obliterated. The vight hawk gave a shriek, alit, and left its bloody meal unfinished in the grass.

A void opened in Zossimus's being. Though a distant part of him sensed still the presence of the Shadow Weave, the absence of the Weave—his original mistress—

tore a hole in half of his being. Spells prepared that morning went absent from his mind, erased clean. He opened his mouth to scream but managed only a strangled gasp. A roar filled his ears. His temples throbbed as if a red-hot coal burned in his brain. He fell to his knees, gripped his head in his hands and tried to jerk it from his shoulders, to stop the pain with death, to fill the emptiness with oblivion.

The minor cantras that preserved the flora in his courtyard began to fail with audible pops. The ornate gargoyle fountain ceased its magically-driven perpetual flow. The ruby and emerald dragonfly constructs he had so painstakingly crafted as a gift for Jennah fell inert to the lawn. The artificial illumination from glass lightglobes fell dark. In a flash of insight, he realized that all magic in Faerûn dependent on the Weave—which meant all magic other than the experimental shadow magic practiced in Shade—was failing.

How? he wanted to shout, but he could manage nothing but a low moan.

Beneath his feet, the floating mountaintop upon which Shade had been built began to fall earthward. Zossimus's stomach lurched. His afternoon meal raced up his throat, but he swallowed it down, tasting bile. Birds of every color exploded from the trees and ferns of his courtyard and took wing, avian rats abandoning the sinking ship of Shade. Screams and shouts erupted from around the city, audible even in Zossimus's secluded inner courtyard. It sounded as though the whole city were screaming as one. Shade was falling. . . .

Zossimus, paralyzed with pain and terror, waited for the impact that would kill them all.

After a few terrifying heartbeats, the city's descent slowed, slowed more, then stopped all together. It took another heartbeat for Zossimus, still disconcerted, to deduce what had happened.

Shadow magic. The disappearance of the Weave had not affected the Shadow Weave. The Twelve Princes must have been drawing on it to save Shade, to keep it from crashing to earth. Even as that thought hit him, Zossimus could see in his mind's eye the other floating cities of Netheril plunging earthward as the magic that held them aloft failed. Their apocalypse would happen in the bright light of the sun, while Shade's salvation would occur in eternal twilight, *because* of the eternal twilight. Netheril's other floating cities, once testimony to the awesome power of Netherese arcanists, would be nothing more than grandiose tombs for tens of thousands.

The city began again to descend, slower this time. Zossimus's sense of satisfaction vanished. The Shadow Weave must have been inadequate by itself to keep the city aloft. Zossimus guessed that in the Palace of the Most High, the Twelve Princes were even now struggling to tap enough shadow magic to keep Shade airborne. They were failing.

Zossimus bit back his frustration. He would have joined them if he could, would have shaken the cobwebs from his head, endured the loss of the Weave, and added his considerable magical skill to theirs, but his teleportation spell had been lost when the Weave had been destroyed. It would take half an hour to traverse the city by foot. By the time he reached them, the issue would already be decided.

The city continued to descend, picking up speed incrementally. Another thousand feet maybe, and all would be over. When it hit the earth, it would kill every citizen, if not the impact, then the aftermath. The partial mountaintop upon which Shade floated had an irregular base, so it would not settle peacefully to earth even if it were somehow slowed to walking speed. It would topple over on its side, and everyone would be crushed under an incalculably massive avalanche of buildings and walls.

Zossimus wanted Jennah, desperately. If he were to die, he would die with his love.

"Jennah—"

A sudden shout—a roar of ecstatic triumph as loud as ten of Kozah's cyclones—carried from the south to drown out his voice. The force of the shout hit Shade like a maul and sent it lurching sideways, a bit of flotsam in the ocean of the sky. Zossimus fell facedown in the grass and cursed through his fear. He knew that voice—Karsus.

"Mystryl! I'll have your power!" boomed Karsus, his voice reverberating through the heavens.

Shade steadied itself, though it continued to descend. Zossimus rose to all fours.

"Karsus, you arrogant ass," he cursed.

Surely this was the end of the world, and Karsus had somehow brought it about.

Again the sound of Karsus's voice thundered through the sky, but this time Zossimus heard only sobs. Bottomless despair.

The crying fell silent, cut off as sharp as a razor. The world seemed to hold its breath, silently waiting. Nothing more.

Shade continued to slip earthward.

Zossimus wanted to hold Jennah in his arms. He had maybe a hundred heartbeats. He leaped to his feet and raced for the villa.

A small winged figure alit from an upper window, frantically flapping—Pleeancis. Zossimus's familiar streaked for him as though shot from a bow, a blur of green scales and membranous wings.

Unable to stop in time, the terrified little quasit crashed into Zossimus's stomach and got tangled in his voluminous violet robes. Man and demon went down in a heap.

Pleeancis's high-pitched voice squeaked oath after oath. "Oh, curse this purple hell! I'll shred you thread-by-thread, wretched robe. Dare you to offend Pleeancis the Mighty—*yeep!*"

Zossimus grabbed the tiny demon by his left haunch and yanked him free of the robes. "Enough!"

The quasit fluttered in his hand. His red eyes shot the robes one last evil glare before giving Zossimus his most winning, fanged smile.

"All right, Boss. Just having a moment there. Easy on the leg, eh?"

Zossimus released Pleeancis and climbed to his feet. The quasit hovered before his face, a scaly, fanged hummingbird demanding attention.

"Boss—"

"Not now, Pleeancis."

He waved the quasit away and hurried for the villa. The city was still sinking. He could feel it in the pit of his stomach. If only he and Jennah had Pleeancis's wings.

Unperturbed, Pleeancis buzzed along beside him while he ran, the demon's fanged mouth moving as quickly as his wings.

"What's happened, Boss? Huh? I can't even teleport. There's something wrong with the ring. Watch this!"

In mid-air, wings still beating, Pleeansis squatted and made as though to . . . do something. He squeezed his eyes shut and clenched his tiny fists with the effort.

"Unh. *Unh.*"

Zossimus would have laughed but for the end of the world. Magic had ceased to function, and Pleeancis was concerned only that his favorite toy was not working.

"See, Boss? Nothing. Nothing at all. Couldn't teleport if I wanted to. I—*ack!*"

Zossimuss stopped, grabbed his familiar out of air, and looked at him with narrowed eyes. "Where's Jennah?"

"What? Who cares? *I'm* here, and my ring doesn't work!"

Zossimus knew the quasit didn't like Jennah, or at least didn't like that Zossimus cared for her, but he had no time for Pleeancis's foolishness. "Where?"

The quasit must have seen his anger. His wings sagged. He ran a forked tongue over his fangs and said, "She was in the sitting room."

Zossimus released the quasit and sprinted for the villa. Pleeancis flitted about his head.

"But, Boss, you don't need her. Didn't you hear me? I can't teleport. There's something wrong with *my* ring."

"I said *not now,* Pleeancis!"

"But, Boss—"

As he ran, Zossimus lashed out and smacked the tiny demon across the midsection. Pleeancis, off kilter, let fly with a stream of high-pitched epithets, spiraled out of control, and finally crashed to the lawn.

Zossimus ran on. From behind, he heard Pleeancis squeak indignantly. "From now on, it's Pleeancis *the Mighty* to you, Boss!"

Despite himself, Zossimus cracked a grin. Not even this Karsus-made catastrophe could quiet his familiar. They should all be so blissfully ignorant.

Before he reached the villa, Jennah burst from the doors. Her long red hair flew wildly behind her; her skin had gone white. Zossimus had never seen such a lost look in her green eyes. She too was a mage. She too had sensed the destruction of the Weave, but unlike Zossimus, Jennah had steadfastly refused to tap the Shadow Weave. She had no shadow magic in which to find at least some succor.

"Zoss! The Weave!"

He raced to her and took her in his arms. "I know."

She pushed him to arms length, looked him in the face, and said, "And the city . . . ?"

He shook his head in the negative. She blinked while that registered.

"Are we doomed then? What's happened?"

Zossimus didn't want to answer her first question and couldn't answer the second. Clearly, Karsus had done *something. . . .*

Pleeancis flitted over and squirmed between them. "What in the name of Asmodeus's arse is going on around here?" He glared at Jennah. "Why're *you* so upset? I'm the one who can't teleport." He shoved his ring finger before her face.

Zossimus did not have the energy to engage in further nonsense with his familiar. He gently plucked him from the air and placed him on his favorite perch—Zossimus's right shoulder. Jennah seemed hardly to see the quasit. Her gaze was far away.

"What now, Zoss? What now? I want to see the flowers again. Like we used to." She looked at him with her gentle eyes.

Remembering their many days spent among the purplesnaps on the plains below—the plains where they would die today—his eyes began to well. He took her in his arms.

"We'll see them again, dearest. We will. I promise."

She sobbed into his shoulder; he fought to keep down his own tears. Shade fell further.

"Oh, for crying out—Your hair is in my eyes, human woman," Pleeancis hissed.

Jennah ignored him or did not hear him. Zossimus shooed the little demon away.

"Be gone, Pleeancis, we've no time for you now."

Pleeancis fluttered away, leaving a stream of curses in his wake. "All right, Boss, now it's *really* Pleeancis the Mighty to you! I was jesting before, but now. . . ."

Zossimus made no reply, merely held his love as she sobbed.

He knew they had only moments. He wanted to tell Jennah how much he loved her, whisper to her how her presence had made his life in the twilight bearable, but he could not give voice to his feelings, not even now. Instead, he stroked her long hair, held her tight, and said nothing. Pleeancis, as usual, spoiled the moment.

"Boss, I think we're falling."

The quasit spoke with such surprise in his tone that Jennah's sobs turned to laughter. Zossimus too began to laugh. What else could they do?

"It's not funny," Pleeancis said. "Did you hear what I said?"

"We heard, little one," said Zossimus.

Jennah leaned back from Zossimus and looked him in the eyes. Her tear-streaked but smiling face looked luminous. He found his voice and spoke before she did.

"I love you, dearest. More than anything."

Jennah opened her mouth to reply, but before she could, a strange silence descended, as though they had filled their ears with wax. The twilight turned darker. The air grew charged.

"What's that?" she asked, her voice dull and seemingly far away.

She disengaged herself from him and looked westward. Curious, he too looked to the western sky.

Above the city, the sky roiled. There, the twilight of Shade gave way to a deeper darkness. Whorls of black and ochre rippled across the sky and expanded toward them. A multitude of miniature cyclones took shape and ran before the ever-expanding curtain of darkness, an honor guard of destructive force. Some of them were large enough to damage buildings. Pieces of roofs flew skyward and swirled in the turbulent air.

Zossimus knew at once what was occurring. He whispered it aloud, awestruck. "They're taking the city fully into the Plane of Shadow."

The cyclones were planar vortices, present anywhere that two planes violently collided.

At the same moment, he realized that Shade was no longer sinking. Moving the city farther into the Plane of Shadow must have strengthened the Twelve Princes' Shadow Magic. The city had stabilized, at least for a time.

Gleeful, he turned to Jennah to sweep her into an embrace.

The look of horror on her face stopped him cold.

"I won't go," she said, and took a step back from him. "I can't live like that—like this."

She gazed skyward, and made a gesture that took in all of Shade.

The curtain of darkness—colorlessness—drew nearer. A peculiar sonic effect preceded it: not silence, but a dulling of sound. Even the destruction wrought by the planar cyclones sounded muted.

"There's nothing else to be done, Jennah. Dearest."

He moved toward her, one hand outstretched. When she recoiled, he struggled to keep the pain from his face and voice.

"We'll die otherwise. The shadow magic won't keep the city afloat. Jennah—"

Something within her seemed to break. Her eyes grew pained, and when she spoke, her voice was thick with the attempt to control her tears.

"I don't care, Zoss. Don't you understand? I can't live like this anymore. I'd rather die. I stayed for you. Only for you. We've lived in the dark too long. I—"

He felt it at the same moment she did. Pleeancis must have too. From high in the air, the quasit let forth a squeal of joy.

"I can teleport, Boss! I can teleport!"

As though to make his point, the little demon began repeatedly to do just that—disappearing from one location only to instantaneously reappear in a different location a stone's throw away. His high-pitched, delighted laughter filled the sky from ten different directions.

The Weave had returned!

Zossimus's soul refilled. The flow of magic that had ebbed moments before, now re-entered his being like a riptide. He smiled fiercely.

Jennah laughed for joy. She spoke an arcane phrase and alit from the earth to frolic in the air.

"We're saved, Zoss! Oh, thank Tyche!"

She spiraled about in the air, as gleeful as a child at play.

Pleeancis teleported onto Zossimus's shoulder. "I'm back, Boss," he said with a fanged smile, "and better than ever."

Zossimus reached over to scratch the little demon's scaled head. "Indeed, little one. Me too."

Beneath his feet, Shade lurched. The sky grew nearly pitch. Pleeancis yelped and teleported under Zossimus's robes. Zossimus looked skyward. The black, colorless curtain of the Shadow Plane continued to rush toward them. Despite the return of the Weave, the Twelve Princes were still taking Shade to the Plane of Shadow. Perhaps the unexpected return of the Weave had caused the spell causing the move to go awry. The latter seemed more probable to Zossimus, because in only a heartbeat the seething darkness that represented the border between the planes had picked up speed and the planar cyclones had grown larger. Whole buildings flew skyward under the force of the roaring winds.

"Jennah! Pleeancis! Get into the villa, down to the wine cellar, both of you. Now!"

Pleeancis poked his head out of the robes, looked at the seething sky, and teleported out of sight without a word. Jennah still flew high above Zossimus.

"Look, Jennah! Look!" Zossimus pointed to the onrushing planar border. "Come down! It's our only chance!"

"I can't, Zoss," she shouted above the rising wind.

She looked at the onrushing darkness and her face went pale. A gust of wind caught her and sent her spinning toward it. Zossimus's throat grew tight. He mouthed the words to a spell that would grant him flight.

Jennah recovered quickly, however, and steadied herself.

"I love you, Zoss, and I always will, but I can't stay here anymore."

Zoss, unwilling to let her go so easily, took flight toward her. "Wait, Jennah. Please, dearest. Don't leave!"

She backed away from him, as though afraid to let him come too close. Another gust caught her, stronger this time, and sent her careening helplessly through the air.

"Jennah!"

Zoss streaked after her as fast as the spell allowed as she cartwheeled helplessly toward the onrushing darkness. She screamed in terror, a sound audible even above the roar of planar collision.

Before she reached the darkness, a planar cyclone, filled with whirling stone debris from destroyed buildings, caught her up. She vanished into the cylinder of roaring wind. Zossimus screamed her name in vain, circled about the cyclone as near as he dared, trying himself to stay airborne in the whipping winds. The darkness engulfed him, but he did not care. His senses went dull. Sound became less clear, sight less crisp. They had entered the Plane of Shadow. The world was muted, but his pain at losing Jennah was as acute as ever.

With the transition to the Plane of Shadow complete, the planar cyclones dissipated as quickly as they had materialized. Stone and wood crashed to the ground. So too did Jennah. Zossimus flew to her side.

He started to speak her name but couldn't bring himself to utter a sound. Her body, twisted by the terrible force of the cyclone, battered by the swirling debris, lay on the ground like a broken thing. He cradled her in his arms and cried.

Pleeancis teleported beside him. "Belial's balls, Boss! What happ—" He stopped and cocked his head. "Hey, where are we? What happened to her?"

He stuck out a foot to nudge Jennah. Zossimus did not have the energy to rebuke him.

"She looks done for, Boss." Pleeancis smiled broadly, his fangs glistening. "I guess that means it's just you and me now, huh?"

The familiar's satisfied smile pushed Zossimus over the edge. His grief gave way to rage. He clutched for Pleeancis, meaning to strangle the little bastard where he stood.

The quasit backed off, eyes wide. "What'd I say?"

Zossimus's rage left him as quickly as it had flared up. "Leave us, Pleeancis. Now."

The little demon must have heard the steel in his voice, for he backed off still farther, then teleported away.

He teleported back an instant later. "It's Pleeancis *the Mighty*," he said, and teleported away again before Zossimus could kill him where he stood.

Lying atop the tall ebony bookcase, Pleeancis woke with a yawn, stretched his wings, and glanced around the Boss's bedchamber to see . . . the usual. Still drab, still utilitarian. There was a disheveled bed with faded blue sheets and worn pillows, a dark dressing table with a tarnished silver mirror, a sturdy but unremarkable work desk, several old oil lamps, the feeble glow from which barely lifted the colorless gloom of the plane, but no Boss. Pleeancis blew out a sigh.

"Not again."

He knew where he would find the Boss. The same place he always found the Boss when the Boss wasn't eating or sleeping. With *her*. Pleeancis rolled his eyes and flicked his tongue angrily. That human woman was more bothersome dead than alive.

He leaped off the bookcase, beating his wings once to ensure a soft landing, and alit on the carpeted floor. He glanced around furtively to ensure that the Boss was not around. Satisfied that he was alone, Pleeancis rolled around on the carpet. The feel of the luxuriant fibers against his scales made him hiss happily. The Boss would not allow him such pleasures were he present.

Succubus teats! thought Pleeancis. The Boss didn't even allow *himself* any pleasures since she'd died—and that had been years ago!

"Succubus teats," he said to himself, still rolling on the carpet. "That's pretty good."

He hissed with laughter. He prided himself on his creative oaths, an invaluable skill in a familiar that the Boss didn't appreciate. Of course, the Boss didn't appreciate much of anything.

Pleeancis climbed to his feet. He would find the Boss in the workroom, pining over the dead human woman. Pleeancis refused to refer to her by name, even in the privacy of his own mind. She was gone, and Pleeancis was glad of it. She had always gotten in the way of he and the Boss anyway. But the Boss would not let her go. Instead, he had dedicated his life to bringing her back.

Pleeancis considered using his magical ring to teleport to the shop, just to startle the Boss, but decided against it. Since her death, the Boss was easily angered. Best just to walk.

Trooping through the once grand villa, Pleeancis wished—just for a moment—that he was no longer bound to the Boss. The villa had fallen virtually into ruin since the move to this plane, and the Boss did not seem to care. Once it had been meticulously kept, with imported rugs and furniture, and all the finest food and drink for Pleeancis to partake of whenever he wished. Now the divans and chairs were old and ill kept, the rugs frayed, and the cupboards bare. If not for the invisible servant valets, the place would no doubt be knee deep in dust. To Pleeancis, who loved the finer things, the villa was empty of everything important. It looked worn, dull, like the plane itself, like the Boss's spirit since her death.

Heavy with self-pity, Pleeancis dragged his clawed feet along the floor as he walked. He made his way through the maze of bare hallways and down the spiral staircase, until he reached the ornate, slightly ajar double doors of the Boss's workroom. His ears perked up. Within, he could hear the Boss mumbling to himself. Pleeancis could imagine well enough what the Boss was doing—the same thing he had been doing for the past two years: poring over esoteric tomes, crafting this or that obscure magic item, scribing one or another theretofore unknown spell, all in an effort to bring her back. That was all the Boss cared about anymore. Pleeancis didn't get it. Who needed her? They had each other.

Of course, the Boss didn't feel that way. He had put her body in stasis immediately after her death and had tried all the ordinary spells—even called in priests—to bring her back from the dead. Much to Pleeancis's delight, something had interfered, and the spells had failed. The Boss thought the difficulty had to do with the fact that she had died while the city had been in the midst of a planar crossover. Interaction of magic and planar mechanics or something like that.

Pleeancis picked absently at an itch behind his ear while he worked up the patience he would need. The Boss just wasn't the Boss anymore, he thought wistfully.

A shout from within the library nearly scared him out of his scales.

"Boss!" Pleeancis flapped his wings, leaped into the air, pushed through the door and found—

—the Boss, seated at his worktable, barely visible behind a pile of stacked tomes, bubbling beakers, and glowing braziers, laughing. Laughing!

Unsure of what to make of this unexpected mirth, but pleased to see the Boss more like his old self, Pleeancis flitted over to the desk and landed on a stack of tomes.

They smelled like dry leaves. The Boss shot him a grin, his tired gray eyes more alive than they'd been since she had died.

"I found it, Pleeancis. I've finally found a way." He nodded at the single gray wax taper, still cooling in its iron mold, which sat on the table before him.

Before Pleeancis could answer, the Boss rose from his chair, took Pleeancis by his tiny, clawed hands, and danced a little jig. Pleeancis could not help but flash his own fangs in happiness. The Boss was as chipper as an archfiend at a feast of souls.

When the Boss finished the jig, Pleeancis leaned down to look more closely at the candle. Except for some unusual gray and brown whorls that ran through the wax, it was ordinary. The mold too appeared ordinary. Nothing to indicate why it made the Boss so happy. Still, Pleeancis did not want to spoil the mood. Maybe the Boss had gone insane, but the good kind of insane, where he would think everything was great. If so, maybe Pleeancis could convince him to set some decent food at the table for a change. Pleeancis smacked his lips and decided to play along.

"This *is* a nice candle," he said, and tried not to giggle at how silly that sounded.

The Boss patted him on the head, still smiling. "It is that, little one. It's the way to bring Jennah back."

He glanced over at the magically hardened glass case set along the wall that held her perfectly preserved body.

Pleeancis followed his gaze and bit back a snarl.

Jennah—*she*—lay there in her little glass case like some red haired doll with alabaster skin. Pleeancis wished he had gouged out one of her eyes over the years. He could've blamed it on a rat or something.

The Boss walked across the room to the case, his face wistful. He reached out and laid a hand on the glass.

"Soon, dearest," he whispered. "Soon."

Pleeancis ground his fangs and squinted his eyes in anger. Damn it! He did not want her back.

Since the Boss's back was to him, Pleeancis took what vengeance he could—he stuck out his forked tongue and made a terribly obscene gesture taught to him by a dretch demon. She, of course, made no response.

Pleeancis used the claw on his forefinger to pop the candle from its mold. He picked it up and held it in his hands. He wondered if it would hurt him to eat it. After all, no candle, no her. He sniffed it. It smelled loamy, vaguely like tenday old mushrooms. He opened his mouth—

"Pleeancis!"

He dropped it with an alarmed squeak. The Boss rushed over and gingerly picked up the candle, as though he were holding an infant.

"I was just smelling it, Boss." Pleeancis took a step back, prepared to take flight, but the Boss didn't seem angry. Relieved, Pleeancis beat his wings and halted his retreat. "It smells funny. Kinda like the dirt covering dead people. What's in it?"

The Boss secreted the taper in an inner pocket of his black and purple robe.

"Souls," he answered cryptically, his eyes aglitter. "Life-force. Enough to overcome the resistance that has prevented the efficacy of my spells. Enough to ensure that my next attempt will bring my love back."

He looked past Pleeancis to the glass case. Pleeancis rolled his eyes.

He didn't understand the human obsession with *love*. What a bunch of tripe. It was neat that the Boss had put souls in the candle, though. No wonder many of the houseslaves had disappeared recently. Pleeancis giggled, then he remembered that the candle would bring her back. He stopped giggling.

"How can it bring her back, Boss?" he asked and stole a quick, hateful glare in her direction. "It's just a candle. If you couldn't do it by yourself . . . ?" He let the rest of the question go unspoken. If the Boss—one of the more powerful wizards in Shade and one of the preeminent practitioners of shadow magic—couldn't bring her back with his spells, how in the Nine Hells could a candle?

The Boss smiled absently, but his eyes burned with intensity. "This is a special candle, Pleeancis, one that draws upon the Shadow Weave. When its light casts a reflection of a . . ." he stuttered over the next word, as though embarrassed to say it aloud, ". . . a corpse, the reflective surface becomes a portal, a doorway to the place where the soul of that corpse resides." He reached into his pocket, no doubt to touch the candle while he spoke. "The soul can return through that portal, re-inhabit the body, and thereby return to life."

Pleeancis wanted to puke. He glared at her, showed her his fangs.

"Now that the candle is complete," the Boss went on, "the critical factor is the reflective surface."

Pleeancis hung his head and snarled softly. He wanted to hear no more. The familiar kicked petulantly at the books on the table. He and the Boss had spent years alone together. They did not need her. Stupid love.

The Boss continued on, lost in his own world.

"In this case, for the shadow magic to work, the reflective surface must be the dusky scales of a living shadow dragon."

Pleeancis's head snapped up. His wings fluttered with perturbation. "A shadow dragon!"

The Boss merely looked down on him, still smiling, and nodded.

Disbelieving, Pleeancis took wing and fluttered before the Boss's face. He snapped his scaled fingers to bring the Boss back from his madness.

"Shadow dragons are tough, Boss. Tough. And there's only one around here—"

"Ascalagon," the Boss finished for him and nodded again. Unbelievably, he did not look afraid.

"But Ascalagon is ancient," Pleeancis squeaked. "And *big*. Can't you use my scales?" He preened to show his green scales to best advantage.

"No, little one." The Boss patted him on the head. "The fact that Ascalagon is big and ancient is the very point."

"You're going to get help then?"

The Boss shook his head. "No."

Pleeancis's voice rose an octave. His wings beat crazily. "You're going to take on Ascalagon alone?"

The Boss chuckled. "Not alone, little one. With you."

Pleeancis's heart raced. He knew then that the Boss *had* gone insane but not in the good way.

❧ ❧ ❧ ❧ ❧

They had been walking for over an hour. The colorless sky hung above them, a featureless roof of slate. Darkbriar trees surrounded them on all sides like walls of dull, gray bark. Nightmarish versions of a Faerûnian cypress, the branches of the dusky leafed darkbriars hung low enough to brush Zossimus's head. The roots of the great trees twisted their way into the soft, marshy earth like giant worms. The smell of organic decay filled his nostrils. A light mist hung in the fetid air. The dull calls of gray birds and bats mingled with the low buzz of insects. Sound was muted; color was absent. The purple of Zossimus's robes and the green of Pleeancis's scales stood out in this murky, otherwise colorless plane like a giant in a halfling's cottage. Despite the trees, the grass, the insects and birds, the Plane of Shadow felt unreal, like a bard's conception of the realm of the dead. There was motion, true, but no life, no color. The plane was a mirror of the real world, a reflection without substance.

"Smells like a dungheap, Boss," Pleeancis whispered from his perch atop Zossimus's shoulder. Quick as a cat, the quasit plucked a black fly as large as a coin from the air and impaled it between his thumb and foreclaw. "Why would the big bastard lair here? I thought dragons were supposed to be smart."

"Quiet, little one," said Zossimus.

He knew that choosing this dank forest for its lair *was* smart. Zossimus had numerous protective and divinatory spells cast on his person, among them a spell that allowed him to see through magically created obscurement, but even his magically augmented vision could not see behind natural barriers to sight. Between the wall of darkbriars, the ubiquitous fog, and the indistinguishable gray hues of every damned thing, Ascalagon could be watching them even now, and Zossimus would not know it. The thought made his heartbeat accelerate. Once again, he told himself that the dragon would be open to reason. He had brought along an incentive to aid negotiation. Behind him, floating on an invisible platform of magical force, was an open mahogany coffer trimmed in platinum. Within lay a king's ransom in dusky opals and black pearls—his offering to Ascalagon.

Of course, Zossimus had prepared for the possibility that the dragon might prove unreasonable. He had cast so many spells on his person that the turgid air around him fairly sparkled. An enchantment had rendered his skin as hard as granite, to fend off dragon fang and claw. A field of invisible positive energy surrounded him, to protect against Ascalagon's vitality-draining breath weapon, and various additional protective enchantments sheathed him too, all of them attuned to some aspect of Ascalagon's nature. He was as ready as he could be.

A short while later, they reached a circular clearing, perhaps two spear casts in diameter. The short, gray grass looked like an age-faded carpet, devoid of color. The soft glow from the Shadow Plane's feeble stars trickled past the wall of darkbriars to cast the clearing in an even deeper patchwork of shadows—the ideal environment for the dragon.

Zossimus knew that he would have to face Ascalagon on the dragon's terms, which probably meant in the clearing. His spells would expire soon. He needed to persuade Ascalagon to show himself.

With a thought, he stepped from the treeline then propelled the invisible platform forward and rested it in the center of the clearing.

"We wait here," he said to Pleeancis.

The quasit looked around the clearing, his eyes darting from shadow to shadow. "How will the dragon know we're here?"

"I suspect it already knows."

Pleeancis's eyes went wide at that. His tail flicked in agitation. He grabbed Zossimus's robes all the tighter.

They did not have to wait long.

Within a few moments, the bats and insects fell silent, leaving only the whisper of the breeze through the darkbriar leaves. Zossimus steadied himself, thought of Jennah's return, and rehearsed in his mind the power-laden phrase that would trigger the first transmutation he would cast—if necessary.

The shadows on the far side of the clearing grew darker. The soft rustle of leaves bespoke the passage of something within the wood. Even with his vision-augmenting spell in effect, Zossimus still could see nothing but darkness, the impenetrable darkbriar boles, and the brush. Pleeancis clutched so tightly to his shoulder that the quasit's hindclaws sunk into his flesh. He ignored the discomfort and peered into the shadows.

He took a few steps forward, farther out from the safety of the treeline. He knew the colors he wore, even the color of his skin, made him easily sighted. He was the splash of color superimposed against the painting of a forest done only in varying shades of gray.

Still, he saw nothing.

A rich, whispered voice from just behind his ear nearly caused his heart to stop. The exhalation of rancid breath was as strong as a mild breeze.

"Consider well your next words, human. For the moment, I find you more curious than appetizing."

Ascalagon.

Pleeancis let out a squeal and teleported himself within Zossimus's robes. "Unholy crap," he muttered. "Unholy crap."

Zossimus ignored the quasit, steeled his courage, and slowly turned around.

Ascalagon's smoke colored eyes, each the size of a man's fist, bored into him like carpenter's awls. Zossimus could have reached out and touched the dragon's scaled muzzle. The sleek reptilian head was the size of a caravan wagon, the teeth as long as broadswords. Its respiration covered his face in moisture.

Ascalagon's head sat atop a serpentine neck that extended from back within the trees. Within the shadows of the darkbriars, Zossimus could only just make out the huge, powerful body—the great wings that walled off that side of the clearing, the powerful shoulders and forelegs that ended in dagger-length claws, and the semi-translucent black scales, some as large as a kite shield.

Zossimus could not believe that such a gargantuan beast could move so gracefully, so quietly, through the trees. Only the thought of Jennah's return kept him from running for his life. Beneath his robes, he could feel Pleeancis shivering in fear. He managed to keep his voice level.

"Mighty Ascalagon, I stand before you to ask a boon. As a token of my good faith, I have brought you an offering." He gestured to indicate the coffer behind him.

"I have already seen your ridiculous gems, little human, and I will take what I wish when I am through with you."

The head snaked forward and sniffed at Zossimus, the fangs only a handwidth from the arcanist's body. Zossimus remained still but recited in his mind the words to a spell.

"I have seen you too, little demon."

Pleeancis squirmed within Zossimus's robes, poked his head out, and piped indignantly, "*Little* demon? My name is Pleeancis, dragon! Pleeancis the Mighty."

Zossimus winced. The dragon fixed Pleeancis with a baleful gaze, and streamers of black energy snaked from his nostrils.

The quasit let out a yelp, whispered, "Get him, Boss," and teleported into the trees to Zossimus's right, *away* from Ascalagon.

Zossimus took a step backward, to prevent premature contact between the dragon's energy-draining breath and his protective spells. Ascalagon reared back his head and showed his fangs. A smile? If so, it reeked of menace.

"The protective dweomers about you are plain to me, mage. Paltry things."

Zossimus endured the slight and stood his ground. "As I said, noble dragon—"

At the word "noble," the dragon hissed in what could only be laughter. Shadows swirled madly about the great head and neck.

Zossimus continued, "I have journeyed from Shade Enclave to ask—"

Ascalagon ceased laughing. His smoky, bottomless eyes narrowed, and he lurched forward from the treeline. Darkbriars cracked under the strain. Zossimus took a step backward.

From somewhere within the trees to his right, he heard Pleeancis exclaim, "Uh oh."

"Shade?" boomed the dragon, his voice low and dangerous. "A native from the city of invaders dares come to my abode to ask of me a boon? A boon! Insolent cur!" Ascalagon threw back his head and roared. The noise was like a roll of thunder. "Here is your boon, mage!"

Jaws wide, Ascalagon exhaled a cloud of seething black energy. The force was enough to paste Zossimus's robes to his body. Blackness swirled about him, and he flinched. When the dragon's breath met the protective sheath of positive energy about Zossimus's person, the contact caused an explosion of golden light, no doubt the most light this dark place had ever seen. The energies sparked and sizzled, opposites at war. Unharmed, Zossimus took the opportunity to incant the words to one of his two most powerful spells.

"Essare telpim."

The world stopped. Silence descended. Around him, the black death of the dragon's breath weapon hung unmoving in the air, frozen in time. The dragon towered above him, a colossal statue of scaled flesh. A halo of motionless golden motes surrounded Zossimus's body.

Zossimus knew he had less than a minute—relatively speaking. To Ascalagon, it would seem as though no time had passed. Unfortunately, Zossimus's spell did not allow him to affect anything other than himself while it was in effect, so he could not yet use the special candle. Instead, he took the opportunity to better prepare for combat. In the end, he had only one spell that would serve his purpose. It was his most powerful, but he needed to weaken the dragon a bit first.

Moving quickly and deliberately, he stepped out of the cloud of the dragon's breath and backed away, perhaps thirty paces. Far enough, he deemed. With deft hand gestures and a sure voice, he renewed all of his protective spells, and also cast a glamour that created six rapidly shifting phantasms of his person, all shifting about his real body. He hoped they would confuse the dragon and attract some of its attacks.

He was out of time.

Sound returned with the rush of an incoming tide. For a fraction of a heartbeat, Ascalagon appeared confused at Zossimus's abrupt movement.

"Get him, Boss!" Pleeancis screamed from the safety of the trees.

Zossimus pulled a pinch of sulfur from his robe, cast it to the wind, and began to cast.

Ascalagon roared, flapped his great wings once, and leaped forward out of the trees to cover the entire thirty paces as quickly and surprisingly as a bolt of lightning. Taken aback, Zossimus stumbled backward, fumbled with the words to his spell, and lost it from his memory. A wall of scales and shadows surrounded him. Fangs and claws ringed him in, seemed everywhere.

Enraged and roaring, the dragon lashed like a mad thing at Zossimus and the illusionary images. The thrice-damned thing moved like whirlwind! A claw ripped through an image and tore great clods of sod from the earth. A backhand lash sent another image to oblivion. Another claw attack, another image. Fangs descended, snapping. Zossimus leaped sidewise and the jaws annihilated another image. Even as he tried to create some distance between himself and the dragon, a claw caught Zossimus full in the chest.

Only his protective spell saved his life. With skin as hard as stone, the eviscerating claw strike only tore a deep, but non-lethal gash down his torso. The impact, however, sent him flying through the air toward the trees, where he crashed into the brush with a groan.

Pleeancis shouted from across the clearing. "Oh, you'll swim up to your snout in Hell's turdpool for that one, dragon."

Zossimus clambered to his feet and began again to cast. He had only two images remaining.

Ascalagon was upon him again. Trees cracked under the dragon's weight as he crashed into the woods. A shower of leaves and limbs fell to earth. Fangs and claws lashed. Zossimus dodged backward and managed to maintain his concentration, determined this time to complete a spell.

With the speed of a striking asp, the dragon's gaping jaws shot earthward, directly at the real Zossimus. He backed off as abruptly as his casting allowed, but he was too slow. The great jaws closed on him and jerked him into the air. Growling, the dragon tossed his head back and forth, trying to devour the human. The powerful teeth and jaws ground against Zossimus's magically hardened skin. Despite the protection of the spell, the teeth pierced his body all over. Warm blood bathed him; pain wracked him. The dragon champed down, trying to crack him open like a stubborn walnut. Bones snapped under the pressure. In agony, Zossimus found himself staring down into the dark tunnel of the dragon's gullet, but he refused to lose his concentration. From somewhere, he could hear Pleeancis's terrified shouts.

"Boss! *Boss!*"

Through the pain, Zossimus managed to mouth the final word to his spell.

"Velendere!"

A glowing, pea-sized ball shot from Zossimus's outstretched hand, flew down the dragon's throat, and exploded into a cloud of fire. Flame and heat rushed back up Ascalagon's throat to envelop Zossimus, but his protective spells shielded him from the worst of it. Not so the dragon. Ascalagon leaped a spearcast into the air, tossing his head madly, roaring in pain, coughing fire. Zossimus flew smoking from his jaws and crashed amongst the trees.

With several fractured bones, Zossimus quickly swallowed a healing potion. Bones and skin painfully recombined. He regained his feet to see the dragon writhing in the clearing, his wings and front legs wrapped around his stomach like a child who ate too many sweetmeats. Smoke streamed from his nostrils and mouth.

Zossimus called to mind the spell he would use to immobilize Ascalagon. The instant he began to mouth the words, Ascalagon focused his eyes on him and rolled to his feet.

"You will die for this, mageling," he said, voice gravelly.

Zossimus paid no heed to the dragon's words. Either his spell would work or it wouldn't. He traced the magical symbols in the air before his face as he incanted the final phrase.

Ascalagon rushed him with a hoarse roar, and closed the distance with a mere two strides.

Zossimus completed the spell, felt his magically augmented will meet with that of the dragon's—and dominate it.

"Stop!" he ordered.

Ascalagon halted in mid-stride.

Zossimus let out a sigh of relief. He could feel Ascalagon fighting against the chains of will that held him immobile, but by the gods Zossimus had done it!

"Remain perfectly still," he ordered, and Ascalagon did, though the smoky eyes seethed with anger.

Pleeancis streaked out of the trees. "Boss! Boss! You did it!" The quasit flitted crazily about him, grinning. "I thought you were a goner for sure when he spit you out."

"Pleeancis, go retrieve Jennah."

"What? Oh." The quasit's grin vanished, and his wings drooped slightly. "Sure, Boss. Just one thing first."

The quasit flew up eye to eye with the dragon.

"Pleeancis *the Mighty*, you lizard! Remember that."

For punctuation, Pleeancis pinched Ascalagon's nostril

with his tiny hand. The dragon, of course, could make no response, but Zossimus felt him fighting against the mental bonds. He did not have much time before the spell would expire.

"Now, Pleeancis."

"Right Boss."

The quasit made an obscene gesture at the dragon and teleported away.

Zossimus spoke a single, power-laden word. The magical candle appeared in his hand. Soon he would hold Jennah in his arms once more.

◈ ◈ ◈ ◈ ◈

Zossimus felt as light as he had in years, despite the ongoing struggle of wills with Ascalagon. Jennah's body lay on a bed of gray grass and leaves before the immobilized dragon, awaiting only the candle's light to cast her reflection on Ascalagon's chest scales. Soon he and his beloved would be together again.

Pleeancis, sulking, refused to speak to Zossimus. Instead, the quasit fluttered around the dragon's head and issued half-hearted insults.

Heart racing, Zossimus positioned himself behind Jennah's body and whispered a word. A stream of flame issued from his finger. He touched it to the candle's wick and held the lit taper before Jennah's body.

The candle flared, burned a quarter of the way down, and sent melted wax pouring over Zossimus's hand. He grimaced but endured the pain. The light of the candle reflected the light in his soul. Today, his life would start over again.

The candle's flame burned brighter still, and chased the dreariness of the plane. A doorway sized area of Ascalagon's scales glittered and shimmered in the glow. Zossimus saw his own reflection, and gave a start. He had not known how pale he looked, how ill kept. He put those thoughts aside.

The reflection of Jennah's body also took shape in the scales. The image roiled, grew brighter, flared.

A scene of beauty materialized. Zossimus gasped at the wave of colors. Colors! Tall grass, dotted with red, yellow, and purple flowers. Zossimus could actually smell their fragrance; could feel the clean breeze on his face. And the sun! The sun! He had not seen sunlight in over a decade. It looked like gold spilling from the sky. Tears welled in his eyes at the sight. The realm of the dead was not colorless! It was beautiful, rich. It was his life in this shadow realm that was colorless. He had lived in the dark so long he had forgotten that.

Men, women, and even a few children walked and played contentedly amidst the waving grass. Among them, he saw Jennah.

He had forgotten too how radiant her hair looked in the sunlight. Dressed in a white gown and smiling, she looked as beautiful as a sunset over a calm sea. Tears flowed freely down his face. He leaned forward, reached his hand through the portal, and called to her.

"Jennah! Jennah!"

She gave a start, looked around in surprise. "Zoss? Is that you?"

"Yes, dearest! Yes. It's me. I'm here. Here." He waved his hand.

She looked in his direction, must have spotted him through the portal on that side, and ran toward him. She reached out to hold his hand. Her spiritual flesh passed through his hand.

"I've come to bring you home, dearest. Come through."

Her smile faded and she backed off a step.

"Zoss, I am home." She smiled and twirled about, arms above her head. "Look at the sun, Zoss. The flowers." She met his gaze through the portal, her eyes troubled but determined. "It's dark where you are. I'm not coming back."

The finality in her voice hit Zoss like a punch in the stomach. He could not breathe. He knew then that the resistance to his prior attempts to bring her back from the dead had not been the result of planar mechanics; it had been her. She had not wanted to come back.

"But . . ."

"I'm sorry, Zoss," she said softly, and brushed his fingers. "I miss you, but I can't live in the dark. You'll come here in your time. I love you still."

She smiled softly, but turned to leave.

Despite it all, Zossimus could not blame her. Seeing the sun, seeing the smiling faces of the spirits, the flowers, all of it reminded him of how empty his life had become. How dark, how muted, how *colorless*. He could not ask her to live in shadows. She belonged in the light.

As she walked away, he made up his mind. Instead of him bringing her back to life, she would bring him back.

"Wait, Jennah!"

She turned. "Zoss, I can't—"

"I know. I'm coming with you."

With a mental command, he released Ascalagon from the spell.

The dragon roared with pent up rage. Pleeancis shrieked. Ascalagon's head snapped down, jaws wide.

The instant Ascalagon's fangs began to rend his flesh, Zossimus's spirit departed his body and darted through the closing portal. When he reached the other side, the sun stung his eyes, but he smiled nevertheless. Now a spirit himself, he took Jennah in his arms and threw her into the air. She laughed like a schoolgirl.

They kissed, then ran off amidst the flowers, under the golden light of the sun.

The dragon must have heard Pleeancis's scream as it devoured the Boss. Ascalagon snapped his head in Pleeancis's direction. Bloody tatters of the Boss's body leaked from between his fangs.

Pleeancis gave the dragon one final obscene gesture and teleported away.

Back at the manor, the quasit stood in the Boss's bedroom and kicked at the ground.

"Damnable lizard. I should've stabbed you in both eyes."

But he hadn't, and now the Boss was gone. The manor felt emptier than ever. Pleeancis thought of all the good times he had once had with the Boss. The memories made his stomach feel funny. Tight. His head hurt too, and . . . what was this wetness on his face?

"Stupid love," he said, and curled up on the carpet to weep.

DARKSWORD

Troy Denning

20 Flamerule, the Year of the Moat (1269 DR)
Lost on the Road Across the Bottomless Bogs

Out of the fog ahead came mist-muffled voices,
many of them and not far off, mothers singing,
children crying, fathers shouting . . . oxen bel-
lowing, hoarse and weary. Melegaunt Tanthul
continued walking as before—which was to say
very carefully—along the road of split logs,
which bobbed on the spongy peat with every step
he took. Visibility was twenty paces at best, the
road a brownish ribbon zigzagging off into a
cloud of pearly white. Not for the first time, he
wished he had taken the other fork at the base of
Deadman Pass. Surely he was still in Vaasa, but
whether he was traveling toward the treasure
he sought or away from it was anyone's guess.

The voices grew steadily louder and more distinct, until the hazy outline of the road ahead

abruptly dissolved into nothingness. Strewn along a narrow band at the end of the road were a handful of head-shaped spheres, some perched atop a set of human shoulders with arms splayed wide to spread their weight. Farther back, two sets of nebulous oxen horns rose out of the peat, the blocky silhouette of a fog-shrouded cargo wagon sitting on the surface behind them.

Melegaunt pulled his heavy rucksack off his back and continued up the road, already fishing for the line with which he strung his rain tarp at night. As he drew nearer, the head-shaped blobs seemed to sprout beards and wild manes of unkempt hair. He began to make out hooked noses and deep-set eyes, then one of the heads shouted out, and with a terrible slurping sound, sank beneath the peat. This cry was echoed by a chorus of frightened wails deeper in the fog, prompting the nearest of the remaining heads to crane around and bark something in the guttural Vaasan dialect. The voices fell immediately silent, and the head turned back toward Melegaunt.

"T-traveler, you would do well to s-stop there," the Vaasan said, the frigid bog mud causing him to stutter and slur his words. "The l-logs here are rotted through."

"My thanks for the warning." Still fifteen paces from the end of the road, Melegaunt stopped and held up the small coil of line he had pulled from his rucksack. "My rope won't reach so far. I fear you have spoiled your own rescue."

The Vaasan tipped his head a little to the side. "I think our chances b-better with you out there, instead of in here with us."

"Perhaps so," Melegaunt allowed.

He peered into the fog beyond the Vaasan's tribe, trying in vain to see where the road started again. As annoying as it was in the first place not to know where he was going, the possibility of being forced to turn back before he found out absolutely vexed him.

"Where does this road lead? To Delhalls or Moorstown?"

"Where d-does the road lead?" the Vaasan stammered, his voice sharp with disbelief and anger. "What about my people? After I saved you, y-you are not going to help us?"

"Of course I'm going to help you. I'll do everything I can," Melegaunt said. Somewhere deeper in the fog, another Vaasan screamed and sank beneath the bog with a cold slurp. "You might, uh, disappear before I pull you free. If that happens, I'd still like to know where this road leads."

"If that happens, the knowledge w-will do you no good," the Vaasan growled. "Your only hope of reaching your d-destination is to rescue my clan, so that we can guide you wherever you are going."

"Something is dragging your tribe under one-by-one and you are trifling over details?" Melegaunt demanded. He pulled his black dagger, then dropped to his hands and knees and began to probe the logs ahead for rot. "This is no time to negotiate. I won't abandon you."

"Then your patience will be rewarded," the Vaasan said firmly.

Melegaunt looked up, his brow furrowed into a deliberate scowl. "Am I to understand you don't trust me?"

"I trust you to try harder if you have n-need of us."

"An answer as slippery as the bog in which you are mired," Melegaunt snapped. "If I am successful, you will have no need of *me*. How can I trust you to guide me then?"

"You have the word of Bodvar, leader of the Moor Eagle Clan," the Vaasan said. "That is all the trust you need."

"Trust has different meaning for outsiders than for Vaasans, I see," Melegaunt grumbled, "but I warn you, if you go back on your promise. . . ."

"You have nothing to fear on that account," Bodvar said. "You have but to keep yours, and I will keep mine."

"I have heard that before," Melegaunt muttered, "far too many times."

Despite his complaint, Melegaunt continued to advance up the road, probing ahead for rotten logs. By all accounts, the Vaasans had been a harsh but honest people until the fabled bloodstone mines of Delhalls and Talagbar were rediscovered and the outside world intruded to teach them the value of duplicity and fraud. Now, save for a few villages like Moortown where a man's word was rumored to be more precious than his life, they were said to be as corrupt and sly as everyone else in this world of liars and cheats.

Melegaunt was beginning to doubt Bodvar's story about the rot when his dagger finally found soft wood. He pressed harder, and the entire log disintegrated, crumbling into red dust before his eyes. Then the one beneath his hands grew spongy, prompting him to push back onto his haunches. The log beneath his knees began to soften as well, and a muddy dome of peat welled up not three feet in front of him, a long line of dorsal barbs breaking the surface as the spine of some huge, eel-shaped creature rolled past.

Melegaunt dropped onto his seat and pushed away, scrambling backward as fast as he could crawl. By the time the wood ceased growing soft, he was five paces farther from Bodvar, distant enough that he could no longer make out even the shape of the Vaasans' heads.

Another clansman screamed, then slipped beneath the bog with a muffled slurp.

"Traveler, are you still there?" Bodvar called.

"For now," Melegaunt replied. He stood and backed away another couple of paces. "Something came after me."

"One of the bog people," Bodvar said. "They are attracted by vibration."

"Vibration?" Melegaunt echoed. "Like talking?"

"Like talking," Bodvar confirmed. "But do not worry about me. My armor muffles the sound—it is made of dragon scales."

"All the same, rest quiet for a while." Melegaunt's opinion of the Vaasan was rising—and more because of the risk he was taking for his tribe than because he wore dragon-scale armor. "I'll get you out. I promise."

"A man should not promise what he cannot be certain of delivering, Traveler," Bodvar said, "but I do trust you to do your utmost."

Melegaunt assured the Vaasan he would, then retreated a few more paces up the road and held his hand out over the road edge. There was not even a hint of shadow. Melegaunt's magic would be at its weakest, and he had already seen enough of his foe's power to know it would be folly to duel him at less than full strength— even in this world of decay and rebirth, wood simply did not rot as fast as had those logs.

Doing his best to ignore the occasional screams that rolled out of the fog, Melegaunt removed a handful of strands of shadowsilk from his cloak pocket and twisted them into a tightly-wound skein. In a century-and-a-half of reconnoitering Toril, he had yet to risk revealing himself by using such powerful shadow magic where others might see—but never before had he been given reason to think his long quest might be nearing its culmination. This Bodvar was a brave one, and that was the first quality. He was also wary, neither giving oaths nor taking them lightly, and that was the second. Whether he was also the third remained to be seen—and it soon would, if matters went as expected.

Once Melegaunt had twisted the shadowsilk into a tightly wound skein, he uttered a few words in ancient Netherese and felt a surge of cold energy rising through his feet into his body. Unlike most wizards in Faerûn who extracted their magic from the goddess Mystra's all-encompassing Weave, Melegaunt drew his magic from the enigmatic Shadow Weave. As universal as the Weave itself, the Shadow Weave was less known and far more powerful, if only because the cloaked goddess—she who must never be named—kept it uncompromisingly secret and maddened anyone who revealed its existence.

When he was sufficiently imbued with the Shadow Weave's cold magic, Melegaunt tossed the skein of shadowsilk out over the bog and made a twirling motion with his fingers. The cord began to unwind but sank into the peat before it finished and continued to spin, drawing long tendrils of fog after it.

An oxen bellowed in alarm, then there was a huge glugging sound followed by the crackle of splintering wood and the shrieks of terrified women and children.

"T-t-traveler?" called Bodvar, sounding weaker and colder than before. "H-have you left us?"

"Stay quiet, Vaasan, or there will be no reason for me to stay," Melegaunt shouted back. "I am working as fast as I can."

Judging by the restless voices that followed, the clan of the Moor Eagle took little comfort from this assurance. Melegaunt urged them again to be patient. While he waited for his first spell to do its work, he prepared himself for battle, girding himself with magic armor and shields of spell-turning, readying power word attacks and casting enchantments that would allow him to walk on mud or swim through it with equal ease. By the time he finished, his spell had thinned the fog enough that he could see a long line of mired Vaasan men and overloaded wagons curving away toward the jagged gray wall of a distant mountain range. The end of the column was perhaps two hundred paces distant, and fifty paces beyond that, he could see the brownish ribbon of logs where the road resumed again.

Instead of looking impressed or grateful, Bodvar and

his equally bearded warriors were all searching the blue sky with expressions of alarmed expectation. Those with free sword arms were holding their weapons ready, while on the wagons, women and old men were stringing long-bows and raising spears. Melegaunt glanced around the heavens and found nothing except snow clouds—then heard two loud slurping sounds as another pair of warriors were drawn down into the muck.

He stepped to the end of the log road and held his arm out. Finding that there was now enough light to cast a shadow, he swung his arm around until the dark line pointed at Bodvar. Though a good twenty paces remained between them, the fog was so thin now that Melegaunt could see that with sapphire-blue eyes and hair as red as bloodstone, Bodvar was both handsome and fair-haired by Vaasan standards.

"You caused this clearing, Traveler?" Bodvar asked.

Melegaunt nodded then lied, "I like to see what I'm fighting." Actually, he was more comfortable fighting in darkness than light, but if he could keep the Vaasans from pondering the nature of his magic, there was a good chance they would be unfamiliar enough with outsider spells to think he was using normal magic. "The battle goes faster."

"Indeed," Bodvar answered. "Let us hope not too fast. There is a reason the Mountainshadow Bog is crossed only in thick fog."

Melegaunt frowned. "That would be?"

"On its way."

Bodvar raised his hand—the one that was not trapped in the bog—and pointed west. The nearby peaks had grown distinct enough that they resembled a line of snow-capped fangs, and curving down from their summits, Melegaunt saw several lines of pale specks.

"Griffins?" he asked. "Or wyverns?"

"You will wish."

"Well, as long as they're not dragons," Melegaunt said. "Anything else, I can handle."

"You have a high opinion of yourself, Traveler."

"As shall you," Melegaunt replied.

With that, he spoke a few words of magic, and the shadow he had lain across the bog expanded to the width of a comfortable walking trail. Melegaunt stepped off the logs, and continuing to hold his arm out, followed the shadow forward. To prevent the path from vanishing as he moved forward, he had to utter a spell of permanency—and that was when the sodden peat let out an explosive glub beside him.

Melegaunt turned to see a pair webbed hands clutching the edge of his shadow-walk, and between them was a slimy reptilian head shooting up to attack. The face itself was rather broad and froglike, save that its dead black eyes were fixed on Melegaunt's leg and its lips were drawn back to reveal a mouthful of needle-sharp fangs. He lowered a hand and spoke a magic power word, unleashing a cold black bolt that drilled a fist-sized hole through the thing's head. The hands opened, and its lifeless body slipped back into the sodden peat.

"What magic is that?" Bodvar gasped, watching from a few steps ahead.

"Southern magic," Melegaunt lied. He stopped at the Vaasan's side and stooped down, offering his hand. "You wouldn't know it."

Bodvar was not quick to reach for the shadow wizard's swarthy arm. "Who would?" he demanded. "We are not so backward here in Vaasa as you may think. We know about the dark magic of Thay."

Melegaunt had to laugh. "You have no idea." He uttered a quick spell, and tentacles of darkness shot from his fingertips to entwine the Vaasan's wrist. "Now come out of there. You made a bargain."

Melegaunt stood and drew the tentacles back into his

fingers, pulling Bodvar's arm along. A muffled pop sounded from somewhere below the peat, and the Vaasan screamed. Though Melegaunt was fairly certain he had just separated the chieftain's shoulder, he continued to pull—pulled harder, in fact. As loud as Bodvar had screamed, the bog people would be after him like a school of snagglesnouts after a waterstrider.

The Vaasan did not budge, and though Melegaunt had the strength to pull the arm off, that would not free Bodvar of the sodden peat's cold clutch. He stopped pulling. Bodvar continued to groan—though less loudly than he had screamed before—and a long ridge of upwelling peat began to snake its way toward the chieftain.

Melegaunt pointed a finger at the head of the ridge and uttered a magic syllable, and a ray of black shadow shot down through the peat. The creature was too deep to see whether the attack hit home, but the ridge stopped advancing in Bodvar's direction.

"Be quiet," Melegaunt urged. "See if you can slip free of your boots and trousers."

Bodvar stopped groaning long enough to cast a sidelong glance at Melegaunt. "My trousers? My *dragon-scale* trousers?"

"You must break the suction," Melegaunt explained. "It is your trousers or your life."

Bodvar sighed but struggled to move his free hand under the peat.

"Can you reach them?" Melegaunt asked.

"No, I can't—" Bodvar's eyes suddenly went wide, then he began to yell, "Pull! *Pull!*"

Melegaunt felt the Vaasan being dragged downward and began to haul in the opposite direction. Bodvar howled in pain and rage, his body squirming and thrashing as he struggled to free himself. There was a muffled crunch that sounded something like a breaking bone, then Bodvar finally came free, rising out of the bog with no boots or pants, but a dagger in hand and his sword belt looped over his elbow.

Melegaunt glimpsed a slimy figure slipping down the hole with the Vaasan's trousers trailing from one corner of its smiling mouth, then the bog closed in and concealed it from view. Melegaunt cast a shadow bolt after it, but it was impossible to say whether the spell hit its target or vanished into the bottomless depths without striking anything.

"Hell-cursed mudbreather!" Bodvar swore. "Look what it did to my sword!"

Melegaunt lowered the Vaasan to the shadow-walk, then looked over to find the man naked from the waist down and one arm sagging askew from the shoulder socket, holding the flopping scabbard of a badly shattered sword in his good hand.

"How am I to fight with this?"

"Fight? In your condition?"

Melegaunt glanced toward the mountains and saw that the distant specks had now become **V**-shaped lines, all angling toward the bog where the largest part of the Moor Eagle clan was still trapped. He opened his cloak and pulled his own sword, a slender blade of what looked like black glass, from its scabbard.

"Use this," Melegaunt said, "but with a light hand. It will cut much better than that iron bar you're accustomed to."

Bodvar barely glanced at the weapon. "I'll use my dagger. That thing'll break the first time—"

"Not likely." Melegaunt brought his sword down across Bodvar's dagger and sliced through the blade as though it were made of soft wood instead of cold-forged iron, then flicked the stump out of the grasp of the astonished Vaasan and replaced it with the hilt of his own weapon. "Be careful not to take off your foot."

Bodvar closed his sagging jaw, and one arm still hanging limply at his side, stepped past Melegaunt and lopped the heads off two bog people emerging from the peat behind him.

"It'll do," he said. Despite the obvious pain from his separated shoulder, the Vaasan did not even clench his teeth as he spoke. "My thanks for the loan."

"Consider it a gift," Melegaunt replied, turning back to the rest of the clan. "I use it so seldom."

To his dismay, the bog people had been far from idle while he was rescuing Bodvar. Half the warriors who had been mired when he arrived had already vanished beneath the surface, while the women and old men were struggling to keep dozens of bog people from clambering onto the cargo wagons with the clan's sobbing children. Melegaunt pulled a handful of shadowsilk from his cloak and flung it in the direction of the wagons, then spread his fingers and waggled them in a raining motion. A dark pall fell over the six closest wagons, and everyone it touched—Vaasans and bog people alike—fell instantly asleep.

"How did you do that?" Bodvar demanded. "Sleep magic doesn't work against the bog people!"

"Clearly, you have been misinformed." Melegaunt held his arm out toward the nearest wagon, extending the shadow-walk to within three paces of the driver's bench. "Do you think . . ."

Bodvar was already sprinting down the shadow-walk, borrowed sword in hand. When he reached the end, he launched himself into a wild leap over the horns of a mired ox, bounding off its half-submerged shoulders, and came down on the seat between the slumbering driver and the old man slumped beside her. Despite Melegaunt's warning to handle the weapon lightly, he set to work on the sleeping bog people with an ardor that left little doubt about the primitive state of Vaasan weaponsmithing.

Melegaunt saw him cut two enemies cleanly apart across the torso and cleave through three of the wagon's sideboards before he could no longer bear to watch and turned his attention to the mired warriors.

The nearest vanished beneath the surface as Melegaunt approached, and two more cried out in alarm. Seeing he had no hope of rescuing even a dozen of the remaining warriors, he tossed his tarp line onto the surface and uttered a long spell. The far end raised itself out of the peat, and the black rope began to slither forward. He pointed at the nearest of the warriors, and the line angled in the man's direction.

"As the rope comes by—"

That was all Melegaunt needed to say. The first warrior snatched the line, and slipping free of his trousers, allowed it to pull him free. He slid across the slippery surface for three paces, then rolled onto his back and began to hack at something beneath the surface with his sword. Seeing that he had at least a reasonable chance of defending himself, Melegaunt directed the rope to the next warrior in line, who also came free without his pants or boots, and there were two Vaasans slashing at their unseen pursuer.

They seemed to get it after a dozen yards, but by then Melegaunt had three more warriors on the line, and two of them were being trailed by the tell-tale rise of a bog person traveling just beneath the surface. He summoned the rope over to his shadow-walk and used his last shadow bolt to kill one of their pursuers, and the warriors themselves took care of the last one before bounding off after Bodvar to help defend the wagons.

Melegaunt glanced toward the mountains. To his alarm, the distant fliers were now so close that he could make out not only the white bodies hanging beneath their wings, but their bandy legs and curved swords as well. Whatever the creatures were—and he had yet to see their like in a century and a half of wandering this world—they were as fast as baatezu. He only hoped they were not as adept as the pit fiends at defeating shadow magic.

Melegaunt sent the rescue rope out again and managed to pull in six more warriors before the bog people claimed the rest. Though he was not happy to fail so many—the number had to be nearly twenty—the Vaasans took their losses in stride, pausing only to grunt a half-understood word of thanks before rushing back to join Bodvar and their fellows in defending the women and children.

Seeing there was no more to be done, Melegaunt retrieved his tarp line and turned toward the mired wagons. With the half-naked warriors he had rescued rushing back to help, the women and old men were holding the bog people at bay with surprising displays of swordsmanship and bravery. No matter how well they fought, though, it was clear that the younger children and older clansmen lacked the agility to leap from wagon to wagon—especially over the heads of panicked oxen—as the warriors were doing.

Melegaunt rushed alongside the caravan, laying his shadow-walk close enough that the trapped Vaasans could jump from their wagons onto the path behind him. The bog people redoubled their attacks, glugging up alongside the walk in a near-solid wall. But all of Bodvar's clansmen were as well-trained and disciplined as his warriors, and they repelled the attacks easily. Though Melegaunt failed to understand why the bog people did not use their rotting magic on the wagons themselves, he was relieved that they were not. Perhaps their magic-user had run out of spells, or maybe the enchantment took too long to cast.

With their panicked masters rushing past, the mired oxen bellowed for help that would never come. Given time, Melegaunt could certainly have freed the creatures and saved the cargo in their wagons, but as things were, he would be doing well to lose no more of their masters. As he neared the end of the caravan, he was astonished to see that the bog people had not pulled even one of the beasts from its yoke. Whatever their reason for attacking the Moor Eagles, it had less to do with hunger than wanting to wipe out the tribe.

Melegaunt was twenty paces past the last mired wagon when a trio of bog people emerged before him, snatching at his legs with their webbed hands. He drilled the middle one with a black shadow bolt, then heard hooked finger-talons clattering off his spell-armor as the other two attempted to slash his legs from beneath him. He brought his boot heel down a sloping forehead and heard a loud pop as the skull caved in, then caught his other attacker by the arm and jerked it out of the peat. Save that the bog-man was covered in slimy brown scales and had a flat, lobsterlike tail in place of legs and feet, it looked more or less humanoid, with powerfully-built shoulders and a navel that suggested it was born rather than hatched.

It slashed at Melegaunt with its free hand several times. When its claws continued to bounce harmlessly off the wizard's shadow armor, it gave up and opened its mouth, attacking with a long, barb-tipped tongue so fast Melegaunt barely had time to tip his head aside and save his eye. He caught the tongue as it shot back toward the creature's mouth, then whirled around to find Bodvar and the rest of the Vaasans staring at him with expressions that were equal part awe and terror.

"Don't just stand there," Melegaunt ordered, "kill it!"

Only Bodvar had possession enough of his wits to obey, slashing the thing across the waist so hard that his borrowed sword came a hair's breadth from opening Melegaunt's ample belly as well. Eyeing the chieftain sidelong, Melegaunt tossed aside the lifeless torso, then pointed at a long line of bog people rising out of the peat beside the gape-mouthed Vaasans.

"Lift your jaws and see to your enemies!"

Without waiting to see whether they obeyed, he turned and extended the shadow-walk the rest of the way to the logs, then led the way to the relatively solid footing of the road. The bog people had no choice but to give up their attack, for all the Vaasans had to do to be safe was retreat to the middle of the road where they could not be reached.

The creatures flying in from the mountains were another matter. Only a few hundred yards distant, they were close enough that Melegaunt could make out scaly white bodies with long, pointed tails and craggy saurian heads with long snouts, swept-back horns, and huge yellow eyes. One of the creatures flung something in their direction and began to make spell gestures.

Melegaunt flattened a ball of shadowsilk between his palms, then flung it toward the approaching dragonmen and uttered a few words in ancient Netherese. A hazy disk of darkness appeared between the two groups and began to bleed black tendrils of shadow into the sky, but Melegaunt had not been quick enough to raise his spell shield. He felt a familiar softening underfoot, and the Vaasans cried out and began to stampede up the road. It was exactly the wrong thing to do. The rotting logs came apart all the faster, plunging the entire tribe to their knees in sodden peat.

In an attempt to spread their weight and slow their descent, they immediately threw themselves to their bellies and splayed their arms. Still standing atop the peat by virtue of the spells he had cast before the battle, Melegaunt cursed and laid his shadow-walk again, then turned to meet the dragonmen.

They were nowhere to be seen, at least not near his

spell shield. Pulling another strand of shadowsilk from his pocket, Melegaunt pivoted in a slow circle and—as expected—found them diving out of the sun. Melegaunt allowed himself a tight smile. They were wise to respect his abilities—much wiser, in that regard, than had been better-known foes in the south. He tossed his shadowsilk into the sky and uttered the incantation of one of his more potent spells.

That whole quarter of the sky broke into a shower of shadowy tears. Instead of rolling off when they fell on a body, however, these drops clung to whatever they touched, stretching into long threads of sticky black fiber. Within moments, the entire column of dragonmen had become swaddled in gummy balls of darkness and was plunging headlong into the bog. Melegaunt watched long enough to be certain that none of the fliers would escape, then turned to find the Moor Eagles rushing onto the log road behind him.

They were glancing at him over their shoulders, making signs of warding that might have kept a demon at bay, but that only made Melegaunt feel lonely and unappreciated. Stifling bitter laughter, he walked across the bog to where Bodvar and three more brave warriors stood waiting for him at the edge of the road.

"I'm sorry for your losses, Bodvar," he said. "I might have saved more, but there was much you didn't tell me."

"And much you didn't tell us," Bodvar replied. He laid the hilt of Melegaunt's black sword across his arm and offered it to the wizard. "My thanks."

Melegaunt waved him off. "Keep it. As I said, I seldom use it anymore."

"I know what you said," Bodvar replied, "but only a fool takes gifts from a devil."

"Devil?" Melegaunt snapped, still not taking his sword. "Is that how you repay my kindness? With insults?"

"What is true is no insult," Bodvar said. "We saw the things you did."

"It was only magic," Melegaunt protested. "Southern magic. If you have not seen its like before. . . ."

"Now it is you who are insulting us." Bodvar continued to offer the sword. "In Vaasa, we are backward in many things—but wisdom is no longer one of them."

Melegaunt started to repeat his protests, then realized he would only anger Bodvar by insisting on the lie—and revealing the truth about the Shadow Weave was, of course, out of the question. If he were lucky enough to avoid being struck dead on the spot, he would lose forever the dark power that had so impressed the Vaasans.

When Melegaunt made no further attempts to argue, Bodvar said, "We will keep the bargain we made." He tipped his chin toward the three warriors with him. "These are the guides I promised. They will take you wherever you wish to go in Vaasa."

Melegaunt started to say that he no longer needed them—then thought better of it and smiled. "*Anywhere?*"

Bodvar looked uncomfortable, but nodded. "That was our bargain."

"Good. Then I want them to take me wherever the Moor Eagles are going." Melegaunt took his sword back. "And no tricks, Bodvar. I'm sure we both know what happens to those who play false with devils—don't we?"

Higharvestide, the Year of the Moat
In the Shadows of the Peaks of the Dragonmen

Bodvar came to the island, as Melegaunt had known he would, late in the day, when the sun was sinking low over the Peaks of the Dragonmen and the shadows of the mountains lay long upon the cold bog. What the wizard had not known was that the chieftain would bring his wife, a young beauty with hair the color of night and eyes as blue as a clear sky. She seemed a little thicker around the middle than the last time Melegaunt had seen her, though it was always hard to tell with Vaasan women—their shape tended to vanish beneath all the furs they wore.

Melegaunt watched them pick their way across his zigzagging boulder-walk until a metallic sizzle behind him demanded his attention. He checked the sky to be certain there were no white-scaled fliers diving down to trouble them, then donned a huge leather mitt and pulled a long narrow mold from the oven he had kept blazing for three days. In the mold, floating on a bed of liquid tin, lay a sword similar to the one he had offered Bodvar all those tendays ago—save that this one was still molten and glowing white hot.

Melegaunt placed the sword on a bed of ice—freezes came early to this part of the world—then waited for the mold to cool. When he was sure the cold would draw the tempering elements down to the underside, he began to lay fibers of shadowsilk on the molten glass, taking care to arrange them first lengthwise, then diagonally in both directions, then lengthwise again so the weapon would have strength and resilience in all directions. Finally, he used his dagger to open another cut on his arm, dripping his warm blood into the mixture and quietly whispering the ancient words that gave the blade its magic thirst.

By the time that was finished, the sword had hardened enough that he could lift it from its mold and plunge it into a vat of slushy water, placed at just the right distance from the furnace to keep it that way. Once the heat had melted all of the slush, Melegaunt removed the sword, then placed it on its bed of hot tin with the opposite side down and returned the mold to the oven again. Such was the art of the shadow blade, heating and cooling a thousand times over, tinting them with shadowsilk until the glass could finally hold no more and began to shed fibers like an unbrushed dog.

A soft boot scuffed the stone at the edge of Melegaunt's work site, then Bodvar called, "I see you are still here, Dark Devil."

"You can see that by the smoke of my furnaces." Melegaunt pulled the sleeve of his cloak down to hide the cuts on his arm, then turned to glower at the chieftain. "Come for a sword, have you?"

"Hardly." Bodvar cast an uneasy glance at the nineteen weapons racked at the edge of the work site. Though all were completed and honed to a razor edge, they were paler than Melegaunt's sword, with a crystal translucence that still showed the lay of the shadow fibers embedded in the glass. "You are wasting your time on that account."

"Am I?" Melegaunt smirked knowingly. "Well, they will be here when you need them."

"Our need will never be that great."

Melegaunt did not argue, only swung an arm toward the furnace behind him and said, "That will be twenty. Twenty warriors is all that remains to you, is it not?"

Instead of answering, Bodvar glanced around the cluttered work area and shook his head. "Only a devil could live out here alone. It is exposed to every wind that blows."

"It's a safe place to work."

Melegaunt glanced at Bodvar's young wife and smiled. Idona smiled back but said nothing. Though Vaasan women were hardly shy, he had noticed that most of them preferred to keep their silence around him. He looked back to Bodvar.

"The bog people protect every ground approach but one, and the dragonmen are easy to spot from here."

"The dragonmen can watch you," Bodvar countered, "and the bog people have you surrounded."

"Vaasans may see it that way." Melegaunt knelt and began to feed his furnace from the charcoal pile beside it. "The way to destroy an enemy is to make him fight in his home instead of yours."

Melegaunt raised his mitted hand toward a white-hot poker, and Bodvar, not thinking, reached for it—then shrieked in surprise as Melegaunt used a cantrip to summon the utensil and spare him a burned palm.

Idona giggled, drawing an embarrassed, though tender, frown from her husband. Melegaunt shook his head in mock exasperation at Bodvar's clumsiness, and she broke into full laughter.

"You see?" Bodvar complained lightly. "This is what comes of treating with devils."

"Of course, my husband," Idona said. "This bearded one is always saving you from something, the mudbreathing knave."

"That is what worries me," Bodvar said, his tone more serious.

Desperate not to let Bodvar's suspicious nature undermine the unexpected openness his humor had won from Idona, Melegaunt poked at the coals, then changed the subject. "Speaking of mudbreathers and saving you, Bodvar, you never did tell me why the bog people and dragonmen were trying so hard to wipe out your tribe."

"*Were*?" Idona echoed. "They still are. Why do you think we stay camped at the other end of your walkway? If it wasn't for you—"

"Idona!" Bodvar snapped.

Hiding his delight behind a tolerant smile, Melegaunt tossed the poker aside—it remained hovering in the air— and began to feed more charcoal into the fire.

"I'm only happy to be of use." Melegaunt fixed his gaze on Bodvar. "But that still doesn't answer my question."

Bodvar flushed and said nothing.

Idona smirked. "Are you going to answer him, Husband, or am I?"

The more Idona spoke, the more Melegaunt liked her.

"By all means, Idona," Melegaunt said, "I would rather hear it from your—"

"I had this idea," Bodvar began. "I wanted to build a fort."

"Fort?" Melegaunt stopped feeding the flames and stood.

"For the treasure caravans," Idona said, rolling her eyes. "He actually thought outlanders would give us good coin just to sleep with a roof over their heads."

"And to have us stand guard," Bodvar added defensively. "When we're out hunting, they're always asking to share our camps and fires."

"Do they pay then?" Idona demanded.

Bodvar frowned. "Of course not. Who'd pay to pitch his own tent?"

"I see." Melegaunt found it difficult to keep the delight out of his voice. At last, he had discovered something that might move Bodvar to take help from a "shadow devil." "But the bog people and dragonmen prey on the caravans, and they have other ideas?"

Bodvar nodded. "The dragonmen sacked our first fort before it was half completed, and when we tried to move south to a more defensible site . . . well, you saw what happened."

Idona took his hand. "We're better off anyway," she said. "Who wants to live one place the whole year? What happens when the herds move?"

"What indeed?" Melegaunt asked absently.

He was looking over his shoulder toward the granite summit of his little island. On a clear day, it was possible to look across the bog clear to where the log road ended—or began, if the caravan was coming from the mountains with its load of treasure. If he could see the road, then anyone on the road would be able to see the top of the island.

"Melegaunt?" Bodvar asked.

Realizing he had not been paying attention, Melegaunt tore his gaze from the summit and turned back to Bodvar. "Sorry. You were saying?"

"He was inviting you to take feast with us," said Idona. "It's Higharvestide, in case you have lost track."

"It's Idona's idea," Bodvar added, though his friendly tone made it clear that he did not object too strenuously. "She says it's only common courtesy."

"And no more than we owe," Idona added, frowning at Bodvar, "considering all you have done for us."

"All I have done for you?" Melegaunt waved a hand in dismissal. "It's nothing, truly, but I can't join you. Next Higharvestide, perhaps."

"*Next* Higharvestide?" Bodvar scowled at the furnace where the last sword lay on its bed of sizzling tin. "If you're staying to watch over that sword, you may as well come, because—"

"It's not the sword," Melegaunt said. "The sword will be done by nightfall. I must have my rest tonight. Tomorrow will be a busy day for me."

Idona's face was not the only one that fell.

"Then you are leaving?" Bodvar asked. "If you are, be certain to take your swords with you, because they will only—"

"I'm not leaving." Melegaunt had to turn toward the island's granite summit—try as he might, he could not hide his smile. "Tomorrow, I start work on my tower."

"Tower?" Idona echoed.

"Yes." Finally in control of his expression again, Melegaunt turned around. "To watch over the treasure caravans."

But Melegaunt knew he would have no rest that night. He had read in the dawn shadows that this would be the evening when the Moor Eagles moved onto the island with him. His divinations proved correct shortly after dark, when the clan's mead-induced revels were interrupted by the clanging of the sentry's bell. Melegaunt lit a signal beacon he had prepared for the occasion, then he went to the front of the work site to inspect the situation.

A cloud of white forms was descending from the peaks of the dragonmen, their wings flashing silver in the moonlight as they spiraled down toward the bog's edge. Their spellcasters were already hurling magic bolts and balls of golden flame at the Moor Eagles, but the rest of the warriors were taking care to forestall counterattacks by keeping their magic-users well screened from Melegaunt's island. A sporadic stream of arrows began to rise from Bodvar's camp and arc into the night, falling pitifully short of their targets.

Melegaunt spread his arms and cast a shadow fog over the camp, more to prevent the Moor Eagles from wasting their time and arrows than to delay the dragonmen. Still, they had not forgotten the sticky rain he had called down on them in the bottomless bog—half their number had sunk beneath the peat and drowned—so they gave the dark cloud wide berth, angling away to land in the foothills on the far side of camp.

Leaving the Moor Eagles to fend for themselves, Melegaunt turned his attention to what he was sure would be the second part of the dragonmen's plan and found a company of bog people slithering up to block his boulder walk. The clan women were gamely rushing forward to meet them, Idona and a few of the others wielding iron swords or wood axes, but most armed with nothing more deadly than fire-hardened spears and cudgels so light Melegaunt could have snapped them over his knee.

"Hold!"

Melegaunt's Vaasan had grown passable enough over the last few months that Idona recognized the command for what it was and called her sisters to a stop. He pointed at a hole in the exact center of the shadow-walk and spoke a single word of magic. A whirling pinwheel of black tentacles erupted from the hole and slashed the bog people into so many chunks of slimy flesh, then withdrew back into the hole.

"*Now* you can come," Melegaunt called, using his magic to project his voice. "And bring those foolish husbands of yours, or the only Higharvestide feast will be that of the dragonmen."

Idona raised her sword in acknowledgement and sent the other women forward with the children, then rushed back into the shadow swaddled camp. Melegaunt waited impatiently for her return. It seemed to take her forever, and he feared the surviving bog people would regain their courage before she could convince her husband to retreat to the safety of the island. Finally, warriors began to stagger onto the boulder walk in twos and threes, often supporting and sometimes carrying each other. Melegaunt thought for a moment that the evening's festivities had simply been proceeding faster than he expected, but then he noticed that one of the men was missing an arm and another had something dangling on his cheek that might have been an eye.

Bodvar came last with Idona at his side, holding an armful of quivers over one arm and a shield over the other, alternately feeding arrows to her husband and stepping forward to intercept the wicked barbs flying their way from somewhere deeper in the camp. Melegaunt allowed them to retreat to the first sharp bend in that fashion, then speaking a magic command word, he pointed at a crooked crevice bisecting the boulder closest to shore.

A wall of faintly writhing shadows shot up from the fissure, sealing the boulder walk off from the Vaasans' camp. Bodvar and Idona turned and raced for the island, moving so fast that they nearly overran the next turn. Only Idona's quick feet—and quicker hands—kept Bodvar from going over the edge and plunging into the cold bog. They took the next corner more cautiously then reached the island and started up the trail behind the others.

By then, the first wave of dragonmen were flying over and around the shadow wall at the other end of the boulder walk, staying low and close to avoid making themselves targets. It was a bad mistake. As they passed by, the writhing shadows struck out like snakes, entwining anything else they could reach. Whatever they touched vanished, and soon arms, legs, wings, even heads were raining down on the shore and into the bog.

The dragonmen's pursuit stopped cold, and the Moor Eagles' women and children began to pour onto the work site. Melegaunt directed them into the shallow shelters he had hollowed out behind the sword rack. When he turned back to the battle, the tentacles in his shadow wall were swirling outward in three separate cones, each spiraling toward a small cluster of dragonmen hovering over the village. The spinning cones tore through the warrior screen as easily as they had the pursuit fliers a moment earlier, then diced the spell casters they had been trying to shield.

"Try to dispel *my* magic, will you?" Melegaunt called in ancient Draconic. "Come hither. I have more of the same waiting here!"

The last few dragonmen sank behind the shadow and vanished. For a time, Melegaunt feared he truly had defeated the attack so easily. The warriors began to reach his work site and check on their families. There were a handful of anguished cries and panicked calls for missing children, but with Melegaunt's help, the Vaasans had managed their retreat without losing many of their number. Three warriors who were too badly injured to fight were given over to the clan's healing witch, then

Bodvar and Idona arrived, breathing hard and supporting each other, but both whole and sound.

"Well, Devil, it seems you have saved us again," Bodvar said. "Whether we like it or not."

Melegaunt spread his hands. "I live to serve."

Bodvar scowled and started to make a retort, then someone called, "Whitescales from the east!" and someone else yelled, "And from the west! Thirty at least, coming in low over the bog!"

Melegaunt rushed to the western edge of his work site and saw a long rank of dragonmen approaching the island, their white scales shining like ivory against the dark peat. Their line curved behind the island, and from the cries behind him, it continued all the way around to the other side. The clan of the Moor Eagle was surrounded. Struggling to bite back his smile, Melegaunt turned to find Bodvar and Idona standing behind him.

"It seems your faith in me was misplaced," Melegaunt said. "My apologies, Bodvar."

"None necessary. I'm the one who brought this on us," Bodvar said. He fluttered his fingers in the direction of the approaching dragonmen. "Just do what you can."

"I am afraid that will not be much, my friend." Melegaunt spoke loudly enough to be sure that nearby warriors, already gathering to eavesdrop, would be certain to overhear. "Even I have my limits."

"Limits?" Bodvar growled.

"I did not expect this. My magic is all but exhausted."

Bowstrings began to thrum around the perimeter of the work site, but they were too few—and their arrow points too soft—to turn back the dragonmen.

Melegaunt drew his black sword, stepped away from the edge, and said, "But I can still give a good accounting of myself."

As he had hoped, the sight of his darksword proved an inspiration.

"The black swords!" Idona cried, turning toward the rack. "Those will balance the—"

"No." Calm though it was, Bodvar's voice was surprisingly masterful and imposing. "Of all the women in the tribe, Idona, you should know better. A devil's gift is no gift at all."

Idona looked as though she wanted to argue, but her respect for her husband—and for her chieftain—was too strong. She bit her tongue and pointed at the hidden shelter.

"Then we had better fall back," she said, "before there is nothing left to defend."

Bodvar gave the order, and the dragonmen were on them, streaming onto the work site from all sides. They flew headlong into battle, thrusting at their overwhelmed enemies with iron-tipped spears and relying on their size and speed to carry the attacks home. Half-a-dozen human voices wailed in pain in the first three heartbeats alone, then the second wave came crashing down from the island summit, and it grew clear that the Vaasans hadn't a chance. When they were lucky enough to land a strike, their brittle weapons either bounced off or broke like icicles against the dragonmen's thick scales.

Still, the Vaasans fought bravely and well, falling back toward the shelter behind the sword racks in good order, defending each other and striking at eyes and armpits and other vulnerable areas whenever the chance came. Within moments, there were as many dragonmen lying on the stony ground as there were humans.

And Melegaunt quickly added to the toll. Protected as he was by an aura of impenetrable shadow and holding a sword that would cut through any armor known on Faerûn, he turned and whirled through the dragonman ranks, slashing legs off here and behorned heads there, dancing past spear thrusts and shrugging off claw strikes like a drow blademaster.

One of the huge saurians managed to clasp him from behind in a bear hug, lifting him off the ground and trapping his arms so that it was impossible to wield his sword. Perhaps thinking to take him out over the bog and drop him to his death, the creature spread his wings and leaped into the air. Melegaunt slammed the back of his head into his attacker's snout, smashing it flat and driving one of the bony horns back into the thing's brain. When the wizard dropped back to his work site, the other dragonmen fell over each other to find someone else to attack.

Then it happened.

A trio of dragonmen spotted the hidden shelter, and battering a pair of human defenders aside with their powerful wings, charged for the children. The first warrior scrambled to his feet and rushed after them, shattering his brittle sword against the back of a thick reptilian skull.

The other Vaasan grabbed one of Melegaunt's glass swords. He sliced one dragonman's legs out from beneath him, then cleaved a second's spine on the backstroke and ran the blade through the third one's heart from behind. As this last saurian crashed to his knees, the warrior let out an anguished gasp. He stumbled back clutching at his heart, and one of the women in the shelter wailed in despair and cried out his name, but he did not fall. Instead, his hair and beard went as white as snow. The swarthiness drained from his face and his skin turned as pallid as ivory, and when he turned back to the battle, his eyes were as dead and black as those of the bog people, and the sword in his hand had lost its crystal translucence. Now it was as dark and glossy as Melegaunt's, with no hint at all of the shadow fibers embedded in its heart.

A dragonman stepped out of the mad whirl, thrusting at the warrior's heart with an oaken spear as thick as a man's arm. The Vaasan brought his sword up to block and slashed through the shaft as though it were a twig, then smiled darkly, opened his attacker across the chest, and waded after more victims.

His success inspired another warrior to snatch one of the weapons, and a woman in the shelter grabbed one to defend her children from an approaching dragonman. They killed their first enemies and underwent transformations similar to the first sword-taker, then they, too, began to cut a swath through the attacking saurians. A dozen dragonmen leaped into the air, angling for the rack of deadly swords. They were met by a like number of Vaasans, all pulling weapons off the hangers and putting them to good use.

Bodvar appeared at Melegaunt's side, nearly losing his hand when he made the mistake of grabbing the wizard's shoulder without warning.

"Stop them!"

"How?" Melegaunt caught a battering wing on his shoulder, then lopped it off and slashed his attacker across the back of the knees. "The choice is theirs. They would rather live than die."

"Not live in your service!" Bodvar objected. "You arranged this."

"Not arranged." Melegaunt pointed his palm behind the angry Vaasan's head and blasted a would-be attacker with a shadow bolt. "You give me too much credit."

"And you do not give me enough." Bodvar stepped close, and Melegaunt felt the tip of a sword pressed to his back. "Release my clan."

Melegaunt glared at the chieftain. "At the moment, Bodvar, you have worse enemies than me." Relying on his shadow armor to protect him, he reached back and snapped the steel sword with his bare hand. "If you want them released, do it yourself. All you need do is persuade them to set aside their swords."

Melegaunt shoved the chieftain away and turned back to the battle. With most of the glass swords now in hand, the Vaasans seemed to have matters well under control. The dragonmen were being forced steadily away from the shelters, and even when they attempted to use their wings to slip over the defenders, they were met with a flurry of flashing shadow. Finally, they gave up trying and took wing—at least those who could.

Dozens of wounded saurians remained behind with wings too shredded or broken to lift them yet still strong enough to fight—and ferocious enough to do it well. The Vaasans quickly set to work on them, herding them into a tight ball and driving them toward the cliffs on the east side of the work site. Seeing that only one sword remained, Melegaunt left them to their work and quietly went to the rack and slipped the last sword into his empty scabbard—and that was when Bodvar choose to assert himself again.

"My warriors, look at each other!" he called. "See what Melegaunt's devil weapons have done to you?"

Melegaunt groaned and shook his head in resignation. Were Bodvar not so stubborn and sure of himself, the wizard supposed, he would not be worth the trouble in the first place. He turned to find the chieftain and his loyal wife standing behind their warriors, Idona holding a cloak loaded with an armful of steel swords, which Bodvar was trying none too successfully to press into his clansmen's hands.

"Finish the battle with your own weapons," he said.

One of the sword-takers—Melegaunt thought it was the first—scowled. "Why would we do that?" He hefted his darksword and said, "These are better."

"Better?"

Bodvar lunged for the sword—and was dropped to the ground by a solid elbow to the face.

"This one belongs to me," the warrior said.

"Does it?" Idona dumped the steel swords on the ground. "Or do you belong to it?"

She glared over her shoulder with a look that sent a cold shiver down Melegaunt's spine then grabbed her husband beneath his arms.

"Come, Bodvar." She pulled him to his feet and turned to leave. "We are Moor Eagles no more."

"Leaving?" gasped the warrior who had struck Bodvar. He looked at his darksword a moment, then, as a discontented murmur began to build among his fellows, lowered the weapon. "Wait."

Melegaunt cursed Idona for an ungrateful shrew, and fumbling in his thoughts for some way to salvage the situation, started forward. As usual, it was the dragonmen who saved him. All at once, they burst into action, hurling themselves at the distracted Vaasans. The first sword-taker and another warrior fell instantly, and the work site erupted into a maelstrom of violence even more confused and ferocious than the first. Melegaunt saw a pair of saurians springing in Bodvar's direction and took the first out with a bolt of shadow, but the second was too quick. This one bowled the chieftain over on the run and lashed out for Idona, then a half-dozen other melees drifted between Melegaunt and the young wife, and he lost her.

He rushed forward swinging sword and spraying shadow, but the battle was as mad and confused as it was quick. Before he could find Bodvar again, he had to slay two dragonmen and use a spell of shadow-grabbing to keep from being dashed lifeless on the rocks at the base of his own cliff.

When Melegaunt did find the chieftain, he wished he had not been so quick to save himself. Bodvar was standing in the midst of a bloody pile of Vaasans and dragonmen, holding two broken swords of steel and searching the carnage around with a look of utter terror on his face.

"Idona?"

Bodvar found a female leg kicking at the ground from beneath a dead dragonman and used a boot to roll the white-scaled corpse away, but it turned out that the leg belonged to the mother who had grabbed one of the swords to defend her children.

He turned away from her without comment and called again, "Idona?"

"There," rasped someone. "They've got her."

Melegaunt spun toward the speaker and found a pallid-faced sword-bearer pointing across the work site to a small knot of fleeing dragonmen. They were just starting down the trail toward the boulder walk, each one with a limp Vaasan body slung over its shoulders. The last body in line was that of Bodvar's young wife, her throat ripped out and her head dangling by the spine alone, her blue eyes somehow still locked on Melegaunt's face.

"No!" Melegaunt gasped. He laid a hand on Bodvar's shoulder. "I'm sorry, Bodvar. Sorry beyond words."

"Why? You have what you came for." Bodvar reached down to Melegaunt's scabbard and drew the last dark-sword, then turned to start after his dead wife. "You have your twenty souls."

LIAR'S GAME

Jessica Beaven

The Year of the Starfall (1300 DR)

*A*t the edge of a city in Faerûn, a sewer main emp-
ties into the swamp. The light reaching inside
gives way quickly; any who enter must proceed by
touch. Deeper, the sewage grows thicker. It sucks
at one's calves. Deeper still, and the refuse is dry.
The procession from wet to dry challenges the
very imperative that water must flow downward.
And yet the sewers go even deeper. Debris has
come to rest here: a shoe with a foot decaying in
it; a head wedged against a pipe protruding from
the floor; worse.

With no heavenly bodies to mark its passing,
time loses meaning. A drip falls, then fades into
the past, dripping forever in its moment.

The pipes give way to catacombs. Sounds of
weeping fill the close air.

From one corridor, light issues; it seeps from the walls. Shifting animal forms inhabit this hall. Bars and wire hold them in, stripe their features. Some of the creatures look normal—cats shivering in shelved cages, mongrels drooping, even a lion cramped in a forward-sloping cell, its hide pressed into the bars.

The weeping creature in one of the larger cells has retreated to a corner to express its grief. Only fur is visible. For some reason, it stops crying and shifts.

It is another cat—or rather, two. One is joined to the other, exactly upside-down on its back—head melting into head, hip into hip, one tail twitching against another limp one. The piggybacker is motionless, legs flopping, tongue protruding, yellow eyes glazed an inch or two above the green ones. The living cat is lacerated, so that its intestines have spilled from its middle and drag behind it upon the floor.

This corridor is long. It passes into more corridors with small carry-cages abandoned here and there, jumbled alongside tables, cushions, and tapestries. A doorway breaks the expanse of one wall.

Inside the doorway, a would-be archwizard turns, as if sensing a presence. Then she returns to poring over a book of beasts. Druidic scrawl covers the pages.

She appears beautiful, with that ruggedness of druids— lithe body, sun-tinted dark brown hair, blue eyes—but that is only the body she chose to wear today.

She is a descendant of a woman and a man who withdrew, with the everdark Shade Enclave, to the Plane of Shadow centuries ago. She had learned the story as a fledgling druid just starting to taste the power that would entice her to archwizardry, and the ancestral memory of Shade Enclave added fuel to that fire.

Now she can hear the enclave sometimes, calling to her, reminding her of its hold upon her. The Shadovar will soon return to her land, the land of the enclave's birth.

When they do, she will make Shade her home.
She rises and leaves her study.

1

"Pain is reality. But false pain is easy to engineer."
                                      —Chever's last notes

The druid rose and glanced about her chamber, following an impulse to leave prematurely for the meeting of aspiring archwizards. The meetings came more frequently of late. Perhaps, like her, the older the dark ones grew, the more the Plane of Shadow called to them.

She strolled through her museum of abominations, following an urge to check upon them. She had thought she felt a disturbance earlier, but no—all seemed in order. She paused before her double cat, which was the most vocal, and closed her eyes to let its pain seethe over her. It had stopped crying for the moment. It had almost forgotten that it once had a life before this, but its despair remained, to confirm reality for the druid-wizard. Only real pain could call forth such misery. This brought the druid-wizard vicious comfort, similar to what a survivor of a shipwreck must feel upon stealing a life raft from a drowning shipmate. She had known doubts about the nature of reality once, long ago. It had been like finding that she could no longer trust the ground to hold her up.

The best specimens were those who had known dejection before she found them—mutations that lived in fear of sounder-bodied predators. Any suffering she could heap upon these abominations compounded that which they already knew. The thrill she derived from their torture could prove almost excruciating, and she would cry out in dark joy. The power she gained from those sessions—the afterglow—lasted for days.

An emissary from the Twelve Princes of Shade had come to her group earlier in the year, having somehow gotten wind of the clandestine organization. After testing the group for sympathy to the Shadovar through various—in some cases fatal—means, the emissary had assigned tasks. After the moot, the druid-wizard would set to her task: to seek out a collection of notes written by the archwizard Chever, who had lived in ancient Netheril. Chever had created the Opus Enclave, which had once housed Netheril's centers of learning.

In his last days, Chever had contacted and conversed with myriad extraplanar creatures and taken down his notes, which made little sense compared to the well-organized books and lectures he had delivered in earlier days. In fact, they allegedly made little sense compared to most anything. His later recordings, especially, disclosed madness.

But the Shadovar deemed the notes valuable, so the druid-wizard would find them. The emissary had given her a starting point: the notes were last rumored to have been in the hands of a scholar living near the northern end of the Desertsmouth Mountains.

The moot passed with relative ease. The would-be archwizards spent most of the meeting clustered, heads bent, over this or that tome, debating the consequences and efficacy of proposed actions. They seemed to have it under control, so the druid-wizard slipped away early, both to prepare for her journey and to escape being assigned a new task.

She had things to attend to—like her beast collection, which would fit so perfectly deep inside the catacombs of the floating enclave. Others might control the enclave's surface, but she would take advantage of the fact that surface has no depth; only one who rules an object's substance truly commands it. She would be the one who whispered suggestions that must be followed, the one who masterminded activities that the enclave's figureheads would consider their own.

She made the trip back to her stronghold automatically, not remembering anything of the distance she had traveled from the wizards' moot to her room. She checked her beasts' water supply, which she had tapped from drainage pipes. The system kept the creatures watered automatically, so she would not need to worry about them dying in her absence. She dressed in the traveling garb of a druid and filled her satchel with the items she would need in the Desertsmouth. She would let her druid aspect ascend for this trip, as she would need to give the wizard full control upon her return.

2

"At the edge of darkness is where the light is greatest."
—Chever's last notes

She chose to walk to her destination—a walk of many nights, but one that allowed her to flex her druidic muscles. She would live off the land and revel in moon, stars, sun, and earth. She supposed some part of her would miss these things when she moved to Shade Enclave, but then it wasn't as if she couldn't leave now and. . . .

Anyway, it didn't really matter. When she reined in the druid again after this trip, the wizard would find satisfaction. Best to please that—the strongest of her two natures—first.

As the Desertsmouths rose on the horizon, the bushes and small trees along the banks of the river by which the druid-wizard had been traveling gave way to meadow grass as she neared the foothills. She curved away from the river and followed a brook through sun-speckled groves and alpine flowers.

After traveling for several more hours, with ground squirrels and meadowlarks as her only companions, she broke free of a small patch of oaks and aspen to encounter a cottage near a dip in the creek she had been following. She had passed several cabins along the way, but until now she had come across none that had the aura of promise she sought. This one, though . . . this one was different.

She peered into a warped-glass window, but the dwelling's single room was empty. A bowl of stew and sheets of parchment on a rough-hewn table told her of recent occupation. In fact, a door between a case of shelves and some gardening tools against the back wall was cracked open, allowing a ray of sunlight to reach in and illuminate dust motes and floorboards.

She would observe the cottage's owner. It had been a while since she had enacted the Change, and it would feel good to assume wolf form again. She performed the ritual and watched lazily as her palms thickened into paws, her fingers withdrew into pads. She felt her nose and mouth pull out as if some god shaped them of clay. Fur sprouted all over her body; she was the earth in spring, shoots of hair emerging from her in a quiet burst. Her bone structure changed, forced her prone. Her knees reversed; her tailbone extended into a plume. The process lasted a mere moment, and a strange voice in her mind wove through it all, as if it, and not she, had commanded the Change.

The druid-wizard veered into the meadow grasses, slunk to a vantage point among them. Her brown ears and blue eyes lifted to just above the grasses' tips.

The man's back was partially turned to her. He was slim yet muscular, and his facial features—silhouetted against the green and yellow of the creek's trees and the sun on the leaves—formed smooth angles against his tousled hair.

He spoke in the voice that had accompanied her Change.

The druid-wizard sidled around to better see what the man was doing. He was crouched near a vegetable garden, shaded under an eave. He spoke to a rose plant.

But his lips did not move.

His voice seemed to fade for a moment, as if the druid-wizard's surprise at the realization forced That Which Was to become That Which Was Not. But then her credulity caught up to her. She had known stranger things than this in her hundreds of years of magic. Why had this affected her?

The voice returned, rising and falling in windlike rhythm. It seemed to *create* a wind, for though no breeze swept the grasses among which the druid-wizard hid, the rose nodded and swayed, almost as though it responded to the man's thoughts.

The druid-wizard swiveled her ears, as if to better catch those thoughts.

. . . fell asleep in my stew and dreamed of music. In that music, you spoke to me. And I tried to tell you "soon," but I don't know if my words reached you. Now I am awake, and I can talk to you only like this. Please understand me. Please know that I am talking to you. Ah! You nod! But I never know if your replies are real or merely figments of my desperation. I have lost my ability to know anything with certainty. I am . . . I am lost. . . .

He broke into quiet sobs. The druid-wizard thought she sensed an image in his mind—an image of a woman. . . .

Clearly the man had gone mad in his isolation. Fascinating.

The druid-wizard could almost imagine that he spoke to her somehow, and not to the rose. Some part of her responded to the idea with a surge of longing so sudden that she could not breathe, an imperative that, for a moment, wiped out all else.

She had not lost control of her emotions in such a way since childhood. To know surprise at a simple hermit's thought-projection! To be blindsided by emotion hitherto suppressed, unsuspected! She should leave; power of this magnitude could ruin her. Even as she thought this, she knew that whatever force was at work here had already secured its hold on her. Plus, she must complete the task for the Shadovar, and that meant exploring every avenue of this country. She must see where this path led.

The man shook himself. Perhaps he chided himself for becoming so emotional over a plant, or perhaps he shuddered in an echo of the druid-wizard's longing. He stood and entered his cabin, closing the door behind him, leaving the rose to nod and twitch alone. It turned to face the druid-wizard—almost as if it knew she was there and regarded her with curiosity. But that was just the way some breeze had blown it.

Angry with herself, the druid-wizard resumed her human shape abruptly enough to cause herself pain and strode to the cottage's back door. She hated her weakness, but she could not deny that she wanted the man—wanted to make him speak to her as he had spoken to the rose.

As she knocked, she forced her turmoil aside and focused upon enhancing her beauty. She drew from the vague image of the woman she had seen in the man's mind, as well as from her own ideal self-image. Her eye color intensified; her hair took on new highlights and curls; the top few buttons of her shirt undid themselves. No man had ever resisted this spell.

The man opened the door, a puzzled half-smile betraying surprise at the appearance of a visitor so soon after his moment with the rose—and at the back door, no less. For a moment his heart had surged with the wild hope that . . . but no, he must not indulge such fantasies.

When he saw the woman, puzzlement gave way to lust and wariness, the latter because one such as this woman would never appear at a place such as this without trouble in the land or powerful magic at work.

❧ ❧ ❧ ❧ ❧

Time for the druid-wizard to play her part, if she was really to make this man her own.

She adopted an expression of uncertainty and stammered a pattern of truths and half-truths. "I . . . I . . . felt drawn to this place. I have no one, and I dreamed that I must journey . . . . I saw you with your rose, and I thought I would like to know love like that. So . . . here I am.

"I'll leave if I came in error," she added, to dispel any doubts that might remain after her speech.

He said not a word—not one word for her in that voice!—but drew her inside.

Now I'll see if I can call forth love as effectively as I can call forth pain, she thought. And, once I do, to see if love can grant me as much gratification. Perhaps, as some attest, even more.

She let her body take control—drew his head to hers, kissed him deeply, felt him kiss back. From there they fell to the floor, and so the day passed.

Afterward, as they sat at the table over fresh bowls of stew and the druid-wizard secretly used her magic to destroy any chance of a child taking root, the man finally spoke to her.

"I dreamed I would meet you," he said.

He had recurring dreams of a woman linked to him with powerful bonds. The bonds, though they kept the woman's spirit close to his, stretched over chasms of time and space. Her features were usually indistinct, but he thought she might look something like the druid-wizard.

"Was that the same dream in which your rose spoke to you?"

He looked at her askance. "No . . . you heard that?"

"Yes, I'm sorry. I couldn't help myself."

He frowned, then shook his head. "It's fine. It's probably good that you came now. I think I might have started to invent things, to hallucinate, if I'd been alone much longer."

Perhaps you already were hallucinating, the druid-wizard thought. She said, "How long have you been here?"

"I don't know. A long time. I got tired of cities and people and just wanted to get away for a while. How about you?"

"I've been alone for a long time, too. I live in the city, though, and I have . . . pets."

"That must help."

They fell into pregnant silence.

"Will you go back to the city, then?" he asked. "To take care of your pets?"

"Oh . . . yeah, I should. It's still home for now, even though I've found true love." She met his eyes and smiled as though at a joke. "Would you like to come with me?"

True love, she had said. The man supposed they were true lovers—he *had* dreamed of a woman something like this one, and this woman had been drawn here. But the words rang crass. He considered expressions of true love best uttered in times of great emotion, great change—not over bowls of half-eaten stew and among garden tools and cupboards. Just because she didn't share this fancy . . . that didn't mean he and this woman weren't destined for each other.

In any case, he had been away from the world long enough.

"I think . . . I think I will go with you," he said.

His thoughts drifted. What did this woman do, he wondered, when she wasn't trying to find her true love in the wilderness? And what city was she from?

He posed his questions.

"I do magic tricks," she replied, "in Phlan, on the Moonsea. I plan to move soon, though."

The druid-wizard watched the man clean up their dishes. Engineering his love had been easy; now she must figure out how to draw upon its power.

3

"Long is the times but there are times when . . . so you see what I'm saying."

—Chever's last notes

In the days and tendays that followed, the druid-wizard grew fond of the man. She enjoyed watching his thin muscles flex as he applied his pickaxe to stones with which he planned to line a walkway from the garden to the creek, for whoever might choose to occupy his cabin after they left. A small application of her magic could have broken the stones much more easily, but the time was not yet right to reveal to him exactly what kinds of "magic tricks" she could do.

One day, he showed her the parchment pages she had seen through the window when she first came upon the cabin—pages he studied in his spare time.

They were the notes of Chever.

The druid-wizard's eyes narrowed.

The man would not say how he had come by them. The druid-wizard guessed the experience must have been horrifying, as his face went gray and slack, and his eyes took on a faraway look, the few times she had tried to get him to divulge on the subject.

The man believed that the notes held some of the universe's secrets, which would be his if only he could unlock the notes' meaning. Sometimes he felt on the verge of something great, but so far his efforts had rewarded him with only enough enlightenment to make him want more.

On sunny days, the man showed the druid-wizard his favorite groves and clearings. When it rained, they toured hidden caves. He told her about strange beasts he had glimpsed higher up on the mountain slopes and about the occasional eccentric he had met while scavenging for food. In most of the places the man showed her, the druid-wizard could detect faint, benign magic—in sharp contrast to the darker magic to which she was more accustomed.

One day, as the man bathed in the creek, an old peddler arrived at the door. The druid-wizard bickered with the woman for a while—the woman was pushy; the druid-wizard didn't want to buy anything—before deciding she had had enough. As the man rounded the corner of the house, hair still wet, torso naked, he was just in time to watch in helpless disbelief as the druid-wizard turned the old woman into a cow.

He ran to the cow, screeching, "What have you done? You've killed her! Where did she go?"

He was making about as much sense as Chever's notes. "She didn't go anywhere. She's right here." The druid-wizard indicated the cow.

"But . . . what about my supplies? How am I going to fix my rake?"

"Your rake . . . ? You aren't going to need a rake in Phlan. Besides, wouldn't you much rather have steak?"

"Steak?!" the man cried, and he seemed to crumple. "What have you done? Who are you? What are you doing here?"

"I told you I did magic for a living."

The man lowered himself to a bench near the front door and held his head in his hands.

The druid-wizard felt, for the first time in a long while, a hint of remorse.

The peddler-cow, who had known a moment of bewilderment, now came to her senses. She lunged for the druid-wizard, but the druid-wizard held her at bay with an invisible wall of magic.

The man didn't notice the cow's expelled breath as she hit the wall; his thoughts lay too deeply inward. The druid-wizard gently prodded him to his feet. He lifted his head to gaze at her, his eyes full of accusation.

"Come inside," she said. "I have something to show you."

Head bent, he obeyed. As the door closed behind them, the shield holding back the cow dissipated, and she began to charge the door.

Thud.

The man jumped the first time it happened, then peered out at the cow.

Thud.

"Is she all right?"

Thud.

"She's fine; just angry with me." The druid-wizard raised her hands to cast a spell. "Here, let me—"

"No! What are you doing?"

"I'm only going to give her rest."

His eyes seethed with mistrust.

"I promise," she assured him, "only rest."

His shoulders relaxed a little. He nodded reluctantly.

The druid-wizard cast the spell, and the cow sank to her knees and quieted, sides expanding and contracting as she took on the steady breathing of sleep.

The druid-wizard returned her attention to the man. She started to speak then paused. Finally, she said, "I know this whole thing might be hard for you, but please don't hate me for what I am." The plea felt unnatural falling from her lips, despite the fact that she meant it only as a way to regain his trust, a way to stay on track with her plan. "It's not as bad as you think," she reasoned. "So that woman wasn't bothering you, but think if she had been—she'd never bother you again. I can give you that—I can take away your troubles."

He just looked at her.

Why couldn't she think straight? This should be merely a case of problem and solution. All right, so . . . what was the problem? The problem was that the man was sad. How does one fix sadness? With cheer. Simple as that.

Relieved to have found solid footing again, she offered, "I can change things in other ways. Imagine what fun we could have with something like this."

She held up her hand, palm forward, and created a handfang—a mouth in the center of her palm. She raised an eyebrow suggestively and quirked a smile.

The man cried out in disgust.

It was just as well, the druid-wizard supposed. He probably wouldn't have been amused to discover the acid that served as handfang saliva.

The man left, slamming the door behind him. The druid-wizard watched him from the window. He tripped on one of the sleeping cow's legs but didn't fall. Nor did he look back.

He would come back, though, she knew. His rose was here—as were Chever's notes.

At least while he was gone the druid-wizard could dispose of the cow. She did so using a burst of combustion.

This whole adventure was proving a little more complicated than she had bargained for. Perhaps it was time she took the notes and left.

But she couldn't stop worrying at the situation. It didn't make any sense! How could the man feel betrayed? Had she not done something he himself must have wished he could do many times—if not to the peddler, then to some other annoyance or enemy?

Not sure whether she planned to leave alone or with the man, she began to pack her things.

4

"It comes and says I say what? i don't understand? and i wish I it hadn't asked. . . ."

—Chever's last notes

The man's greeting, when he returned, was flat and pained, the result of an hour's soul-searching.

"I can't stand to be apart from you." He saw that the cow had gone, but he suppressed the urge to ask whence. "I couldn't stand to have you out there in the world without knowing whether you lived or died, whether you loved or hated me. I can't allow this to end bitterly."

He noticed her mountain gear, packed and almost ready to go. She had not yet added Chever's notes.

"I'll come with you," he said. "You're going home?"

"Yes, but first I'm going to try to find one of those creatures you told me about. The ones that live higher up in the mountains."

It had occurred to her that it might be nice to bring home a little something for herself, an addition to her collection.

"Then I'll go home," she said after a while. "If you really want to honor our love that far, you should bring anything you wouldn't want to lose."

She nodded meaningfully toward the back door—the rose.

The man nodded, tucked the notes into a pack, and took a shovel and a large pot through the back door.

The druid-wizard removed one of the spellbooks from her pack and studied it idly. She had time to wait. Her only imperative was that she return when the Shadovar summoned her, and that wouldn't be for a while yet. She would sense it when that time drew near.

After an hour or so, the man reentered carrying the newly potted rose plant and a leather sling he had fashioned for carrying it mounted upon his pack. The rose had flinched as he had cut it from the ground, as though the unavoidable loss of some of its roots brought it conscious pain. It had wilted in his garden the past few tendays, largely neglected for the company of a flesh-and-blood lover. Its leaves had yellowed, and some of its petals drifted to the floor.

"I'm ready," the man said.

He eased into his pack and rose-carrying contraption, and the druid-wizard closed and repacked her book.

5

". . . Shapes and sizes, things make no sense yet all make together fit AAARGH! Can't think in two places at once. Can't lose either one, either."

—Chever's last notes

They found one of the horrors they sought during the third day out. They watched the beast for a while, and the druid-wizard remembered when she had crouched as a wolf to watch the man in much the same way, not so long ago. She would not lose him now.

She directed the man to a position opposite her in the undergrowth, so that the creature's path would lead it directly between them. She imbued her arms with a spell of strength, removed her boots, and formed her feet into panther claws.

After a few minutes, the creature emerged and shambled down the path.

One of its heads swung from side to side, on the lookout for food. The other head lay at an unnatural angle off of its shoulder, bobbing limply whenever the creature took a lurching step with a clubfoot. It already looked as though it had spent several sessions in the druid-wizard's spell-testing chamber—its creator, whether it had been evil magic or nature, had done much of the druid-wizard's work for her. She particularly appreciated the lolling second head—the irony of death in such close proximity to life. Many of her own creatures possessed similar features. It was almost as though she had been destined to capture this very beast—but she saw destiny everywhere now, ever since she had met the man.

The druid-wizard tensed as the creature's live head swiveled to peer her way, but then a crackle sounded in the opposite direction—that would be the man. When the creature's head pivoted toward the sound, the druid-wizard sprang.

The creature snuffled when the druid-wizard landed on its back and choked its live head in her arms, scratching at its sides and back with her panther's feet. She closed her eyes to better feel its spirit casting about within its body. She felt its fear—its confused thoughts grasping to regain the contentedness it had felt moments earlier.

Already its thrashing lessened. The best moment passed, but the druid-wizard could still feel the pulse of power she had gained from the hunt's climax. She would remember it every time she visited the creature in her museum.

The druid-wizard suspended the creature, gasping, at the end of a magical tether. The man approached it with curiosity verging on awe. He saw its anomalies, but he also saw its original design. A graceful neck. Tapered fingers. Deep, brown pools of wisdom in its eye sockets.

"Can you relieve its pain at all?" he asked.

The druid-wizard shrugged and cast another spell. The creature fell back on its tether, still panting but calmer for the moment.

The druid-wizard was pleased that the man felt comfortable calling upon her magic—his request told her that he was growing accustomed to it.

"What kind of a creature is it?" the man asked.

She had no answer. She remained silent.

The man didn't seem to notice. He had begun to whisper to the creature, as he used to do with his rose. It watched him—looked into his eyes—and its breathing evened out.

The druid-wizard felt a pang of envy and stood.

"We should go," she said. "The sooner it settles into its new home, the better."

She yanked the creature after her and turned to hike back down the mountain.

The man followed, admonishing her to treat the creature gently.

She smiled fondly through her annoyance. The man never failed to amuse her with his concern about such insignificant things.

6

"So much darkness, darkness . . . can't see and . . . light! but it's only more darkness!"

—Chever's last notes

"Do you think you can help it?" the man asked one day. "Can you make it whole?"

They had just rejoined the river the druid-wizard had followed to the mountains, and the man had grown increasingly concerned about the beast's welfare.

The druid-wizard affected an expression of sorrow.

"I'll try," she said.

She could make it whole, but that would defeat her purpose.

"That's all I ask."

At long last they glimpsed Phlan. It was just in time, by the man's reckoning. The creature had eaten and drunk little and appeared on the verge of starvation or dehydration. Its eyes had grown glassy, as if it found the world no longer worth seeing.

"Is your home near this side of the city?" the man asked.

"Part of it is," she said. Then she added, "We only have to get through this swamp."

They had been slogging through muck that only loosely fit the definition of land. Early on, the man had lost both boots to the squelching mud. The druid-wizard had removed her own boots long before, to give her druid aspect a little direct contact with the earth—before she must sequester it once more to the backwaters of her mind. The Plane of Shadow felt near, so very near. She wondered if the Shadovar were preparing to bring their enclave over even now.

The man and the druid-wizard finally reached the sewer pipe. The druid-wizard paused, gauging the man's expression. He glanced around, mildly interested in the new surroundings but anxious to reach their destination. The druid-wizard ducked into the pipe.

She glanced back at him. He looked surprised but did not question her, even when the smell of sewage rose to his nostrils. Perhaps he thought she was taking the back way to some sprawling mansion.

When they reached the museum and she stopped to deposit the new denizen into an empty cage, realization dawned.

"This is it?" the man cried. "This is your home? The sewers?"

"I couldn't bring myself to tell you before: people don't take well to magicians in this city," she lied. "I've been forced underground."

"Why'd you lock them in cages like this?" he continued, as though he had not heard her. "You could give them better treatment than this!" He gestured at a random cage, then gasped as he glimpsed the monstrosity inside. "What *is* this? What's wrong with this turtle?"

It was a giant tortoise, but it had four heads, spaced equally apart around the rim of its shell. The heads, each one independent of the others, could not agree upon the direction in which to travel. It must have managed occasionally to drag itself to a bowl of water near the front of its cage, or it would not have survived in the wizard's absence, but when the original head won out and made for one of the four food dishes in each corner of the cage, the turtle could not reach the food, as the dishes were enclosed behind wire mesh. When the original head made for a different bowl, a head on the side would discover the last bowl and make for it instead. The scene would have been ludicrous had the turtle not been straining so hard against itself, and for so long, that a couple of its legs had scraped themselves raw in its attempts to gain ground.

"I'm trying to cure it," she answered. "I found it like this—"

"Then why not bring its food to it?" The man sprang to do just that but couldn't find a door of any kind in the bars. "Open it!" he commanded.

She did so with a gesture, bemused. The man tore the wire mesh from the food dishes and slid them toward each of the tortoise's four heads. The tortoise choked down the morsels as the man squatted near it, watching.

"I know you can fix this," the man said over his shoulder. "I saw you turn an entire woman into a cow. Why can't you just wave away three of this turtle's . . . ?" He stopped. "Unless you did this to it," he whispered. He looked at her. "You didn't find the turtle like this, did you? It was fine when you found it, wasn't it? You took it . . ."

The druid-wizard didn't like the way this was going. The tortoise was nothing compared to some of her other tenants. She must keep him from seeing the others.

"I did what it's my nature to do," she finished for him, coaxing him to her chambers, holding his eyes with hers. "Surely you knew on some level. The things that give me joy—they aren't joyous things, but I can't help that they bring me joy."

"How could you . . . ? Never mind. What did you really plan to do with the creature we captured? No, never mind that, either."

He paused to think. They had entered her bedchamber, and she eased him down into a chair.

"After your trick with the peddler, I thought . . ." He trailed off. "But this . . ."

She let him mull things over without interruption.

After a few moments, he said, "I guess maybe I did know on some level. Maybe that's one of the things that attracted me to you, but that doesn't mean I accept it! I mean, I can find joy in trees, birds, and flowers . . . Why can't you?"

He had meant the question rhetorically, but she answered anyway. "Because I can't deny what I am."

"But why resign yourself like that? Somehow you had to become what you are. You only need to backtrack to the point where things went wrong . . ."

She turned his face gently toward her. His eyes ceased wandering about the room and focused on hers.

"It doesn't work that way," she said tenderly.

He looked back into her eyes fully for a moment then wrenched his face from her grasp.

"I have to go," he choked.

He stumbled from the room.

7

"It's inside the walls. It's behind every door until you open it. It's under everything, but, if you look inside everything, you can't see it, because you're always seeing it."

—Chever's last notes

The man fled whence he had come, his vision bleared by tears. When he passed the corridor of horrors, the faces all seemed to rise up in myriad yawning grimaces, crying and moaning, and sometimes screaming.

But the imprisoned creatures made no sound. Those sounds came from him.

He found himself back outside, pant legs splattered in sewage, the light of an overcast afternoon searing his dilated eyes. He jogged blindly, heedless of swamp mud and brambles, until he found himself in a small clearing. The clearing was dead. No water softened its ground, stagnant or otherwise. No grass grew. No swamp insects buzzed. Overhead, where branches protruded, green leaves gave way to bare, dead limbs, almost as if someone had drawn a line: life on one side, death on the other.

The man found the absence of all life—all magic—comforting. He sat cross-legged at the edge of the clearing and let the nothing embrace him, soothe him. The emptiness would be complete if only . . .

He removed his backpack, which he had hoped to remove in a roomy suite in the wizard's nonexistent house. It carried his two treasures. He pulled out Chever's notes, traced the lines of the handwriting with his fingers, then crumpled them and sent them flying. A breeze lifted them, and a couple of pages caught on tree branches. A thin rain had begun to fall; it would mold that parchment to the trees soon enough.

It felt good to be rid of the magic; he hated it now. Magic meant lies and betrayal. Magic meant loving, then finding that you love a stranger, then discovering that you cannot stop loving even when nothing of the illusion remains.

He touched the rose, whose petals had begun to collect raindrops. It was crying—no. It was only a flower that had collected a little rain. With a tortured cry, he hurled it, too, as far as he could throw it, then broke into wracking sobs.

In her den, the druid-wizard looked up, sensing something amiss. The notes . . . ? She closed her eyes and focused upon them. She saw the swamp . . . the man, weeping and trudging back toward the sewer . . . the notes sagging in a drizzle in a clearing he had left behind! She immediately teleported to the clearing and gathered the notes under her robe.

As easy as that, they were hers.

8

"We make it little by little, until it's too big and over-whelms . . . us . . . then goes away aging."
—Chever's last notes

As the druid-wizard dabbed the notes dry while waiting for the man's return, she could not help but consider his misery. In spite of herself, she wanted to alleviate it. How to accomplish that? Well, what had he loved before she had come along? His rose. Chever's notes. Those were all. The rose was gone, broken in the swamp, its crime its failure to convince the man that it was more than what it seemed. The notes, though . . .

Perhaps if the man had the time to study them more, he would find the answers he sought, the answers he had felt were just beyond his reach back when he first showed her the notes at his cabin.

Maybe she didn't need the notes for her own purposes just yet. Maybe she would have him study them a while longer. In fact, if he reached a breakthrough, that knowledge might prove invaluable to the Shadovar, put the citizens of Shade Enclave in the druid-wizard's debt. Yes. . . .

She couldn't wait long, though. During the last few days, she had begun to hear the Shadovar's call, and it grew louder with each day.

When the man returned, he first paused at the cage of the creature they had brought back from the Desertsmouth Mountains. He held his hand up to the bars, and the creature mirrored the gesture. Their gazes locked for a moment, then the man tore his away and made his way to the woman's chambers.

She looked up when he entered, and he nodded as though nothing had happened; indeed, as though he had been entering just this way for many years, coming home after a hard day's work. She seemed a little damp, as if she had been out in a mist or sweating over a difficult spell.

She reached out her hand, and in it were Chever's notes. "You shouldn't leave such valuable things lying around," she said.

A few days ago, he might have railed at her, accused her of spying. Instead he just stared dully, waiting for her direction.

"You should keep studying these," she continued. "They may help you find completion."

Back in the world of magic and lies, he could not refuse. He took the notes to the nearest table and began to read over the familiar words for the first time in what seemed like months. The woman left him to his thoughts.

When the druid-wizard peeked in later, she thought that perhaps the intermission had done the man good. He was poring over the notes avidly, as though he had never thrown them away.

The days passed.

The druid-wizard rarely went out. She had skipped the last few archwizard moots.

The man ventured out to obtain food or to wipe his mind clean in one dead clearing or another. Each time he returned, he paused at the same creature's cage, took what silent wisdom he could glean from it, and pushed on.

The man did not know of the floating city. The druid-wizard would not stand for him to accompany her to it. She had watched him grow paler each day, watched his hair turn grayer and lose its luster, watched the dark circles grow under his eyes and his shoulders slump. He would not live long in the darkest catacombs of the city of darkness.

But she would not allow him to live without her, either.

One windy, magic-strewn evening, the woman approached the man.

"I have something to show you," she said.

She clasped his wrist, and they teleported to the edge of a cliff.

Stars sang their distant song, and the waxing moon was bright. The man stood at the edge, cloak whipping about him. He could feel her presence slightly behind him; possibly she had taken on her wolf form, which had become a familiar event to him. When he turned, she was human.

"Why did you bring me here?"

"Have you by chance made any breakthroughs with Chever's notes?"

"What? . . . Oh. No, nothing significant. Why do you ask?"

"No reason." She sighed and moved up beside him. "I wanted to show you that, because of you, I can take joy in more than pain. The stars . . ."

She gestured, then turned to him.

"I was a druid once, you know. I still am, in many ways, but I'm a wizard more. When I was only a druid, I loved the stars, but they didn't give me joy as they do now. It's a gift I'll treasure."

She flowed to him, and she kissed him long and hard.

The kiss tasted like poison, and the man quailed, sensing his life spinning out of his control. He broke the kiss with a small cry.

The woman held him at arm's length for a moment, looking into his eyes.

And she was gone.

The man's heart wrenched, grieved and painful. Power left him—something sucked it out. Loss overwhelmed his senses, and he fell to the ground.

9

"And that's how . . . we . . . it . . . all makes sense. I mean, how—we make sense with the things we see. So it really does make sense when you look at it that way."
—Chever's last notes

The man awoke on the cliff top and picked his long way back to the sewers in a daze. The sewers had become home to him so easily. . . .

In the days that followed, the woman did not return. Perhaps her evil deeds had finally caught up with her, or perhaps she had found a more suitable mate. The man made some perfunctory inquires about her in the town, but rarely did anyone know of her. Those who had heard of her grimaced as at a bad taste and would not speak to him. She had wanted to leave, in any case, and who was he to come upon her unwanted? He thought of the peddler-turned-cow and shuddered.

Days poured one into the next with nothing to distinguish them from those gone before or those come after, except that, on some days, he imagined he could sense the woman from whatever place she had gone to. What was he to do now?

He could not open the cages of her museum, since only magic could open them. Rather than leave the prisoners to wither, he slipped all but the newest member of their congregation poison purchased from a street vendor with gold coins he had found in one of the woman's robes. He told himself it was mercy-killing.

He attended to the newest creature's needs better than he attended to his own. He took violently ill, leaving trails of coughed-up blood on the cold floors. His disinterest in his own life might be conspiring to bring about his demise, or perhaps something in her final kiss. . . .

As the lackluster days continued to drag, the stench of the dead in their cells grew thick, until the man thought sometimes that he must have fallen into the Nine Hells in error, the sole living being among the Hordes. Only his creature companion kept him from being alone—and one day it, too, died.

10

"When truth comes, knowledge leaves. Truth is big."
—Chever's last notes

The day the last creature died, the man climbed from the sewers into the city. Twice along the way, he encountered sickly plants that seemed to move of their own accord. He wondered whether they were endowed with sentience as he had once thought his rose was, or if they had once been people who had found themselves on the wrong end of a wizard's spell.

He wandered into a tavern, oblivious of the wrinkled noses and the patrons who got up to move or leave when he sat near them. He stared blankly into a mug of mead for a while, and, following sudden dizziness, the world became blank and utterly white.

*". . . go now. Can't keep holding to this . . . keeping, I
mean, to . . . together."*

—Chever's last notes

When he came to—when the white dimmed to the colors
of earth—the man lay curled up in swamp mud. The first
thing he saw was the rose—a hallucination. An illusion.

He reached out, palm up. The illusion's head rested
softly upon his fingers. He wept.

When the tears ceased, the rose was still there.

He felt something hard beneath his ribs, lodged in the
mud, and shifted to push it aside. A rock. A light touch
brushed his cheek. When he had shifted, he had come
nearer to the rose, and now it touched its face to his.

He pushed himself to a sitting position and cupped the
bloom between his palms. It had taken root at a slant; it
had fallen on its side when he had thrust it from himself
in a time that seemed so long ago. Its stem had curved to
enable it to capture what rays of sun it could through the
swamp's mossy ceiling.

He gradually became aware of his hands; something
about them had nagged at the back of his mind ever since
he had awakened.

There: they had begun to rot. He felt no pain, and yet
the skin hung from them in tatters. He thought he could
see the bone of one of his knuckles.

So this was it. The woman had given him a disease as
her parting gift, and he would die soon.

It had been worth it.

Now he would remain here. He would not leave his
rose again.

Time passed. He did not count cycles of light and dark.
Sometimes he lay on his back and stared through the
moss and branches at the sky. At night, he saw the stars

and thought of his love on their last night together. During the day, he imagined that certain strands of the whitish green moss overhead might be the remnants of Chever's notes, caught and molded to the trees in the rain. But no—the woman had brought them back after he had tossed them away.

Why had she done it? Why had she come to his house, lied, stolen his heart, brought him to the sewers, infected him with rot?

His only regret was that he had never reached an epiphany over Chever's notes. He thought longingly of the table in the sewers where he kept them, where they doubtless rested even now. Or . . . did they?

He strained to see into the blur of days between her disappearance and the present. And . . . yes, the image came: himself, standing over a table empty of all but a stump of a candle, frowning slightly, thinking vaguely that something was missing but not caring enough to think on it further.

An empty table. No notes.

She had taken them.

Of course. It made sense. What else of value had he to offer her? He had nothing special, no powers or insights. His rose was valuable only to him, but Chever's notes. . . .

He could imagine those would be valuable to many of the woman's kind. He had been so caught up in his little world of garden, studies, and mountain cabin that he had failed to think beyond it. This was the price of that failure. To ensure he would not come after his treasure . . . a poison kiss.

But why had she not taken the notes sooner? He would never know. Perhaps he had been the one brief flash of light in her otherwise dark existence, her chance to know love before losing her life to whatever pit dark wizards swarmed in. Perhaps, having known love, someday she might also know remorse, penance . . . and, somewhere beyond that, peace.

Yes . . . that's what he would believe.

He had propped himself up on one elbow, and now he let his head fall back to his pillow of mud. Leeches clung to his face, and he smiled. Now the end would come.

THAT CURIOUS SWORD

R.A. Salvatore

The Year of the Shield (1367 DR)

"It is not so different from Calimport," Artemis
Entreri insisted, somewhat stubbornly.

Across the table from him, Jarlaxle merely
chuckled.

"And you call my people xenophobic," the dark
elf replied. "At least we are not so racist toward
others of our own species!"

"You talk the part of the fool."

"I talked my way into the city, did I not?" Jarlaxle replied with that mischievous grin of his.

It was true enough. He and Entreri had come
north and east, to the region known as the
Bloodstone Lands. There, word had it, adventur-
ers could do a fine business in goblin ears and
the like, taken from the wild lands of Vaasa to
the north of the kingdom of Damara and this

city, Damara's capital, Heliogabalus. Liberally invoking the name of Gareth Dragonsbane, and reminding the city guards that the Paladin King of Damara was a man known for tolerance and understanding, a man known for judging all people by their actions and not their heritage, the dark elf had convinced the city's stern protectors to allow him entry.

They had agreed mostly because Jarlaxle was like no other dark elf they had ever heard of—and none of them had ever seen one. Outrageously dressed with a flamboyant wide-brimmed hat capped by a huge purple feather, a flowing cape—blue on the day he had entered the city, since turned red—an eye patch that daily changed from eye to eye, and with no apparent weapons, the drow seemed more a conversation piece than any threat to the security of the great city. They had let him and Entreri, with his magnificent sword and jeweled dagger, enter the city but had promised to watch over them carefully.

After a couple of hours, the assassin and the drow knew that promise was one the lazy guards didn't intend to keep.

"You're taking far too long!" Entreri yelled across the somewhat crowded tavern, at the hapless waitress who had taken their order for drinks and food.

They knew she was in no hurry to return to them, for she had been trembling visibly at the sight of a drow elf all the time she was trying to concentrate on their words.

The woman blanched and started toward the bar, then turned around, then turned around again, as if she didn't know what to do. At a nearby table, a pair of men looked from her to Entreri, their expressions sour.

The assassin sat calmly, almost hoping that the pair would make a move. He was in an especially foul mood over the last couple of months, ever since he and Jarlaxle had destroyed the Crystal Shard. The road had been boring and uneventful, even with his flamboyant companion, and Jarlaxle's plan to come to the Bloodstone Lands to make a reputation and some coin by killing goblins and other monsters sounded more to Entreri like a job for his former arch-nemesis Drizzt and his "gallant" friends.

Still, Entreri had to admit that their options were a bit limited, since Calimport was shut off to them and they'd have a hard time truly establishing themselves in the bowery of any other city.

"You've flustered her," Jarlaxle remarked.

Entreri just shrugged.

"You know, my friend, there is a saying among the drow nobles that if someone treats you well but is wicked to the peasants, then he is truly a wicked person. Now, in my society, that is a compliment, but here?"

Entreri sat back and lifted the front of his round, thin-brimmed hat—Jarlaxle called it a "bolero"—high above his eyes, so that the drow could clearly see his stare, could see the skepticism in his dark eyes.

"Do not pretend you don't care," Jarlaxle said against that smirk.

"Now my conscience is a dark elf?" Entreri asked incredulously. "How low must I have sunk."

"Artemis Entreri is a better man than to whip a serving girl," was all Jarlaxle said, pointedly turning away.

With a frustrated growl, Entreri shoved back from the table and started across the room, his small form moving silently and gracefully, almost as if he was floating across the room, heading for the serving girl. He passed the table with the two loud onlookers, and one of them started to stand as if to block the way, but a look from Entreri, so cold and strong, was enough to alter that plan.

"You," Entreri called to the girl.

She stopped, and everything in the place seemed to come to a complete halt, all conversations ending abruptly.

Well, except for the knowing chuckle from a peculiar looking dark elf at the back of the room.

The serving girl slowly turned to watch Entreri's approach. He moved right up to her and fell to one knee.

"I beg your pardon, good lady," he apologized.

He held out his hand and dropped a few gold coins onto her tray.

The young woman stared at him in disbelief.

Entreri came up from his bow to stand before her. "I expect that you've forgotten what we ordered," he said, "which is understandable, given the . . ." He paused and glanced back at Jarlaxle, then finished, ". . . unusual look of my friend. I will tell you our preferences again, and with my apologies for not seeing your dilemma earlier."

All around him, the patrons went back to their private conversations. The waitress beamed a great smile, obviously relieved.

Entreri started to go on, to ask her forgiveness, but he couldn't quite bring himself to do that.

"My thanks," he said, and he reiterated the order, then turned back and rejoined Jarlaxle.

"Wonderful!" the dark elf said. "I do believe that I will have you in a paladin's order within a year!"

Entreri narrowed his dark eyes to which Jarlaxle only laughed.

"Thinked I was gonna have to kick yer arse outta here," came a voice from the side.

The companions turned to see the innkeeper, a burly older man who looked like a good portion of his chest had slipped to his belly. Still, the large man held an imposing aura about him. Before either of them could take his words as a threat or an insult, though, the man widened a crooked, gap-toothed smile at them.

"Was glad ye made me girl, Kitzy, happy." He pulled out a chair, reversed it, then straddled it, placing his huge elbows on the table and leaning forward. "So what's bringing a pair like you to Heliogabalus?"

"I just wanted to see a city that could boast of such a stupid name," Entreri quipped, and the innkeeper howled and slapped his thigh.

"We have heard that there is fame and fortune to be made in this country," Jarlaxle said in all seriousness, "for those strong enough and cunning enough to find it."

"And that'd be yerself?"

"Some might think so," the dark elf replied, and he gave a shrug. "As you can imagine, it is not easy for one of my heritage to gain acceptance. Perhaps this is an opportunity worth investigating."

"A hero drow?"

"You have, perhaps, heard of Drizzt Do'Urden?" Jarlaxle asked.

Once before, he had tried to use that name for himself, to impress some farmers who, it turned out, had never heard of the unusual drow warrior of Icewind Dale.

Entreri watched his friend's performance with budding anger, recognizing the ploy for what it was. Jarlaxle had been frustrated with his inability to impersonate Drizzt, or at least, with the lack of gain he would derive from impersonating someone that no one had ever heard of, but perhaps if this man knew of Drizzt, Jarlaxle could assume the identity anew, and begin this phase of his journey a bit higher on the feeding chain of Heliogabalus.

"Drizzit Dudden?" the man echoed badly, scratching his head. "Nope, can't say that I have. He another drow?"

"Another corpse," Entreri put in, and he shot Jarlaxle a glare, not appreciating that Jarlaxle kept bringing up that one's name.

Artemis Entreri was done with Drizzt. He had beaten the drow in their last encounter—with help from a dark elf psionicist—but more importantly than killing Drizzt, Entreri had exorcised the demon within himself, the need to ever deal with that one again.

"It does not matter," Jarlaxle said, apparently catching the cue and bringing the conversation back in place.

"So ye're here to make a name for yerselfs, eh? I expect ye'll be headin' up Vaasa way."

"I expect that you ask too many questions," said Entreri, and Jarlaxle tossed him another scowl.

"You do seem rather inquisitive," the drow added, mostly to downplay Entreri's tone.

"Well that's me business," the innkeeper replied. "Folks'll be askin' me about the strange pair that came through."

"Strange?" Entreri asked.

"Ye got a drow elf with ye."

"True enough."

"So if ye're tellin' me yer tale, then ye're really saving yerselfs some trouble," the innkeeper went on.

"The town herald," Jarlaxle said dryly.

"That's me business."

"Well, it is as we have already told you," the dark elf replied. He stood up and offered a polite bow. "I am Jarlaxle, and this is my friend, Artemis Entreri."

As the innkeeper replied with the customary "Well met," Entreri put another frown on and glowered at the dark elf, hardly believing that Jarlaxle had just given out their names. The innkeeper offered his name in reply, which Entreri didn't bother to catch, then began telling them a few tales about men who had gone up to fight in Vaasa, which interested Entreri even less. Then, after a call from the bar area, the man excused himself and walked away.

"What?" Jarlaxle asked against Entreri's frown.

"You are so willing to give out our identities?"

"Why would I not be?"

Entreri's expression showed clearly that the reasons should be obvious.

"There is nobody chasing us, my friend. We haven't

earned the anger of the authorities—not in this region, at least. Were you not known in Calimport as Artemis Entreri? Do not be ashamed of your name!"

Entreri just shook his head, sat back, and took a sip of his wine. This whole adventure on the road was too out of place for him still.

Some time later, the inn clearing out of the nightly patrons, the innkeeper ambled back over to the pair.

"So, when're ye off to Vaasa?" he asked.

Entreri and Jarlaxle exchanged knowing looks—the way the man had spoken the words showed it to be a leading question.

"Soon, I would expect," Jarlaxle replied, nibbling at the bait. "Our funds are running low."

"Ah, ye're lookin' for work already," said the innkeeper. "Killin' goblins only? Well, goblins and orcs, I mean? Or are ye in the game for more subtle forms?"

"You presume much," said Entreri.

"True enough, but ye're not tellin' me that ye're fighters of the open road, now are ye?"

"Would you like to see?" Entreri offered.

"Oh, I'm not doubtin' ye!" the man said with a broad grin. He held his huge paws up before him, warding the dangerous man away. "But ye look like a pair who might be doing better work for better pay, if ye get me meaning."

"And if we do not?"

The innkeeper looked at Entreri curiously.

"If we do not get your meaning," Jarlaxle explained.

"Ah, well, there're plenty of jobs about Heliogabalus," the innkeeper explained. "For the right crew, I mean. The authorities are all up at the wall in Vaasa, fighting monsters, but that leaves many citizens wronged back here in town with nowhere to turn."

Entreri didn't even try to hide his smirk, and in truth, just hearing the man ramble on made him feel a bit more at home. Heliogabalus, after all, wasn't so different from

Calimport, where the laws of the land and the laws of the street were two very different codes. He could hardly believe that he and Jarlaxle had been sought out so quickly, though, with no reputation preceding them, but he didn't think too much about it. Likely, most of the fighters of the region were away in the north, along with most of those who had made their living by keeping order on the street, as well, whatever order that might be.

"And you know of these jobs?" Jarlaxle asked the man.

"Well, that's me business!" said the innkeeper. "In truth, I'm a bit short o' help right now, and I got a friend askin' me to hire out a job."

"And what makes you think that we are capable of such a job?" Jarlaxle asked.

"When ye been doin' this as long as ol' Feepun here, ye get to know the look," he explained. "I watch the way ye walk. I see the way ye lift yer drinks, the way that one's eyes keep movin' side-to-side, watchin' everything about him. Oh, I'm guessin' that the work I have for ye, if ye want it, will be far beneath yer true talents, but it's a place to start." He paused and looked hopefully at the pair.

"Well, pray tell us of this job," Jarlaxle prompted after a lengthy pause. "Nothing against the law of the land, you understand," he added, a typical and expected disclaimer that any self-respecting thief or assassin would be quick to add.

"Oh, no, not that," Feepun said with a laugh. "A bit of justice sorted out, that's all."

Jarlaxle and Entreri exchanged knowing smirks—that was the common disclaimer response, usually meaning that someone either deserved to die, or to be robbed.

"Got me a friend who's lookin' to get an idol back," the innkeeper explained, leaning in and whispering. "He's paying good, too. Hundred gold pieces for one night's work. Ye up for it?"

"Keep talking," said Jarlaxle.

"Seems he's had a dispute over a little statue. Got stolen by a guy near here. He wants it back."

"How do you know that we are capable of doing this?" Entreri asked.

"Telled ye I knowed how to read me guests. I think ye can. Shouldn't be too hard a job, though this thief, Rorli, is a nasty one."

"Perhaps a hundred is not enough, then," Jarlaxle put in.

The innkeeper shrugged. "Said he'd give a hundred. Seems like a fair price to me. I can ask—"

"First tell us the particulars," Entreri interrupted. "We have much to do and need to buy supplies for the road north."

The innkeeper grinned and leaned in even closer, detailing all he knew of Rorli, including the location of the man's apartment, which was not far away. Then, on the request of Jarlaxle and Entreri, the innkeeper left them alone for a bit.

"It might be fun," Jarlaxle said when he and his friend were alone.

"Might get us killed or get Rorli killed."

The dark elf shrugged, as if that hardly mattered. "A hundred gold is a pittance," he said, "but so begins a reputation that might suit us well, perhaps."

"Give me a hundred gold now, so I might buy the items I'll need for the work," Entreri said.

Grinning widely, Jarlaxle reached into a tiny pouch and pulled forth some coins, then some more and some more—more than the purse could possibly hold, except that it contained an extra-dimensional pocket within—until Entreri had closer to two hundred.

"And we're doing this for a hundred?" the assassin asked skeptically.

"The things you buy will be reusable, yes?"

"Yes."

"An investment, then."

It occurred to Entreri that his companion was enjoying this a bit too much. He knew that usually meant trouble.

Still, he shrugged and motioned for the innkeeper to come back.

Deftly working his housebreaker harness and the ropes he had set with a grapnel on the building's roof, Entreri scaled the two-story structure, setting himself at the ledge of the second story window that he knew from observation to be Rorli's bedroom. A quick check had him confident that there were no pressure traps on this side of the glass.

In perfect balance and with amazing dexterity, the thief pulled forth his other newly-acquired tools, pressing a suction cup delicately against the center of the glass, then attached a swivel arm, with its diamond-tipped glass cutter. He traced a perfect circle and tugged lightly, though the cut piece didn't immediately pull free.

Jarlaxle calmly levitated up beside him. "An interesting contraption for one who cannot levitate," the dark elf said, indicating the harness.

"I make do," Entreri replied.

"But such a waste of money for the darksuit," the drow went on, shaking his head and sighing. "The cloak I gave you is far more effective, and the hat even more than that."

Entreri knew he shouldn't be surprised by anything Jarlaxle said concerning magic items, and he had been fairly convinced that the cloak he wore was some improved version of the concealing drow *piwafwi*. The remark about the hat, though, had him completely off-guard.

"The hat?" he asked. He brought his free hand up to the short and stiff brim of his bolero.

"Tip it down and to the left with your left hand and it will shield you from prying eyes."

Entreri did as the drow instructed and an immediate chill washed over him, bringing a shudder.

"There," Jarlaxle announced. "When you feel warm again, just tip the hat."

"I feel like a corpse."

"Better to feel like one than to be one."

Entreri tipped his hat in agreement, and shuddered again, then went back to his work on the window, this time popping the cut circle of glass free.

"Tight fit," Jarlaxle said dryly.

The assassin tossed him a smirk and gingerly reached through the glass, moving his hand slowly and gently, so gently, about the pane in search of a trap.

"Seems like a lot of work," said Jarlaxle.

He reached up to his huge hat and pulled forth a small black piece of cloth. Seeing it, Entreri just lowered his head and sighed, for he knew what was coming.

Jarlaxle spun the cloth about and it elongated, grew larger and larger. The drow threw it against the wall, and the whole area of the structure that the black circle covered simply disappeared. The typical portable hole, a rare and valuable item, created an extra-dimensional pocket, but as with most of his items, Jarlaxle's device was far from typical. Depending upon which side the drow threw down, the portable hole would either create the pocket, or simply put a temporary hole in whatever surface it had struck. Jarlaxle casually stepped into the room and pulled his hole in behind him, securing the wall once more.

So flustered was Entreri that he almost moved too quickly across the trapped part of the window pane, feeling the slight lump that indicated a pressure trap.

Regaining his wits, the man's hand worked with perfect movements, and in seconds, he had the trap disarmed and even opened, revealing a small needle, no doubt poisoned.

He had it free and safely stuck through his cuff in a few more seconds, then finished his check of the window, clicked the lock, and entered the room.

"At least I put the wall back," Jarlaxle quipped, indicating the circle of glass in Entreri's hand.

A flick of the assassin's wrist sent the glass piece crashing to the floor.

"So much for secrecy," said Jarlaxle.

"Maybe I'm in the mood to kill someone," Entreri replied, staring hard at the frustrating dark elf.

Jarlaxle shrugged.

Entreri scanned the room. A door was set in the wall across from the window, in the corner to the left, with an open closet beside it. Halfway down the wall to the right of the window stood a chest of drawers as high as Entreri's shoulder. A bed and night table across from the bureau completed the furnishings. Entreri went for the chest of drawers as Jarlaxle moved to the closet.

"Poor taste," he heard the dark elf say, and turned to see Jarlaxle rifling through the hanging clothes, most of them drab and gray.

Entreri shook his head and pulled open the bottom drawer, finding some linens, and under them, a small pouch of coins, which disappeared into his pocket. The next drawer was much the same, and the third one up held assorted toiletry items, including a beautiful bone comb, its handle made of pearl. He took that, too.

The top drawer held the most curious items: a couple of jars of salves and a trio of potion bottles, each filled with a different colored liquid. Entreri nodded knowingly, and looked back to the window, then he shut the drawer and moved along to check the bed.

"Ah, a secret compartment," Jarlaxle said from the closet.

"Let me inspect it for traps."

"No need," said the dark elf.

He stepped back and produced a silver whistle, hung about his neck on a chain. Two short blows and there came a *pop* and a flash as the secret compartment magically opened.

"You have an answer for everything," Entreri remarked.

"Keeps me alive. Ah, yes, and look what we have here."

A moment later, Jarlaxle walked out of the closet carrying a small statuette, a curious figurine of a muscular man, half white, half black.

"Back to the inn and our reward?" Jarlaxle asked.

In response, the statue began laughing at him. "Doubtful you will be going anywhere, Artemis Entreri!" it said, and the fact that it was addressing Entreri and not Jarlaxle tipped both off that the speech had been preprogrammed, and with foreknowledge of the assassin.

"Um . . ." Entreri remarked.

The door to the room opened then, and Jarlaxle fell back toward the window. Entreri stayed to his left, over by the bed. In stepped a muscular, dark-skinned man dressed in long and ragged-edged black robes, a many-crested helm on his head. Behind him loomed a horde of huge gray and black dogs, blending in and out of the shadows in the hallway as if they were made of the same indistinct stuff as those patches of blackness.

Entreri felt a pull from his belt, from Charon's Claw, his magnificent sword. It didn't feel to him as if the sword was relating its eagerness for battle, though, as it usually did, but rather, almost as if it was greeting an old friend.

"I take it you were expecting us," Jarlaxle calmly stated, and he presented the statue as his proof.

"If you give it over without a struggle, you may find us to be important allies," the large man said.

"Well, I am not endeared to it just yet," Jarlaxle replied with a grin. "We could discuss price—"

"Not that worthless idol!"

"The sword," Entreri reasoned.

"And the gauntlet," the man confirmed.

Entreri scoffed at him. "They are better allies to me than you could ever be."

"Ah, yes, but are they as terrible foes as we?"

"Us? We?" Jarlaxle cut in. "Who are you? And I mean that in the plural sense, not the singular."

Both the dark man and Entreri looked at the drow curiously.

"The sword your friend carries does not belong to him," the dark man said to Jarlaxle.

The drow looked to Entreri and asked, "Did you kill the former owner?"

"What do you think?"

Jarlaxle nodded and looked back to the dark man. "It is his."

"It is Netherese!"

Entreri didn't quite know what that meant, but when he looked to Jarlaxle and saw the drow's eyes opened very wide, as wide as they had been when the pair had encountered the dragon to destroy the Crystal Shard, he knew that there might be a bit of trouble.

"Netherese?" the drow echoed. "A people long gone."

"A people soon to be returned," the dark man assured him. "A people seeking their former glory, and their former possessions."

"Well, there is the best news the world has heard in a millennium," Jarlaxle said sarcastically, to which the dark man only laughed.

"I have been sent to retrieve the sword," he explained. "I could have killed you outright and without question, but it occurred to me that two companions such as yourselves might prove to be very valuable allies to Sh—my people, as we shall be to you."

"How valuable?" asked Jarlaxle, obviously intrigued.

"And if I ally with you, then I get to keep the sword?" Entreri asked.

"No," the dark man answered Entreri.

"Then no," Entreri answered back.

"Let us not be hasty," said the deal-maker drow.

"Seems pretty simple to me," said Entreri.

"Then to me, as well," said the dark man. "The hard way, then. As you wish!"

As he finished, he stepped aside, and the pack of great dogs charged into the room, howling madly, their white teeth gleaming in stark contrast against the blackness of them.

Entreri fell into a crouch, ready to spring aside, but Jarlaxle took matters under control, tossing out before the dogs the same portable hole he had used to enter the room.

With howls turning to yelps, the beasts disappeared through the floor, tumbling to the room below. Jarlaxle bent immediately and scooped up the hole, sealing the floor above them.

"I have to get one of those," Entreri remarked.

"If you do, don't jump into mine with it," said Jarlaxle.

Entreri fixed him with a puzzled expression.

"Rift . . . astral . . . you don't want to know," Jarlaxle assured him.

"Right. Now, where does that leave us?" the assassin asked.

"It leaves you with an enemy you do not understand!" the dark man replied.

He laughed and moved to the side, disappearing so quickly, so completely into the shadows that it seemed a trick of the eyes to Entreri. Still, the assassin did manage to flick his fingers and knew his tiny missile had struck home when he heard a slight chirp from the man.

"You favor the darkness, drow?" the dark man asked, and as he finished, the room went perfectly black.

"I do!" Jarlaxle responded, and he blew on the whistle again: a short burst, a long one, and another short one. Entreri heard the door slam.

It was all happening quickly, and purely on instinct, the assassin drew out his sword and his jeweled dagger and moved protectively back against the bed. He tipped his cap again, though he understood this to be magical darkness, impenetrable even by those who had the ability to see in the dark. It was fortunate he did, though, for right after the chill enshrouded his body, he felt the sudden intense heat of a fireball filling the room.

He was down and under the bed in an instant, then came out the other side as the burning mattress collapsed.

"Caster!" he yelled.

"Seriously?" came Jarlaxle's sarcastic reply.

"Seriously," came the dark man's cry. "And I fear not your little stings!"

"Really?" Entreri asked him, and he was moving as he spoke, trying hard not to give the dark man any definitive target. "Even from the needle off your own window tr—?"

His last word was cut short, though, as complete silence engulfed the room. Profound, magical silence that quieted even the yelping and howling dogs below. Entreri knew that it was Jarlaxle's doing, the drow's standard opening salvo against dangerous magic-users. Without the ability to use verbal components, a wizard's repertoire was severely limited.

But now Entreri had to worry about himself, for his magical sword began a sudden assault upon his sensibilities, compelling him to turn the blade back on himself and take his own life. He had already fought this struggle of wills with the stubborn weapon, but with an apparent representative of its creators nearby, the sword seemed even angrier.

The assassin wore the gauntlet, which minimized the effect the sword could have on him, and he was able to hold the upper hand—somewhat. For he also had to keep exact track of where he was in the room. He had one good shot because of his previous actions and words, he knew, and to miss the opportunity would make this situation even more dangerous.

He aligned himself with the heat emanating from the bed, turned in the direction he guessed to be perfectly perpendicular to the window, then took three definitive strides across the room, finally sheathing the stubborn sword as he went.

He struck once, he struck fast, and he struck true, right into the back of the dark man, his vampiric, life-stealing jeweled dagger diving in deep.

A strange feeling engulfed Entreri as the dagger pumped forth the life-force of the dying man, dizzying and disorienting. He fell back, then stumbled silently to the floor, and lay there for a long while.

Soon after, he heard the dogs barking again from below.

"It's over," he announced, fearing that Jarlaxle would drop another silence on the room.

A moment later, the darkness lifted as well. Lying on the floor, Entreri looked straight up to see his dark elf companion similarly lying on the ceiling, hands tucked comfortably behind his head. Entreri also noticed that the scarring on the walls and ceiling ended in a bubble about the drow, as if he had enacted some shield that magic, or the fireball at least, could not affect.

The assassin wasn't surprised.

"Well done," Jarlaxle congratulated, floating down gently to the floor, as Entreri stood and brushed himself off. "Without sight or hearing, how did you know he was there?"

Entreri looked over at the dead man. He had pulled out the top drawer of the dresser as he'd slumped to the floor, its contents spilled about him.

"I told him I had hit him with the needle from the window," the assassin explained. "I guessed that one of those bottles contained the antidote. He wanted to use the cover of the darkness and the silence to take care of that little detail."

"Well done!" said Jarlaxle. "I knew there was a reason I kept you around."

Entreri shook his head. "He wasn't lying about the sword," he said. "It held an affinity to him. I felt it clearly, for it even tried to turn against me."

"A Netherese blade. . . ." Jarlaxle mused. He looked at Entreri, and his eyes widened for just a moment, then a smile spread across his face. "Tell me, how does your sword feel about you now?"

Entreri shrugged and gingerly drew the blade. He felt a definite closeness to it, more so than ever before. He turned his puzzled expression upon Jarlaxle.

"Perhaps it thinks of you as more akin to its original makers now," the drow explained. When Entreri gave him an even more confused look, he added, looking at the fallen enemy, "He was no ordinary man."

"So I guessed."

"He was a shade—a creature infused with the stuff of shadow."

Entreri shrugged, for that meant nothing to him.

"And you killed him with your vampiric dagger, yes?"

Entreri shrugged again, starting to get worried, but Jarlaxle merely laughed and produced a small mirror. Looking into it, Entreri could see, even in the dim light, that his normally brown skin had taken on a bit of a gray pallor—nothing too noticeable.

"You have infused yourself with a bit of that essence," said the drow.

"What does that mean?" the alarmed assassin asked.

"It means you've just become even better at your craft,

my friend," Jarlaxle said with a laugh. "We will learn in time just how much."

Entreri had to be satisfied with that, he supposed, because there seemed nothing further coming from his oft-cryptic friend. He bent over and picked up the discarded idol. This time it remained silent.

"We should go and collect our money from the innkeeper," he said.

"And?" the drow asked.

"And kill the dolt for setting us up."

"That might not go over well with the Heliogabalus authorities," Jarlaxle reasoned.

Entreri's answer was one so typical that Jarlaxle silently mouthed the words along with him.

"Then we won't tell anybody."

A LITTLE KNOWLEDGE

Elaine Cunningham

19 Marpenoth,
the Year of Wild Magic (1372 DR)

Long rays of morning sun slanted through Halruaa's ancient trees, reaching out like tentative fingers to waken the rain-sodden village. But Ashtarahh was already long awake and bustling with activity.

The summer monsoon season was over. The village diviner decreed that yesterday's storm would be the last. Already the rice fields and brissberry bogs were alive with harvesters, moving barelegged through ankle deep water as they sped their task with morning-glad songs.

Mist clung to the fields and swirled around the small buildings, pinned between land and sky by the hot, dense air and the swiftly climbing sun. No one wondered how the moisture-laden skies could absorb yesterday's rains; the answer was in the lush Halruaan landscape, and in particular the tall, thin trees lining the forest's edge, swaying dreamily to music only they could hear.

The vangi trees came with the first rains, sprouting up overnight like verdant mushrooms. They grew with incredible speed—two or three handspans a day. By the end of the monsoons, they were ready for harvest. Several children, agile as monkeys, shimmied up the segmented trunks to pluck the fist-sized purple fruit at the top. These they tossed into the canvas sheet held taut and ready by the four glum-faced, land-bound boys who'd drawn short straws. Several young men stood ready with machetes. Once the fruit was taken, the trees would be cut, dressed into lengths, and dragged to the road. The village streets were cobbled and the forest roads deeply sheltered, but the path leading through the fields was slow to harden. Each year fresh rows of vangi trees were pressed into the muck, forming a bumpy but mostly dry path for market traffic.

This path ended between two shops: the blacksmith and the wheelwright. Smoke rose in billows from the heating forge, and two apprentices busily rolled new wheels into waiting racks. A trip down the vangi corduroy road was a bone-rattling gauntlet, and more than one of the expected market carts would not survive it unscathed. But visiting merchants and artisans shrugged off splintered wheels, unshod oxen, and broken axles as the cost of doing business in Ashtarahh.

The late summer market was especially busy. Market stalls and tents rapidly took shape under the hands of carpenters and minor wizards. The owners of more permanent shops folded back the protective canvases, wielded brooms, and set out their wares. The clack of looms and the tart aroma of ripe cheeses filled the air. Bright glass vials of brissberry cordial stood in lines, looking like enormous ruby necklaces. Lengths of fine white linen gleamed in the morning sun, and skeins of brightly dyed yarn hung in arched windows in deliberate imitation of rainbows. But the most famous of Ashtarahh's crafts were its cunningly woven tapestries. These hung at every third stall, transforming the market into a veritable gallery.

Villagers who were not otherwise engaged strolled along the cobbles, admiring the woven art. Most of the tapestries depicted scenes from Halruaan history and legend. Skyships were commonly depicted, as were the magical creatures common to Halruaa: the brilliantly colored, many-legged crocodilians known as behirs, the winged starsnakes, even the dreaded laraken. Some of the tapestries depicted famous and infamous wizards. Small magical effects enlivened some of these scenes, sending bursts of light arching between spell-battling foes. A large weaving of a quite-literally blazing phoenix— the new standard of King Zalathorm—drew admiring attention. The biggest crowd, however, was the group stealthily converging upon the southwest corner of the square, where Ursault the All-Seeing sat with his crooked, cast-off loom.

Ursault was a thin, unassuming man of indeterminate age. His long, rather stringy locks had gone gray, and his face was unmemorable but for his pale eyes—a hazel more gray than green, an oddity in a land of dark-eyed, black-haired people. The title "All-Seeing" held gentle mockery, though it was rumored that it had once been spoken with respect. Once, it was said, Ursault had been a powerful diviner, one who saw many possible paths with equal clarity. But the vast and various potential of the future was a burden too large to carry, and Ursault had retreated to this sleepy village, content to weave his confused visions into tapestries no one wanted, and only he could understand.

A band of boys wove through the stalls as they crept

toward the wizard, their grins wide and white in small dirty faces. Several of them scooped mud from between the cobbles and readied the first wave of attack.

The wizard looked up and smiled in gentle welcome. No knowledge of the coming mischief was written in his pale eyes, but a small, ominous gray cloud appeared directly over the head of the band's leader, a stocky little urchin who answered to Dammet.

The unwitting boy hauled back for the throw. Instantly the cloud exploded into a tiny, belated monsoon, drenching the boy and sending his comrades skittering away, hooting with delighted laughter. Liquid mud dribbled between Dammet's fingers as his weapon dissipated.

A second boy darted back and hurled his mud ball with a deft, side-armed toss. Ursault moved one hand in a vague little gesture and the mud changed in midair to a crystalline white. He caught the snowball and tossed it back to the urchin. The boy yelped with surprise and tossed the ball from hand to hand, marveling at the unfamiliar sting of cold.

"Taste it," Ursault suggested.

Uncertainty flooded the small face, but the mixture of encouragement and taunting from his friends decided the matter. He took a tentative lick, and his eyes rounded with delight.

"Mazganut cream," the boy announced grandly.

He dodged several grasping hands then darted off, his prize clutched possessively. Two of the boys started to give chase but abandoned the notion after their first few steps. There was a bigger game to be played, and their faces were smug with anticipation.

Dammet pushed a smaller boy forward—an ungainly lad with an intense but unfocused stare. Dammet flipped a lock of wet black hair off his face and draped an arm around the boy's tensely-hunched shoulders.

"Here's my man Tad," he announced. He leaned down

to scoop up more mud, which he slapped into the boy's hand. "You might say he's skittish. If he kept his mind stuck to one idea for more'n a heartbeat, the shock of it would likely kill him. And he can't throw worth goat dung. There ain't no way you could know where this mud ball's gonna hit."

Indeed, the wizard's face furrowed as he contemplated the possibilities. An expression of near panic seeped into his pale eyes.

"Mebbe not, but you can figure out where *I'll* hit sure enough," announced a thin, nasal voice. A short, stout man stepped out from behind the stall's tumble-down wall, brandishing a vangi switch. "Now git."

The boys got, scampering off with scant regard for their less agile champion. Tad stumbled after them, howling protests against his abandonment.

Ursault glanced at his rescuer. Though the wizard was seated upon a low stool, he was eye to eye with the newcomer, a man whose barrel-chested torso was supported by uncommonly short, bandy legs. He was about the height of a dwarf but was most definitely not of that race. His face was as beardless as a boy's though he was well into adulthood. There was no hint of any other race about him to explain his stature—he lacked the small frame and hairy feet of Luiren's halflings, and the bulbous nose and blue eyes common to gnomes. Yet some wag had called him a Gnarfling—an unlikely combination of all three races—and the name had stuck.

Something that for lack of a better name could be called friendship had grown between the two village misfits. Gnarfling was the only person who regularly sought out Ursault's company and who actually seemed to enjoy the old wizard's tales. He leaned in and regarded the tangle of thread on the wizard's loom.

"What do you make of this?"

"Melody Sibar's peacock chicks," Ursault said, pointing

to a matted blob of gray thread. "They'll hatch today or perhaps tomorrow. At least, those that intend to hatch at all."

"That ought to cover it."

Gnarfling uncorked a flask, which they passed back and forth a couple of times. He belched companionably and settled down, preparing to enjoy the morning's story-telling. His look of contentment faded when he noted a stout woman bustling purposefully toward them.

"Landbound skyship a'comin' under full sail," he muttered.

The description was not far off. Vilma was Dammet's mother, a cheery, chatty woman who frequently—and jus-tifiably—looked a bit flustered and windblown. Wisps of black hair escaped her single braid and her round face was rosy-cheeked from her morning's work. Like her son, she was always busy, never still. But unlike many of the villagers, she made time to chat with Ursault now and again, mostly because he was one of the few people in Ashtarahh who tolerated Dammet's pranks.

With a grateful sigh, the woman shouldered off the straps that held a basket of newly-harvested brissberries to her back. The fruit was heavy, covered with a thick rind and a nut-like shell, and extracting the juice was a long process. She unhooked a small cleaver from her belt—a needed tool for the task ahead—and began to smooth a whet stone over it.

"What's coming to this little corner of Zalathorm's realm, lord wizard?"

"A white dog," Ursault said mildly.

"Fearful doings," she said with a grin.

He nodded somberly. "That dog will be the death of more than half the people in a neighboring village."

A small brindle pup ambled by, not far from the wizard's stall. Vilma gave a good-natured chuckle. "That's Dammet's mongrel pup, and the closest thing we got to a white dog hereabouts. Not much of a threat there."

"Not for several seasons, no, but then the dog will wander far from the village and mate with a renegade wolfwere. Their offspring will have pure white fur and look more dog than wolf. In human form, she will be a comely maid."

Vilma responded with a thin smile. "My man Tomas will enjoy this tale, that's for sure and certain! His eye for a pretty girl will be the death of him." She shook her cleaver, an unconsciously lethal gesture.

"True enough, but his death will not come at your hands," Ursault replied.

The woman's smile faded, and fear crept into her eyes. When a wizard—even a mad wizard—spoke of death, it was time to start kindling the funeral pyres.

"Of course, if your boy Dammet remembers to tie the brindle dog when the harvest moon blooms full, the white maid will never be. A lot of trouble that will save." Ursault cocked his head, as if listening to unseen voices. "But on the other hand, a lot of trouble that will cause. This same wolfwere maid could bring doom to the floating city. A lot of trouble that will save. On the other hand—" He broke off with a grunt, momentarily silenced by a sharp, warning nudge from Gnarfling's elbow.

The woman's smile returned, edged with both relief and pity. "Floating cities now, is it? Here in Halruaa?"

Ursault shrugged. "Sometimes yes, and sometimes no."

"That ought to cover it," Gnarfling said meaningfully.

Vilma's gaze darted toward the short man and moved quickly away. Her tolerance did not quite embrace the odd little man. Everyone in Ashtarahh knew most everything about everyone else, and found comfort in this universal lack of privacy. But not even the most imaginative gossip among them could invent a story that could in satisfactory fashion explain Gnarfling, or define his purpose in coming to Ashtarahh. Vilma had a limited imagination and a healthy suspicion of anything than lay beyond its bounds. She gave Ursault a tentative smile, then hauled up her basket and took off at a brisk pace.

Gnarfling reached for his flask and gestured with it toward the loom. "What else you see in there?"

A forlorn expression touched the wizard's face. "Everything," he said softly, his voice sad and infinitely weary. "Everything."

The small man cleared his throat, uneasy with his friend's pain. "Well, how about you start a new weaving, and let's see where it goes."

Ursault obligingly drew a small knife and cut the tangle from his loom. He made a complicated arcane gesture, and a new set of vertical threads appeared on the crooked frame. For a long moment he studied the warp threads, as if examining and discarding many possibilities. Finally he took up a shuttle and began to layer in the weft.

His hands flashed with a wizard's exquisite dexterity, adding a thread here and a new color there. Before long a pattern began to emerge. Glowing, silvery threads connected in a fine web. The fabric between this web, however, remained a dark and indeterminate color, deep as moon-cast shadows. Gnarfling frowned in puzzlement as he noted that Ursault was threading in some mud-splattered crimson. Even this bright color disappeared into the shadowy gloom.

"What do you make of that?" he demanded.

"That's the Weave," Ursault replied, naming the web of magic that surrounded and sustained all of Halruaa, and for all Gnarfling knew, the rest of the world as well. "At least, it's Ashtarahh's place in the Weave."

Gnarfling leaned in and squinted. Sure enough, he could make out the faint outline of the village, as it might appear to a soaring hawk, carved out of the tightly packed web that represented the jungle. Fainter, thinner silver threads connected the fields and buildings, and tiny glowing dots seemed to mill about the open area—an uncanny representation of the market square and the people who readied it.

This was the first discernable picture Gnarfling had ever seen on Ursault's loom. For some reason that worried him. So did the intense expression on the wizard's face as he tossed colors haphazardly into the pattern, only to have them swallowed by the strange, shadowy void that separated and defined the silvery Weave.

In short order a small tapestry hung on the loom. Ursault studied the weaving intently, and Gnarfling studied Ursault.

"You see something, don't you?"

"Everything," the wizard responded again in wondering tones. "Everything."

The response was familiar, but there was a new note in his voice, something that sent tiny fingers of cold dancing down Gnarfling's spine.

After a moment, Ursault moved one hand in a flowing circular pattern. The unseen colors shifted, and a man's face took form in a gap between the glowing silver threads, a face depicted with precision and clarity that the best of Ashtarahh's weavers could not match.

The man was young and exceedingly lean. His high, sharp cheekbones leaned precariously over the deep hollows below, and the thin black mustache on his upper lip looked as tremulous and impermanent as an alighting moth. His face was exceedingly pale for a Halruaan, and a sharp contrast to the feverish brightness of his black eyes.

"Trouble coming," muttered Gnarfling. He was well acquainted with trouble and plenty familiar with wizards—which, to his way of thinking, was two ways of saying the same thing. "When?"

In response, Ursault merely shifted his gaze from the loom to the market square.

The square was filling rapidly. Visiting merchants strolled along the paths, eyeing the tapestries and sampling bits of cheese. The trundle of carts over the corduroy filled the air with a pleasant rumble. Already two of these carts had been hauled off the path to languish by the wheelwright's shop, listing heavily over shattered wheels. A young man stood by one of them, arguing with the apprentices and punctuating his complaints with overly dramatic gestures.

Gnarfling's eyes went straight to a thin young man, narrowing as they took in the too-familiar theatrics. The newcomer didn't have the look of a merchant or artisan. He was tall and thin, not much past twenty summers, and obviously possessed more money than sense. He traveled alone on in an expensive covered cart drawn by matched horses. His emaciated form was draped with fine robes of purple-trimmed black, and jewels flashed on his gesticulating hands. All of these things fairly screamed "wizard."

Even without the trappings, there was an intensity about the newcomer that suggested magic, yet Gnarfling could sense no hint of Mystra's Art about the young man. His nose for such things was as keen as any hound's— and more to the point, as keen as any magehound's. These instincts, and the permanent disguise offered by his stunted form, had kept him alive for over thirty winters.

Why then, he wondered, was he so uneasy?

"He's looking for you," Ursault said, as mildly and as matter-of-factly as if his companion had spoken his question aloud.

The small man shot to his feet as if he'd just sat on a hedgehog. The sudden movement seemed to draw the newcomer's eyes. Recognition flared in his strangely burning gaze, and for a moment Gnarfling stared into the youth's face like a hare mesmerized by a hawk.

Then, suddenly, the young man was standing directly in front of Ursault's stall.

Gnarfling blinked once in surprise, and a few times more to adjust his vision. He instinctively sniffed for the scent of magic, but all he smelled on the newcomer was the cumulative effect of several days on the road: the faint odor of wet cashmere, the musty stench of dirty clothes, and a perfume that smelled of dangerous herbs and pending lightning—a scent no doubt meant to mask the other, more mundane smells.

"I am Landish the Adept," the young man announced grandly.

Gnarfling collected himself and folded his stubby arms. "Good for you. Me, I got no business with the outlandish or the inept. You want I should ask around, and see if someone else might?"

Pure fury simmered in the man's intense gaze, a rage out of scale with the small insult. "Are you certain you have no business with me?" he said meaningfully. "Absolutely certain? Tell me, *jordain*, what am I?"

A small sizzle of panic raced through Gnarfling, quickly mastered. Surely this revelation was nothing new to Ursault the All-Seeing, and no one else was close enough to hear the damning secret.

"What are you?" he echoed. "The back end of an ox, so far as I can tell."

The man's eyes narrowed. "'Outlandish and inept,'" he repeated. "A strange choice of words for someone who purports to be an itinerate field hand."

Gnarfling stared for a moment, then his shoulders rose and fell in a profound sigh.

"A magehound," he muttered. "And here I'm thinking I'd outrun every thrice-damned half-wizard busybody in Zalathorm's realm. Well, even a slow and stupid hound sometimes blunders into a vhoricock's nest."

"A jordaini proverb," Landish said smugly, clearly enjoying himself. "You should guard your words more carefully."

"Don't see what harm it could do at this point. A magehound," Gnarfling repeated in disgust.

No," stated Ursault.

There was a conviction in that single word that dismissed all other possibilities. Gnarfling sent a puzzled look at the wizard and was astonished at the simmering wrath in the old man's usually vague, mild eyes.

"Mirabella," Ursault said grimly.

The small man's heart seemed to leap in his chest like a breaching dolphin. Mirabella was the woman who'd saved an outcast jordaini babe, one whose stunted form was deemed unsuitable for the rigorous physical training given Halruaa's warrior-sages. But there was nothing wrong with his mind, and the soft-hearted midwife charged with his destruction knew enough of jordaini ways to give him a bit of the training. Enough to keep him aware and alive—until now, at least.

Landish's gaze snapped to the wizard's face and for a moment he looked deeply troubled. His face cleared.

"Ah. A diviner, I suppose. You see the results of my work, if not the actual workings."

"Your work? What'd you do with Mirabella?" roared Gnarfling.

He threw himself into a charge, his stubby hands leaping like twin hounds for the man's skinny throat.

Then he stopped, stunned by the white, leprous growth that had appeared on his short digits. As he stared, the small finger on his left hand listed to one side, then broke off entirely and fell to the muddy ground.

"That," Landish said succinctly. "She won't be missed. Just as you weren't missed, until now—and won't be missed after."

"Mirabella is not yet dead," Ursault said as he rose to his feet. "She may not die. The old speckled hen, the one destined for the soup pot, is going to lay her first egg since the last new moon. If she lays it in the hencoop, Mirabella will die. If the hen ventures into the gardens, a tamed hunting kestrel will see her and swoop. This will draw the eye of a passing hunting party. They will follow their hawk and find Mirabella. The hunter has a terrible fear of the plague. If he is the first to see the woman, he will flee in panic and the others will follow, never knowing what he saw. But if his horse throws a shoe—there is a loose nail and the shoe could be lost any time today or tomorrow—his greenmage daughter will be the first to find Mirabella. She can mix the herbs and pray the spells that will cure the woman. The herbs grow near Mirabella's cottage. She may find them, provided that—"

"Enough!" howled Landish, his dark eyes enormous in his too-pale face. "What madness is this?"

"He's mad, that's for sure and certain," Gnarlish said, jerking a leprous thumb toward Ursault, "but that don't stop him from being right. His way of telling the future is like throwing a really big fireball—the target can be found somewhere in the big, smoking black hole, if there's anyone left to look for it."

Ursault turned the loom around, revealing the weaving and the scenes depicted in it. Landish's face was still there, and so was a small, snug cottage, complete with speckled hens and an elderly woman sprawled, facedown and still, in the courtyard. A soft moan escaped Gnarfling.

"You named yourself an Adept," Ursault said to Landish, "and so you are. You are a Shadow Adept, though this is not known to your master, the necromancer Hsard Imulteer. You intend to ambush and destroy your master, but fear that your growing powers will give you away before you are strong enough to prevail. Desiring to test your shields, you prayed to dark Shar, the goddess of shadows and secrets, and she led you to a hidden jordain. You wished to see if a jordain could perceive your true nature, and you believed that my friend here presented a small risk. Obviously he is gifted at perceiving magic in others, or how would he evade the magehounds for these many years? If he had been able to perceive you for what you are, what harm could come of it? He could not accuse you without also giving himself away."

The young man's face paled to a papery gray. "This is not possible. No one could know these things!"

"They don't call him Ursault the All-Seeing for no reason," retorted Gnarfling.

Landish began to pace. "Yes, I have heard that name," he muttered in a distracted tone. "A wizard who sees so many possibilities he cannot discern the truth, paralyzed, driven mad, finally fleeing into a hermit's life. Seeing all, knowing all—the possibilities are staggering!"

Gnarfling began to see where this was headed. He'd met wizards before who believed they were the exception to every rule, magical and otherwise.

He sniffed derisively and said, "If you're thinking the bat guano in your spell bag don't stink, think again."

But the Adept was no longer interested in his intended quarry. He stopped before Ursault and fixed his intense black gaze on the older wizard's face. "You can see all possible futures—including those influenced by practitioners of the Shadow Weave. This is a great gift, my friend!"

"Gift or curse?" said Ursault softly. "It is difficult to say."

Landish shook his head vigorously. "Halruaa is famed for wizardry, but few know of the Shadow Weave. We who are blessed by Shar can move in secret."

"But as you gain power, your ability to perceive the workings of Mystra diminish," Ursault concluded. "You may be hidden from wizards, but their ways, in nearly equal measure, are hidden from you."

"You grasp the salient point," the young Adept said, nodding approvingly. "Clearly, you do not want this gift and—forgive me—you have not proven strong enough to handle it. It has become a burden, one I would gladly lift from you."

"A little knowledge," cautioned Ursault, "is a wonderful thing."

Landish let out a sardonic chuckle and dismissed this notion with a wave of one skinny hand. "Come, let us make a bargain. I will give you the herbs needed to cure your short friend and the old dame who raised him."

"No deal," said Gnarfling sternly. "Ursault already knows what herbs are needed. He can find them himself, no help from you."

"Of course he can find them, and of course he can cure you and the old woman—'if this, and if that,'" mocked the Adept. "And let us not forget 'unless this and the other.' Count your fingers—how many remain? Are you willing to trust your life and the woman's to a mad old wizard, and the whims of fate?"

"Same question, back at you." The small man folded his arms. "That mad old wizard could just kill you and have done with it."

"No," said Landish smugly, "he couldn't."

The wizard considered this claim for a moment then agreed with a grim nod.

"You see? This discussion is a mere formality. I could simply take this man's powers from him. He knows this, and he knows how. It would be easier for me, and far more pleasant all around, if he yields them willingly."

"Mageduel," Ursault said curtly. "Take the three of us to Mirabella's glen, and we will do battle for the title of All-Seeing."

"Done!" the Adept said gleefully.

He stepped behind the wizard's stall and conjured an oval portal, gleaming with dark, purple-black light. He made a mock-courtly gesture for the others to precede him.

Gnarfling charged through the portal and hit the ground running. He bolted toward his foster mother, dropped to his knees, and gently turned her over with hands that felt strangely numb. He recoiled in grief and horror at the ravaged mess the Adept's spell had made of her face. He lifted one hand to stroke the old woman's hair away from her eyes, and grimaced at the sight of his own hand. He didn't look much better off.

He looked to the center of the courtyard. The wizards faced each other, an expression of intense concentration on each face as they attuned themselves to each other and to their competing Weaves.

A sly smile crossed Gnarfling's face as he perceived the wizard's stratagem: an Adept of the Shadow Weave would have little power in a mageduel arena.

Indeed, a dazed expression crossed the Adept's face as he ventured into the older wizard's convoluted mind. His feverish eyes started to dart about, as if tracing the paths of a hundred startled ground squirrels.

Landish pulled himself together with visible effort and said, "As you yourself observed, I am apprentice to a powerful necromancer. There is still enough of Mystra's art remaining to me to vanquish you, old man. Surely you foresee this."

"It is a possibility," Ursault admitted, "but only one of many."

The younger man sniffed. "A cube, fifty paces on all sides. I could manage more, but the smaller the arena, the swifter my victory."

"As you wish." Ursault smiled faintly. "And in defiance of the rules, you may take your spellfilcher gem into the arena with you."

He did not point out that the man was intending to do precisely that, but the meaning was there all the same.

Landish's face flushed at this gentle rebuke, but he spun around and began to stalk off his portion of the arena. Ursault did the same. A translucent, faintly glowing red cube began to take shape around them, growing on all sides as they moved farther apart.

"Just let him rob you and be done with it," muttered Gnarling. "That'll serve him right and fair."

Landish began to mumble the words of a spell. A brilliant golden flame erupted from the ground before him. Bright droplets turned into insects—deadly magical fire gnats whose touch could raise blisters and whose bite could set living flesh aflame.

A faint blue mist surrounded the older wizard as the glowing insects swarmed in. Each one met the aura with a faint, sharp sizzle and flared out of existence.

Tremors shook the ground as invisible fingers of necromantic magic reached deep into the soil. The clearing stirred, and small puffs of dirt and sod exploded upward as long-dead bones fought their way into the light. The older wizard countered with a quick gesture, then he clapped his hands sharply together. A thunderous rumble echoed through the clearing and the old bones shattered to dust.

On the battle raged, and each spell Landish cast was anticipated and countered. The young man's thin, wolfish face contorted with rage, and he hurled his remaining spells one after another, so quickly that spell and counterspell seemed to follow each other as quickly as two sword masters' thrusts and parries.

So intent was Gnarfling on the battle that he did not at first notice the glowing gem on the Adept's hand. A large amethyst, brilliant purple, was taking on light and power with each of Ursault's counterspells.

"The spellfilcher gem," he muttered, cursing Landish as a cheat and coward.

The light intensified until it filled the arena and

spilled out into the clearing. Finally Ursault collapsed, falling to one knee and drawing in long, ragged breaths. As Landish has promised, the process of taking his magic from him had not been easy or painless.

The Adept stood triumphant in the eerie light. The hand bearing the glowing gem was fisted and held high, and his eyes shone with the bright, multifaceted dream that was his future.

Gnarfling eased Mirabella from his arms and went over to haul the old wizard slowly, painfully to his feet.

"You shoulda thrown the fight," he grumbled.

"And willingly pass this curse to another, even such a man as this?" Ursault shook his head.

"You knew he was going to win, though."

"It was a possibility. One of many."

With Gnarfling's help, the wizard made his way over to Mirabella. After a moment he shook his head. "She needs more help than I can give her."

The short man sat back on his heels. "If that and if this," he mused.

Suddenly he leaped to his feet, went to the hencoop and kicked it resoundingly. A half dozen hens exploded from it, squawking in protest. One old biddy scurried into the field.

Landish's howl of protest cut through the clearing like a machete. Even before he looked up, Gnarfling knew what he would see.

The small form of a kestrel circled against the clouds. Within moments the hawk went into a diving stoop, tempted by the plump, slow-moving meal below.

The rumble of horses hooves turned thunderous as the hunting party burst from the forest and onto the old corduroy path. Gnarfling blinked in surprise at the size of the entourage: at least six wizards, plus squires and a plain-faced young woman in simple tunic and trews. That would be the greenmage.

Her gaze fell upon the old woman, and she let out a small cry. A bolt of lightning sizzled toward her—and was stopped just short of a strike by an answering bolt flaring from one of the mounted wizards. The hunters spurred their horses toward Landish. They dismounted and began to circle the young adept.

"You didn't mention the other wizards," Gnarfling said.

Ursault smiled faintly. "Knowledge is not quite the same as wisdom. It is not necessary or wise to speak of everything you know."

But Landish had not yet acquired this wisdom. He advanced swiftly, his hand fisted and his spellfilcher ring held out to capture the first spell flung at him.

"The first of many," Ursault observed. He sighed in resignation.

"What's going to happen?" Gnarfling asked. He suddenly seemed to hear his own words and grimaced. "Sorry. Old habit."

"The only thing that could happen," the wizard replied. "The ability to *recognize* several possible futures does not grant a corresponding ability to *avoid* them.

Gnarfling responded with a nod and an evil grin. When several powerful wizards were concerned, one possible future apiece seemed more than enough to ensure the Adept's thorough and messy demise.

The battle that followed was swift but violent enough to meet Gnarfling's expectations. When all that remained of Landish the Adept was a smoking, greasy circle on the blasted clearing, the greenmage came up and took Gnarfling's hands between hers.

"The same blight," she murmured, her brows pulled down in a deep frown. "It is a necromantic spell, but not one I have seen before."

"Are you not Suzza Indoulur, niece to Lord Basel of Halar?" asked Ursault.

Her eyes widened, and she responded with a nod.

"Your name is spoken as a capable greenmage, but did I not also hear that you are studying for the priesthood of Azuth?"

"News travels swiftly through this forest," she said cautiously.

"The herbal potions and prayer spells of Constandia of Azuth against the leprous blight may prove efficacious," suggested Ursault. "Even a novice priestess might be granted such a spell. I believe I saw some wild priestcap flowers just off the path. Shall I gather some for you?"

She considered this, nodded, then set to work. In short order Mirabella was sitting comfortably, sipping a steaming herbal brew as the greenmage gently smoothed priestcap ointment over the old woman's face. Gnarfling was grinning like a gargoyle and flexing his ten pink fingers, which were longer and more dexterous than they'd been before Landish's spell and Suzza's healing ministrations.

"I can make more ointment for your legs, if you like," the greenmage offered. "It may lengthen them, as it did your fingers—to match the rest of you," she said hurriedly. "I mean no offense. Everything else seems just fine. That is, a man as handsome of face and form . . . What I meant to say was . . ." She trailed off a second time, her lips folded tightly together and her face blooming a vivid pink.

Gnarfling considered this, astonishment and hope dawning in his eyes. "Might not hurt to even things out a mite," he said casually. "Kind of you to offer."

The greenmage sent him a tentative smile and set to work with a wooden bowl and pestle. She scooped the ointment into a small pot and pointed to a curving mark carved into the pottery.

"This is my family sigil. Trace it with one finger and repeat the words I will give you, and it will bring you to our estates near Halar. I would like to see you again to make sure the cure is progressing."

"And if it doesn't?" asked Gnarfling, gesturing to his stubby limbs.

The greenmage's soft smile didn't falter. "Even then."

She spoke a short, strange word and had Gnarfling repeat it. When she was satisfied with his pronunciation, she rose in one swift, surprisingly graceful move and strode to the impatient band of wizards. Her father's squire handed her the kestrel, and she tied the little hawk's jesses to her saddle pommel. They rode off without a backward glance, their horses clattering over the rough corduroy path.

Gnarfling watched them go, and for the first time, his future seemed bright with possibilities. He turned to his wizard companion.

Force of habit prompted him to ask, "What now?"

Ursault's smile held a world of contentment. "I have no idea."

ASTRIDE THE WIND

Philip Athans

7 Alturiak, the Year of Wild Magic

Astride the Wind tucked his wings close to his body and felt his dive accelerate. Below him, the strange boat grew rapidly as he fell toward it. He could feel Atop the Sky next to him and could feel the cool rush of air from his own wake buffet the other kenku. To his credit, Atop the Sky rode the winds well. His dive was tight and fast—almost as tight and fast as Astride the Wind's.

He focused on the men in the flying boat, and his vision narrowed. The first barrage of arrows from Astride the Wind's brother kenku flashed among the soldiers. The arrow shafts ricocheted off the soldiers' gleaming gold armor, snapping and bouncing uselessly away without harming a single one of the startled humans.

Astride the Wind tightened his grip on his

scimitar and continued his fast dive. The arrows shot by the three kenku archers were meant as a diversion anyway, but Astride the Wind was disappointed and concerned that of the three none had found a mark.

Two of the soldiers looked off the starboard side of the flying boat and pointed in unison in the direction of the kenku archers. Astride the Wind risked a glance in that direction and saw the archers—Embracing the Clouds, Whirling on High, and Above it All—fluff their wings to slow and pull to their right and down.

As he watched this, Astride the Wind muttered the ancient words passed from chief to chief for all the history of the Soaring Heights Clan. From the corner of his eye he saw Atop the Sky pull farther away from him, knowing well enough to give him a bit of room. In the air around Astride the Wind appeared first one, then a second, then a third and a fourth identical kenku to himself. The images mimicked his every move, sliding through the air around him in a swirling dance guaranteed to confuse any opponent.

It might have been the sudden appearance of the images or maybe he was just well trained, but one of the soldiers finally looked up. Astride the Wind had always had some difficulty telling one human from any other, but these six men were nearly as identical to each other as the magically conjured images were to Astride the Wind. The soldier who looked up had the same close-cropped black hair as the other five. His eyes, though, were bright green.

Astride the Wind expected the man's eyes to bulge in surprise or even fear. He expected the man to have some reaction to the sight of six kenku is a sharp dive in the direction of the top of his head, but there was nothing. The man with the green eyes took note of them and drew his black sword. He opened his mouth to say something and pulled his sword back to strike, but Astride the Wind was there. The kenku felt his blade take the man's head off, and there was a spray of red as Astride the Wind swished past and down.

The magic images followed Astride the Wind down along the side of the flying boat. An image came within reach of one of the gold-armored soldiers, who slashed back and around without even looking and took the image under its right wing. If that had really been Astride the Wind, the slash would have gutted him. Instead, the image burst painlessly in a flash of green and disappeared.

At the same time, Atop the Sky spun his carved wooden staff in a circular blur at his side, away from his wing and smashed the wood into the side of a soldier with crooked teeth—or he tried to, at least. The soldier with crooked teeth took one quick step back and placed the wide, heavy blade of his black sword into the blur of the spinning staff. The staff was cut cleanly in two. Atop the Sky followed Astride the Wind down and under the boat with a squawk of frustration.

The kenku—Astride the Wind, his three remaining images, and Atop the Sky—pulled their wings out to their sides and twisted them to slip under the boat and begin a gentle arc back up the other side. They were as tall and nearly as heavy as the humans they fought, but they were birds. Astride the Wind opened his beak to taste the dry air over the burning wastelands of Anauroch and sensed a storm brewing in the distance. The clouds were over the mountains and would stay there.

They'll need to be drawn there, Astride the Wind thought to his companion.

To the mountains, Atop the Sky responded directly into Astride the Wind's mind. *To the storm, yes?*

Draw them there, Astride the Wind told him.

The soldier with the crooked teeth looked over the edge of the boat just in time to meet the last two of the party of seven kenku. Borne on the Drafts and Suspended in Air were coming up from below almost as fast as Astride the Wind and Atop the Sky came down from on high. Suspended in Air's scimitar was out in front of him, and though Astride the Wind was sure his friend was going for the soldier's face, the tip of the scimitar drove hard into the man's chest. The human with the crooked teeth fell back hard into the boat.

As Astride the Wind came up along the opposite side of the flying boat, he saw the man with the crooked teeth sprawled on his back in the bottom of the strange vessel. He was breathing hard but was already starting to stand. Suspended in Air's blade had failed to penetrate the ornate gold armor.

Astride the Wind turned his attention to the human who had eliminated one of his images. Again, this human looked like a copy of the others, but he held his black sword in grotesquely hairy hands, hands like the hands of an ape—which is what these creatures were, after all.

Astride the Wind, his three magical images dancing around and through him, swooped in at the boat. The man with the hairy hands tried to follow them all. His jaw was set, and his eyes were narrow. He was obviously trying to figure out which was the real Astride the Wind but was having no luck. He'd seen one of the images disappear into thin air and didn't seem to want to be fooled again.

Astride the Wind's scimitar rang against the human's black sword, and the blow sent a vibration up the kenku's powerful arm, rattling the humanoid bird's skull and momentarily blurring his sharp vision. The human's grunt made Astride the Wind think he'd felt the same thing.

One of the images passed in front of Astride the Wind, and another passed through him. Astride the Wind turned one wing down to move out of the range of the hairy-handed human's blade. The kenku made the motions of a duel to keep the images active. The human stepped back, still trying to figure out which kenku was real and which illusion.

Astride the Wind took a second to scan the other soldiers and saw one of them, a man wearing a shiny copper ring, pull something small from a belt pouch. Atop the Sky and Suspended in Air were swooping in to engage the other soldiers and were coming in for another pass. For some reason Astride the Wind realized just then that none of the humans were speaking. Astride the Wind's experience with humans was limited, but he remembered them doing a lot of shouting and talking. Atop the Sky, his staff in both hands, shrieked a war cry and pulled around to face the boat. The man with the copper ring threw whatever it was he'd taken out of his belt pouch at Atop the Sky and Suspended in Air. Astride the Wind cracked a peel of kenku laughter realizing it was a small stone. The human was throwing rocks at them.

Atop the Sky ducked the thrown rock easily and Astride the Wind thought to him, *Careful, Atop the Sky, they're throwing rocks at—*

The flash was white at first, followed quickly by a roiling mass of orange brilliance. The light burned Astride the Wind's vision and made him close his eyes. He heard Atop the Sky and Suspended in Air scream in unison and felt a wave of thought from them that was the beginning of their dying wishes. It was their good-byes to the Soaring Heights Clan.

The orange fire broke apart in the air to reveal the blackened forms of Atop the Sky and Suspended in Air, feathers gone from their wings. They fell impotently, dead. Atop the Sky's steel scimitar whirled, spinning down next to the bodies.

Astride the Wind had come with six seasoned warriors

of the Soaring Heights Clan, the clan that called him chief, to confront six of the humans. One of the humans was dead, but now Astride the Wind had lost two of his own.

The man with the hairy hands growled something in his indecipherable human tongue and Astride the Wind saw that another of his conjured images was gone.

Some seventeen hundred years before, the kenku who would one day form the Soaring Heights Clan were an undisciplined, barbaric race who lived high in the Columns of the Sky and hunted in the Myconid Forest north of Shade Enclave. The kenku sometimes harassed the citizens of the town of Conch, which sat on the eastern slopes of the Columns of the Sky.

They could not speak. They had no written language, and their manners were more like the birds they resembled than the humans they stole from. They had mastered fire and were carving crude tools from shale and wood. Strangely, they were devoid of religion and superstition. They had no mythology or philosophy. They had no fear of gods or mortals.

Kaeralonn Jurneille was determined to put an end to that.

He was called "General," though the title was more ceremonial than a real military rank. The men he commanded were assassins, scouts—the sort of soldiers who went in either first or last, but never in the middle, and never in force. Not all of them were human. Kaeralonn drew his operatives from whatever race or construct was most suited for the mission at hand. He employed everything from enormous, powerful, and mindless golems to fickle and wily sprites.

The kenku were brought to his attention by a farmer who sold barley to Shade Enclave and kept an eye on the village of Conch for the Twelve Princes. Kaeralonn paid the farmer well for a dead kenku, then he erased the man's memory and began studying the bird-men in great detail.

Scouts, Kaeralonn thought. These creatures would make exceptional scouts.

Kaeralonn put the dead kenku on ice and started to think. He walked the streets of Shade, sailed through the cool skies on his private skiff, and haunted the libraries of House Tanthul.

The plan formed quickly enough. It was a simple plan and one he'd used before. Kaeralonn was three hundred years old and did very little quickly. It was months before he opened the self-freezing casket and began to thaw the dead kenku.

As the bird-man thawed, Kaeralonn removed the arrows and sealed the wounds. He set the creature's broken wing and helped some missing feathers to grow back. When the time was right, he brought in a priest of Shar, who muttered his prayers and waved his hands and brought the kenku back to life.

The creature burst up from the table and the sound of its wings unfurling echoed in Kaeralonn's laboratory. The priest grumbled and stepped back, but Kaeralonn smiled and stepped forward. It was a beautiful beast, and Kaeralonn knew it would serve him well.

The kenku twitched its head to take in the chamber, crowded with glass and apparatus. It glanced sideways at the priest, then fixed its eyes on Kaeralonn, who had just finished a hastily-cast spell.

Release me, a voice, shrill with panic and indignation, vibrated in Kaeralonn's mind.

"Is that you?" Kaeralonn asked the kenku, then he thought, *That was you, wasn't it?*

Release me, the kenku repeated into Kaeralonn's mind, the voice less shrill now and more insistent.

Kaeralonn could feel the spell he'd just cast fill his own mind, wrapping around the kenku's silent speech.

You are among friends now, Kaeralonn thought to the kenku. *I would like you to stay.*

"I will take my leave now," the priest said, almost startling Kaeralonn, certainly annoying him.

Kaeralonn waved the chubby little man away and didn't watch him shuffle out and slam the door behind him.

Who are you? the kenku asked.

Kaeralonn stepped closer to the kenku and held out his right hand. *I am Kaeralonn Jurneille of Shade Enclave. I would like us to be very close friends. Please, tell me your name and take my hand.*

The kenku tipped its head to one side and stared hard into Kaeralonn's eyes. *I am known as Amidst the Blue*, the creature responded.

Amidst the Blue, Kaeralonn sent. *That is a beautiful name.*

The kenku reached out with one feathered arm and put its strong hand into Kaeralonn's.

Good, Kaeralonn thought. *You will be a leader among your people, Amidst the Blue. Your name will be written in all the histories of the kenku, for a thousand generations to come—a thousand-thousand.*

Leader? Amidst the Blue asked, obviously confused. *Written? Histories?*

Kaeralonn smiled and responded aloud, "First among many . . . chief. . . . The rest, you'll learn. I'll teach you magic, as well. And you will teach your people."

Teach, Amidst the Blue repeated. *Magic. Yes. You are a friend.*

Kaeralonn laughed and drew back so the kenku could step down from the table. There was another rustle of wings, and Amidst the Blue sank to the floor, still a good head taller than Kaeralonn.

The human didn't want to give himself away so he kept the words "charmed" and "enchanted" out of his mind. He never let himself think the word "slave." He knew what the kenku was and what his people would be—the kenku would figure it out soon enough.

Astride the Wind smashed his curved blade at the human's midsection, but the man with hairy hands was fast enough to drop his heavy black sword to his side and smash the kenku's weapon away.

The mountains, brothers, Astride the Wind sent to the other kenku. *Withdraw and let the fools follow.*

Astride the Wind faked another slice to the man's midsection, and when the human drew his blade around to block it, the kenku tucked his wings tight against his side. Astride the Wind fell back and kicked up with one thin, bony leg. At the end of the frail-looking leg was a formidable four-toed talon. His own red cape billowed up behind him and momentarily blocked Astride the Wind's vision. The talon scraped against the human's golden armor with a thin shriek that made the fine feathers along Astride the Wind's spine fluff.

The human dodged backward a step, though, so was unable to take advantage of Astride the Wind's ill-considered, failed attack.

Under the clouds, brothers, Astride the Wind sent as he slid his wings through the air and drew himself back up—just in time to see the hairy-handed human whip his black blade at his neck.

Astride the Wind spanked it away with his scimitar and grabbed the flying boat's thick-walled gunwale with one talon, lifting himself up and out of the way of the human's follow-on attack. One of the magical images passed through him and drew itself up as well. The human's sword connected with the image's scimitar. The resulting clang made the savvy human squint with suspicion.

A flash of green and brown drew Astride the Wind's attention sharply upward. Borne on the Drafts passed close over his head and flew fast away. Looking back down, Astride the Wind sent his scimitar fast and hard in an overhand chop at the hairy-handed human's unprotected head. The two images followed, and the human made a startlingly effective attempt at blocking all three of them. The result was that he actually dodged two of the triple chops—including Astride the Wind's very real and very deadly strike. The human slid his sword up the second image's blade and found the weak space under the image's left wing. The image popped out of existence, eliciting a frustrated grimace from the human soldier.

Two of the other soldiers stepped up, their heavy-booted footsteps sending resounding thumps through the dense wood of the flying boat. Astride the Wind turned and flapped his wings furiously at his sides. The remaining magical image did the same, of course, and the result was three startled, confused human soldiers. Unfortunately the confusion didn't last long—at least for two of them. The human with the scar on his cheek danced forward and pushed the tip of his wide black sword into the image's abdomen. The phantasm disappeared, leaving Astride the Wind alone, standing on the gunwale with his wings outstretched behind him.

The human with the hairy hands came on strong and fast, and Astride the Wind parried one attack after another until the human's blade finally found a way in, slashing the kenku across the chest. The cut wasn't deep, but blood and feathers flew, and Astride the Wind cawed in pain.

Astride the Wind's cry turned into a more complex vocalization as he kicked out with the talon that wasn't still locked onto the gunwale. He spun to the right and kicked at the man with the hairy hand. The human dodged back, and the kenku's claws pinked harmlessly off his gold armor. The man with the scar on his face tried to take advantage of Astride the Wind's failed kick and attempted to cut the kenku's wing off. Astride the Wind tucked his wing in and down quickly, sending the man with the scar on his cheek off-balance.

Astride the Wind brought his scimitar around fast into the stumbling human with the scar on his cheek. At the same time he kicked his free talon back up into the face of the recovering man with the hairy hands. The kenku took hold of the hairy-handed soldier's face as the scimitar bit deeply into the throat of the man with the scar on his cheek. Blood flew from the scarred man, and Astride the Wind released the power of the spell he'd cast. The man with the hairy hands kicked impotently, and there was the smell of burning flesh. The man's black hair stood up on end as if he were fluffing his plume in some sort of dying ritual.

Both of the humans fell to the deck, dead. One pumped his blood in ever-decreasing gouts onto the old wood of the deck. The man with the hairy hands shivered and tensed, his face black, and his eyes rolled back white.

Astride the Wind saw the man with the copper ring—the man who'd killed Atop the Sky and Suspended in Air with magic fire—pulling another stone from his belt. The human was stepping backward and was pressed against the rail farther along the boat and on the other side. The human's legs touched the solid rail. The copper ring glinted in the sunlight, and Astride the Wind twitched. The man brought the stone up, and Astride the Wind tensed to spring but felt confident he'd be blown to bits, burned, frozen, or disintegrated before he could cut diagonally across the boat. The human's mouth drew up in an unreadable expression, then his eyes rolled back in his head and his eyelids flittered closed. The soldier slumped back, sitting on the rail for half a second before he flipped back and over the rail.

Astride the Wind opened his mouth in surprise and looked back. The other kenku were riding the currents forty yards or more from the boat. Astride the Wind made eye contact with Whirling on High, who had cast the spell.

My thanks, brother, Astride the Wind sent.

Whirling on High's thoughts drifted silently across the distance to echo in Astride the Wind's head, *Are you with us?*

Without bothering to answer, Astride the Wind folded his wings tight against his body—the soldier with crooked teeth swiped at him with his black sword, but missed—and let himself tip over off the side of the boat. The man with the copper ring, still sound asleep, was spinning to his death thousands of feet below.

Astride the Wind fell after him but not very far. He closed his eyes just long enough to will himself invisible, and he faded from the sight of others. It was something he'd been able to do for a while. It had just come to him— come naturally—one day.

Astride the Wind flew fast toward his brothers, zigzagging tightly in case one of the soldiers had another one of those dangerous stones. The other four kenku were already flying fast and in a wide formation toward the distant mountains. Astride the Wind let himself be seen again just as he slid into the head of the formation. There were only two soldiers still alive of the six. Under normal circumstances, two humans who'd seen four of their friends killed would flee or surrender. Astride the Wind knew, though, that what set his people against these humans in the first place was an old and heartfelt hatred. These humans would not flee, and they would not surrender. Astride the Wind was confident that these soldiers would follow them.

Ahead were the low mountains, dry and brown. The Soaring Heights Clan were from the Turnback Mountains, higher than the dry crags ahead of them. They had spent centuries avoiding contact with humans and hunting in the nearby Frozen Forest. Now the old enemy was back—Netherese soldiers in a flying boat.

Astride the Wind looked back and saw the two soldiers turn their boat. The vessel came about, and they followed the kenku. Astride the Wind sent out a roaring call of challenge that faded into a satisfied, avian laugh.

❧ ❧ ❧ ❧ ❧

Amidst the Blue was beginning to understand the human language. He'd been with his new friend Kaeralonn for a year and in that time had brought dozens of kenku to Shade Enclave—the massive flying city of the impressive archwizards. Kaeralonn was his friend and had taught him much, but there were things that gave the proud kenku pause.

They were back in the cage room again. Amidst the Blue had been there four times over the past few months. He was there simply to watch, which was all he did. The first time he'd been brought there Amidst the Blue was unable to understand what he was seeing. The second time he was nervous, and Kaeralonn had to speak to him in soothing tones to help calm him down. The third time he started to understand what Kaeralonn was doing. The fourth time he felt . . . offended . . . confused . . . unhappy.

"They can just fly out through the ceiling," the old man said, waving a hand at the cage with the open roof.

Kaeralonn shrugged and said, "They'll try."

The old man was visiting and Amidst the Blue understood that Kaeralonn was concerned about the stranger's opinion. Amidst the Blue had never seen his trusted human friend so concerned about the opinion of another.

"You devised this . . . protocol yourself, then?" the old man asked. Amidst the Blue could feel his suspicion and doubt.

Kaeralonn shrugged and said, "There is some precedence in the literature, but it's best when modified where appropriate to the subjects."

Amidst the Blue wasn't sure what the humans were talking about. Spoken language was still uncomfortable for him, and some of the words they were using were too complex for the kenku to understand.

Kaeralonn waved to a young assistant who pulled a lever that opened a steel door in the wall of the cage. Suspicious and twitching, four naked kenku passed through the doorway and into the cage. The door slammed shut behind them, startling them, and they scattered to the corners of the cage. One looked up almost immediately and saw the hole in the ceiling. Amidst the Blue thought the kenku prisoner would soar through the opening and out into the free air, but he'd seen the process happen too many times. Though he knew it pleased Kaeralonn when the kenku responded to his teaching, Amidst the Blue was secretly disappointed when the kenku cowered in the corner.

"They'll stay in the cage?" the old man asked.

"They've all tried to fly out at one time or another," Kaeralonn explained. "Every time one tries it all four are subjected to low-level lightning magic they find most unpleasant. Eventually they stop trying to get through."

"How long does that expensive and bothersome process go on?" the old man asked, rubbing his chin and looking at the trapped kenku in a way that made Amidst the Blue feel bad, despite the fact that this was Kaeralonn's friend.

Kaeralonn shrugged. "Some are more persistent than others, but I think this group is ready to move on," he said, then turned to the assistant. "Send in the new subject."

The assistant nodded and opened a second steel doorway in the cage. A young male kenku burst through the opening with a defiant shriek that made Amidst the Blue's heart leap in response. The strong young kenku grabbed the bars of the cage with both talons and used his wings to shake the bars violently. The cage held, and eventually the vital young male looked up. When he saw the opening in the roof, the young kenku leaped into the air—

—and all four of the other kenku dived on him. Talons tore and wings buffeted, and soon the young male was overwhelmed, held down firmly to the floor by shrieking, terrified kenku. Amidst the Blue could hear the mind-screams of the attacking kenku—a cacophony of single words lacking the complexity and subtlety of Kaeralonn's human tongue.

Pain.

Stop.

No.

Pain.

"Extraordinary," the old man said.

Kaeralonn smiled and said, "They learn slowly, but they learn."

The old man ran a hand through the wispy remnants of his white hair and said, "But you had the lightning ready just in case."

Kaeralonn laughed. "No," he replied. "No need. Not now. They'll be their own jailers now."

The old man nodded, and Amidst the Blue began to silently weep.

Astride the Wind's laugh was still hanging in the high air when he turned back to look at the flying boat. There were only two soldiers left alive, the one with crooked teeth and the other with sketches of gray in his black hair. They were following quickly.

Keep them on our tails, brothers, Astride the Wind told the other four surviving kenku, *but not too close.*

Ahead of them, deep gray clouds roiled over the jagged tops of the rugged mountains—fertile fields for Astride the Wind's purposes. The soldiers were following them there, and though they'd suffered losses, Astride the Wind had reason to be optimistic. All that was left was for the Enemy to appear. Astride the Wind was sure he would. He had to.

The fog that appeared before them in a supernatural burst of billowing yellow-green set Astride the Wind's feathers on edge. It smelled of poison and foul magic. Astride the Wind tipped the leading edges of his wings down and drew his taloned feet in tightly. His head dipped and the rest of his body followed in a tight, fast dive. He missed the front of the conjured fogbank and twisted in the air so he could see it pass above him. Borne on the Drafts and Embracing the Clouds swerved past it, smart and agile enough to keep even the tips of their wings from cutting the mist. Whirling on High and Above it All were nowhere to be seen. Embracing the Clouds shrieked an audible warning.

Where are they? Astride the Wind asked the minds of his comrades.

They couldn't turn in time to—Borne on the Drafts began then stopped when Embracing the Clouds shrieked again.

Whirling on High and Above it All, proud kenku warriors both, fell from the bottom of the cloud trailing sickly mist and shriveling feathers. Even from a distance Astride the Wind knew they were dead and knew his instincts were correct when he'd avoided the strange fog.

Steel yourselves, brothers, Astride the Wind sent.

The reply was a feeling without words, Borne on the Drafts and Embracing the Clouds would fly with him to destroy the enemy. Astride the Wind never thought otherwise.

Astride the Wind pulled up past the back end of the cloud, facing the flying boat. A breath caught in his throat when he saw the third man there. He was tall and lithe, young but not youthful, wrapped in the confining robes of human mages. His hands were clasped in front of him and his eyes blazed with a commanding light. His face was a mask of jagged scars. The two soldiers were turned to face him and Astride the Wind could see the newcomer's mouth moving. He was giving them orders and they were listening intently. This new human was the Enemy, the slaver, the general.

Jurneille.

He is come, brothers, Astride the Wind told the other kenku. *To the mountains. To the heavy sky.*

Borne on the Drafts and Embracing the Clouds beat their wings furiously as they passed the slowly sinking cloud of yellow-green poison and tore off in the direction of the mountains. Astride the Wind hung on a thermal and chattered a series of words passed from chief to chief. Bolts of blue-green energy burst from his chest and flashed through the sky faster than the fastest swift. Their path took them unerringly toward the hated enemy.

The human looked up from his soldiers and fixed his eyes on the onrushing missiles.

See them coming, slaver? Astride the Wind thought. *The last thing your eyes will—*

The archwizard held out a hand and the bolts of energy, which in Astride the Wind's experience had never failed to hit their mark, veered off and passed only a few inches from the man's blowing robes. The curve of their deflected path brought the missiles slamming into the face of the soldier with the gray in his hair. The soldier's head exploded in a burst of light and his body fell limply onto the deck of the flying boat.

Astride the Wind screamed in frustration and turned back to join Borne on the Drafts and Embracing the Clouds, the mountains now looming close ahead.

Well done, Chief, a voice echoed in Astride the Wind's head.

It couldn't be the human, Astride the Wind thought.

But it is, was the man's response.

Enemy! Astride the Wind raged back, not turning to look at the man.

The man sent a laugh into Astride the Wind's mind that tickled the kenku's throat.

Your father taught you well, Chief, the man persisted, *as his father taught him, and his father taught him, back along the lines of your flea-speck generations to when I taught your savage ancestor the glory of the Weave.*

In the name of what your father's father's father did to my people, Shade, Astride the Wind sent, *I will send you back to the hell you've been—*

It was me, Chief, the man interrupted. *I live now as I lived then. For every spell you cast, for ever sorcery you inherit, I have a thousand more at my command. Only a savage like yourself, a low thing, would think it difficult to live a thousand years, or two thousand, or three.*

Astride the Wind beat his wings rapidly to press farther on, his eyes glued to the prize ahead. If what this man claimed was true, his victory would be all the sweeter.

Do you not remember me, kenku? The man sent.

Astride the Wind swallowed in a dry throat and saw in his mind's eye the paintings on the wall of the High Cave, the home of his people. The paintings were as old as the Soaring Heights Clan, and told the story of the city on the floating mountain, the soldiers in their flying boats, the misery of servitude, and the disappearance of the hated city just before its neighbors were thrown to the unforgiving ground by the hand of a dying goddess.

They remembered. They all remembered.

Ahead the blackening air above the ragged mountains beckoned. Astride the Wind flew faster, and Borne on the Drafts and Embracing the Clouds were alongside him.

You are certain, Astride the Wind? Borne on the Drafts asked, a wave of uncertainty accompanying the thought.

Astride the Wind did his best to transfer a sense of purpose and confidence, but he couldn't feel if Borne on the Drafts took it all in or not.

We are our only hope, he added.

Borne on the Drafts's shiver sent a tremble through the air. Whirling on High was his older brother, born in the same mother's nest three years before. And Whirling on High was still spiraling, inert, to a dismal, lonely death on the desert sands below.

Astride the Wind felt a wave of heat pass up his back and he dropped a couple feet to let whatever it was pass. There was a flash of orange light in front of him—an oblong bolt of fire as long as his forearm had rocketed over him. He glanced back and saw several more arcing toward he and his comrades from the outstretched hands of the Enemy. A bolt of flame narrowly missed Embracing the Clouds and another passed within a handspan of Astride the Wind. Borne on the Drafts cawed when one caught the hem of his tunic and singed it, nearly setting the garment ablaze.

He means to burn us! Borne on the Drafts sent, the thought edged with panic.

I mean to get your attention, hatchling, the man replied, the alien voice like stagnant water in Astride the Wind's mind. *It has been a long time, but there is much to do now, and Shade Enclave requires the efforts of all those who serve her now or served her then. You are recalled.*

Blood boiled in Astride the Wind's feathered head. *You*

ask us to fly into your chains merely because you wish it? And I thought your hateful arrogance mere legend.

The kenku heard the Enemy laugh in both his mind and ears.

I offer you the opportunity to participate in the refounding of the greatest empire this world has ever known. If that's arrogance, then so be it.

Astride the Wind, Borne on the Drafts sent, the thought jittery and unsure, *are you certain? If what you said is true, then . . .*

Speak it, hatchling, Kaeralonn prodded.

Astride the Wind realized that he and Borne on the Drafts had been circling, the boat gaining on them rapidly. He glanced at Embracing the Clouds, now circling himself some fifty yards or more closer to the roiling, gray mountain air.

The mountains, brothers, Embracing the Clouds urged.

Come with us, Borne on the Drafts, Astride the Wind sent. *This human would own you. He has nothing to offer us but misery. Come.*

But he made us . . . Borne on the Drafts replied, the young kenku's eyes fixed on the rapidly approaching boat. *He gave us what we . . .*

Astride the Wind looked back at Borne on the Drafts as he came around the far end of the circle he was making in the air. The boat was moving with a purpose toward Borne on the Drafts, who twisted in the air and brought his own gentle arc closer to the vessel. Kaeralonn smiled through his scars with a toothy, feral grin.

With a curve of one wing, Astride the Wind broke his gentle circle and dived toward Borne on the Drafts, racing the flying boat to his confused, frightened, overwhelmed clanmate. Kaeralonn reached out a hand to Borne on the Drafts, who was passing slowly down toward the boat, his wings ballooned out at his sides to slow his descent. Astride the Wind tucked his wings in tight and reached out with his free left hand to grab for Borne on the Drafts's rustling tunic.

The soldier with the crooked teeth leaned far over the rail of the boat, holding his black sword out in front of him. Astride the Wind, too intent on grabbing Borne on the Drafts out of the way of the Enemy, flew dead into the blade. The sword bit deeply into Astride the Wind's side, but he managed to spin in the air so that the fine edge clicked off a rib.

The maneuver saved his life but made it impossible to grab Borne on the Drafts. Astride the Wind let himself fall a few feet, trailing a spray of blood and looking up. The boat eased past the slowly descending Borne on the Drafts, and the archwizard's fingers brushed the side of the young kenku's beak.

No! Astride the Wind screamed into the minds of friend and foe alike, but there was nothing he could do.

Borne on the Drafts's body stiffened at the touch and the light went out of his eyes. Like his brother, Borne on the Drafts began to fall, stiff and lifeless, to the dry ground below.

Kaeralonn made that hideous human sound they called a laugh and looked down at Astride the Wind. *All I want is you this time, Chief, descendant of Amidst the Blue.*

No! Astride the Wind screamed again. He shot both wings out to grab the air and turned away from the sight of Borne on the Drafts's falling corpse. With strength born of anger and revulsion, he beat his wings furiously against the uncompromising air and soared to meet the circling, impatient Embracing the Clouds.

We're alone, Embracing the Clouds, the kenku sent to his last comrade. *The time has come to finish this.*

Embracing the Clouds gave a ragged squawk of agreement and flew fast toward the mountains, Astride the Wind lagging behind.

Fly, Chief, the hated Enemy called. *There's nowhere you can go where I can't chase you, no lifetime you can resist that I can't wait out. You will come to me as your ancestor did, and you'll deliver the rest of your people as he did, and you will teach them to serve me as he taught them to do. It's your destiny to serve as it's my destiny to command—in the name of Netheril, in the name of Shade, in the name of common sense.*

Astride the Wind's beak clamped shut, his feathers ruffled, and a wave of hot blood flooded through his tingling body. His vision narrowed to a focused point, and he flew faster than he'd ever flown before.

No, brother! Embracing the Clouds called from behind him. *This way!*

Astride the Wind ignored him. Instead of following his own instructions, his own plan to lead the human to the heavy, energy-rich air above the mountains, he shot at the boat like an arrow and smashed into the side. The flying vessel tipped violently and the impact sent a wave of pain burning through the kenku's injured side. Blood flowed and bright stars exploded in his vision.

The last remaining Netherese soldier fell from the boat but managed to grab the side. His face twisted in a red, sweating grimace, he hung there, his life depending solely on the strength of his left hand. The headless corpse of his comrade-in-arms tumbled over the side and spun madly, trailing blood as it fell.

Astride the Wind recovered quickly from the impact and though the pain in his side was still intense, he managed to get his wings back onto the air. He caught a fast rising thermal at the edge of the mountain range and rode it upward. Behind him, the Enemy snarled through a string of nonsensical words. Astride the Wind honestly couldn't tell the difference between an incantation and the human's normal speech, so he braced himself for anything. He smelled a faint whiff of sulfur and before he took the time to make a conscious decision, he tucked and dived out of the way.

The world exploded in heat and roiling red-orange fire in a rapidly-expanding sphere above him. Singed but not blistered, Astride the Wind swooped out of the way even as the fire burned itself out into a single puff of black smoke that fouled the air.

Astride the Wind looked back at the boat and saw the soldier with the crooked teeth get his right hand onto the edge of the still teetering boat. The soldier's sword was safely in its scabbard at his belt. The man's face was more relaxed, confident that he had avoided a mile-long fall to his death.

An arrow came from behind Astride the Wind and above his head and slammed into the side of the boat. Splinters shot into the soldier's face and he gasped. The edge of the boat broke off and the soldier seemed to hang in the still air an inch off the side of the flying boat. Then he screamed as he fell, his arms twirling and his body spinning.

Astride the Wind looked up and back at Embracing the Clouds, who was banking back toward the mountains holding his longbow in his left hand.

Well shot, brother, Astride the Wind sent.

I serve the clan, was Embracing the Clouds's reply. *The mountains? The heavy air?*

Astride the Wind flew fast toward his clanmate, glancing back to see an obviously irritated, scowling arch-wizard in the flying boat, giving chase.

The mountains, yes, Astride the Wind responded. *The heavy air.*

Amidst the Blue twitched under the ministering hands of the human while Kaeralonn paced angrily across the aviary. Behind him, the clear sky sparkled with stars that moved as one as the floating city gently turned. Warmth spread from the human's hands and Amidst the Blue twitched again when the now familiar nettling itch of the priestly healing magic closed his oozing wounds.

There were more than you told us there would be, Amidst the Blue sent to the pacing human.

Kaeralonn stopped pacing and spun on him angrily. "That's what I sent you to determine, you pea-brained fool. You killed as many of your own men as the enemy did. Need I remind you again of the cost to train you feathered savages, to keep you and equip you?"

Amidst the Blue looked away, his feathers ruffling. He had no answer. He'd been sent to lead a flight of his brother kenku against a small flotilla of flying boats set into the sky by a neighboring enclave. The battle had gone badly from the start. The enchanted maidensthigh melons they'd been given to drop on the boats from above instead exploded in the hands of a good dozen kenku—blasting them apart in a blaze of green-white flame. Only two actually managed to land on a boat, neither working the way Kaeralonn had planned. All they did was illuminate the invisible shields with which the enemy mages had encircled their boats. Arrows both enchanted and mundane ripped more kenku apart, and the small spells of the kenku and their weapons and talons took some toll on the enemy, but in the end it was Amidst the Blue who broke off and retreated, with only a quarter of the force he'd flown out with. Kaeralonn had reason to be displeased, but so did Amidst the Blue.

"Silence?" Kaeralonn asked with a sneer. "You have nothing to say for yourself?"

What is there to say, General? Amidst the Blue answered.

"I am finished here," the priest muttered to Kaeralonn,

who waved him off dismissively. "Your slaves are well cared for, General."

Kaeralonn stepped closer to the priest and grabbed his arm with a tight, commanding grip. "Hold your tongue, priest," Kaeralonn said through tight lips, "and get out."

The priest looked offended but left quickly. Kaeralonn went back to his angry pacing and Amidst the Blue was left to ponder the priest's words.

Slaves.

He had heard the word many times in the last two years. He had heard it uttered by his own people—kenku whom Amidst the Blue had brought to Shade Enclave himself, brought into the service of Kaeralonn. Amidst the Blue had been confused, baffled by his brothers' inability to see the warmth and friendship in Kaeralonn or the value in service to his cause. The other kenku regarded Kaeralonn with fear and suspicion, even hatred—but why? Amidst the Blue was beginning to understand.

He sat up on the cold metal table and looked next to him at the young kenku, Along the Thermals, who was lying next to him, bandaged and writhing in pain. Their eyes met and Amidst the Blue could feel the emotions of the young kenku, wrapped in a psychic package of pain and pleading.

You're the only one, Along the Thermals sent.

The only one? Amidst the Blue asked, a tear coming unbidden to his bruised eye.

You brought us here, the young kenku replied, *and only you can take us out. Resist him. Break our bonds, Amidst the Blue, and we will follow you to—*

"Silence!" Kaeralonn shouted just as a flickering, jagged string of blinding blue-white luminescence leaped from the tips of his fingers and smashed into Along the Thermals hard enough to lift the young kenku off the table and pound him into the mudbrick wall. The wall cracked and the kenku screamed, twitching madly in the hold of the vertical lightning. The bolt was gone in less than the space of a heartbeat, but its path was burned onto Amidst the Blue's vision. Along the Thermals lay dead and smoking, a melting black ruin on the scorched floor.

Amidst the Blue felt a hand on his shoulder and turned to see Kaeralonn smiling at him in a condescending, twisted, evil way. "Don't listen to these slaves, my friend, they're just—"

Kaeralonn went down hard from Amidst the Blue's kick. The human grabbed at his midsection and tried to breathe in but couldn't.

You, Amidst the Blue dropped into the gasping human's mind, *are not my friend.*

Kaeralonn reached up with his right hand, his fingers moving through the traces of a spell and he found his voice in time to utter only the first arcane syllable before Amidst the Blue grabbed his face with one sharp-taloned foot.

I'm no longer your slave.

The kenku ripped down and tore into the silky flesh of the general's face. Blood flew everywhere and the other kenku—nearly a hundred of them lying around the open room in various states of disrepair and despair—stood up and took notice.

"Stop!" the human gasped, his face a bloody ruin, his hands pressed against his cheeks to hold the flesh on.

Amidst the Blue drew his sword and raised it over the head of the archwizard. *You have taught us well, Kaeralonn, but you have taught us too much.*

As the blade came down fast and hard at the human's neck, Kaeralonn pulled something from inside his mouth—a tooth, Amidst the Blue saw—and when the sword came down past where his neck should have been, the human was gone.

Amidst the Blue let himself laugh. *There will be a time, slaver. We will not forget.*

With that Amidst the Blue led his people to freedom.

⊛ ⊛ ⊛ ⊛ ⊛

The jagged brown mountains loomed before them. The sky directly above seethed with potential energy and Astride the Wind and Embracing the Clouds found it difficult to maintain altitude. Astride the Wind's side burned and his head ached, but still he fought on.

Where are you going? Kaeralonn asked the kenku's reeling mind. *Leading me back to your nest, in hopes that your clanmates will overwhelm me? You're as foolish and as vain as Amidst the Blue.*

Astride the Wind ignored him. Instead, he thought to Embracing the Clouds, *This is it. It ends here.*

Astride the Wind fluffed his wings, bringing himself up short—and his wings were pressed hard against his sides by some heavy, outside force. He was covered in a mass of white silk like a spider's web, but the web had appeared out of nowhere, in the air all around him. The source of it was obvious, even before Kaeralonn's gloating statement, *Wrapped like the gift you are, thrall.*

Astride the Wind squawked in defiance and began to fall. Unable to spread his wings, he couldn't fly. He could twist his body enough to control his spin, though, and he managed to see what Kaeralonn was doing. The flying boat was moving fast on a course obviously designed to bring it under Astride the Wind. Kaeralonn had immobilized him so he could drop like a bundle into the open boat.

Arrows whistled through the air from a circling Embracing the Clouds. Kaeralonn didn't even bother to hold up a hand. The arrows—which should have lodged deep in the man's chest—whirled around him and down like water caught in a drain. Embracing the Clouds cawed in frustration, though they both had always known this enemy would be harder to kill than that.

Astride the Wind slammed onto his back on the wooden deck of the flying boat and his vision spun from the impact. Above him were the deep black clouds, below two thirds of a mile of open air then the stony foothills. Astride the Wind struggled against the web, but it held his wings and arms tightly to his sides. Kaeralonn looked down at him and said something in his vile human speech that Astride the Wind couldn't understand.

The bound kenku managed to sit up in the gently rocking boat, and he could see Embracing the Clouds wheeling in the distance against the backdrop of the barren mountains. Embracing the Clouds's bow was around his shoulders and a dagger was in his right hand. His wings arced and he turned to fly fast at the boat.

No, brother, Astride the Wind sent to him. *Keep your distance.*

Embracing the Clouds whirled around in the air and started back the way he'd come without a moment's hesitation. The human had the audacity to laugh.

Astride the Wind ignored them both, only barely feeling the boat lift and turn in the direction of Embracing the Clouds's flight. The human meant to give chase.

Astride the Wind felt the energy building within him. The human, for all his great power, was still dependant on spells. Spells required hands, a tongue, and sometimes items of focus or power. What Astride the Wind had drawn the hated human here to do required none of those things. It was a natural progression from the seed of power planted in the ancient kenku by Kaeralonn himself, as shortsighted as he was long-lived.

The kenku's reverie was deep, but not so deep that he failed to hear Kaeralonn begin the chanting cadence of a spell—from this close so obviously different from his normal monotone, mumbling speech. Astride the Wind's legs were still free, though not entirely. He could, and did, kick out and up just enough to jostle Kaeralonn's elbow, knock him just enough toward the edge of the boat to startle him—and in the process ruin the spell.

The archwizard spun on the restrained kenku, his scarred face blazing with anger.

Know, the archwizard screamed into Astride the Wind's mind, *when you're beaten, slave!*

The human reached down and grabbed Astride the Wind's shoulder roughly. The human wore a ring on that hand, a ring that started to burn when it touched Astride the Wind's feathers. Kaeralonn was obviously immune to the heat, but Astride the Wind was being burned painfully. He couldn't help but call out a single pained shriek.

Astride the Wind . . . Embracing the Clouds sent, concern making the thought spiky and urgent.

Go, brother, Astride the Wind replied. *Tell them what happened here.*

Indeed, "brother," Kaeralonn interceded. *Tell them all that the master has returned and their service is required once more. Your clanmate—or what's left of him—will be waiting for you on Shade Enclave.*

No, Kaeralonn, Astride the Wind replied. *When Amidst the Blue took your face and your slaves from you, he remembered everything. When that ragged band of kenku flew from your hated aerie and found a home in the high caves far away, they painted his memories and his warning . . . and his wishes for the future, on the walls. He told us the manner of the death of the slaver, should the day come that he or his kin returned.*

The burning subsided and the archwizard smiled in a condescending, unimpressed way. *How lovely for you all.*

The manner of your death was decreed by your first slave, Kaeralonn. You will share the fate of the martyr, Along the Thermals.

Along the . . . ? Kaeralonn responded, confused.

Astride the Wind closed his eyes, the power inside him linked to the heart of the clouds. He could feel Kaeralonn's hand come off his shoulder. The first half of the first syllable of a spell certainly designed to get him away whispered off the tip of the human's lip—and the sky exploded in blinding light.

The lightning bolt held all the fury of the heavy mountain clouds. It slammed into the boat and through Kaeralonn with force enough to blast the archwizard into a spray of flaming gobbets of sizzling flesh. The wood of the boat shattered, exploded from within. Astride the Wind's body tensed and he could feel small bones break in his hands, his jaw, his talons. The web boiled away, taking rows of feathers with it, and Astride the Wind screamed at the pain of his unprotected flesh burning.

He tumbled madly away, laughing through the pain and loss, knowing that he'd taken the slaver with him.

The hands that grabbed him grabbed him hard and a flood of emotions flowed into his mind from Embracing the Clouds. Astride the Wind opened his eyes and found that he could only see out of one of them, but he could see his clanmate.

It is done, highest of brothers, Embracing the Clouds told him, his arms gently circling Astride the Wind's burned, limp form. *The clan awaits.*

Astride the Wind could feel Embracing the Clouds's wings carry them both higher, turning to the west and home.

THE FALLEN LANDS

Murray J.D. Leeder

19 Ches, the Year of Wild Magic

I remember sitting in the class of my mentor, the
wizard Maligo of Mistledale. Retired from his
adventures to the clergy of Azuth, he occasionally defended the Dale from its enemies but
mostly was content to live quietly and teach a
new generation of mages. He would die several
years later of a miscast spell during the Time of
Troubles, a hard blow to me. I learned almost all
I know about magic from him. In this particular
class, I took it upon myself to ask a naughty
question:

"If Mystra is a goddess of good, why does she
allow evil people to use magic?"

The other children around me tittered that I
asked such a question, but not Maligo. He was a
man of infinite patience.

"What do you children think?" he asked.

"It is not for Mystra to deny magic to anyone," answered another mageling, the son of one of the Council of Six and certainly my archnemesis of the moment. Despite his best attempts, he never became nearly as close to Maligo as I did. "She teaches us wisdom instead," he explained, "and if we do not heed her wisdom, if we use her power for destructive means, she is not to blame."

This was the usual answer to that question. It wasn't the first time I'd heard it, nor the last. I had to hear that answer many times before it started to sound reasonable....

I woke up to the sun stabbing me in the eye. Assessing my situation as best I could, I found I was wrapped in some kind of animal fur and naked underneath. The chill air on my face kept me awake. I tried and failed to sit up, so badly was I aching, though I knew my wounds had been healed.

Wounds. Where did I get them?

The orcs. I remembered the orcs. They attacked us at night. Hundreds of them, far more than I had seen at one time, moved toward us in waves. Many were riding flightless avians, like ugly featherless ostriches. My spells slew many, but they kept coming. These orcs looked unusual. In their eyes, shining in the torchlight, I did not see the manic bloodlust typical of their kind. Instead their eyes were glassed over, faraway.

I remembered Neril slipping between the orcs, slashing at all sides with his great broadsword and cleaving them by the dozens. Mystra! There was a moment when they were around him on all sides, separating him from the rest of us. That was the last I saw of him.

"The others," I croaked, my throat parched. "The others."

"Did you hear that?" said someone with a deep male voice. "He speaks our language!"

"Are you sure?" somebody else said.

"Please . . . the others." I was regaining my faculties, and I attempted a complete sentence: "Are the others all right?"

A man stepped over me. My eyes widened as I stared up at him. His head eclipsed the sun, so I couldn't make out his features clearly. He was tall, probably a head above me, and in the Dalelands I was considered a tall man. His hair was long and black, and he was clad in the pelt of a wolf. A barbarian.

Yes! I remembered the barbarians. They rushed out of the night like ghosts and joined the fray, their spears and axes and hammers sailing across the battlefield. Just before I passed out, a warhammer shattered the skull of the orc with its sword to my throat. It likely saved my life. Now, a similar hammer was in the hands of the man standing above me.

"Do not move, Civilized. Stay still, or you will taste Uthgardt steel. How did you come to speak our language?"

I heard Common, but his lips moved in his native tongue.

"I don't," I said.

I ran my weak hand up to my chest and confirmed that I was still wearing the amulet. I pulled it out from under the fur. It glowed serenely, and gave off a certain amount of warmth, something I was glad for in these northern winters.

"This makes it possible for me," I explained.

The amulet was a gift from my mentor, many years ago. It translated my language into that of the listener and his language to mine. It had served the Blazing Band well over the years, even though it had limitations. The barbarian's use of "civilized," for example, was probably the best translation it could manage of a concept not present in Common.

"I knew we should have taken it away from him, Thluna. It's magic!"

"I knew it was magic, Gar," answered the barbarian above me. "That's why I didn't touch it. I was afraid it might poison me."

"It is not a weapon. It's not a danger to you or anyone," I said. "Tell me, who else from my company survived the battle?"

"No one," he said.

My heart sank, though I wasn't surprised at his answer. I reviewed them all in my mind. I had known Neril the longest, since we were children. The two of us formed the Blazing Men together in Mistledale—it wasn't until we took on our first female member that we amended the name—but somehow I felt saddest for our youngest member, dear young Shalinda. She had joined us in Sundabar barely a month before. She was just a northern farm girl, eager to see the world and with a minor aptitude for the longbow gained from shooting wolves. It was her first battle that killed her, and I doubt she was able to slay even a single orc before they reached her.

Sundabar. That's where we were when we heard the news. The Lords' Alliance was dispatching troops—even the Blackstaff was rumored to be on the move. Neril suggested we take an unusual route—east of the High Forest—to Evereska, one that would get us there quickly while avoiding major roads, which might be compromised. We were lucky to get through the Nether Mountains before the blizzards began.

"Ask him if he's a mage. Ask him if this is a magic book."

I forced myself to sit up and saw the other barbarian, an equally brutish-looking fellow. He had my spellbook, my one possession of true power, my one defense, lying closed in front of him, with my quarterstaff and robes beside it. My mind was empty of spells. I could not fight my way out if I wanted to.

I recalled the advice a seasoned adventurer once gave us. We met him in a tavern in Neverwinter. He said, "If you ever want to commit suicide easily, tell an Uthgardt you're a mage."

But I suspected they had a still lower opinion of liars.

"I am a mage," I confessed. "My name is Arklow of Ashabenford."

I turned my eyes to the barbarian above me. As he moved his head out from behind the sun, I realized that he was very young; probably barely fifteen winters. His scars told me that at this young age he had seen more combat than I had in my thirty. In his eyes, I saw an odd mix of revulsion and something else. Curiosity?

"A mage? We've saved a mage, Thluna," said the other barbarian. "Sungar will skin us for this. He won't be happy that the shaman healed him before some of our own."

"He was the most badly wounded, and he fought fiercely against the orcs," replied Thluna, "even if he is a mage."

I filled in the appropriate adage- -the enemy of my enemy is not my enemy—but I detected a strange under-current to Thluna's voice that made me suspect there was more to it than that.

"Arklow of Ashabenford, I am Thluna, son of Haagra-van, of the Thunderbeast tribe. That is Garstak."

Thunderbeast. I'd never heard of that tribe before, and I was happy for that since the most famous tribes were generally those who raided civilized settlements. Some-how, though, the name made something click in my mind. There were mountains visible in the distance, and I knew they were among the northernmost of the Greypeaks. I

turned and looked behind me, and I saw an expanse of
dry, dead earth stretch off to the horizon. There was some
shifting snow but not much. The area seemed almost
devoid of weather. I knew the name of the place we were
cutting through to get to Evereska. It was a dismal, little-
visited corner of Faerûn civilized men called the Fallen
Lands.

Once I was ready to walk again, Thluna and Garstak
let me dress. They did not return my spellbook or staff,
and for the moment I didn't ask for them. They led me
through the Thunderbeast camp, a hodgepodge of
portable dwellings of animal skins, filled with a selection
of stocky barbarians, all male and mostly wounded in
some way or another, and all looking at me with fear and
contempt. They took me before their chieftain, Sungar
Wolfkiller.

A fiercely bearded man, probably younger than me but
looking decades older, Sungar was slighter than many of
the Uthgardt but still an imposing figure. He had a huge
gash across his cheek, fresh from the battle. Apparently
the tribe's shaman had yet to get around to healing his
wounds. He clutched a huge battle-axe in a single hand, a
weapon so heavy I expected few men could even lift it. The
forgery looked almost dwarven, but in a human's size. I
wondered where it came from. The chieftain thanked
Thluna and asked them to leave us alone in his tent.

"Mage," he addressed me. "We Uthgardt despise your
magic. It is a terribly distasteful thing to talk with you
through that magic device of yours." He pointed at my
amulet.

"I understand that," I said. "I thank you and your tribe
for saving my life. I owe you everything. I owe you enough
to leave your company immediately."

"Normally, that would be the best you could hope for, but . . ." His eyes drifted to the ground. "Circumstances are not normal.

"We are far from the rest of our people and farther still from the bones of the beast that watches over our tribe. We set out into this dead region to battle the orcs. Our tribe generally embarks on such a campaign every two or three winters as a test of our mettle. This is Thluna's first time and my seventh. I believe I have seen almost everything of orcs a man may encounter. Thousands have fallen to my axe, but I have never seen anything like the orcs we battled last night.

"Orcs are cowardly beasts. When the tide of the battle is turned against them, some of them will retreat. This is the case, always, but these orcs fought to the last. I lost many warriors to their spears and swords, and not one orc fled the battle.

"None of us have ever known orcs to mass in such numbers. This dead region in particular is noted for its constant feuds and rivalries, orc tribe against orc tribe. Never have they been so united.

"Finally, some of my men have observed, and I concur, that these orcs did not look like orcs. Orcs are disgusting, drooling creatures. In their eyes there is nothing but hatred and evil, but these orcs had nothing of that. Their eyes were distant. It was as if their minds were not theirs. My experience has no explanation for this. Perhaps yours does."

Sungar stared me in the eye. I took a deep breath, and told him what I knew.

"My company was passing through this region, which we call the Fallen Lands, on the way to Evereska. It is an elf settlement to the south. We received word in Sundabar . . ." I paused, wondering if I should explain either elves or Sundabar, but I decided against it, ". . . that something had happened near there—an eruption from the underground of an unusual type of monster, the phaerimm."

"Phaerimm?"

"I don't know much about them. They were more legend than reality for most of us. They're thought to live beneath Anauroch . . . the desert to the east." Sungar nodded in understanding. "They're said to be intelligent, wicked and powerful, and excellent magicians. Some say they even subsist on magic itself. The arrival of such monsters could have devastating consequences for us all. We heard that many forces of good were proceeding to Evereska to counter this invasion and decided to head there ourselves.

"It's also known that the phaerimm are masters at enslaving other races to their will, even highly intelligent creatures like dragons and beholders. If their object is one of simple destruction, it does not surprise me that they send their servants where they cannot go themselves. If they can control the mind of a dragon, it should be no trick to bend the will of an orc."

Or a barbarian, I thought, or a mage.

Sungar shook his head in disbelief. "Uthgar protect us. These phaerimm . . . they can be killed?"

"I'm sure they can, but even the strongest wizards in the world fear the phaerimm. I am no match for them, I am certain of that, and neither are your men. Our only hope is that none of them are here in the Fallen Lands; that instead, it is one of their servants who is enslaving these orcs."

"But the orcs are dead. We killed them."

"Were they all the orcs in the Fallen Lands? All the other monsters besides? Maybe they were just an exploratory force. There could be another army out there, probably even larger. What would you do if some of your men were slaughtered, and you were in a position to strike back? How would you react?"

"I would seek revenge." Sungar leaned pensively on his battle-axe. "What do you recommend we do, mage?"

"We could move north. I could rejoin civilization; you could rejoin your tribe, that is, if the phaerimm's forces do not intercept us on the way. They could make us their slaves, just like those orcs." I paused to let my words sink in. "Or we could—"

"We will move south and confront this army before it expects us. If we perish, we will perish defending our tribe. Come with us, Arklow of Ashabenford. We have seen your valor in battle and know you to be a worthy warrior. I promise no Uthgardt warrior will molest you if you ride as one of us."

My staff and spellbook were returned to me, and as soon as all the Uthgardt were properly healed by the shaman, they were ready to mobilize again. Only Thluna's friend Garstak did not join us but was instead sent back north to warn the tribe. The Uthgardt buried their dead in the dirt of the Fallen Lands and a few of them helped me dig graves for the Blazing Band. I had thoughts of recovering some of their magical items, perhaps the enchanted dagger from the thief Jarok, but with the Uthgardt watching I decided otherwise. Barely a trace was left of the encampment by the time we left.

I was provided with a horse, its rider killed by the orcs. It was a far less domesticated animal than most of the horses I had ridden, but I think I impressed the Uthgardt by handling it as well as I did. The Uthgardt were not horse barbarians like the far-off Nars and Tuigan, and clearly had come only recently to the art of equestrianism. My father was one of the Riders of Mistledale, and he had taught me well. There was something perversely amusing about the situation. Two tendays before, I was wintering in Sundabar and would never have expected to find all my friends and companions dead, and myself riding into the depths of the Fallen Lands with a barbarian tribe to battle the phaerimm.

My mind frequently drifted back to poor Shalinda. How irresponsible we were for taking the young woman, barely more than a child, into such danger. She should have stayed in Sundabar; she should have stayed a farmer. If she had, she'd still be alive.

The Blazing Band had accomplished many glorious things. It deserved better than to be massacred by orcs in some godsforsaken corner of Faerûn. Or did it? When Neril had come to us with the news that phaerimm were assaulting Evereska, we all agreed to proceed there immediately. Why? Was it selfless concern for the elves of Evereska? Or was it just another opportunity for glory? Maybe even a chance to fight next to Khelben Arunsun himself?

The farther we went into the Fallen Lands, the more barren the place became. A vast expanse of dirt and cracked earth—no wonder all sensible men avoided it. Only magic could leave a place so infertile. I understood it was once a Netherese survivor state. Perhaps that's why the Uthgardt regarded it with such suspicion. Physically desolate as it was, though, it teemed with magic. I could feel it in the air, just as I could sense the absence of the Weave the instant I stepped into the dead magic area in Tantras. There I developed a throbbing headache, feeling my separation from the Weave and the glory of Mystra, but here I felt the opposite, a heady feeling verging on euphoria. I didn't doubt that the phaerimm would feel very much at home in this place.

Thluna rode his horse up next to mine. He was wearing a silver war helmet and clutching a warhammer. Of all the Uthgardt I had met, he was the only one who went out his way for my company, and I was glad for it. Some of the others looked as if they'd quickly put an axe to my head if it weren't for Sungar's instructions. I was worried that some of them thought I might try to corrupt Thluna's young mind with my civilized philosophies, but they didn't express this as far as I saw. To their credit, they trusted their dogma to keep him on what they defined as the right path.

"Do you know about the Blue Bears?" he asked me.

"The Blue Bear tribe? A little."

"My father pried this helmet off the body of one of their warriors, whom he killed with his bare hands. Of all the degenerate Uthgardt tribes, the Blue Bears are the worst."

I was happy to hear that. The helmet was marked on one side with an emblem of Everlund, and I was a trifle concerned about how he'd got it.

"I understood the Blue Bears are extinct now. The tribe crumbled after Hellgate Keep was destroyed."

By a group of magic-wielding "civilizeds," I silently added.

Thluna nodded. "This is true, so far as we have seen. We passed through their territory a tenday ago and saw nothing of them. It is said that when they learned their bitch chieftain Tanta was not human at all, but some foul fiend of the Hells, they were too twisted to even care." He turned his eyes to me. "Is that what we will be like if these phaerimm enslave us?"

"I don't know," I answered truthfully.

"Any of us would rather fight to the death than to allow that to happen to us or to happen to the rest of our tribe."

"You'd even rather fight beside a mage." When he didn't knock me off my horse as I suspected he might, I thought I would press my luck farther. "What is your people's objection to magic? You have priestly magic."

"Priestly? Our shaman's spells are a gift from Uthgar.

Your magic is not the same."

He was right, in a sense. Clerical magic did not come from the Weave like my spells.

"Magic isn't just a tool of destruction," I said. "It can be helpful, beneficial. This amulet is a good example. Without it, we couldn't be talking to each other like this."

"Were it not for your magic object, we would have to learn to communicate on our own level. We'd be forced to accomplish something. Instead, the amulet does it for us. Magic does not make your life better, only easier."

" Magic is an Art. It's a gift of Mystra."

"Mystra," said Thluna. "We are aware of this goddess, though we do not think of her often. When we do, it is of a trickster who lures men with offers of tremendous power, power without restrictions. These powers grow and grow and eventually become impossible to control. She is a ruiner of men and tribes alike."

My anger rose, but I knew this was Thluna's way of getting me back for what I had said a moment ago. Things were settled between us, so I didn't dare to say what we thought of his god.

It was later that day that one of the Uthgardt pointed out a plume of smoke rising to the sky in the distance.

"Could be orcs," said Sungar. "But there are so few trees. Where are they getting the wood for a fire?"

He had a point. Orcs ate raw meat but preferred it cooked. "It's probably magical fire," I reasoned. "A gift from their new masters."

One of the older barbarians chimed in with his advice. "We should attack now, while there's still light. In darkness they will have the advantage."

"I'd like to know what we're up against first," said Sungar.

"I have a spell for that."

Some of them began to object, but Sungar silenced them with a glance.

"I'll need silence for a minute or two," I said and crouched on the ground, facing the direction of the smoke.

I cast my spell and felt my consciousness propelled over the fields of the Fallen Lands with increasing speed. There was a large plain ahead of us, featureless but for a small ruin rising maybe eight feet above, like the tip of something mostly buried under the ground. But for that, there was little cover in any direction. Surrounding the ruin was an impressive force made up mostly of orcs, with a few stray bugbears and gnolls in the mix, probably acquired somewhere between there and Evereska. A lot of them were tending to their mounts, those ugly bipedal birds, and some were cooking meat over a series of magic bonfires. Still, they looked like they were ready to fight at a moment's notice. I estimated at least ten of them for every one of the barbarians.

My mind slipped between a set of orcs and continued toward the ruin, barely more than a few cracked walls and broken columns. A few huge and bulky masses were standing nearby like statues, and on the ruin itself was a long, thin serpentine body, a dark blue-purple in color, ending with a human face that was buried in the belly of its meal, a dead orc.

How do we know this civilized is not warning our enemies?

He is luring us into a trap!

The voices shot through my mind and sent me hurling back to my body so hard that I fell backward.

"Silence!" shouted Sungar at the offending Uthgardt, who slunk away in submission.

Sungar was a strong ruler but smart enough to know that some of the ill-tempered barbarians would not tolerate my presence much longer. Barbarians lived for battle. It was the only pleasure in their harsh lives, and battle was the only thing that would protect me. These Uthgardt would much rather fight beside me than ride with me.

"It's all right," I said, pulling myself to my feet. "I saw enough. There are maybe four or five hundred orcs in the army, and a few other humanoids as well, but I did not see any phaerimm. We can be relieved at that. They're being led by a dark naga."

"A dark what?"

"A naga. They're snakelike beings who hoard magic items and knowledge. They're born collaborators. This one probably works for the phaerimm in exchange for new spells, including the mind control spells that are keeping that army in line. Nagas have poison stingers on the end of their tails, and they bite. They also have powers of telepathy and can read your thoughts if you get too close to them. They're dangerous foes."

"Have you ever fought one before?" asked one of the Uthgardt.

"No," I admitted, "but I did fight something similar—a water naga—back home. I've read accounts from those who've fought others. The naga's being guarded by two umber hulks. They're large, underground monsters. These I have fought before. They can be deadly in close quarters but are slow and awkward out in the open. Never meet their eyes. They have powers of confusion. I bet the naga brought them with it from the Underdark as bodyguards. It's nice to know it can make such a mistake."

"These monsters can be killed?" Sungar asked, clutching his axe.

"I think so." The barbarians shouted in approval. "I said the naga's spells were controlling the minds of the orcs. I can't be certain, but that may mean that if the naga died, the control would end. If the orc tribes in the Fallen Lands are as divisive as I've heard, then that army must contain a lot of enemies. We can capitalize on the confusion. After all, we can't kill four hundred orcs, but two hundred orcs can kill two hundred orcs."

Craftiness in strategy was not a skill much admired by barbarians as a rule, but I think the Uthgardt realized that their usual direct approach would not be successful here. I fetched my staff from the back of my horse and drew in the dry dirt a rough overhead sketch of the army as I had seen it. Soon we had formulated a battle plan.

"None of us will leave the field before the battle is won," said Sungar as the sun was just about to set and our campaign was about to begin, "or none of us will leave it at all."

The sentiment frightened me, but I could not improve upon its eloquence.

Sungar, myself, and a dozen others separated from the rest and circled south and to the west, keeping out of the army's view. As there was no cover close to the battlefield, we had to move quite a distance. After a few tense minutes' wait, we moved on the orcs. The sound of weapons clashing was audible from the battlefield. Dimly we could see the mounted figures of the others beset by throngs of orcs, dodging their spears and arrows, and could hear war cries mix with the clanking of orcish armor.

"There." I pointed out the ruins where I had seen the naga.

It seemed our plan was working. The defenses along the flank had thinned as the others drew more orcs forward. We charged. As I looked back at the Uthgardt, horses galloping, weapons held high, their long black hair flying in the breeze, I felt an instinctive terror of my allies. That's what made barbarians the potent force they were, why they were feared across the North. In truth most of them were probably less skilled as fighters than many I'd fought beside or against in my life, but as a spectacle they had no equal—but I knew their fearsome visage would have little effect on these enspelled orcs.

Some of the orcs noticed us almost immediately and started moving in our direction on foot or mounted, but on the whole they continued engaging the others. They did not count on my presence, but they would learn of it soon enough. At this point I offered one discreet prayer to Mystra, and another to Torm or Tempus or Uthgar, or whatever god would help us win the battle.

Sungar used his mighty axe to knock the first blank-faced orc to reach us off its avian as he rode past it, while I prepared my first spell. I had searched my spellbook for something that would impress on the Uthgardt that magic need not be destructive. Perhaps something with weather control, a mighty wind to blow the orcs away from our path, but I went back to one of the most common offensive spells in the Realms, which has no match when it comes to removing larger numbers of enemies and quickly. I had rarely cast it from a horse before, let alone one charging at its top speed, but I managed to summon a large fireball and send the orange-red sphere sailing high through the air. Silhouetted against the darkening sky, it was a thing of tremendous beauty. I even think I heard some of the Uthgardt around me gasp. It landed dead ahead of us in a dense group of orcs, tearing through them with waves of flame. Cries of pain drowned out all other noise.

A spear caught the flank of the horse of the barbarian riding beside me. He went tumbling to the ground, and I hoped he managed to stand before the orcs rushed over to slit his exposed throat, but I couldn't turn back to look. Sungar rode up beside me, and together we led the charge toward the ruin growing larger in the distance. Most orcs instinctively dodged the feet of our horses, and I sent a few magic missiles whistling across the plain to clear those who didn't. Soon a very definite path between us and the ruin formed.

As we passed through the scorched spot where my fireball had landed I could see the two umber hulks loom ahead of us, but I could not see the naga.

A purple tail snaked out of the lines of orcs ahead of me and swung at me. Its stinger came so close to me I could smell its poison. My reflexes were faster than my spells, and I pulled my staff from behind me, bashing the naga's tail as hard as I could. It immediately slipped away, back between the orcs and vanished from my sight.

"Where did it go?" yelled Sungar.

The point where it attacked me was now some distance behind us. We both looked backward just in time to see the naga leap out of the fray onto one of the Uthgardt following us. It caught him by surprise, sinking its fangs into the side of his head. It flexed its long, thin body backward, pulling him from horse and sending him flying backward onto the orcs' waiting blades. I fired a magic missile and struck the naga in its side. With lightning speed, it retracted once again into the safety of the ranks of orcs.

The lines of orcs around Sungar and me were far too close together for us to turn around and confront the naga at this speed. We looked forward again and found we were nearing the ruin where the two umber hulks stood waiting for us. Sungar jumped from his horse just in time for it to run straight into the huge, outstretched arms of an umber hulk. It grasped at the horse's head, crushing it instantly, but the momentum hurled the unsteady creature backward and off its feet while badly damaging its claws.

The other hulk tried to pull me off my horse, but I dodged, rode a small circle around the ruin, and came back at it, letting a flame arrow fly directly at its ugly face.

My spell met its mark, but the creature was unfazed and reached out for me again. I leaped off my horse and landed hard on my back, swearing. My staff went flying off somewhere, and the hulk's huge mandibles were closing in on me.

Sungar's battle-axe impacted the hulk's scaly hide, eliciting a tremendous moan of pain from the beast. The creature turned to face its attacker.

I shouted, "Avoid its eyes," as Sungar struck again.

The orcs were keeping their distance. Normally they would have swarmed us, but the naga's spells and the presence of the umber hulks kept them at bay.

No sooner had I pulled myself to my feet than I felt the umber hulk's arms close around my middle. The monster was badly injured in its collision with the horse, but its hug was crushing enough even in its wounded state. Without my hands free, I couldn't cast my spells and I felt my breath start to fail, my ribs ready to crack.

I heard a loud impact just above my head and the hulk's grasp loosened. I wormed my way free and quickly whirled about, ready to fire another magic missile at the monster's foul heart, but I didn't have to. It fell on its own, and the ground shook as its huge mass landed. An Uthgardt throwing axe was embedded in the back of its skull, likely thrown by someone from the other, larger force, at last making some headway in its push for the ruin.

I turned in time to see Sungar's axe finish off the other hulk, slicing it through its thick belly. Almost immediately, the orcs surrounding us stopped being spectators and charged. Sungar and I retreated up into the ruin, a more defensible location since the broken pillars and ancient walls provided protection from some sides. I slipped into a corner to preserve the few spells I had left, while Sungar held the entrance with his axe.

"Why does the naga not show itself?" asked Sungar. "It's a coward."

"It wants to survive," I said, "but it also wants to win. It will not disappoint its phaerimm masters. It can read our minds and knows our—"

The wall behind me collapsed. I barely kept my balance enough to stay standing. I turned around and saw the naga coiled ahead of me, hissing at me with its fanged mouth. The orcs backed away once again.

"Something's wrong," I mumbled to myself as I prepared another magic missile.

I launched the spell-bolt at the monster's face, but it never impacted. Instead it bounced off the air surrounding the naga and flew back at me, striking me in the chest. I went flying backward, agony radiating through my torso to all parts of my body. I screamed and fell hard onto the stone of the ruin. Sungar rushed over to my aid, while the naga licked its lips in amusement.

"What has it done?" the chieftain asked me.

"It's wrapped itself in some kind of magical field," I answered, teeth gritting in time with my throbbing pain. "It turns magic back on its wielder."

"That's no match for Uthgardt steel!" Sungar shouted and ran forward, swinging his mighty battle-axe and letting out a loud war cry. The naga tried to dodge, but the battle-axe caught it in the neck. The field around it flickered, and I saw the axe energized with a red burst of energy shooting down to its wielder. Sungar and the naga both writhed in pain, and both seemed on the verge of collapse. The naga desperately swung around its tail, but Sungar, the agony obvious in his every move, sliced through its flank with his axe, sending the stinger flying off into the crowd of orcs. Sungar collapsed from the pain, letting the axe fly away. The naga came about and prepared to rip his throat out with its fangs. I watched helplessly.

A rain of Uthgardt spears, hammers, and throwing axes flew at the naga's thin, serpentine length, a few of them striking their mark exactly. The creature writhed in pain and let out a sharp scream that could have shattered glass. The Uthgardt at last penetrated the row of orcs behind us, and I felt arms strain to lift me from the ground onto the back of a horse. It was Thluna.

"You saved a mage," I said weakly.

"The second time I've done that," he answered.

I saw one of the other barbarians pull Sungar from the ground and bury a warhammer into the naga's ugly face, killing the monster at last.

Thluna brought his horse around and started charging away from the battlefield. I turned my eyes to the orcs and saw that it was happening just as I predicted. When orc after orc realized that it was armed and standing beside a member of a rival tribe, its instinct was not to ask questions. By the time we were clear of the area, orc-on-orc fights were breaking out like a string of Shou firecrackers.

Only fourteen of us left the battle, about a third of those who entered it. Sungar was the most badly wounded and took up most of the shaman's spells, so the rest of us were left to heal on our own. We set up camp nearby. Food was running scarce, the Fallen Lands offering little in the way of vegetation or wildlife. Whatever the orcs usually ate, it was likely consumed by the naga's army, so several of the most able-bodied Uthgardt set off for the Greypeak Mountains to the west to hunt.

Thluna, myself, and a few of the others went back to the battlefield to recover the honored dead from among the piles upon piles of orc corpses. Surely there were some survivors of the battle, but so few that the Uthgardt considered this among the most glorious victories in their tribe's history, one about which great songs would be sung. I doubted, somehow, that Arklow the Civilized Mage would get a verse.

I inspected the ruin and found it was even more badly

damaged than before. However, I did notice for the first time that the wall that the naga had brought down was marked with a single star etched into the stone; an ancient symbol of Mystra. Perhaps the ruin was once a piece of her temple, part of some ancient city. A new feeling rose in me, a quite blissful peace. I smiled, and I felt privately certain that someone divine had taken measures to ensure our victory.

"Here it is!" one of the barbarians shouted, and we all rushed over to see.

He found Sungar's great axe, lying beneath a dead orc.

"Wonderful," said Thluna. "We can present it to the chieftain when he awakens."

I asked Thluna about the axe, and he explained that it was ancient, going back many generations among the chieftains of the Thunderbeast tribe. No one could remember where it came from or when it was forged.

The hunting party returned with game and plenty of firewood just in time for Sungar to awaken. I wasn't there at the time, but I heard that his first words were, "Was the battle won?"

"Yes," he was assured, "the battle was won with Uthgardt steel."

A feast was held as soon as the chieftain was well enough, a final celebration before the tribe would go back north, back home. For my valor in battle I was allowed to take part, and I was gratified that even the gruffest of the barbarians accepted my presence. All attended the feast in their frequently bloodstained armor, fresh from battle.

Sungar offered a prayer. "We thank Uthgar for the victory he has given us, and in Uthgar's name we ask that we may be strong in battle against our enemies. May we resist the unholy temptations of civilization, of magic, and may we keep the North pure, always."

That night, as the festivities continued, my mind started wandering and I gazed intensely at Sungar's huge battle-axe. I remembered how it hurt Sungar when he swung it at the dark naga, just as my magic missile came back at me, and in a flash I understood why.

I should not have done what I did next. I'm not entirely sure why I did it. Maybe it was an act of spite. I cast a spell, one that would show the aura of enchanted items, and the axe started glowing a light blue. All around us, too, some of the barbarians' weapons, armor, and gear glowed. There was silence, and all eyes turned on me.

"It's magic, Sungar," I said. "Your battle-axe is enchanted, a magical weapon. That's why it hurt you when you struck the naga. You may not approve of magic, but whoever forged that axe certainly did."

"What have you done, mage?" threatened Sungar.

"Nothing. I've done nothing. I've changed nothing. I've merely revealed what was always there. You have always used magic. You just didn't realize it. Don't you see, chieftain? That battle was not the first time magic saved your tribe. It probably has hundreds of times before."

Sungar's face gradually turned from anger to resignation. "You have done us a service, mage. We know what needs to be done."

He stood, taking his axe in hand. He walked away from the camp, raised it above his head, and with impossible strength, hurled it far away onto the barren earth of the Fallen Lands.

One by one, the others followed suit. This is an image that will never leave me. They took their swords, axes, spears, hammers, their helmets and their armor, anything that radiated magic, and threw them all away. Soon, a veritable treasure trove of magical items lay in the dirt. Thluna was among the last to go up. He flashed a sad but nevertheless quite determined glance at me before removing his father's helmet and hurling it to join the rest.

I never shared another word with Sungar, but the next morning, Thluna gave me a horse and escorted me to the edge of the High Gap. From there, I could travel on down the banks of the Delimbiyr River to Loudwater, if such a place existed any longer. Perhaps there I could join another adventuring company. Perhaps I would end up at Evereska after all.

"Our people have a story," Thluna told me. "It is that this region you call the Fallen Lands was once a kingdom of magicians who lived in shining cities. They grew in power till they no longer did anything for themselves. Instead, they would have magic do it for them. They were proud and thought themselves capable of anything. Then one day, the well that they drew their magic from went dry. Their civilization crumbled overnight, and those who survived were set upon by orcs and other foul creatures. All that was once their shining cities has vanished beneath the dirt.

"I cannot tell you if that story is true, mage, but I do know this: Uthgar commands us to resist civilization wherever we find it. Civilization breeds leisure and decadence and magic, all of which seem like strengths but will eventually prove weaknesses. We Uthgardt will outlive all civilization. All civilizeds will eventually become like us."

I sat in silence for a long time, pondering what he had told me, and what I had done. I wanted to tell him everything I knew about Netheril and about the creation of Anauroch, that possibly his ancestors, and very likely mine as well, were survivors of a civilization dead from magic.

Somehow I said nothing.

As I rode away from Thluna, I felt my spellbook under

my robes. For a brief moment, I wondered if I would ever take it out again.

Oh, Lady Mystra! Command me. How could you grant us a gift so destructive, a gift we so rarely use properly? For Thluna was right. It is magic that might some day turn all of Faerûn into the Fallen Lands.

WHEN SHADOWS COME
SEEKING A THRONE

Ed Greenwood

1 Kythorn, the Year of Wild Magic

A hundred tiny stars flashed and sparkled, their reflections crawling silently along bright-polished silver all around the room.

The Queen of Cormyr set down her tallglass, plucked aside the dark shimmerweave cover even before the Lady Laspeera could ready a royal spellshield, leaned forward, and asked gently, "Yes, Mreen? Are you well?"

The Lady Lord of Arabel looked haggard in the depths of the crystal ball. The dark, ragged line of a recent sword-cut across her cheek was all Queen Filfaeril and the senior war wizard needed to see to know the truth.

Myrmeen Lhal shrugged, smiled, and replied simply, "Highness, I live."

Myrmeen was still in full armor, and they

could see the large, well-worn hilt of her warsword where it lay on the table within easy reach.

Filfaeril shook her head at the grim jest. "Not good enough, Mreen—and lay aside my titles. It's *me*, lass, Fee. Your old friend, remember?"

"Highness," the Lady Lord of Arabel said stiffly, "I perceive that you're not alone."

It was Laspeera's turn to sigh. "Myrmeen," she said with just a hint of weariness, "it's just the two of us. Put your boots up on the table, fill your goblet, and tell us: how fares Arabel?"

There was a muffled thud as two mud-caked boot heels crashed into their field of view, daintily crossing at the ankles, and swiftly-moving gold flashed back candlelight as a man-sized goblet was plucked up from out of sight beneath a table edge.

"Very well," Myrmeen said flatly, saluting them both with the drink in her hand. "As you command."

The Queen of Cormyr chuckled in the same soft, deep way her husband had so often done. The Lady Lord of Arabel almost shivered at the sound. Azoun was dead and buried, yet any moment she expected him to stride around the corner, laughter in his eyes, and—

"Mreen," Filfaeril said softly, as if she could read minds, "I miss him too. More than anyone, though I know full well how much I shared him. For his sake, I go on, day after day, to keep Cormyr strong. How fares Arabel?"

"My Queen, I'm so sorr—Fee." The Lady Lord of Arabel slapped the table in anger at herself, took a quick sip—no, a warrior's gulp—of wine, and said crisply, "The city's retaken. Steady patrols remounted, Crown law restored, we're done fixing roads and bridges, and most of your troops are now out among the crofters, with barn-raisings well underway and folk lifting their voices in thanks for your generosity. Now the *real* rebuilding can begin."

Filfaeril smiled, and Laspeera sat back, nodding in satisfaction. "Ah, Mreen, it's such a pleasure to talk with someone who thinks, sees, and speaks directly. You've no idea . . . these courtiers. . . ."

"Oh, yes, I do," Myrmeen Lhal replied fervently. "Were it not for the peril their recklessness and treasonous ambitions would bring down upon us, with the Stonelands so close and this new dark magic outdoing the Zhents, I'd press you to agree to my old pet plan."

It was Laspeera's turn to chuckle. "Clap all our courtiers in armor and ship them out to you, to work their hands dirty and face war-fear and hear a few harsh orders? Don't think we haven't been tempted."

"So do it," the commander of Arabel said. "If I make loyal and useful men out of half a dozen courtiers and die in the doing, that's six replacements for one down—and a lesson that might just cow the rest into keeping mute and out of the way, lest they be 'volunteered' to follow."

"And lose Arabel again?" Filfaeril asked gently. "How many good men would pay the price of winning it back even one more time?"

Myrmeen nodded, took a long drink from her goblet, and said, "Right enough, your—Fee. Gods damn, Filfaeril, but I just can't call y—"

"Oh, yes, you can," Filfaeril said, sudden iron in her voice. "Courtiers down here call me 'the Whore of Ice' behind my back, just loud enough to make sure I hear, and I was 'Lonelybed Longtresses' for years to throw Azoun's amours in my face, and I'll be flayed on the altars of Loviatar before one of my few true friends can't call me by my own name."

"Don't let the lords who linger at Court hear you use that expression," Laspeera said with another chuckle. "So few ideas fall into their heads as it is."

Filfaeril rolled her eyes. "So true. I've tried dropping choice phrases where their spies can overhear, to start them thinking, and all they do is wonder what I meant—aloud and over drink after drink, until they get the words all wrong and twist what they thought I meant all around—and I have to watch Lous fight down the urge to strangle them barehanded, one more time."

It was Myrmeen's turn to chuckle. "Doth the Steel Regent's temper grow . . . more tempered?"

The queen sighed. "Yes, more credit to her, yet being away from the saddle and the sword and her young lords to fence with smiling lies every day . . . I can see it building in her. Someone, someday soon, is going to say one wrong word or do something small and only slightly offensive—and the storm inside Lous is going to break."

"It won't be the only thing in the realm to break that day, I doubt not," the commander of Arabel agreed. "But I fear I waste too much of your time, Fee. You should know some other things, of events up here."

The queen nodded and smiled. "Speak."

"Sightings of terrified Zhents fleeing out of the Stonelands," Myrmeen replied. "Oh, yes; hard to believe, but I saw some myself. They've apparently been babbling about great magical battles, therein, between mighty wizards and horrible flying beasts."

A royal eyebrow lifted. "Apparently?"

"So the jailers say, and they're good ones. I'll make time tomorrow to question the lone live captive we have."

Laspeera had been watching the Lady Lord of Arabel intently through the crystal. "That was your better news," she said quietly. "Now tell us the rest."

Myrmeen held up one scarred, long-fingered hand. "Just one thing, gods be thanked for small mercies. Our patrols have scoured the east."

"And?" The queen's voice was as gentle as if she'd been soothing a crying child.

"Tilverton is gone," Myrmeen said bluntly. "Truly, utterly *gone*."

"Destroyed," Filfaeril murmured. It was not a question. The Lady Lord of Arabel nodded sadly back at her through the scrying-glass, as the queen sighed, threw back her head, and added evenly, "Thank you, Mreen. It's good to hear truth, and not . . ."

"Courtiers' honeyed words," Laspeera said quietly. "Our thanks, Myrmeen. Get some sleep."

The Lady Lord of Arabel gave them a wry smile and a derisive grunt together. "This *was* my sleep, ladies. Gods keep you well, and Cormyr better." She raised her goblet in salute, swung her legs back down to the floor, took up her sword—and the crystal went dark.

"Gods keep *you*, Mreen," the queen said quietly, staring at it. "One of the few true blades we can trust. Oh, they are so few . . ."

"Lady Queen," Laspeera said crisply, "we can only wallow in despair when the needs of the realm permit us time for such indulgences."

Filfaeril's head snapped around, her eyes blazed up into flames, and she gave the senior war wizard a twisted smile.

The queen bowed her head, and murmured, "Right you are, Laspeera. Command me."

"My *Queen!*" Laspeera said, truly shocked.

Filfaeril rolled her eyes and said, "Well then, good Lady, what now is your advice?"

"Alusair must be informed," Laspeera said, nodding at the crystal. "As must the Mage Royal, so she can best order the War Wizards to proceed."

The Queen of Cormyr lifted both her eyebrows. "You've forgotten how to give orders?"

The senior war wizard sighed. "She was Vangy's choice, and we can't expect her to stand strong and loyal when next our need is greatest, if we don't let her so much as give a simple command here and there. I don't want to be Court Wizard, High—Fee. I never have. And what's better, Caladnei doesn't either."

The Queen nodded. "The reluctant serve the best."

Laspeera nodded at the old maxim instead of making a face or sticking out her tongue, as she might have done at another time and in another mood. She merely added in thin, tired tones, "There's still a ghazneth out there . . . and I don't think any of us are hungry, just now, for any more magical tumult in our back pastures."

Filfaeril nodded again, and rose in a shifting of silks. "I'll tell Alaphondar as much as he needs to know."

Laspeera smiled. "Leaving Lous for me? *Thank* you."

"You're welcome," the Queen of Cormyr replied sweetly.

She swept out of the room, in the space of an instant somehow becoming every inch the grand dowager once more.

Laspeera gave the serene royal back a crooked smile, and turned in another direction to go out a darker door.

❧ ❧ ❧ ❧ ❧

Offices breed, somehow. The huge, interconnected fortress of the Royal Court now sprawled larger than the palace itself, and almost entirely shielded—or cut off, rather—the seat of the Obarskyrs from most of the proud city of Suzail.

Yet, gargantuan though it was, courtiers bred faster. They spilled out its great arched doors, across the courtyard between, and over into the palace itself. Two of them, dandy-cloaks swirling brightly around them, stood by a shimmering tapestry—a lambent turquoise scene of crawling blue dragons that Laspeera had always liked. They were obviously waiting for her, so Laspeera strode on toward them, not letting them see the slightest hesitation in her step.

On their faces were the easy smirks of men who airily considered themselves masters of the realm, and for a moment, as she bore down on them, the senior war wizard hated them enough to turn them into mice—or ashes under her boots.

How dare they sidle into the the private chambers of the royal family to warm themselves closer to the flame of power than their fellows, to whom they'd pretend that they enjoyed the personal confidences of the Obarskyrs. At what time had they lost their fear of guards, or for that matter, of swift-striding war wizards?

"Good Lady—" one of them began, as he moved to block her path, his smile almost a sneer.

"My lords," Laspeera interrupted, not slowing or moving aside, "have you personal business with the queen? Or are you merely lost?"

"Ha ha," the courtier replied, in the eager, empty mirth that by its tone announces that its utterer is about to say something important that should—nay, *must*—be heeded.

"Lady Laspeera," the other courtier said firmly, stepping directly into her way, "it was actually you we came to see. It's a matter of some urgency and delicacy . . . ah . . . involving authority over magic."

Laspeera called on the power of the ring that adorned the hand she kept low and behind her—and marched straight into him.

Her shield, unseen and noticeable only as a faint, high singing sound, thrust the man back, startling him into momentary silence. The tall, slender woman in the dark gown was reputedly a powerful mage, yes, but he must weigh almost twice what she did, and how by all the gods—

"Yes," the laughing courtier's voice sprang into the uneasy moment of his fellow's stumbling retreat, "you see, we need to see the Royal Mage."

"I fear you have the wrong realm, gentlesirs," Laspeera told them over her shoulder, as she strode on down the passage. "In Cormyr we have a Court Wizard who is also our Royal Magician, also known as the 'Mage Royal.' We have no 'Royal Mage.'"

"Oh, come, come," the laughing courtier demurred. "Lady, you know well to whom we refer!"

Laspeera swung around, a warning in her eyes, and replied, "Yes, as it happens, I do—and am therefore puzzled as to why you've come to me. The Mage Royal grants audiences to all at times well known to you, and more private appointments with her may be made through the clerks of the court. Their offices lie considerably to the south of here."

She leveled a pointing finger through a handy window at the impressive bulk of the Royal Court, then turned on her heel, and strode on.

"Lady!" the mirthful courtier protested, with a derisive little laugh. "We're not children! We—"

"—have gotten lost to the extent of wandering across a wide courtyard into the wrong building for some other reason, lords? Excessive drink, perhaps?" a new voice said smoothly, as its owner stepped out of a doorway to block their pursuit. He was a Ready Sword of the Palace Guard, and he was not alone.

In the space of a swiftly-drawn breath the two courtiers found themselves ringed by unsmiling Purple Dragons. Guardsmen, in fact, who held weapons half-drawn and looked like they had never in all their long, weather-beaten lives known how to smile.

Laspeera allowed herself a satisfied grin at the alacrity of the response to the song of her rising shield, which would have been very loud in that guardroom, but kept it inside. Her face was its usual pleasant mask as she swept past another courtier—a son of the Helmstone noble family, this one, with rather more right to be on this floor of the palace—even before he could look up from the servant he was snarling threats of dismissal at, and cry hastily, "Lady! Lady Wizard!"

Laspeera neither replied nor slowed, and so—of course—he came hopping along in her wake.

"Lady Laspeera, I must speak with you!"

Not letting her sigh reach her tone of voice, she asked, "Must you, Lord?"

"Well, ah, *yes*, actually."

Laspeera turned a corner without slowing. "Then do so," she replied calmly.

"Here? In the middle of a hallway?"

"Why not, Lord? Do you find hallways somehow . . . tainted?"

"No, no, you misunderstand me, lady. Why, I almost fear you do so deliberately. I-it's just that the matter I must speak with you about is, *ahem*, regarding, ah, future actions of some delicacy involving the Lady Caladnei, and—"

"Lord Helmstone," the senior war wizard replied, "I fear discussing a marriage proposal with anyone other than the lady you wish to become attached to is less than prudent—as is considering anything at all of the sort without first acquiring the approval of your rather formidable father."

"Wha—*marriage?* To such as *her?* Lady, you wound me deeply—"

"No, Lord, not yet," Laspeera murmured, passing through an archway and rounding another corner. "Not yet."

The younger Lord Helmstone was bustling after her, still sputtering in outrage. "Lady, I *protest!* Nobles of the realm are not to be trifled with, not even by—"

Laspeera spun around so swiftly that he was forced to snatch at a voluptuous statuette on a pedestal to slow himself, lest he crash into her. Seeing what rondure he'd laid his hand on, he snatched his fingers away in cringing haste.

Her voice was low and calm when she spoke, but it drained the high color entirely from his face nonetheless.

"Young men of even less prudence than manners? I say again, Lord Helmstone: before you open your mouth again in the palace, seek the wise counsel of your father."

The War Wizard turned on her heel, stepped through the next archway—and discovered that it was her turn to come to a swift halt.

"He did," a deep voice said, in tones as challenging as a sword-thrust, "and is now doing *exactly* what I bade him to. He is attempting, in his own way, admittedly less direct than it could be, to tell you a plain truth. Lady Laspeera, you we know and accept, though some among us mistrust a secretive woman—and a commoner, at that—holding so much power. You have demonstrated your loyalty to the Crown time and time again. You we would accept as Mage Royal, but not another mysterious woman—*another* commoner worming her way into office over us—not this motherless Caladnei. I but seek to warn you of the general mood. King Azoun is gone, lady, and our tolerance for the excesses of those he's left behind wanes—it does indeed. We won't take much more of this."

"King Azoun *the fifth* is alive and well, I assure you," she replied. "And who, my most gracious Lord of Helmstone, is 'we'?"

Laspeera's voice was a razor-sharp dagger of ice, but the elder Lord Helmstone did not flinch. A scuffling sound behind Laspeera told her that his son had, but her shield was still up around her. If sudden ambition—or "patriotism"—should move him to fell a hated war wizard to in some small way cleanse the realm, her back was not unprotected.

"The heads of most of the noble houses of Cormyr, Lady Laspeera," Helmstone said quietly. "The flower of the realm. The swords and coins upon whose support the Dragon Throne stands—or falls."

"And if I was to loudly denounce this treason, Lord?"

"Lady, as King Azoun—the *fourth*—himself said to us

all, 'tis not treason to seek what is best for the kingdom."
Helmstone regarded her gravely, and murmured in tones
that barely reached her ears. "You should now be Mage
Royal, Lady—not some uplands upstart."

"Do you know so clearly, my lord, what's best for
Cormyr?" Laspeera asked him softly, her voice still icy.
"Better than does the wizard Vangerdahast, perchance?"

Helmstone shook his head. "I have no love for the old
wizard, Lady, but with him at least I knew what I was
mistrusting." He drew back, and waved his hand in a gesture that was clearly a signal to his son to depart, swiftly
and upon the instant. "I see our time here is wasted. You
too must be mind-mazed by the spells of the new witch."

Laspeera shook her head, almost as amazed as she
was pretending to be. "Do you misunderstand what wizards do *that* much?"

Helmstone's response, as he drew aside a hanging to
step through a door he should not have known was there,
was a growl of menace.

"Our beloved Forest Kingdom is falling on dark days,
indeed," he said, "if the last withered branches of the
decadent Obarskyrs are now cozened by scheming
witches. Steps must be taken."

A startled servant stood blinking in the revealed doorway, a tray of decanters in her hands. With a snarl of
anger the noble let the hanging fall right in her face,
whirled, and strode past Laspeera, back down the passage in his son's footsteps.

Timidly the hanging was lifted aside. Laspeera gave
the servant a wordless, "I don't know about these nobles,
either," shrug and swept on in search of the Steel Regent.
The short route to where Alusair would be seemed to
have grown very long.

Passing a certain doorway, she gave the face regarding
her from its shadowed depths a discreet nod and strode
on without speaking.

Out of that way, in the senior war wizard's wake, stepped a man whose answering nod was even more subtle. Glarasteer Rhauligan, dealer in turret tops and spires, strolled nonchalantly after the storming noble, humming a popular song of the streets as he went.

Far down the corridor, Laspeera stiffened as she recognized it—and, slowly and ruefully, let a real smile touch her lips. The name of that tune was *Wizards, Kings, and Doom, We All Rush to Seek the Tomb.* Indeed.

The noble faces staring down into the pit were pale and sweating. It's one thing to sneer at terror-tales heard in youth, deeming them sheer lies spun by the weak-minded. It's quite another to see them come to life and writhing in pain below you—wounded, yes, but so large and mighty in magic and so terrifyingly near.

Netheriloursonce. Heed, humans. Greatevil returned shadows shadowmen darkwizards, city of Shade now back. In desertofourdevising. Will reachout seizebetter-lands—this one! Soon, plotting evennow! Storm back from exilehidingcravenstealth to seize whatrightfullyyy-ours togreat acclaimproperrank bards'esteem Weak women on throne ignorant willdither willbetoolate youCormyr's only hope YOUher salvation!

The hissing mind-voice fell silent, but its echoes still thundered in their heads, and it was only with difficulty that Halvundrar Cormaeril managed to speak, his voice thick, slow, and awkward.

"What . . . must we do?"

Keepsecretkeepsilent heedmy words!

The voice slowed, mind-speaking each word carefully and firmly, as an angry father might deliver a warning of great importance to a child.

Royal Magician must be slain. First get from her key to

Iltharl's Vault. Very powerful magic therein. Take it, cleanse your fair land, and set someone suitable on the throne. Yourselves, for instance. Soon it will be time to strike. Very soon.

In their minds appeared a sudden, vivid image—of a long-barreled key, its silver plate tarnished with age, its wards large and fluted, its handle worked into a dragon's head, jaws agape.

Darkness descended like a curtain, and their minds were their own again. They could see nothing of the pit and the ridiculous-looking, trumpet-shaped bulk shuddering in it, clawed arms and stinger moving restlessly.

Maerlyn Bleth shivered. So that was a phaerimm.

His mind whirled the image of the key they must seize from the Mage Royal in front of him and took it away again.

A flying city of shadow wizards come back from ancient Netheril. All the Realms endangered, Cormyr the closest prize . . . it was using them, that thing down in the pit, using them like the brainless cattle it so obviously and scornfully believed them to be. When the time was right, its spells would lash out or it would stab at their very minds.

But plots are easily spoken and harder in the doing. Mistakes inevitable—oh, hadn't the gods taught far too many Cormyrean nobles *that*. Mighty magic is always a weapon worth having—and if Cormyr was doomed, after all these centuries, at least the House of Obarskyr could be driven down in richly-deserved slaughter first, every last screaming woman of it, those sneers wiped off their faces as they saw the nobles they and their forebears had so wronged working revenge upon them at last.

He was grinning like a wolf, Maerlyn knew. Teeth flashed in the dim light around him as they hastened out of the cavern together. Every last one of his fellow conspirators was grinning savagely too.

Ah, but it would be good to see the Obarskyrs get theirs at last.

The Steel Regent struck again, grunting with the effort, and Caladnei reeled. Every blow of Alusair's onslaught was like a hammer in her head, and the Mage Royal was fast acquiring a blinding headache.

Both women were drenched and staggering as they circled each other, cotton tunics plastered to their curves and errant hairs escaping sodden headscarves. Gods, but the princess was as fast as a striking snake!

Her wooden practice blade swept around again, and this time Caladnei dodged away to avoid parrying, stumbling in her weariness.

Her own sword was an edgeless bar of force, maintained by her will alone, and—

Alusair thrust past her guard, their blades binding, and Caladnei shouted in pain.

"No," the Steel Regent snarled, as the Mage Royal gasped and held up a hand in a gesture of surrender, "don't give up on me now! A murderous noble won't stay his steel because you wave to him that you're winded."

They were circling each other again, both caked with the sand of the practice-floor where they'd clinched, kicked, and tumbled earlier in their bout. Shamra the Healer stood watching them carefully, ready to step in if either woman lost her temper and went too far, or took a wound through a slip at the wrong instant.

"I did not . . . seek this office," the Mage Royal snarled between gasps. "I didn't want this title . . . these duties . . ."

The Steel Regent's grin was as wry as it was fierce. "I've heard those very same words before, echoing back at me from my own bedchamber mirror."

Her blade skirled and thrust. Caladnei shouted again

at the pain in her head—and a wooden blade slid home to touch her just under her breasts, thudding painfully up and in, at her heart. She put a hand on Alusair's weapon and bent over to catch her breath, reflecting ruefully that she wasn't half the swordmaster the princess was.

"Did you die gloriously?"

The calm question made both of the panting, sweating women look up. The voice belonged to Laspeera, and she never disturbed them at practice unless matters were urgent or of the utmost importance.

Caladnei waved away the question with a smile as she struggled for breath.

Alusair handed her sword to the healer, strode up out of the sand, and asked, "What news, Lasp?"

The senior war wizard reported the news from Arabel and her encounters with various murmuring critics of the Mage Royal on the way to them, as the two women did off their tunics and headscarves, washed with mint-water, toweled down, and put on fresh tunics.

Shamra was holding out a hair-ribbon to Caladnei as Laspeera recounted the words of the elder Lord Helmstone, her mimicry of his tone as exact as her recall of his utterances.

The Mage Royal frowned, stiffened, and snapped, "Later, ladies!"

The place where Caladnei had been standing was suddenly empty. Shamra was holding out a ribbon to emptiness. She blinked once, and calmly turned and put the ribbon back on the side table from which she'd taken it. Alusair and Laspeera were exchanging raised-eyebrow looks.

"One of her telltales went off," the war wizard murmured. "I wonder what disaster's unfolding now?"

The princess sighed as she made for the door, binding back her hair as she went.

"I miss Vangerdahast," she said. "He never told you

anything either, but he had this sneering, testy way of doing it that somehow reassured you that he had everything under control. I miss that feeling."

Laspeera's smile, as they went out of the practice hall together, was thin. "You're not the only one. Nor am I. The nobles were never so restless under Vangy's eye."

Behind them, the healer smiled. Out of habit she turned to make sure nothing vital had been forgotten, and struck Alusair's wooden sword against the door post. It was still slick with sweat, and slipped from her fingers—but it never clattered to the floor.

Just for an instant, Shamra's hand blurred into something dark and very like a tentacle, that plucked the blade from the air and reshaped itself once more into the healer's fine-fingered hand.

She was alone, Laspeera's back just disappearing through an archway.

Hefting the wooden sword in her hand, the healer let her smile broaden. Not so wide as to show fangs or seem strange—but as eager and deadly as the sudden glitter in the eyes above it.

Soon it would be time to move at last . . . very soon. With magic enough, she could hold the throne if she took it. And taking it would be so easy. Wring the neck of a babe, and catch Alusair alone and treat her to the same fate before word spread of little Azoun's doom . . . and slay Filfaeril, take her shape, and play the sorrowful queen waiting to be wooed by the right noble.

It would not be such a bad thing, to rule a kingdom as fair as this one, if she could keep all these idiots from shattering it around her.

"What can I say, good my Lord, to convince you to join us?"

The elder Lord Helmstone was angry—gods above, couldn't the man see this was the right thing to do? He wasn't a dullard, after all.

"Nothing that comes to my mind," Lord Everran Summertree replied, in a voice that was sharp with disapproval. "Cormyr can ill afford—Helmstone, *we* can ill afford—another war right now, with so many dead and their crops unplanted, and Sembians eager to snap up land in return for just enough coin to see starving crofters warm and fed through the coming winter. Our realm needs peace to rebuild, not another petty squabble over whose shoulders carry this or that title, or even whose backside warms the Dragon Throne!"

Lord Helmstone sighed—the angry gust of a man exasperated by obstinate idiocy. He drew a slow, simmering breath, threw his chin forward like a weapon, and growled, "The time will come, Summertree, when you see sense. I only hope 'twill not be too late. In the end you'll find you simply must turn against these witches and foolish women who now misrule us, and so sully the bright memory of Azoun and Cormyr's greatness—before it ebbs entire!"

Out on the balcony—or rather, just beneath it, where he was clinging by his fingertips—Glarasteer Rhauligan rolled his eyes. Did all of these nobles learn their bombast at the same school? Or did the Lord of Traitors answer their prayers by filling their minds with the same grand speeches of self-righteous "for the good of the realm I do this" blurf?

"If you truly cared for the good of Cormyr," Lord Summertree replied coldly, "You'd court Alusair and set your son to wooing the Mage Royal—and win or lose their charms, you'd gain yourself ample opportunity to fill their ears with the policies and stances you think the realm should adopt."

"Take that spitfire to wife? Harness my son to a *commoner?*"

"Oh, stop *squeaking*, my lord. Barely two centuries have your kin held nobility—and right now you scarcely seem suited to it. We were all commoners, once. As for taming princesses—think of it as better sport than sticking your lances through stags and a few scrawny boar. 'Twould keep you busy, at least, and—"

"And out of your regard? That much I *can* do, my lord! Good day to you!" Lord Helmstone's parting wish was delivered at a roar as he whirled and stormed out, backhanding a wine-bearing manservant out of his way so fiercely that one of Summertree's best decanters clanged off the passage wall.

Its owner waved the servant away with a reassuring smile, firmly closed the door, set its lock bar in place, and strode to his desk.

Lord Summertree was not in a writing mood at this moment, it seemed. He went around behind his chair, kept going—and with surprising speed for a man so muscular and of graying years—snatched aside the tapestry that concealed the door to his cloak closet. His sword was half drawn as he stared into the wide eyes of the still-sweating Mage Royal.

He asked pleasantly, "I trust you heard everything you wanted to. Have you a good reason to give me why I shouldn't just run you through with this good blade right now—as I would any sneak-thief?"

Caladnei cleared her throat. "Are you not afraid of my Art?"

Summertree smiled back at her wryly. "Shouldn't you be afraid of mine?"

The larger of the two ornate rings on his left hand winked, and a singing, glowing aura appeared around the noble. He stepped back and drew his sword. In silence they both watched a radiance that matched Summertree's shield awaken in his blade, and start to silently race along its bright, sharp edges.

"No," the Mage Royal said flatly, tossing her head. "I know you stand loyal for the Crown—and so I have nothing to fear."

Summertree raised an eyebrow. "I know not where you stand," he replied gently, lifting his sword so that its tip was a whisker away from the cotton cloaking her breast, "so I think you do."

The blade lifted, to menace her throat. "Who is Caladnei, really?" the noble asked, his voice almost a purr. "How do any of us know if Vangerdahast *really* chose you—or if he did, what he intends for our fair realm? Who's he truly loyal to, and whom do you serve? I ask again: why shouldn't I just run you through now, as many of the hotheads among we who bear titles desire me to do?"

Steel flashed as Glarasteer Rhauligan stepped into the room. "Because, my Lord Summertree," he said firmly, "to do so would be the act of a traitor—a man I would be forced to cut down, even in his own manor, for so cruel a murder and deliberate treason against the Crown."

Everran Summertree was not accustomed to being surprised by the silent approaches of strangers—least of all in his own study, and with daggers poised in their hands to throw in his direction. If the old lord was astonished, Caladnei was even more so.

"Who are *you?*" they said, more or less together.

Glarasteer smiled an easy smile, and replied, "I think you really mean to ask me *what* I am or rather whom I serve. Well, then, I harp from time to time, and bear with me both a Purple Dragon ring graven with my name by Azoun IV himself, and a Crown commission from Vangerdahast."

Lord Summertree shook his head. "It seems my private chambers have become a popular wing of the court, this evening," he observed, spreading his hands to include both of his guests. "Will you join me in wine?"

Two heads shook in unison, politely declining. The man who'd stepped in from the balcony raised his other hand from behind him, and Lord Summertree watched the light of his favorite lamps gleam along the edge of a very sharp long sword. As he wondered for the first time if he might die this evening, there came a whirling of a different sort of light from closer at hand—and the Mage Royal vanished.

The two men looked at each other—and both shrugged.

"A pleasant evening to you, Lord," Glarasteer said softly, ere he took two swift steps and vaulted over the balcony rail into the gathering dusk.

"A bit late for that, don't you think?" Lord Summertree murmured, after a moment of standing alone with his sword raised against no foe.

Setting it carefully on the desk, he went to a sideboard, poured himself a goblet of a favorite wine with hands that shook not at all, and strolled thoughtfully out onto the balcony to watch what bards liked to call "the soft summer stars coming out."

The tentacle that slapped around his eyes and mouth, and broke his neck with a quick, brutal jerk before snatching the noble's shuddering, spasming body back out of sight, was accompanied by a calm, slightly husky, feminine murmur.

"Far too late, my Lord Summertree, but not too late for you to have a change of heart and go to join the conspirators."

For just a moment, as it flexed a pair of tentacles and casually tossed the large, limp body up onto the manor roof for the crows to rend, the shape that had spoken resembled Shamra the Healer. The moment was gone, and it dwindled and thickened, taking on the burly bulk of the much-respected, childless bachelor noble. Barefoot it padded to the robing rooms to choose clothes, plucking up the fallen goblet as it went.

When it set off across the study toward the door and its lock bar a few breaths later, it moved with utter confidence, and a fair approximation of Lord Summertree's stride.

At least she had this one dusty chamber, spell-shielded by Lord Vangerdahast to keep everyone else out, as a refuge.

Right now, Caladnei of the Raging Headache sorely— and that was a mild word for what she felt—needed it.

She clutched at her temples as her head rang and rolled, softly cursing all of the grasping nobles that Cormyr seemed so richly over-endowed with. Gods *damn* and blast them all!

Even here in the palace, they circled like vultures around Azoun's tomb, eyeing the throne. She didn't want any of this, Royal Magician and Court Wizard and Lady Master of the War Wizards—and all the other barbed, honeyed words at court.

The Forest Kingdom was a beautiful place, and it felt like home—it *was* home—but why couldn't she just take over an old, ramshackle upcountry house in the woods and be left alone there to work magic?

Every month it surged in her more strongly. Just plain Caladnei could do wondrous things, she knew, if she could take the time to try steering her sorcery thus and so, observe, and try again, unleashing magic that was truly Art, not these dry inscriptions the wizards so loved.

Yet all around her in the gloom were the spells Vangerdahast had left her. Shelves after shelves of fat, mysterious-looking books and pigeonholes of yellowing scrolls. Hundreds of both. Dusty tomes and cryptic symbols and crabbed inscriptions, the things book-wizards loved, true—but to read even one of them awakened things in her, stirred her sorcery to eager life, and left her able to do more . . . even if it had nothing to do with the written spell. She'd never have been allowed access to such treasures if Lord Vangerdahast hadn't named her his successor.

"Why, take this scroll, here," she murmured aloud, knuckling her head against the pain. She'd found it yesterday, in a cobwebbed corner that didn't look as if it had been disturbed since the palace was built . . . whenever that was. A translation—by Baerauble himself!—of *Names of Power*. Words bound into enchantments woven into the Weave in ancient Netheril itself. To utter one of them would summon a Netherese archwizard to you, to render a single act of aid. Doubtless most of those words would bring only a cloud of tomb-dust and perhaps a few crumbling bones, now, but still . . . *think* of it! Magic spun when there was no Cormyr and dragons ruled most of the realms of today. Carefully stored here—forgotten, yes, but guarded as the treasures they were—for someone, long centuries later, to find them.

Someone called Caladnei, a wandering adventurer and spellcaster-for-hire. A commoner, a nobody . . . *one more lowborn wench put in office over us*.

The Mage Royal sighed, and let her eye run down the list of Names of Power, wondering if similar intrigues had beset their long-ago owners. Probably, if Netheril was anything like Cormyr or Halruaa.

Brathchacelent. Cathalegaunt. Tarane. Who had they been?

Caladnei sighed. That was the sort of thing she wanted to know, not which blustering noble wanted her horsewhipped and hanged this morning.

Gods, but she might just welcome that about now! The Mage Royal put her head down on a reading desk and moaned, wondering how to master her Art to quell headaches.

Eyes shone like pale moons in the gloom, over the wet scarves that kept them from sneezing in the thick, cobwebbed dust. This secret passage had been forgotten even by the Obarskyrs, just as the phaerimm had said. Maerlyn Bleth looked up sharply as he sensed, more than saw, a blade drawn. Halvundrar Cormaeril gave him a silent glare over it, and jerked his head sharply, pointing at its tip—which slowly, and ever so faintly, began to glow.

Maerlyn stared at it, and by its softly growing light saw the wooden swivel-catch next to it—one of three around the edges of a door or panel that Cormaeril was now patiently tracing. Halvundrar's hand closed on one, and he pointed with his blade at another.

Maerlyn reached for it, but one of the others—Ilryn Merendil; Maerlyn could just make out the line of his short, upcurled beard—was there already, leaving Maerlyn to take the next. Klasker Goldsword and Aldeth Dracohorn squeezed past, their own swords grating out with a sound that was startlingly loud among all the gentle breathing. It earned them a fierce glare from Cormaeril, and he was gesturing again at the catches.

Together, with slow care, they turned, freeing the dry, crumbling wood from where it had rested for perhaps a century, and the panel shifted under their fingers. At a nod from Cormaeril—and who'd named *him* lord of their little band, anyway?—Maerlyn pulled gently on the catch in his hand, using it as a handle, with Merendil at his side.

The panel came away easily, spilling light into their passage—light tinted crimson by the tapestry in front of them. From beyond it, as they set the panel carefully aside, they could hear female voices. Two: the princess, and the Mage Royal, discussing possible traitors at Court, and what to do about them.

Maerlyn saw Cormaeril grin savagely at the irony, and met it with a mirthless smile of his own. He freed the weighted cloak from his belt and shook it out ready in his hand. The cloak would be his own contribution to the plans of the phaerimm. It would go over the Caladnei wench's head as quickly as he could get it there, to keep her from blasting them with magic before they could get their blades into her. Risky, yes, but he'd far rather be skirmishing with a young, untried Mage Royal than crossing blades with the Steel Princess!

Halvundrar Cormaeril ducked his head, brought his blade up over his shoulder, and burst forward in furious silence—and they were all pounding forward into the light, waiting for the screaming to start.

Seeking screams that did not come.

Glarasteer's hands trembled as he set down the call-crystal he'd just shattered. "If I'm wrong," he muttered, "I'll take the blame."

"If you're wrong, good Rhauligan," the Queen of Cormyr said firmly, "*I'll* take the blame. Lord Vangerda-hast still owes me much, and—"

There was a flash of purple and white flame from the far side of the bed. Silhouetted against it, they saw Laspeera and the four trusted Highknights writhing in agony. Writhing—and falling.

Then the light was gone, and in the searing after-glow fitful lightning crackled over the sleeping infant King. Laspeera's spell-shield was collapsing.

"Lasp!" Filfaeril snapped as she glided forward,

snatching a dagger out of her bosom with a speed that made Glarasteer blink. "Lasp! *Speak to me!*"

Only silence answered her—for the triumphant, merciless laughter that was suddenly rolling all around them sounded only in their heads.

So disgustingly easy *thisbestpulinghumanscando? Notworthytorule evenenoughgroundfor theirowngraves hardly worthmytrouble* die *thenweakhumandross!*

Fire was lashing them, *inside* their heads, and Filfaeril's scream was a high, unearthly stabbing at Rhauligan's ears. Purple-white fire blossomed again, around the royal bed, and by its light he saw the queen, dagger fallen, trying to claw out her own eyes.

Then his own hands were coming up at his face, sharp steel still clutched in them—and he threw himself sideways, knocking Filfaeril onto the bed with his hip, driving on to roll away from her soft limbs and into a hard, bruising meeting with the floor. His arms were trembling as he fought against the phaerimm's dominance— *gods*, but it was strong!—and there was a sudden roar and flare of golden light so bright the chamber seemed filled with the sun.

The vice tightening around their minds was gone.

Glarasteer blinked. Across the chamber, something clawed and bestial was thrashing as it died, a last smoldering agony that framed the grim smile of a bearded, robed, rumple-haired man with a very familiar face.

"Vangerdahast!" half a dozen throats gasped as one.

"You summoned, and I came," the wizard growled, as he stepped over what was left of the phaerimm with spell-smoke still rising from his hands. *"Bah!* Why should Elminster get all the fun?"

Glarasteer Rhauligan looked back at the shards of the call-crystal, then over at the crisped and riven remains of the phaerimm. Drawing a deep, shuddering breath, he put down his sword. He'd sworn to defend the lives of the Obarskyrs with his own, so long as he could still draw breath, and for the first time since he'd taken up vigil over the king's bed, he began to hope that he just might live to see another morning come to Cormyr.

The pride of Cormyr's exiled nobility were halfway across The Chamber of Frostfire Candles, with the Steel Regent and the Mage Royal both whirling to meet them, beautiful eyes flashing with anger and something else—eagerness?—when the tapestries on the *other* side of the room boiled, and a nightmare of black tentacles burst forth, snaking around the princess.

Alusair's sword was already drawn. She spun around with a speed that made Maerlyn Bleth gulp, hacked twice, and smoking ichor spattered to the ghost rothé rugs, followed by a thrashing, severed tentacle.

Maerlyn swerved and charged at the Mage Royal, shaking out the cloak as he ran, just in time to bring it up in front of his face as Caladnei snarled something, and the world exploded in a hissing roar of ice.

Cormaeril shouted in pain and fell back, sheathed in sparkling frost, Goldsword toppled without a sound, and Dracohorn staggered once and became still, stiff and white and staring. Maerlyn flinched back from the searing cold, gasping out a curse, and—

There was a sickening wet splintering sound from his left, and the princess sobbed. It was a sound Maerlyn had never thought to hear; he couldn't help but turn and look.

A dark, rippling figure that had a gloating human face but nothing else human about it leaned toward Alusair, its front a forest of writhing tentacles. One of them flailed in shredded uselessness, another wore the regent's sword like a high lady's hatpin as it coiled and whipped in pain—and the rest were tightening around the struggling princess herself.

Gods! This couldn't be the phaerimm, surely, so what was it?

Alusair was snarling, more anger than fear on her face, but one of her arms dangled uselessly, shattered somewhere below the elbow. The other was plying a dagger as fast as she could, keeping those deadly coils from her throat, but a dozen snakelike arms were already tightening around her, and she was being bent back like a straining bow.

In a moment, Maerlyn knew, he would hear Alusair's spine make the same sound that her arm had.

"Caladnei!" the princess cried. "Aid! Aid, unless you want to be regent, too!"

Tightening tentacles slapping around her breast, she had breath left only for a scream of rage and pain.

Gods, yes, Caladnei! He was supposed to be—

Maerlyn whirled back toward the Mage Royal, bringing the cloak up again—but Caladnei, her eyes two dark flames of fury, was rising from a hastily-clawed-open drawer with a wand in her hand, shouting something.

A beam of flame scorched across the room so swiftly that the air made a sound like parchment being torn—and the black, glistening shape exploded in a rain of gore and tangled tentacles, flinging the Steel Regent over a couch and away.

There would be time to make sure of her later. His task remained clear before him. Maerlyn flung the useless cloak aside with a snarl and snatched out his blade—in time to see Ilryn Merendil, a soft smile on his face, slash aside Caladnei's vainly-warding hand with a vicious sword cut, and bring his slim, bright steel around in an elegant thrust that plunged right through the Mage Royal's midriff—to emerge, glistening, from her back.

Her eyes widened in astonishment and agony, and Maerlyn Bleth grew a smile of his own as he stepped forward in a perfect thrust and made his own hole in yielding flesh, crossing his blade over Merendil's to come out the witch's side and pin her arm.

Caladnei reeled, and her eyes found his—eyes awash in pain and sadness and regret. Trembling lips drooled blood, and gasped, *"Tarane."*

The word seemed to rush away across the room, echoing as if across vast distances—and to roar back into a thunderclap that shook the Chamber of Frostfire Candles.

There was someone else in the room—a man Maerlyn had never seen before. He was tall and very thin, wore robes of strange cut and dark but shimmering hue, and his skin was the color of smoke. His eyes seemed almost milky-white as he glanced at the dying woman and at Maerlyn and Merendil. Almost lazily he raised one hand, and it seemed to the astonished noble that shadows clung to it, somehow; shadows that shouldn't have been there, in all this lamplight.

The man smiled a cold, unlovely smile, and something bright blue and bubbling sprang out of his empty palm, washing over Cormaeril and Merendil and—Maerlyn himself!

The youngest son of House Bleth felt a moment of intense cold, and a burning that rose savagely to choke him—and as the world slowly went dark and he stared at the exposed bones of his own sword arm, Maerlyn felt nothing at all.

Done. The mind-voice was calm and triumphant and somehow sneering, Caladnei thought, through the red claws of agony, as the wizard of shadows watched her sag back against a couch with two swords through her. She struggled to reach out a hand to him, and he calmly watched her efforts, smiled that cruel smile, waved a hand, and was gone as if he had never been.

Despairing, Caladnei let the pain take her, shuddering around the swords whose sharp points would not let her lie back against the splendid upholstery and rest.

So this is what it feels like to die . . .

There was noise, fast approaching, an uneven running that ended in a skidding crash into one end of the couch. Spitting blood as the world darkened around her, the Mage Royal felt no pain from that jarring—nothing more than the raging wall of agony that was bearing down, crushing her.

Silver flashed in front of her nose, and soothing fire passed her lips.

"Caladnei!" a voice hissed.

The Mage Royal struggled to focus, to see the face of the princess. Alusair dashed a second healing potion down her throat—gods, but it felt good—and set one booted foot against Caladnei's breast and pulled.

Coming out, the blade tugged the Mage Royal half upright, and if she'd thought she'd tasted pain before, she knew better now. Steel rang and clattered far down the room—Alusair must have just flung the blade away over her shoulder—and without pause the princess bent forward and snatched out the second sword.

Someone very near was shrieking in agony, a raw and horrible sound, and as Caladnei writhed and shuddered on the couch, biting her lips and tongue uncontrollably, she very much feared that it was her.

The pain-creased face of the princess was in front of hers again.

"Hold on, Mage," Alusair was snarling, as Caladnei shrank back from the light and noise and pain, drifting down toward the dark.

"You're one of us now," the princess roared, "and Cormyr needs you! *Don't* you die on me! I so much wanted to gallivant around and have adventures while my father ruled over a placid realm of ever-richer farmers and nobles so adrip with gems that they tossed handfuls of them to their servants . . . but somehow I'm not surprised that the gods had other ideas. If there's to be a Cormyr tomorrow—without Vangerdahast—I need you. *Cormyr* needs you! *Damn* you, Caladnei!"

Strong fingers shook Caladnei like a rag doll, but it all seemed so far away.

Alusair whirled away from the Mage Royal's body and sprinted across the room, shouting at the pains that stabbed through her legs and ribs and shattered arm with each step, until she reached a statuette crowning a mantelpiece—a sculpted likeness of a Purple Dragon.

"Blast you, Vangerdahast," she sobbed, snatching it from its perch and wincing her way back down the room, "this had better not have been one of your sly lies!"

With trembling fingers she snatched one of the enchanted rings off the hand at the end of her broken arm—on her knees and gasping with pain by the time she got it off—and thrust it into one of her open wounds, tearing at her flesh until oozing blood ran freely again.

Tucking the statuette into the crook of her good arm, the Steel Princess reached up to hold the ring in her wound, reeled to her feet, and lowered herself as gently as she could atop Caladnei's limp body. They were going to slide off this bloody couch together, if she didn't.

Grimly Alusair fumbled the purple dragon—one of three in all Faerûn, if Vangy had told her truth—into her good hand, raised herself awkwardly with her broken arm grinding into her dying friend, and the ring held there in her own gore, and smashed the statuette against the back of the couch with all the strength she had left.

It took two sobbing blows before the thing broke. Weeping, Alusair brought the jagged fragment still in her hand around—and stabbed herself with it, right into the ring.

It had been trailing blue fire. So the old wizard hadn't lied, and this just might—

Blue flames burst through her, like fire and ice, cooling and soothing. The pain was gone!

Alusair shuddered as cleansing power raced through her, and—and—gods, Caladnei! Swiftly, ere it ebbed!

She fell forward again and kissed whatever bare skin she could find—Caladnei's left cheek, as it happened, just beneath one staring eye—and held herself rigid to be sure their contact did not end. With tantalizing slowness, almost lazily, the healing magic stole out of her, washed back into her, and rippled into the Mage Royal and stayed there.

The body beneath hers jumped, spasming and moaning gently and trying to rise. Alusair held her down, clawing at the carved back of the couch to hold herself in place as Caladnei sobbed, shuddered, and gasped, "Princess? Alusair?"

The Steel Regent smiled then and let go her grasp to start the slow slide toward the floor.

Tingling, all pain wondrously banished, Caladnei lifted her head to look around, through swimming eyes—as Glarasteer Rhauligan stepped smilingly into the room with his drawn sword raised and ready, and Laspeera looking over one shoulder, and Vangerdahast peering over the other.

Behind them was Queen Filfaeril with the infant king in her arms and the sage Alaphondar at her side—and there seemed to be an inadvertent contest between the infant Azoun and the patrician sage as to who could look the most dazed and just-awakened.

Rhauligan shook his head as he slid his sword back into its sheath and went to help them. He was still two steps away when the Steel Princess bumped down onto the floor.

"Y'know," he remarked, reaching down a hand to help her up, "there're some folk who'd look upon this touching scene and draw quite the wrong conclusions, but . . ."

Alusair gave him a level look, and said crisply, "It's a good thing for *you*, sir, that Vangerdahast, my father, and Elminster all carefully took the time to separately and in the utmost secrecy explain to me just who you are. It's kept you alive these past few months, when certain folk very strongly urged you be rendered dead."

As she spoke, blue flames of healing magic swirled from between her lips.

Weakly, from the couch, Caladnei muttered, "So I was mistaken. Not one of my larger mistakes, I'm afraid."

She looked up at Vangerdahast apologetically. "Are you still sure you made the right choice? I knew nothing about these nobles, and—and that tentacled *thing*."

Her predecessor smiled, shook his head, and said, "The Blood of Malaug are everywhere these days, it seems, and Cormyr is always entertaining noble traitors and exiles who think regicide will win them back their estates and titles with a sword stroke. You'll get used to them."

Caladnei sat up and said almost pleadingly, "I failed the Crown! I didn—"

Vangerdahast snorted. "Nay, nay, lass—don't think to get out of being Mage Royal *that* easily! The mistakes are all yours to make now. I'm not watching over you all, ready to appear in a puff of spellsmoke to save your various shapely behinds whenever you stumble."

He turned slowly on his heel, to favor everyone in the room with his stern gaze, and added, "Consider this a lucky chance that I was passing through. Cormyr is yours now. With the passing of Azoun, my duty was done, and I've so little time left to cram all my neglected tasks and whims and unfinished business into. Farewell!"

Amid a vain chorus of protests, he smiled again, wiggled his fingers playfully at the child king, and vanished.

Filfaeril broke the little silence that followed with a sigh, and turned to Caladnei and asked, "How do wizards *do* that? I've always wanted to just begone into thin air, too—usually when particularly obnoxious nobles were approaching. 'Twould be very handy—"

It was not considered polite to interrupt the Queen of Cormyr, but Caladnei was suddenly lost in a flood of giggles—mirth that begat laughter from others, a rising chorus of guffaws through which the Mage Royal only dimly heard Glarasteer Rhauligan remark in gloomy tones, "She has a flaw after all, our Royal Magician: she *giggles.*"

❦ ❦ ❦ ❦ ❦

In a room that swirled with shadows, Tarane of Shade stood watching the scene in the Chamber of Frostfire Candles through a whorl of scrying magic.

"Well, well," he said, smiling faintly. "An interesting place to rule, to be sure. Let it mature awhile, to grow strong and prosperous again first. Waiting for the right moment is one thing I know very well how to do."

He picked up a ring that had until recently adorned the hand of Maerlyn Bleth from a flaring, flute-topped pedestal table beside him. Turning it so that its half-aroused enchantments—magic the young fool had been utterly unaware he was carrying—made it flash in the backwash of the scrying spell, the Shadovar added with a smile, "Unlike so many of the fair flowering of Cormyr's proud noble houses. Or the last Obarskyrs and their handful of loyal servants, for that matter."

KING SHADOW

Richard Lee Byers

11 Kythorn, the Year of Wild Magic

The old knight and his squire hobbled their weary destriers through the charred and shattered gate. They walked the rubble-choked streets of the murdered city, where even a fresh horse would likely lose its footing.

At first Kevin felt numb and sick. The short, sandy-haired youth had yearned his whole life to ride to war, had felt feverish with excitement on the long, difficult ride from Kirinwood to Tilverton. But he had never imagined war's aftermath: broken buildings and broken bodies reeking of burning, evil magic, and rot, the stink perceptible despite the drizzling rain.

Gradually, though, pure stupid horror lost its grip on the squire, and he regarded his master, only to discover a new cause for dismay.

Before forsaking martial endeavors to run the family farm and make fern-and-mint wine, Sir Ajandor Surehand had seen other scenes of carnage nearly as grim as this. Yet he trudged along without a word, his thin, wrinkled face with its drooping white mustache ashen, his gray eyes lost and empty beneath his shaggy brows.

Kevin was appalled. He had always thought the gaunt old knight indomitable, but apparently the loss of an only child could overwhelm anyone.

"Sir," he said, picking his way around a spill of field-stone, "you know, it may not be possible to find him."

If Ajandor heard, he gave no sign.

"There are so many dead people," Kevin continued, "some disfigured by fire and the like. Others no doubt lie inside the collapsed buildings."

"Is that what you think?" snapped Ajandor, who had never before spoken harshly to Kevin in all their years together. "That my son was cowering indoors when he died?"

"No! I'm sure he died fighting the enemy."

"Then shut up."

As Kevin wondered what to say next, a gray form sprang up from the ground, where it had apparently been lying flat as a sheet of parchment. A pair of vague limbs outstretched, it pounced at Kevin.

The squire tried to dodge and draw his sword at the same time. He managed neither. The dark thing slammed into him and bore him down to the ground. Raking claws shredded his mantle and surcoat and ripped at the hauberk beneath.

Something flashed. The creature leaped away, and Kevin saw Ajandor standing over him with Gray Dancer, his sword of gleaming mithral silver, in his hand. The knight had used it to drive the phantom back.

Kevin scrambled to his feet and yanked out his own

blade, a plain steel one, devoid of pedigree and with only the simplest of enchantments. The humans and the creature stood and regarded one another.

Kevin could see that the shadow resembled an enormous cat, though perhaps that was only one of many possible forms, for its murky substance seemed to flow and shift from moment to moment. The refugees whom he and Ajandor had encountered on the road had warned them of such shadow creatures, phantoms apparently engendered by the same wizardry that had destroyed Tilverton and the army assembling inside its walls.

Evidently hoping to flank the apparition, Ajandor edged to the left. Kevin moved to the right. The cat sprang at him, its entire head opening like an oyster to become nothing more than a set of jaws.

Sidestepping to throw off the shadow's aim, Kevin cut at its shoulder. Though he had felt the phantom's weight and strength, his sword swept through it as if it were made of smoke. That should have been good, but he knew it wasn't. Some supernatural beings were all but impervious to mundane weapons, and this was apparently one of them.

The phantom clawed at him, and he jumped back. Ajandor rushed in and drove his point into the shadow's flank.

The creature spun, reared on its hind legs like a bear, and raked at Ajandor with talons grown long as daggers. Scarcely giving an inch of ground, the knight met the shadow's attack with savage stop cuts. At least his blade seemed to be biting something solid, though whether it was doing the phantom any real harm was impossible to say.

Kevin could tell that his master was trying to get inside the shadow's reach for another stroke to the head or torso, where, perhaps, some vital organs resided, but the creature was holding him back. For his part, the squire couldn't hurt the phantom, but perhaps he could distract it. Yelling at the top of his lungs, he charged and beat at it.

The shadow whirled, loomed above him like a mountain about to give birth to an avalanche, then it jerked, and the point of Gray Dancer popped out of its belly. Ajandor had seized his opportunity to bury the mithral weapon in its back. The cat toppled, and Kevin scrambled aside to keep it from dropping on top of him.

Panting, his heart pounding, the squire was content to stand clear and hope that the shadow wouldn't get up again, but Ajandor was not. Seemingly contemptuous of the cat's flailing limbs, he kept on attacking. The shadow stopped moving and still he hacked at it, until the body abruptly melted away to nothing.

Only then did Ajandor turn to Kevin. The knight's eyes had gone from dull and dazed to fierce and hard.

"Are you all right?" Kevin asked. The collar of his tattered cloak chose that moment to tear completely apart, dumping the garment around his boots.

"Yes." Ajandor inspected his blade of "true silver," only to find that, except for drops of rainwater, it didn't need cleaning. The phantom hadn't possessed any blood to foul it. "Let's move on."

"Move on? After a fight, if it's practical, a warrior always rests and recovers his strength. You taught me that."

"Don't throw my own words back in my face."

"I'm just saying . . . look, further wandering may be a bad idea. We've just seen that the survivors told us the truth. Tilverton is haunted. We should—"

Ajandor turned away, his patched, faded war cloak swinging, and headed up the street. Kevin mouthed a silent curse, snatched up his ruined mantle, threw it around his shoulders like a beggar's rag, and hurried after him.

They prowled until darkness began to envelop the city,

creeping up on them as stealthily as the shadow cat, or so it seemed to Kevin. With the sun hidden behind the perpetual gray cloud cover, he had seen no hint of its setting.

"We should get back to the horses," he said, "and make camp for the night."

Ajandor shook his head. "I want to walk."

"The mounts need care, assuming that some horror hasn't killed them already."

"You can tend them. It is part of your duties, is it not?"

"Yes. Still, what's the point of searching for Pelethen"—Ajandor flinched almost imperceptibly at his son's name—"in the dark? You could march right past his body and never notice."

"I still feel like wandering."

"But the shadows will be more active in the dark, for that's the way of shadows, and without a single light burning anywhere about the streets, you'll never see them coming. They'll kill you before you can even lift your sword!"

Ajandor frowned, considering. At length he said, "I wouldn't want to fall without striking a blow. That would make a poor end to the tale of my line. We'll return to the Cormyr Gate."

On the way back, they passed one of the sets of stairs that climbed to the Old Town, a precinct built on high ground. Famed for its picturesque beauty, it was likely as ruinous as the rest of the city. Partway up the steps was an Altar of Shields, unmarred by the devastation that prevailed on every side. To Kevin, it almost seemed a mockery, as if Helm, god of guardians and protectors, had preserved his own little shrine while permitting the rest of the city to perish.

The squire's mood soured still further when they reached the gate. Redwind, Ajandor's charger, lay dead. No shadow had come to rend the faithful animal. Rather his heart had given out and small wonder. At the knight's insistence, the two riders had pushed their mounts unmercifully once they heard about the destruction of Tilverton, even though, from a coldly practical perspective, they no longer had any reason to hurry at all.

Ajandor gazed down at the horse that had borne him for the past ten years, an animal that, Kevin believed, he had loved.

"Poor old fellow," murmured the knight.

"It's too bad," Kevin said.

Ajandor turned away from the fallen steed. "The animal got me here. I suppose that's all that matters."

"Until we want to ride away."

Ajandor didn't reply.

"Well," said Kevin after a pause, "after I see to my horse, we'll want a fire and our supper."

"Do as you like." Ajandor walked back to the east end of the stone tunnel that was the gate, where the rain created a sort of shimmering, pattering curtain and stood staring out as night swallowed the city.

By the time Kevin finished preparing a meal of fried ham, crumbly yellow corn cakes, and dried apples, the vista beyond the gate had gone utterly black. He tried not to think of what might be lurking unseen just a few feet away. A faint cry came from the opposite direction, out in the countryside, making him jump. Some of the refugees hadn't fled very far from Tilverton, and perhaps shadow creatures were ranging outside the broken walls as well.

At the sound, Ajandor glanced over his shoulder then turned away once more.

"Supper's ready," Kevin called.

His master didn't answer.

For a second, annoyed, the youth was tempted to let it go at that. The gods knew, he was hungry enough to eat both portions himself. He rose from the fire and carried the two tin plates to the end of the gate.

"Here," he said, thrusting one dish forward.

Thus prompted, Ajandor accepted it. He took a token nibble of corn cake then stooped to set the plate on the ground.

"No!" Kevin said. "Sir, you need more than that, or you'll get sick."

"I'm not hungry."

Kevin took a deep breath, screwing up his courage. He had never hesitated to speak his mind to the kindly mentor who had taken him in after his own parents drowned in a boating accident, but this taciturn stranger daunted him a little.

"Sir, I think I know what's in your mind. We couldn't have gotten here any faster."

"That's a convenient way to think."

"It's the truth. We left home the same day the herald brought us word of the call to arms, and we had to ride from one corner of Cormyr to the opposite one, slogging down muddy roads and fording swollen rivers." That, of course, was why the kingdom of Cormyr and its allies were going to war. A city of wizards was tampering with the weather, producing constant rain that ruined crops, birthed floods, and made travel a nightmare. "Despite it all, we did arrive before the date specified in the princess's decree."

"But not in time to fight."

"Obviously, no one anticipated that the shades would lay siege to Tilverton before our forces could march on them. Anyway, do you think we could have changed the outcome if we *had* been here? Do you think you could have saved your son?"

Ajandor sneered. "You're glad you were let off, aren't you? Glad you weren't obliged to die in the service of the Crown."

Kevin groped for a suitable answer. Nothing sprang to mind.

"Get away from me, coward. Leave me to mourn in peace."

The squire obeyed then found that suddenly he, too, had no appetite.

He took the first watch as was customary and his duty, even though Ajandor did not avail himself of the opportunity to rest. Afterwards, the youth found it so difficult to sleep that he almost felt that he shouldn't have bothered, either. The occasional anguished cry from beyond the walls kept jarring him awake.

At daybreak, or what passed for it beneath the perpetual overcast, the two men-at-arms headed back into the streets. It was raining harder, but the stink of the bloated dead seemed worse than ever. At first it churned Kevin's stomach. Eventually, though, he forgot about it, when he noticed something about his master's demeanor.

When they'd first entered what remained of Tilverton, Ajandor had paid particular attention to any dead warriors clad in the wine-colored surcoats of the Purple Dragons, the company of knights to which Pelethen had belonged. Now he paid little heed to any of the pathetic corpses sprawled on every side. Instead, he scrutinized doorways, windows, and rooftops, low walls and the mouths of alleyways, a wagon with two dead mules slumped in the traces—everywhere a foe could lie in wait.

That, Kevin reckoned, was only prudent, but when Ajandor caught a glimpse of a shadow crouching over the burnt corpse of a mother with a blackened, shriveled infant in her arms, his response wasn't prudent at all.

"*Ho!*" bellowed the knight, throwing back his cloak and taking hold of Gray Dancer. "Shadow! Come and fight!"

The murky form rose from the corpses—had it been eating their decaying flesh?—and Kevin saw that it was shaped more or less like a man. It glided forward through the rain, and four more shadows slipped from the ashy ruins of a bakery to fall in behind it.

"Sir!" said Kevin. "There are too many."

"Not for me," Ajandor replied.

Gray Dancer hissed from its scabbard, the mithral blade luminous even on this dreary, rainy morning. The thin man strode forward.

"My sword might not even hurt them!" Kevin called after him.

Ajandor didn't bother to reply, nor did he falter in his advance. Kevin cast away his hindering rag of a mantle, drew his own quite possibly useless weapon, and trotted to catch up with the knight.

As they closed to fighting distance, the phantoms spread out to encircle their human foes. Resolved to prevent that, Kevin pivoted and cut at the one on the left.

The impact felt as if his blade were shearing through cloth, not sinking into flesh, but at least there was resistance. The shadow reeled back with a rent in the middle of its chest.

Kevin cried out in satisfaction—he was still afraid of the cursed apparitions, but at least this time he was fighting something he could damage—and the shadows responded with a piercing, silent shriek. It wasn't sound, but he could hear it inside his head. He flinched at the pain, and two of the phantoms sprang forward and clutched him by the wrists.

Their fingers were burning cold, but the chill was the least of it. Something, strength, or life itself, perhaps, drained out of Kevin and into his assailants. His vision blurred, and his knees buckled. Inside his mind, the shadows squealed in greed and triumph.

He tried to wrench his sword arm free, but the shadow maintained its hold. As Ajandor had taught him, he heaved up his leg and stamped, raking his boot along the ghostly creature's shin and smashing it down on its foot.

It seemed to Kevin that with so much of his strength leeched away already, the stomp kick was a puny, fumbling effort. Still, perhaps startled, the shadow loosened its grip. The squire shoved that one away and turned to the other. It scrambled in even closer, wrapping its arms around his torso, making it impossible to bring the point or edge of his sword to bear. For a moment, weak, frozen, he couldn't think what to do, and Ajandor's lessons came back to him again. He bashed the shadow's head with the heavy steel egg of his weapon's pommel, and losing its hold, the shadow slumped to one knee.

Kevin swayed and stumbled backward. He desperately wanted a moment to collect himself, but the shadows didn't give it to him. Shrieking their psychic shriek, they rushed him.

Gripping his sword in both hands—otherwise, he might not have been able to swing it—the squire swept the weapon in a horizontal arc. The cut decapitated one shadow, and its body and tumbling head vanished. The other phantom nearly succeeded in darting in close enough to grapple, but backstepping frantically, Kevin kept enough space between them to use his blade. He plunged it into the shadow's heart, or the spot where a man would carry his heart, anyway, and it too melted away to nothing.

Gasping, shuddering, he looked about for other foes, just in time to see Ajandor dispatch what was apparently their last adversary. For a few seconds, the knight looked satisfied in a grim sort of way, but then restlessness or hunger crept back into his expression.

"Let's move on," he said.

"No!" Kevin said. "Not yet. This time, I must rest. Did none of the shadows get its hands on you?"

"No."

"Well, they did me, and . . ."

The world seemed to tilt on its axis, and he realized that if he didn't get off his feet, he was going to fall. He tottered to a horse trough overflowing with rain and sat down on the rim.

"Are you wounded?" Ajandor asked.

"Not exactly. I'm not bleeding. I think I just need a few minutes."

Ajandor's mouth tightened with impatience, and Kevin was sure that he meant to walk away and abandon him, weak and helpless, here in the midst of the haunted city.

Instead the knight said, "Very well."

They waited for a time, Ajandor standing, Kevin sitting, the only sounds the drumming of the rain and the creaking of some damaged building shifting toward collapse.

Finally, when the youth felt that mere talking wouldn't constitute an intolerable strain, he said, "I figured it out. You aren't just watching out for the shadows, you're hunting them."

"Correct."

"With Princess Alusair's army defeated, you have no way to strike a blow against the wizards who killed Pelethen, so you're taking it out on the spooks they left in their wake."

"It's a chivalrous act to purge the land of shadows, wouldn't you agree?"

In Ajandor's tone lurked an irony that mocked the entire notion of knightly duty, and never mind that he had always taught his squire that honor was everything.

"I suppose it should be done," the squire said. "Whatever you think, I'm not afraid to help, but is this a sensible way to go about it? According to your own lessons on tactics, we should have a company of men-at-arms sweeping Tilverton systematically, block by block. We should have priests and wizards to support them with their magic. We—"

"Perhaps," Ajandor replied, "but I'm not in the mood for that much company."

"That's mad! I understand—"

A shadow fell over them. Startled, Kevin looked upward.

Something huge was soaring over the wreckage of Tilverton, eclipsing the attenuated light sifting through the clouds. Was it a dragon? Kevin couldn't tell. He had never seen a wyrm, and in any case, the titan's form was as indistinct as that of the lesser shadows. All he could truly discern were tatters of darkness that reminded him equally of a bat's wings and a jellyfish's trolling tentacles. That, and a sense of awesome power and malevolence.

It suddenly occurred to Kevin that the giant shadow might look down and see them, and he cringed, but the thing passed on over the gapped wall encircling Old Town and disappeared.

"The king shadow," murmured Ajandor. "In the end, if I must, I'll come to you."

"Not without an army behind you," Kevin said, "and Vangerdahast, too." Then he remembered the rumor they'd heard along the road, that Cormyr's famous wizard had likely perished in the destruction of Tilverton with the rest of the defenders. "Well, some mage, anyway."

"Ready to go?"

He wasn't, but he was reluctant to irritate his master by asking for more time. He struggled to his feet, and they wandered on.

Ajandor took to shouting challenges whether any shadows were in view or not, and from his perspective if not his squire's, it paid off. Alone or in groups, sometimes vulnerable to common steel and sometimes not, the phantoms slunk out of their hiding places to fight.

Somehow Kevin survived half a dozen of these confrontations, until to his profound relief, it started to get dark, and Ajandor agreed to return to the shelter of the gate. Not that the squire had any particular reason to think that they were truly safe there, either, but at least they weren't actively looking for trouble.

After he prepared another supper and watched Ajandor set his portion aside largely uneaten, he said, "If you mean to continue hunting spooks, we could at least do it beyond the walls. The folk out in the countryside need protection."

"I imagine the shadows slip out of the city to seek their prey," said Ajandor, staring out at the night and the hissing rain, "but they all lair inside, where the stink of necromancy lies thick on the ground. Therefore, I'll be protecting the refugees just as effectively by killing the phantoms in here."

"The people may have other problems." Kevin shifted position, and his shoulder, bruised by a phantom's attack, gave him a twinge. "They may need a leader to sort them out."

"I told you, I don't feel like bothering with other people right now."

"I know they'd respect your grief. Each of them surely has griefs of his own."

"Grief," said Ajandor, as though the word were a paltry, inadequate thing. "Do you know why Pelethen joined the Purple Dragons?"

"Because you did the same thing in your youth. Sir, that does not make you responsible for his fate."

"It's funny. I was happy when Princess Alusair's summons came. To me, the war, with all its perils, was simply a fine excuse for a reunion with my boy."

"I know how much you wanted to see him."

"I wanted to give him this." Ajandor drew Gray Dancer an inch out of its scabbard then shoved it down again. The guard clicked against the mouth of the sheath. "As my father gave it to me. As we have handed it down in our family for four hundred years. What am I supposed to do with it now?"

"Use it to defend the weak, as you have always done."

Ajandor chuckled an ugly little chuckle. "As I have

always done. And here at the end, what do I have to show for it?"

"Sir," said Kevin, "with all respect, you've lost much but not everything. Kirinwood is full of folk who love you. Mistress Waterthorn. Old Nobby. Galen Oakfriend." He could have added himself to the list, except that it would make him feel like a whining child.

"I suppose it ought to shame me," replied Ajandor, "but I just don't seem to care, not anymore. My heart is empty."

"I don't believe that," Kevin replied. "At the moment, all you feel is pain, but when it loosens its grip a little, the gentler emotions will return."

"You're prattling."

Kevin felt his cheeks flush. "Sir, I just don't want to watch you commit suicide, and that's the true objective of our shadow hunt, isn't it? It's a miracle the creatures haven't slain the both of us already."

"If you're afraid, then leave. I release you from my service." Ajandor turned away.

That night, Kevin did indeed consider saddling his horse and trotting away back down the highway called the Moonsea Ride, but he couldn't quite bring himself to do it. There had to be a way to snap Ajandor out of his trance of despair!

After considerable pondering, the squire thought of one ploy that might serve. He was certain—well, reasonably so—that deep down in his heart, Ajandor still did care for all the same folk he'd cherished a tenday ago. If so, then perhaps a threat to one of those dear ones would bring the affection to the surface and restore the old man's perspective. It would show him that his son's death, tragic as it was, hadn't crushed all the meaning out of his life.

Though the scheme did have one drawback: Kevin himself would have to play the role of friend in distress.

All the other candidates were back in Kirinwood.

A nasty voice inside the squire's head whispered that his notion would never work, because Ajandor actually didn't care about him. Hadn't his brusqueness the past few days made that clear? In times past, Ajandor had been kind to his foster child but had really only cherished his son by blood.

No, Kevin insisted to himself, it wasn't so. He could conjure up a thousand memories that proved Ajandor's love for him, and that meant he could make his scheme work. He'd slip away, his foster father would chase after him, and in the end, everything would be all right.

As the night wore on, weariness at last overtook Ajandor. He sat down with his back against the wall, and, gradually, his head drooped until his chin rested on his breast. A soft buzzing issued from his mouth.

Moving quietly, Kevin rose, unlaced one of the saddlebags, and took out a stick of chalk, which Ajandor had packed to sketch out battle plans, duty rosters, and the like. Wincing at the faint scratching sound, the squire scrawled a message on the wall:

I HEAR KING SHADOW CALLING ME, AND I MUST GO TO HIM. FAREWELL.

That accomplished, the youth tiptoed to the arched entrance to the city, thought of all the shadows presumably lurking in the darkness, took a deep breath, and forced himself out into the rain.

To his surprise, he didn't blunder into any phantoms, and after a few minutes, he reached the foot of the Cormyr Stairs. Halfway up, he came upon Helm's shrine. Reflecting that some kindly power certainly seemed to have protected him thus far, he silently apologized to the deity for his earlier irreverence and laid a copper piece atop the Altar of Shields.

He crept on to the top of the steps, peered through the wall, and surveyed Old Town. If any beauty remained to its burnt and battered houses, he couldn't see it under these conditions, nor did he care. He reckoned he'd come as far as required to give Ajandor a nice anxiety-ridden chase, and now he needed a place to wait for him—somewhere indoors, where no passing shadow would spot him.

At the far end of a little plaza stood a cottage, its eaves encrusted with carved roses and its door standing ajar. He scurried to it, ducked inside, found a stool, and sat down behind a window that looked out at the head of the Cormyr Stairs.

Soon, he assured himself, Ajandor would come bustling to the top. The knight would probably be furious when he realized Kevin had tricked him, but it wouldn't matter. The shock of his fosterling's disappearance would still restore him to himself.

Suddenly, a wail of anguish broke into Kevin's imaginings. Unlike all the others he'd heard, this one sounded close by.

Looking in all directions, the squire peered out the window. After a few moments, the source of the noise stumbled into view.

Roped together to form a coffle, a matron with gray curls, two men, and a little girl trudged across the plaza, passing only a few feet from Kevin's vantage point. Slinking around them, shoving and prodding them on, were several of the man-shaped shadows he and Ajandor had fought before. The youth couldn't tell precisely how many. In the darkness, he was lucky to glimpse the shadows at all.

He wondered if the prisoners had still been living somewhere inside the city, or if the shadows had captured them out in the countryside. Not that it mattered. The only thing that did was helping them. But how?

Charge out and attack? Ajandor might have managed it, but he'd been honing a genius for swordplay for forty years. Kevin had been training a modest talent for five.

He doubted he could handle so many of the shadows all at once.

What he could do was follow the shadows and hope that an opportunity to free their captives would present itself. Not that he wanted to. Not only would it be risky, it would mean he likely wouldn't be in position to greet Ajandor if—no, *when*, curse it—the latter climbed the Cormyr Stairs, but Kevin couldn't see any alternative.

As he waited for the shadows to lengthen their lead, he prayed to Helm for aid and wished he'd given the god the sole silver piece in his purse instead of a measly copper.

It was time to go. He crept out onto the porch, and a plank groaned beneath his foot. He cringed, but the shadows didn't seem to hear, so he slunk on.

The stalking proved to be a nerve-racking business. Kevin was no woodsman or housebreaker, schooled in the art of sneaking soundlessly, and no matter how he tried, he couldn't avoid making little noises, each of which threatened to reveal his presence. Nor could he shake the nagging fear that as he concentrated his attention on the shadows ahead, some other phantom would spot him and take him unawares.

But none did, and eventually the shadows and their coffle led him to a drum-shaped keep notorious throughout Cormyr. When Kevin perceived that it was indeed their destination, he nearly laughed in dismay, because it figured, didn't it?

The ruin—now no more ruinous than the rest of Old Town—had once been the residence of the enchantress Tilvara. According to rumor, it was now home to strange beasts and the restless dead, and hellishly dangerous. Few would-be explorers ever even got past the "Medusa's Garden," the field of statuary in front of the entrance. The figures animated and attacked them.

Though many of the statues lay shattered on the ground, a goodly number remained intact. Still, the shadows and their prisoners passed them unmolested. Maybe they knew the trick of it, or perhaps the tides of battle magic washing through the city had somehow rendered the effigies inert.

The procession vanished through an arched door, and Kevin wondered whether or not to keep following. He was sorely tempted to go look for Ajandor, but what if he couldn't find the knight, who by now might already be wandering the city, either to find his errant squire or simply in search of his own destruction? Or what if he did locate Ajandor, and the knight just didn't care? Or what if the shadows slew the captives while Kevin was off searching?

No, curse it, he had to go in.

Kevin headed for the statues. He realized he was breathing hard, tried to control it as Ajandor had taught him, and couldn't quite. He started down the path.

Stone warriors, rocs, manticores, wolves, and double-headed ettins surrounded him on every side. If they all came to life at once, he wouldn't stand a chance, but only one of them even tried. A lion shuddered as he passed but could do no more. Some power had indeed rendered them harmless.

Kevin tiptoed up to the doorway and peeked beyond the threshold into a murky hall. As far as he could tell, no sentries waited there, just as none patrolled the battlements high above. Kevin found the shadows' want of caution peculiar, but perhaps they didn't think like human beings. Maybe they considered themselves so secure in their possession of Tilverton that an assault was inconceivable.

Not that Kevin contemplated anything so grand. Could he simply spirit the captives away, he would be well satisfied.

Onward he skulked, groping his way through stygian chambers that would have been entirely lightless save for the gaps in the ancient walls. Legend peopled these spaces with watchghosts and round, floating, many-eyed beholders, but he didn't encounter any of those. He wondered if the shadows had destroyed even them.

He did soon come to the conclusion that the keep was larger inside than out, but the paradox didn't particularly unsettle him. He'd heard that powerful mages could create such effects. At least the doorways weren't sealing themselves behind him. He'd heard that could happen, too.

A vague form moving on four legs, or perhaps six or eight, prowled out of an arched opening not twelve feet ahead of him. His heart pounding, he flattened himself against the wall. The phantom turned in the opposite direction and disappeared into the blackness.

When his nerves ceased their jangling, Kevin crept on, peeked into the archway, and finally saw the prisoners, those he had been tracking and maybe fifteen others as well.

Tilvara had probably maintained a perfectly good dungeon beneath her residence, but for some reason, the shadows had opted to hold their captives in a spacious chamber where eight or ten looms stood at regular intervals about the floor. Some still supported unfinished bits of weaving, the weft and woof rotting away and tingeing the air with the smell. The humans were still bound, but not with ropes, which lay in careless tangles on the floor. Instead, the prisoners stood enmeshed in strands of darkness, which, anchored to the back wall, floor, ceiling, and looms, were nearly invisible in the gloom.

Kevin didn't know what the black cables were made of—perhaps the same shadow-stuff as the phantoms themselves—but he assumed he would be able to cut them once he disposed of the jailer. For as best he could tell in the darkness, only one shadow lingered in the weavers' workroom, and it had its back to the door.

Kevin crept over the threshold. Evidently sensing his presence, the shadow began to turn, and he cut at it. The sword sheared into its head, and it staggered and disappeared.

The prisoners started to babble, and he frantically tried to shush them, so intent on the need for quiet that it took him a moment to take in what they were saying.

"Look up! The spider! It's right above us!"

As soon as he did understand, he looked up instantly, galvanized by a jolt of terror. He didn't like spiders, and if such a creature had spun the strands holding the captives, it must be huge.

Yet he couldn't see it. The room was too dark, and the ceiling too high. His mouth dry as sand, he pivoted back and forth, trying to spot it.

"Does anybody see it?" he asked the others. "Do you? Do you?"

Evidently they didn't. They simply knew from bitter past experience that it was there.

It occurred to Kevin that he could back out of the room and leave them to their fate. He'd tried to help them, no one could say that he hadn't. It was possible that his sword couldn't even cut the spider.

But he knew he couldn't really abandon them. It wouldn't be chivalrous. Ajandor—the old Ajandor, anyway—would never have countenanced such a selfish, craven act.

Kevin glimpsed motion from the corner of his eye. Impelled by pure reflex, he jumped to one side, and the leaping spider pounced on the spot where he'd just been standing. Some of the prisoners wailed.

Made of the same shifting murk as the other horrors infesting Tilverton, the spider was perhaps the size of a child, its fused bulbs of head and body hanging between arched, segmented legs. Hoping he could land a blow before it reoriented on him, Kevin hacked at its abdomen.

Quick as a cat, the shadow wheeled to face him. His blade slashed through one of its legs, but without encountering any resistance, and without severing the limb.

The spider scuttled toward him and he retreated, cutting and thrusting as he went. It was still like sweeping his sword through empty air. In the dimness, he could just make out a hint of the shadow's ring of bulging eyes, the jagged mandibles opening and closing around its maw.

He backed into one of looms, which banged, rattled, and shed choking, eye-stinging dust into the air. As he started to flounder around that obstacle, he collided with strands of the shadow webbing. The stuff was as sticky as he would have expected, and it had hold of his sword arm, not that his sword had done him any good.

He struggled to pull free. The glue began to give but not quickly enough. The spider scuttled forward to plunge its no-doubt poisonous fangs into his flesh.

Just as the shadow's mandibles were about to close on his knee, he heaved his legs up, evading the bite. The weakened adhesion couldn't support his weight, and he fell free of the webbing and onto the shadow.

He plunged right through the creature just as his sword had done. For an instant, as they were joined, his mind blazed with inhuman sensations. He slammed down on the floor beneath the spider's underbelly.

The shadow started to scuttle off him. Gripping his sword by the blade for use in such close quarters, he jammed the point into the crack between the spider's abdomen and cephalothorax.

For some reason, this time, the steel bit into solid matter, and the phantom jerked and thrashed. Kevin used his sword to roll the spider onto its back, then he kept pressure on the weapon until the ghastly thing stopped moving.

The squire needed to rest but knew he didn't have time. Panting and trembling, he cut the captives free.

Most of them, anyway. On closer investigation, he found that a couple were but dry, shriveled husks.

But the majority were alive. Some were even strong enough to help the weak ones along. Kevin reckoned that with luck, he could get them all out.

He nearly did.

Scouting ahead for shadows, he led the prisoners back the way he'd come. Once, as the procession passed beneath a tattered gonfalon, a toddler started to cry, and everyone froze in terror, certain the noise would bring shadows down on their heads. The child's mother quickly put her hand over his mouth, and no shadow came to investigate the sound. Later on, the fugitives came upon a bellpull, and a scrawny, gap-toothed fellow, who seemed a bit mad from his ordeal, stared at the velvet strap in fearful fascination, as if he didn't want to ring it but felt a compulsion to do so. The matron with the gray ringlets took him by the arm and led him on by.

At last Kevin spied the marble bust of a sharp-nosed, crafty-looking fellow siting on its pedestal. He'd noticed it coming in, and it meant that the exit into the Medusa's Garden was just ahead. He smiled, and a psychic shriek stabbed into his head.

Some of the prisoners cried out. Others clutched their heads and sobbed. Though equally pained by the silent caterwauling, Kevin yelled at them and shoved them. He had to keep them moving, had to get them out the door before their pursuers arrived.

He chivvied them down the long rectangular entrance hall and almost to the arched exit before instinct impelled him to look back. He couldn't see shapes, not yet, but the darkness boiled with movement. Shadows were pouring out of the doorways along the walls.

Kevin reckoned he needed to delay the phantoms for at least a few seconds. Otherwise, few if any of the captives would make it outside. He turned and tried to bellow a war cry, but it came out as more of a weary, frightened squeak. He strode toward the far end of the chamber, and a wave of shadow hurtled out of the gloom to meet him.

He drove his sword into a shadow's chest but never knew whether he'd slain it, for the next instant, the rest of them swept over him, and after that, he was no longer able to keep track of specific adversaries. There was only a pack, a many-limbed mass, striking and snatching at him from every side, as he lurched and whirled and slashed at it.

Once, for a split second, a narrow gap appeared in the mass, and Kevin glimpsed other devils loping toward the door. He wished he could intercept them as well, but knew there was no chance of it. Cold hands seized hold of his arms and shoulders, and the strength began to flow out of him.

Even as he struggled to pull free, other shadows clutched at him, and it was hopeless. He resolved not to scream, but did it anyway, sure the phantoms were sucking out the final traces of his life.

In time, he woke to cold rain spattering his face and hard, wet floor beneath his supine body. He pried open his gummy eyelids. Gray clouds floated directly overhead, but walls rose at the corners of his vision, as if he was in a pit. He tried to lift himself for a better look around but failed. He was horribly weak, and cold deep inside in a way that even his soaked attire couldn't explain.

"Young man!" someone whispered. "Don't move!"

He rolled his head to the side and saw the goodwife with the curly gray hair, who was also lying on the floor.

"Why not?" he whispered back.

"You'll provoke it!"

Somehow Kevin knew without asking what "it" was. King Shadow. The lesser phantoms had borne him and his fellow human into the titan's lair. The fancy he'd scrawled inside the Cormyr Gate had more or less come true.

"Did the shadows recapture all of you?" he asked.

"No," the woman said. "Most of us made it out the door."

Kevin surprised himself by smiling. "Helm gave me good value for my penny then. Better than I had any right to expect."

The matron frowned. "What are you talking about?"

"It doesn't matter. Tell me where we are and what's going on."

"We're in a large chamber at the top of the keep. The roof is gone, and this huge . . . thing apparently makes its lair here."

"Go on."

"The lesser shadows dumped us here for the monster to eat when it's ready, the same way you'd put down food for a dog. It already gobbled up Quinn and Evaine while you were unconscious."

"It's not gobbling us at the moment, and if it's not paying attention, perhaps we can slip away."

"It is paying attention. Evaine tried to sneak out, and that's when it snatched her up."

"Oh. All right, I understand. Now try to rest while I figure a way out of this."

"That's mad. If you were facing the way I am, if you could see the creature—"

"Ajandor, the knight I serve, taught me that if a man keeps his head, he can think his way out of almost any peril, and I might as well try. Why not? What do we have to lose?"

The matron smiled. "When you put it that way, lad, not a thing. Think away."

Kevin lay and pondered, wondering what Ajandor would have done in his place, and if the knight had actually come looking for him. Probably not, for by the cold light of this joyless morning, he recognized that the trick he had attempted to play was a puerile one, born out of desperation rather than sense. No doubt the shrewd old man had seen through it at once and simply bade good riddance to the impudent ass who had hoped to gull him.

No, Kevin could only pray that Ajandor would come to his senses by himself, before his one-man campaign against the shadows destroyed him. His squire had another problem to address.

He waited until a little strength seeped back into his muscles, enough, he hoped, to stand, run around, and yell.

"I'm going to distract King Shadow," he said. "You get out of here. I'm hoping the other prisoners will follow your lead."

Her blue eyes widened. "But the shadow will kill you!"

"It's going to do that anyway."

She hesitated. "We'll still have all the smaller shadows, the ones shaped like men and cats and wolves, barring the way out of the fortress."

"Run. Hide. Throw rocks at them. Whatever it takes to get away."

She swallowed. "All right, and may Helm take you into his keeping. The knight you serve must be very proud of you."

Kevin smiled at a pang that had nothing to do with the mauling the shadows had given him. "Well, he used to be. Get ready."

He gave her a moment to gather her strength, then, wishing the shadows had left him his sword, he scrambled to his feet, and spun around.

As the matron had advised him, the room was big and

essentially circular, with a ragged hole where the ceiling once had been. Scraps of it were lying about the floor, and painted pentacles adorned the plaster walls. In the middle of the space, taking up a goodly part of it, hulked King Shadow.

Kevin was prepared for the hugeness of the shadow and for the strangeness of its tangled limbs, like fat, flexible feathers writhing in all directions. However, he had had no inkling of the true nature of King Shadow's flesh. He hadn't been able to make it out when the titan drifted past high above his head.

Within the shadow's murky substance flowed human faces distorted and jammed together. Despite the stretching, twisting, and squashing, it was somehow possible to discern their grimaces of agony, madness, and rage. Ilmater's tears, was this what became of the people King Shadow destroyed? Did their souls wind up trapped inside the shadow's body?

Kevin stood frozen with horror as King Shadow reached for him, one amorphous arm dipping down above his head and another curving in on each side. At the last possible moment, the youth snapped out of his paralysis and flung himself backward. The three tentacles closed on empty air, and all the faces inside the titan's body began to rave and howl in a silent cacophony.

Bearing the psychic din as best he could, Kevin made his own noise, shouting and shifting back and forth. King Shadow stretched out more of its members to seize him, and the gray-haired woman jumped up and ran for a doorway. Several other prisoners did the same, and the rippling hillock of a shadow ignored them all.

Kevin grinned. It was satisfying to have played a trick that worked, even if it was going to cost him his life.

King Shadow clubbed at him with blows that flattened its boneless arms and shook the floor. The squire dodged and dodged again, knowing it was only a matter of time before one of the tentacles connected. Once his evasions carried him near a doorway, and he dashed for it. The shadow extruded a great slab of itself between its prey and the exit, cutting him off as effectively as a wall.

Something shattered, flashed, and roared on top of King Shadow, and all the faces inside the devil shrieked in agony, for the immense phantom wore a crown of crackling blue and yellow flame. Kevin looked up at the hole in the ceiling, where Ajandor was preparing to throw another keg of oil. Unlike the first, this one didn't need a fuse. When it broke, the contents would feed the fire that was already burning.

Ajandor heaved the barrel, and the conflagration boomed and flared higher. A man drenched in burning oil would likely thrash about and expire, but the titan floated up toward its tormentor. The falling raindrops shone yellow in the firelight.

Kevin picked up chunks of debris and hurled them at the shadow. Several of the smaller phantoms appeared along the edge of the hole. Apparently trusting them to dispose of Ajandor, King Shadow dropped back onto the floor to confront the squire, who wished he hadn't just wasted his only chance to bolt.

Its ragged tendrils squirming, King Shadow spread itself to either side of Kevin, pinning him against the wall. The titan looked like a pair of hands poised to catch a ball, albeit with fire dancing on the upper surfaces and spatters of burning oil dripping off the sides.

Kevin saw no possibility of escape, so he spat at King Shadow. It was a feeble gesture, but better than nothing.

The twin masses of shadow-stuff began to close on him like the covers of a book, then Gray Dancer fell at his feet, hitting the floor with a clank.

Kevin stooped and grabbed the mithral sword by its leather-wrapped hilt. He was sure that Ajandor had dropped Gray Dancer intentionally, to give his fosterling some semblance of a fighting chance, even though the knight needed the weapon himself to battle his own opponents.

The squire came on guard, and a wave of vitality washed the soreness and weakness out of his muscles. Gray Dancer was bolstering his strength. Ajandor had occasionally permitted him to handle the blade, but it had never done anything like this. Apparently it took a foe to wake its magic.

The adversary in question had faltered momentarily when the sword fell between them, but now the twin arms of its V-shape began to converge once more. The squire ran to the member on the right and swung Gray Dancer in a vertical cut.

The weapon's razor edge split the churning shadow-stuff and scrambled the writhing, flowing faces inside it. King Shadow screamed, and its limb twitched backward, creating a gap between itself and the wall. Kevin dived through.

Once out of the trap, he immediately turned and renewed the attack, cutting and cutting for all he was worth. Drops of burning oil spattered and blistered him, but he scarcely felt the pain. Then a column of shadow-stuff exploded out of the mass before him, slammed into his chest, and hurled him across the room.

If not for his hauberk, the impact likely would have shattered his ribs. As it was, as he dropped on his rump, he started to black out, then felt Gray Dancer's magic grip his mind like a powerful hand and heave it back to wakefulness.

When Kevin looked up, King Shadow had pulled itself up into a gray-black fiery sheet curling over at the top like a huge, tempest-driven wave. The youth saw that he wouldn't have time to roll out from underneath, so as the shadow began to fall, he raised Gray Dancer's point to meet it.

King Shadow impaled itself on the sword, and no more balked than surging water would have been, crashed down on Kevin, swatting him like a fly. He lay in a pool of seething, gibbering, burning ghost-faces. He was dazed, vaguely surprised to still be alive, and Gray Dancer hauled him back to full consciousness again, with more difficulty this time.

Though the blade had no real voice, not even a silent one like the shadows, he somehow sensed what it wanted to tell him: *Look, look, look at King Shadow now, look, you only have a moment!*

Kevin did look. The shadow-stuff splashed across the floor was still humping and slithering, but not with its former nimbleness. Evidently the fire, Gray Dancer, or both had finally done the titan some significant harm. Moreover, the soft, murky substance was converging from all directions toward a sort of bulb, as if to rebuild the creature's body around it. Unlike the seepage, the node contained no tortured human faces. It was pure black.

The squire reckoned he knew what to do, but then hot pain washed over his ribs and leg. He looked down and discovered that his clothing was on fire. He could attempt to extinguish it, or he could ignore it and strike while King Shadow was vulnerable.

He tried to rise, and other pains balked him. His left arm and ankle throbbed, sprained or broken, he supposed. He tried again and this time made it to his feet.

He limped forward. The shadow-stuff was flowing faster now, and had nearly succeeded in coating the titanic creature's heart with itself. He drove Gray Dancer's point into the one sliver of absolute blackness still showing.

All the faces screamed, and King Shadow vanished. Kevin threw himself on the floor and rolled until he was free of the fire.

Then he just sat, too sore and spent for anything else, the strength Gray Dancer had lent him expended, until a shout reminded him that his had not been the only battle. He peered up through the smoky air. The rain felt good on his singed, sweaty face.

Ajandor peered back down at him through the hole. "Are you all right?" asked the knight.

"I could be a lot worse. Thank Helm for wet clothing! We have to move. The other shadows—"

"Seem to have disappeared along with their king," said Ajandor, "dead or fled, who knows? Or cares? I'm coming down."

He stepped away from the hole and came through one of the doors in the room a minute later.

"You're sure they're gone?" the squire asked.

"Well, the ones I was fighting just melted away, and I don't see any of them bursting in on us, do you?"

"Now that you mention it, no. How did you find me?"

"It wasn't difficult. I discovered your note and smelled a trick, but I still didn't want you wandering around alone in a city of shadows. I came after you and ran into one of the captives you freed. He told me where to look for you, and I sneaked into the witch's keep. Eventually, I figured out where you were, but I couldn't reach you. Too many horrors blocked the path. However, I did find a way to get above you and the great flying pudding, and I hoped that if I hurt the thing, you might be able to escape in the resulting confusion. I located some oil old Tilvara had laid in, carried it up to the roof, and the plan fell apart." He grinned. "You jumped up prematurely, and some shadows picked up my trail and followed me up to my perch."

"How did you hold them off without Gray Dancer?"

"With my dagger and a torch. Not the more formidable of weapons, but sufficient to give the creatures pause."

"Evidently." Kevin hesitated. "Sir, are you angry at me for trying to fool you?"

"I was, but . . . I know why you did it, and maybe it did shake something loose inside me. Maybe it was meeting the fellow you rescued. That shamed me, by reminding me what a knight is supposed to be. Perhaps seeing King Shadow die has made me feel a little better. At any rate, I still sorrow, but I guess I'm no longer in such a hurry to join Pelethen on the other side. I'll see him when I see him."

"I'm glad." Kevin's gaze fell on Gray Dancer, lying ingloriously in a pool of rainwater. He picked it up and proffered it.

Ajandor made no move to take it.

"Keep it, lad, it fits your hand quite well. I was puzzled what to do with it, but now I see that I have an heir after all."

THE SHIFTING SANDS

Peter Archer

13 Kythorn, the Year of Wild Magic

The camel's hooves kicked up clouds of dust that added to the swirling mist surrounding the travelers. A hot wind howled around them, tearing at their robes, driving the dirt into every crevice of their clothing, probing them with harsh fingers, seeking to hurl them across the rolling plains into oblivion.

Both men clung to the swaying saddle, their heads bent against the storm. The camel soldiered onward, its head bowed stoically before the blast. Its footsteps were almost immediately buried behind it by sheets of fine gray that blew across the desert steppes, making it appear that the travelers had never been there.

One of the men, the taller of the two, turned in the saddle and shouted something to his companion, who bent his head to hear. The smaller man shook his hood and gestured forward. The other gave a shrug and again bent against the wind.

A flash and thunderous report echoed across the dunes of Anauroch, almost knocking the men and their faithful beast over.

The tall man turned and shouted to his companion, "Lighting! In the middle of the godsbedamned desert! We must stop."

"No!" The other was equally vehement. "We keep on."

He reached behind him and slapped the camel's rump. The beast started forward again, and another report knocked it to its knees, tumbling the travelers to the sand. The camel panicked and darted forward.

The tall man recovered first and lunged after the beast. He had not gone five steps before a third thunder blast, much louder than the previous two, electrified the air around them and hurled them facedown in the sand. Their robes whistled and snapped with the impact.

The shorter was the first on his feet this time. Through the whirling sands of the storm, he could see a black mass a few yards from where he lay. Smoke rose from it and was whipped back by the wind, which also carried to his nostrils the sickening smell of burnt camel meat. The saddle and other accoutrements that had been on the creature had been hurled aside by the lightning strike.

As if the storm had expended its last ammunition with this disaster, the wind dropped and the sand settled around them in a fine rain then ceased. The howls and shrieks of the sandstorm wandered to the west, passed over the next dune, and faded from their ears.

Both men walked forward on unsteady feet to view the remains of their mount. The taller glared at the shorter.

"I told you we should have stopped."

The other shrugged. "If we had, we'd be lying there,

cooked to a turn. You don't suppose that lighting was hurled by chance?"

"What do you mean?"

Instead of answering, the merchant was probing amid the supplies that had been scattered around the carcass. The taller man—whose face the desert sun now revealed as scarred and pitted, worn by weather, age, and drink—glared at him and repeated the question.

"What do you mean by that, Avarilous?"

"I mean, my dear Garmansder, that we're dealing with people who would think no more of killing you than of stepping on a spider. You'd do extremely well to keep that in mind. You'll probably live longer if you do."

Avarilous's eyes flickered from side to side, and his fingers, laced across his fat belly, wore a complicated gesture.

Garmansder's eyes widened, then he glared at the merchant and raised his voice. "I know *precisely* what I'm dealing with: a twisted little serpent who can't tell the truth without his forked tongue falling out of his mouth. I should never have agreed to travel with you, even for the gold you're paying. You'll regret it."

From the sash around his waist, he had drawn a scimitar and brought back his arm for a blow. There was a sudden crack of a whip, and the blade flew from his hand to land sticking in the desert sand twenty feet from where he stood. Garmansder cursed volubly and spun around.

Behind him, in a dark line, stood a band of Bedine. Their black robes flapped in the wind, but apart from that they were motionless as statues. One, clad in a robe of red, was clearly the leader, standing a bit forward of the others. In his upraised hand was the whip with which he had disarmed Garmansder.

Avarilous cautiously raised one hand, palm outward.

"Peace be upon your tents, my friends. I stand in your

service. My friend and I have lost our camel and had despaired of finding our way when you . . ."

His voice trailed off as the Bedine moved around them, surrounding them and efficiently disarming them. From Garmansder's robe, the tribesmen pulled a pair of ugly looking daggers. From the merchant, they took three throwing stars and a slender blade that had been strapped to one of his stout legs. All this was done in unnerving silence. The travelers' hands were bound tightly behind them, and they were linked together by a short rope. One of the Bedine took the end of the rope and gave it a sharp jerk.

At a gesture from the red-robed leader, the party started forward in the direction Avarilous and Garmansder had been travelling. They mounted the next dune and saw a herd of camels, standing quietly, chewing their cud. Two or three Bedine stood near them, guarding the pack. Without a word, they mounted and rode on.

Like most Bedine settlements, the travelers did not really see this one until they were upon it. The dun-colored tents blended with the endless sands and revealed their presence only by a soft flapping in the wind. A few faces peered from the tents to look upon the strangers and their silent captors as the tribesmen led the caravan to the largest of the tents. Avarilous and Garmansder were jerked roughly from their perches and dragged inside.

A small fire burned in a brazier at the center of the tent. Some of the smoke escaped through a hole in the roof, while the majority swirled and eddied on air currents. The strong smell reminded Avarilous that the Bedine, in common with most desert dwellers, used camel pads for fuel. Garmansder coughed and retched then coughed again. His face was scarlet and shiny.

Around the edge of the tent were seated a row of robed figures, who stared coldly at the two strangers. Avarilous sat quietly on the floor as his captor muttered in the ear of one of these observers. Garmansder, having recovered from his coughing fit, gazed wildly around the scene.

"What are we doing here? What do they want?" he snarled to the merchant.

"Be silent." Avarilous's voice was cold and decisive, unlike his usual whining tone.

Garmansder sat in silence for a moment then made a desperate lunge for the tent entrance. Half a dozen hands snatched him back in an instant, and a curved dagger appeared at his throat. Avarilous did not move a muscle.

One of the robed figures—he to whom their captor had spoken—flicked back his hood, revealing a head of graying hair and dark, smoky eyes.

"Why do you come here?"

The words were dropped like rocks into a silent well. Their ripples spread outward through the tent across the ring of seated figures.

Avarilous waited a moment before replying then said calmly, "I am the merchant Avarilous of Calimport, and I am delivering goods from Loudwater to Whitehorn. This man is my companion, one Garmansder. Our route led across Anauroch, since we did not wish to detour far to the south, and—"

"Stop!"

The Bedine held up a hand.

"It is true that you are Avarilous, but we know too well the sort of goods you deliver. You are a dealer in information and stolen goods. You may have come from Loudwater, but your home is not in Calimport. Reports of your intrigues range from the passes of Icewind Dale to the jungles of Chult, from the Utter East to the Sword Coast."

"Nonsense!" Garmansder snorted. "I've traveled with this man for months, and he's no more a spy than I am!"

Avarilous said nothing.

The tall man looked at him in amazement then in fury. "Bastard!"

He lunged at the merchant and was brought up short by a trio of hands that clamped him in place. He glared angrily at Avarilous and snapped, "Next time I'll know better than to take up with a fat man with a shifty eye."

The Bedine who had spoken turned to Garmansder and said, without change of tone, "You know little of your companion, it seems. He travels the lands, meddling in the affairs of people whom he does not know. He has performed commissions for the fallen Azoun of Cormyr, for the rulers of far Ulgarth, for the Red Wizards of Thay. He is a horse waiting for hire, on sale to the highest bidder. Some say Avarilous is not his real name, but none know precisely who he is."

Avarilous ignored the outburst of his companion and stroked his chin before conceding the point. "Very well. Let us suppose there is some truth to your statement. What has this to do with you?"

The Bedine shrugged. "It is of little concern to us," he said. "Your reputation is that of a man who dabbles in political intrigue for money. We have little or no interest in the affairs of the rest of the world, except when they affect the tribes."

Avarilous nodded thoughtfully. "I see. From the fact that we are here, I suppose you have something in mind. Something that affects *your* tribe, at least." He stretched, and Garmansder was suddenly reminded of a cat unsheathing her claws.

The Bedine leader made no response, but Avarilous nodded, as if he had received confirmation of his statement. "Perhaps you might tell me, first, with whom I have the pleasure of dealing."

The Bedine leader bent forward and said, "I am Sheik Omar Lhassa Bin-Daar, ruler of the Bin-Daar Bedine, counting two hundred and seventy-five camels, six hundred and twelve goats, one hundred and fifty-four sheep—"

Avarilous raised a hand. "Quite. That's sufficient. Proceed."

It was startling to note how the fat man had taken control of the discussion. To Garmansder's eyes, though, Bin-Daar showed little resentment. He leaned back against a cushion and drew on a hookah that lay near to hand before resuming his speech.

"As you doubtless are aware, the Zhentarim, they of the black robes, have long maintained a route through Anauroch. We Bedine have tolerated its existence out of consideration for the people it supplies, though we could have destroyed it long ago—"

"So you say," interrupted Avarilous. "In fact, allowing it to exist provides you with a steady supply of caravans for raiding."

Bin-Daar ignored the comment and continued, "At various oases along the route, bands of Zhentarim have created their own settlements, extracting tolls from travelers along the road. For the most part, we ignore them, though we have sometimes raided them, thus serving the interests of the righteous of Faerûn."

Avarilous's cynical smile informed Garmansder in what spirit the fat man received this statement.

Bin-Daar coughed gently, as one approaching the heart of the matter. "Of late," he said, "we have seen much activity at one of these oases, one near our lands. The dark-robed ones are becoming increasingly bold, striking out against our tribesmen. Where before they were content to leave us in peace, now they seem determined to destroy us. It would almost seem as if there is something they have found of which they do not want us to learn."

Avarilous's body was relaxed, his pudgy body stretched

out along the ground, resting on one elbow. His eyes were sleepy, half hooded, but the observant might have noticed a glitter within their depths.

"Rumors have come to us of a great excavation by the Zhentarim in this place." Bin-Daar snapped his fingers, and one of his councilors thrust a roll of goatskin into his outstretched hand. "They are digging . . . here."

His finger jabbed a spot on the crude map that adorned the goatskin. Avarilous looked at it.

"Humph. Near Hlondath. One of the Buried Realms."

Bin-Daar nodded. "Precisely."

Garmansder broke into the conversation. "What's Hlondath? And what does this have to do with kidnapping us?"

Avarilous spoke without looking at his companion. His voice was far away.

"Hlondath was a mighty state that existed centuries ago, after the fall of Netheril. It faded away, buried by the desert sands, but some say that there was buried with it some of the mighty magic of lost Netheril. Many have come searching for those items, but few have been found, and most of the explorers have vanished into the sands." He looked carefully at Bin-Daar. "I take it you think the Zhents have found something."

Bin-Daar shook his head. "I do not know if they have found anything, but I suspect they are looking for something. Something they do not wish others to find. Something that might make them a more powerful force in Anauroch."

"Why should they have any more success than in the past?"

"Because—" Bin-Daar dropped his voice—"because of the coming of the City of Shade. Its return may herald a new rise of Netherese magic, one the Zhentarim hope to take advantage of. If they found an artifact of ancient Netheril, they could use it to forge an alliance with the

Shadovar. That would be disastrous for my people. They must be stopped."

"What does that have to do with us?" growled Garmansder, though he suspected he already knew the answer.

Bin-Daar's eyes never left the fat merchant's face.

"I have a proposition for you, Avarilous."

The merchant stretched his pudgy legs, which had grown cramped from kneeling. "I'm aware of that."

For the first time, Bin-Daar's face showed surprise. "You are *aware*? How—" He stopped and nodded slowly, as if satisfying himself on some point. "So," he continued, "we did not find you. You found us."

Avarilous shrugged. "I had heard you were looking for me. I simply put myself in a place where we were likely to meet."

"Why?"

"Your situation interests me. I've heard of this excavation, and I suspected you or one of the other Bedine tribes would try to stop it. An outright attack on the site would be disastrous for you, so you had to resort to other means. As I say, I heard you were looking for me."

"You might have told *me*," growled Garmansder. "If I'd known who and what you were, I'd have run from you as fast as I could. As it is, I want nothing to do with any of this."

Bin-Daar chuckled softly. "You will aid Avarilous in his mission," he told the mercenary. "Your reward will be far more than whatever he has promised you."

Greed flickered in the tall man's eyes, but he held his ground. "It's all very well to talk, but where there's Zhents, I don't want to be watching my back all the time, and I don't trust him."

Bin-Daar's mouth curved in a smile that did not reach his eyes. "I do not trust him either, but he is a powerful weapon. A warrior in battle does not ask where a sharp sword came from, only that it cut true."

Garmansder snorted. Avarilous sighed, and his stomach rumbled.

"Can't we do this over food?" he asked plaintively. "I'm starving."

The Zhent guards had had a sleepy afternoon, basking in the shade of their tent, shielded against the blazing sun. They passed the time throwing dice and drinking *raki*, a powerful liquor distilled from the stunted bushes that covered the hills around the oasis. By midafternoon they were dozing, half drunk, and not in a mood to be disturbed.

One nudged the other then roused him with a kick. The two men rose and stood, swaying slightly, watching the travelers approach.

They were mounted on a camel, but the one riding in front, the stouter of the two, had his hands bound tightly together, while the other held the end of the rope. As the pair drew nearer, the Zhentarim could see that the fat man had a streak of blood down one cheek and an ugly bruise over his left eye.

The camel halted before the guard's tent, and the thinner man jumped down easily, leaving his bound companion seated on the beast.

"Hail!" he said, in a voice scraped raw by the desert winds. "I want to see your commander."

The more sober of the two guards spat in the sand. "Hah! What for?"

"I have something for him." The traveler jerked the cord he was holding, pulling his prisoner off the camel. The captive crashed to the ground with a loud grunt of pain.

One of the guards sauntered over, trying not to appear unsteady on his feet. "Wasss this?" He stirred the fallen man with his foot.

"I'll tell your commander. Trust me, he'll want to see this one right away."

The Zhents exchanged glances, then turned away. One turned back, while the other disappeared into the tent.

"We'll get Lieutenant Thass."

"I want to see the commander, not some lieutenant."

"You'll see Thass. He'll 'cide who you see next. He'll be here in m'nit." He slumped back down on the cask he'd been sitting on.

The tall man looked beyond the guard tent at the rest of the oasis. It was bustling with activity. A long line of Bedine tribesmen were passing buckets filled with sand from hand to hand, supervised by purple-robed Zhents, many of whom bore whips or clubs. The sand was being drawn from a central excavation, perhaps fifty feet wide. Even from a distance, the visitor could see a network of ladders and ropes descending into it. A heavy wooden framework had been erected over it with a wheel to haul up the buckets of sand from the shovels of unseen diggers. The air was full of the groan of the wheel, the creaking of the wooden supports, the moaning of the tribesmen, and the shouts and curses of the Zhents.

A Black Robe with an air of authority strode toward the guard tent, his clothing snapping with impatience. He glanced at the sentries then dealt one of them a slap that spun the man around and knocked him bleeding to the ground.

"Fool! Drunk on duty!"

He lifted a hand and inscribed a gesture in the air. The guard screamed, and his hand came up to one cheek. A thin stream of smoke spurted between his fingers as he shrieked with pain. When he brought his hand down, the visitor could see the raw, red mark of the brand that had been magically inscribed on the guard's skin.

The lieutenant turned his attention to the two men before him, while the other guard splashed liquor on his companion's wound and led him back into their tent.

"Who are you, and why are you traveling this way? It's prohibited to come near this place, on pain of death. By rights, I should flay the flesh from your bones here and now, but I'm in an exceptionally good mood today, so I'll listen to your story before I kill you both."

The tall man did not back down.

"I think you'll be happy to have custody of this one." He kicked the recumbent figure before him. "This is Avarilous, a so-called merchant. In fact, he's a spy. He was paid by the Bedine to come here and find out what you're up to."

The lieutenant looked at him in astonishment then burst into a bray of laughter.

"A spy! A nice job he seems to have made of it. What did the Bedine scum offer to pay him with? Camel dung? Goat meat?" His eyes narrowed as he looked at Garmansder. "Who are you, and why are you telling me this?"

"I am Garmansder of Luskan. I'm a mercenary, hired by this fool to be his guard. When I found out what he was up to, I thought I'd get a better price from the Zhentarim for his head than anything the Bedine—or he—might pay me." He shrugged. "So here he is for you to play with."

Lieutenant Thass crouched by Avarilous's head and stared thoughtfully into the merchant's eyes, which were reddened from the blowing sand of the desert.

"So the little Bedine fools are getting worried about what we're doing here," he said, as if to himself. "Good. Good. Fear will feed on itself. Especially when I send their spy back to them in a basket, or several baskets." He chuckled. "Perhaps they'll pass on their concerns to the Shadovar, who will be more willing to deal with us.

"What's that?" He bent his ear near Avarilous's cracked, bleeding lips.

"Shadovar . . . would never . . . deal with Zhentarim . . . crush you first." The words dropped like tears in the dust.

The lieutenant chuckled and rose to his feet. "We'll see, fool."

He twisted his hand, and Avarilous's body was jerked to its feet. The rope binding the merchant flew from Garmansder's hand to that of the lieutenant.

"Drashka! Get your lazy carcass out here this instant, unless you want to wear your entrails for a necklace!"

From a shelter farther within the encampment, another guard emerged cautiously and saluted. "Yes, sir?"

"I'll take this scum to Commander Hesach's tent. The commander will want to talk to him in a few minutes, so you'd better have someone bring the instruments. I'll keep an eye on him until Hesach's ready—he's slippery as an eel. And Drashka . . ." He tossed the end of the rope to the lieutenant. "I've got my eye on you. You watched those two idiot guards drink on duty and did nothing to stop them. Let me catch that sort of thing again and you'll be scorpion bait!"

Garmansder cleared his throat loudly. The lieutenant glanced at him.

"Ah, yes. Your reward."

Thass fumbled inside his robe for a minute and produced a pouch, tossing it to the tall man. Garmansder looked inside it and opened his mouth to argue when he caught the lieutenant's icy eye and thought better of it.

He swept the pouch out of sight and said, "I'd like a bed for the night."

Lieutenant Thass grunted and turned to the guard. "Drashka, take this fellow and find him a place to sleep, but be sure he's on his way tomorrow at first light." He looked at Garmansder with narrowed eyes. "After all, a traitor might find the habit of betrayal hard to break. Perhaps it might be simpler to return *two* traitors to the Bedine."

Garmansder shook his head vigorously. "Trust me, my lord. I'm heading west and south for friendlier lands, where an honest mercenary can make a living. I've no desire to get mixed up in the affairs of wizards—whether Zhentarim or Shadovar."

The lieutenant's shout of laughter was tossed over his shoulder as he stalked toward his tent.

Left alone, Garmansder and the guard eyed one another with the cautious looks of two dogs circling before a fight. The mercenary dug into the recesses of his robe and produced a stoneware bottle that sloshed pleasantly with liquid.

"*Raki*, lifted from the Bedine. Know somewhere we can share it in peace?"

Avarilous, bound to a crude chair, sat facing Commander Hesach across a rough wooden table. The Zhentarim commander was stocky, running toward fat. His black robes stretched tight across his ample belly, and his face was pitted and scarred, creased with lines that the harsh candlelight of the tent emphasized. He paced about a table, in the center of which were a variety of implements. Their purpose the merchant needed no one to explain. Despite their disconcerting presence, however, his face was composed, and he spoke calmly.

"I have no objection to telling you what I was sent here to do. After all, the Bedine have no claim to my allegiance beyond what price they offered to pay."

"What price was that?" Hesach snorted.

"A thousand pieces of gold," the merchant said.

The commander snorted in disbelief. "I wouldn't have thought they had anything like that."

Avarilous shrugged. "Raiding against caravans seems to have been successful this season. In any case, I haven't seen a copper from them yet. Perhaps the Zhentarim might find more use for my services. It would hardly be the first time I've dealt with those of the Black Network."

"Perhaps. Tell me precisely what you were sent to find, and I may consider it. Then again, I may simply agree to give you a quick death and let it go at that."

Avarilous stretched against his ropes and glanced casually around the interior of the tent. It was richly furnished with rugs and tapestries. Hesach lounged near one wall on a richly carved sedan covered in the skins of desert lions.

"The Bedine seem to feel you are looking for an artifact from the Buried Realms. They seem to think you may have found it."

"Why?"

"Why what?"

The commander gave a negligent gesture, and Avarilous's head jerked back as if he'd been slapped. He shuddered.

"They believe you're trying to build a power base here. Are you?"

"Kindly remember that I'm asking the questions. It will go better for you if you do."

Hesach bit into a pomegranate and let the juice dribble down his chin in a pink stream.

Grinning at his prisoner, he said, "The desert rats are more right than they know." He rose and plunged his hand into a silver-bound chest. "What do you think of that?"

In his palm rested a tiny amulet. It seemed, to Avarilous's weary eyes, to twinkle and glitter, almost as if a star had been imprisoned within it.

He said cautiously, "It's obviously magical. What of it?"

"What of it? What of it?" The commander laughed. "You fat idiot, do you know what this is?"

"A magical amulet." Avarilous sounded bored.

"Ha! This amulet would allow me to control the very sands of the desert, to raise them in a storm, to level them in a sheet of sand that could sweep my enemies before it. It would make me master of the desert."

"It *would*," observed Avarilous, "but it *won't*. It's chipped and cracked. In that condition, I doubt you'd get more than a handful of copper pieces at any market in Calimport.

"True, fool, but where there's one, there must be more!" Commander Hesach tossed the amulet into the chest and sank back onto his couch. "For years, we Zhentarim have searched beneath these sands for the treasures of Netheril. Now, at last, I've found them!"

"You haven't found anything more than a cracked amulet yet," said Avarilous.

His body was relaxed against the ropes, but his eyes flickered back and forth across the tent as if seeking a means of escape.

"Not yet, but soon. Soon our diggers will break through into the hoard that rests below this place. I will control it. I will rise in power. Even Fzoul Chembryl himself will speak with me, will treat with me as an equal. In time, perhaps even I shall take his place at the head of our order."

His voice had risen in volume, and he was now shouting, flecks of spittle spraying from his juice-stained lips. In full cry, he caught himself and smiled nastily at his captive.

"But you. What shall I do with you?"

Raki is a liquor not for the faint of heart or stomach. Its taste is foul, even to those used to it, and in some parts of Faerûn it is used as rat poison. But it does have the virtue of getting one drunk extremely quickly.

Garmansder and Drashka staggered out of the shadow of the tent against which they had been sitting and came into the afternoon sunshine, casting long shadows across the desert. The air was still warm, but a chill wind was beginning to blow, portending the bleak night to come.

Drashka flung an arm around Garmansder's shoulders.

"So. Wha'sh a fine fellow like you doing working for a . . . a *shpy?* Coo'nt you tell something was wrong with him? I mean . . ." He stopped, turned, and vomited copiously before resuming his speech as if nothing had happened. "I mean wha's he doing wandering around in the middle of the desert? Din't you ever *ask?*"

Garmansder swayed slightly. "He was paying good gold. A mercenary never asks. Not if he wants to keep being a mershenary." He laughed inanely. "I mean, if it comes to that, what're *you* doing working for the Zhents out here in the middle o' nowhere?"

Drashka looked around carefully and put a finger against his lips. "*Shhh.* It's . . . a . . . *secret!*" He nodded impressively. "Wanna know what it is?"

Garmansder shook his head. "Nah. Better not tell, if it's a secret and everything."

"Right. Right. All right, I'll won' tell you." He grabbed Garmansder's arm. "I'll *show* you."

The two men made their way across the camp to where the scaffolding loomed over the excavation. Activity around the site had ceased, and as the evening grew darker, a few torches flickered around the site, making the gloom seem even blacker. Here and there, campfires glowed. The Bedine had been herded by their Zhentarim overseers back to some unseen camp, but in the distance the two men could hear the unearthly wails of their singing. The sound floated over the desert and hung like crystal in the dark air.

Drashka made his way unsteadily to the edge of the excavation. A flimsy rail ran between the wooden uprights that held the scaffolding in place, and a few torches on long poles thrust into the sand illuminated the scene. The lieutenant staggered, and Garmansder grabbed his arm.

"Careful. You wanna fall?"

Drashka considered the question for a moment then shook his head. "You fall in there, you'd have a long time to think before you hit the bottom. Lissen!"

He groped for a loose stone and dropped it into the pit. Both men held their breaths until at last, far away, magnified by the walls of the shaft, they heard the distant *thunk!* of stone on stone.

Garmansder nodded, impressed. "So wassit all 'bout?" He leaned against an upright and took another draught of *raki*.

Drashka gestured toward the pit. "We're lookin' for magic. Magic stuff from Netheril. You know. Stuff they lost when the cities fell down and th' empire crashed."

"So?" The mercenary held out the bottle to his companion. "Ever'body knows that stuff was lost a long time ago. Why d'you think you can find it now?"

" 'Cause we already found part of it." Drashka swigged from the bottle and snickered. "We already found stuff, and we're gonna bring up more stuff. Magical stuff."

Garmansder snorted. "I'll believe it when I see it."

"Maybe you'd like to see it." Drashka straightened up and hurled the *raki* bottle into the pit. It smashed against the far side, and the fragments fell into the gulf.

"Hey!" cried the mercenary. "There was more in there!"

"That's all right." The guard's voice was strong, without a trace of slurred, drunken speech. "You can go after it."

He lunged forward with the speed of a striking snake. One hand thrust against the mercenary's shoulder, shoving him back into the blackness beyond the upright. Garmansder shouted, as one hand darted up to clutch at a dangling rope. He swung out and over the pit, then back, landing farther around the rim, some ten feet from where he'd started. A sword was already glittering in his hand when he landed.

Drashka stared then laughed. "I see I wasn't the only one pretending to drink that rot gut." He drew his own blade and stepped forward.

Garmansder retreated cautiously around the pit, his eyes on his opponent's sword. Drashka came on, slashing, his blade whistling through the night air. The guard thrust savagely, and the mercenary, barely avoiding being spitted, stumbled and struck against the rail. The wood shattered, and Garmansder, with a cry, fell sideways into the pit.

With a yell of triumph, Drashka rushed to see the body of his foe hurtling downward. Then he staggered back, blood spurting from a long cut along his cheek. The mercenary was clinging with one hand to the support timbers that lined the side of the pit. In the other hand he still held his sword.

His muscles bulged and he gave a groan of effort as he pulled himself one-handed from the darkness. He heaved his torso onto solid ground and rolled sideways as Drashka struck at him. The soldier's blade left a trail of red in the sand as it slashed across Garmansder's ribs.

The mercenary rolled to his feet. With his free hand he grasped a torch and threw it.

The flames touched and ignited the guard's flowing robe. He tried to beat out the fire with one hand, but it engulfed him. Shrieking, he dropped his sword, whirling, staggering. The sands gave way under his feet and he fell into the darkness. Garmansder could see the sides of the pit lit by the flames as Drashka, still screaming, fell and fell, until there was a faint crash, then silence.

The mercenary tore a rag from the hem of his robe and bound up his wound, cautiously glancing around to make sure the battle had roused no one. Apparently the

Zhentarim guards kept a loose watch—or they were drunk on *raki*—for no one came to investigate the disturbance. Garmansder sheathed his sword and disappeared into the night.

Taking another bite of his pomegranate, the commander stared at the bound merchant, who did his best to preserve an air of detachment. At last, the commander gestured, and a small, glittering knife rose from the table and moved slowly forward in the air, hovering in front of the helpless merchant's face.

"What would the Bedine like back first from their spy?" he mused, nibbling on his pomegranate. "His ear? His nose? His upper lip?"

The knife swayed and dived through the air, humming. It whirled around the merchant's head, snipping a lock of hair from his brow.

"I know," chortled the commander. "An eye. That's it. To be followed by more . . . interesting parts."

The knife drew back and prepared to plunge into Avarilous's left eye. The merchant, watching beyond the knife to the commander's face, saw the stream of pink juice dribbling from his lips turn suddenly red. The knife dropped to the floor with a clatter as the commander, a bite of fruit still caught between his teeth, fell stiffly forward, facedown on the floor.

Through a narrow slit in the tent stepped Garmansder, holding a stiletto. He kicked the body of the commander aside and sauntered over to Avarilous, who glared at him.

"Well, you took your sweet time. Were you going to let me lose an eye? Or did you just find it funny to wait that long before doing anything?"

" 'Thank you, Garmansder. Thank you for saving my

life.' That's how you say it, Avi. It's quite simple, really."

Garmansder's blade made short work of the ropes, and Avarilous rose, massaging his wrists.

"We haven't time for nonsense. Someone will be missing him soon. We'd best be about our business."

The tall man stirred the body of the late commander with his foot. "Did he tell you anything?"

"A good deal. Here's a piece of practical advice for you, Garmansder, if you ever decide to become an agent of evil. When you have your enemy in your power, just kill him and get on with it. I don't know why it is that servants of evil simply *can't* resist the temptation to gloat. It's a very bad habit, one they should get out of."

Garmansder nodded. "It's basic human nature, I suppose. He wanted to tell someone how clever he was, and it didn't matter if that person was a friend or an enemy. I was hoping my guard might tell me after I was kind enough to deliver the Zhents a Bedine spy, but he was pretty vague. I must not be as persuasive as you."

Avarilous had been searching the tent swiftly, his fingers flying everywhere, turning out boxes and bags. His eyes, glittering with a hard light, were drawn back into his head, and the shadows played over his stout form. A rivulet of sweat coursed down his forehead. Garmansder too was looking about, lifting tapestries and cushions with swift, decisive movements.

"How did you get away from the guard—Draka, or whatever his name was," Avarilous asked.

"Not too difficult. We shared some *raki*, and he began showing me the excavation site." He shrugged. "Last I saw of him, he was trying to learn to fly." He gestured toward the body. "Can we make this look like a murder? There doesn't seem to have been any love lost between any of the guards and their officers."

Avarilous ignored the question and countered with one of his own. "How much did you see of the excavation?"

"Some. After Drashka went for his flight, I wandered around. It's deep and very impressive. They're using smokepowder to open up some of the more difficult bits. The whole thing's a bit on the shaky side though."

"Meaning."

"It would be a great pity," observed Garmansder absently, "if anything happened to the scaffolding. Probably bring the whole thing down around their heads. I know I wouldn't care to be in there when it happens."

Avarilous cursed softly. "Where in the Nine Hells could he have hidden it?"

"Ah. I don't know. By the way, what exactly are we looking for? More of those amulets?"

The merchant shook his head. "The amulet's not important. Even if it weren't damaged, our late friend there couldn't have done much with it—not as much as he thought, anyhow. Controlling sandstorms in the desert isn't much of a feat compared to the kind of magic the Shadovar are throwing around these days. No, there has to have been something else. Something he might not even have been aware of. . . ."

Garmansder gave his companion an odd look as his voice trailed off. "What d'you mean? Surely he knew what he was looking for or if he'd found it. You make it sound as if he wasn't the one in control."

Avarilous stopped. "I'm not at all sure he was. In fact, I'm sure he wasn't. He was too stupid, for one thing."

"Oh, come on! If stupid people couldn't control matters, half the cities of Faerûn would be leaderless."

"No, my point is that even if he'd found a powerful magical artifact from Netheril, I didn't get any sense from him that he'd really know what it was or how to use it. Someone had to be pointing him in that direction. I wonder who."

A shadow fell across the entrance to the tent, and Lieutenant Thass entered. His hand rested on his scimitar, while his eyes calmly took in the details of the scene before him.

Garmansder was the first to break the tableau. He dived to the left in a swift roll that brought him standing to Thass's right, a knife in his hand. The lieutenant pivoted and swept a foot around in a savage kick that struck Garmansder's wrist with a crack of snapping bones. The tall man gasped in pain as the knife flew and stuck in a wooden chest, quivering. At the same moment, Avarilous twisted to his right and hurled a dagger. It barely missed Thass's shoulder, slicing through his dark jerkin and clattering to the ground.

Without a pause, the lieutenant cartwheeled behind Garmansder, drawing his scimitar in a single fluid movement. One arm came up clutching the tall man's broken wrist. The other held the scimitar's point just behind Garmansder's ear.

Avarilous caught up the knife that earlier had almost taken one of his eyes. His hand flashed back to throw it then halted abruptly as he saw his friend held hostage.

There was silence, broken only by another soft groan from Garmansder.

Thass spoke first.

"Very good. I didn't think you'd figure things out. Your reputation is well justified, Avarilous."

"Thank you. Now suppose you release my friend, and we sit down and talk things over."

Thass laughed. "I think not. This arrangement suits me very well. But by all means, let us talk. I gather you have been wondering what it was we found here."

Avarilous pursed his lips. His forehead wrinkled in concentration. "I don't think it's an object. If it had been, you wouldn't still be here. You'd have taken it, killed your friend the commander, and brought it to whomever you're working for. Who *is* that, by the way?"

Thass shook his head, smiling. "Go on."

"If it's not a thing, it's more likely to be a place." Avarilous's eyes narrowed. "You've found . . . a way down. A way down into one of the Buried Realms!"

"Excellent!" Thass shifted his stance slightly to match a careful movement of Avarilous's to the left. "A road leading to a hoard of magical power left from Netheril. We've just uncovered a bit of it thus far, but once it's open, there's no telling what we might find."

Avarilous nodded. "I see. That gives me a clear idea of who's behind you. You're working for—"

A series of yells and screams from outside interrupted him. The earth shook beneath their feet, jarring them. Garmansder used his good hand to take advantage of the interruption, driving an elbow into Thass's gut, doubling him over. He ducked himself as Avarilous's knife whizzed past, burying itself in the lieutenant's neck.

Blood spurted, as the tent swayed in a sudden wind. Both men fought to keep their feet. The rumbling intensified.

"Earthquake!" gasped Avarilous.

Garmansder shook his head as he fell to his knees. "Not exactly," he shouted over the tumult. "I set a couple of smokepower charges near the scaffolding with a long fuse. It looks like nobody found them."

Avarilous glared at him. "You idiot! Are you trying to get us killed?"

"No," his friend snapped, "I'm trying to get us out of here! Suppose we go. Now."

He looked at Thass, lying half-conscious on the floor of the tent in a pool of blood. "Shall we finish him?"

The decision was made for him. A wisp of darkness spread beneath the lieutenant. It grew in size until it was a pool of blackness. His body became shadowy and indistinct then disappeared altogether. Slowly the blackness faded.

Avarilous turned toward the entrance. "Come on!"

The two men raced across the oasis, Garmansder doing his best to cradle his broken wrist. Their camel was tugging frantically at his tether and had succeeded in pulling its stake half out of the sand. Other beasts milled about, their grunting adding to the commotion that filled the air as black-robed Zhents shouted and slashed angrily with their whips at Bedine workers. From what Avarilous could see, the Bedine had taken the opportunity to rebel against their masters, and dozens of small battles had broken out across the settlement.

From where the excavation had been rose a thick column of black smoke, partly masked by clouds of dust thrown up by the cave-in. Avarilous had little time to marvel at the results of his companion's sabotage. Already he could hear frantic shouts from the direction of the commander's tent that told him their escape had been discovered. He boosted Garmansder atop the camel, cut the tether with a slash of his knife, and leaped up himself.

A Zhent rushed at them, blade swinging. Avarilous pulled back on the camel's reins, and the beast reared, striking out with its heavy hooves. The Zhent fell with a crushed skull, and the pair of escapees galloped forward. Slowly the shouts and confusion faded behind them.

They rode for several miles before Avarilous insisted upon stopping to bandage Garmansder's wrist, tying it up with a stick to keep the bones rigid. The tall man endured the operation without complaint, though his eyes dilated with pain as the merchant manipulated the bones into place.

When they were remounted and trotting on their way, Garmansder said, "So Thass was working for the Shadovar."

Avarilous nodded. "Yes. They seem to be looking for

access to the magic of the Buried Realms, though I don't know for what purpose. In any case, we should probably be glad we stopped them."

"We?" growled Garmansder. "I think I deserve the credit here." They rode in silence for a mile, and he said, "What are you going to tell Bin-Daar?"

"Nothing." Avarilous half turned in the saddle. "As far as he's concerned, we eliminated his problem. That should be worth the price he offered."

"So we keep this information to ourselves."

"Not at all." Avarilous was looking dreamily at the horizon, where the sun was setting, a flaming ball of orange and yellow that turned the desert sands to gold. "Information, my dear Garmansder, as I have never ceased to explain to you, is the most valuable commodity in this world. One merely has to know what to do with it."

"Uh huh. What are we going to do with this bit?"

Avarilous shrugged. "One thing. Possibly another. I hear Waterdeep is lovely this time of year, and I've always been curious to meet Khelben Arunsun."

Return of the Archwizards

When ancient wizards of extraordinary power return from centuries of exile in the Plane of Shadow, they bring with them an even more powerful enemy and a war that could destroy the world.

Don't miss the beginning of Troy Denning's exciting Return to the Archwizards series! Now available:

THE SUMMONING
Return of the Archwizards, Book 1

THE SIEGE
Return of the Archwizards, Book 2

THE SORCERER
Return of the Archwizards, Book 3
By Troy Denning

Tilverton is no more. Phaerimm surround Evereska. The High Ice is melting. Floods sweep through Anauroch. Elminster is still nowhere to be found. The greatest heroes of Faerûn are held at bay, and a flying city has taken up permanent residence in a world on the brink of destruction.

November 2002

Travel to the far-flung corners of the FORGOTTEN REALMS® with these two new titles!

THE WIZARDWAR

Counselors & Kings, Book III
By Elaine Cunningham

Beyond the gates of the Material Plane, the wizard Akhlaur marshals his forces against Halruaa. By his side is the former magehound Kiva, with her own plans for the destruction of the king. Against these deadly foes is Matteo, jordaini counselor to the king, and his friend Tzigone, the street waif with a mysterious past.

Available now!

THE JEWEL OF TURMISH

The Cities
By Mel Odom

When an ancient evil rises from the grave to stalk the streets of Alaghôn, only a druid with nothing but contempt for the city has the power to save it. The third stand-alone novel in the series that explores the mean streets of the cities of the FORGOTTEN REALMS world.

Available now!

For five hundred years, Elminster has fought evil in the FORGOTTEN REALMS.®

Now he must fight evil in Hell itself.

ELMINSTER IN HELL

By Ed Greenwood

An ancient fiend has imprisoned the Old Mage in the shackles of Hell. Bent on supreme power, the demon is determined to steal every memory, every morsel of magic from the defender of the Realms. As the secrets of Elminster's mind are laid bare, one by one, he weakens unto death.

But Elminster won't go without a fight.

And that is one instance for which his captor may be woefully unprepared.

Available in paperback May 2002

FORGOTTEN REALMS®

Travel with
Drizzt Do'Urden
behind enemy lines in the
first book of an all-new
R.A. Salvatore series

THE HUNTER'S BLADES TRILOGY
Book I: *The Thousand Orcs*

The *New York Times* best-selling author of *Sea of Swords* returns
with an exciting new trilogy that pits the dark elf Drizzt against
his most dangerous enemy. And this time he stands alone.

October 2002

The *New York Times* bestseller
now available in paperback!

SEA OF SWORDS
Paths of Darkness series

For the first time since *The Silent Blade,* Wulfgar and Drizzt cross
paths again, both bent on recovering the hammer that's been
stolen away on a pirate ship that sails the Sea of Swords.

August 2002